SUSAN'S WAR

SUSAN'S WAR

DENISE MICKA

GOLETA
PRESS

ST. LOUIS

Published in the United States by Goleta Press, St. Louis, Missouri

First Edition

This is a work of fiction. Names, characters, places and events either are the product of the author's imagination or are used fictitiously. Any similarity to real persons, living or dead, is coincidental and not intended by the author.

Library of Congress Control Number: 2019914675

ISBN 978-0-9972110-4-7

Cover design by Jamie Wyatt, imnotskippy.com

Edited by Karen L. Tucker, CommaQueenEditing.com

To Ann:
Your smile and humor make rainbows after even the heaviest rains.

To Cosette:
You came and changed everything.

PART I

ONE

"It's closing time, chief." Bobby drummed his fingers on the hood of the car, waiting for Henry to roll out from underneath it. They had both worked for several hours on the mayor's Plymouth, and they had the bloody knuckles to prove it.

"Just another ten minutes, I'm almost there ..." Henry grunted, his voice muffled from under the vehicle. "Go ahead and lock the front door, though. You can work on closing up the shop while I finish up here." He rolled out from underneath the car to grab a tool and found an oily rag being thrown at his head instead. "Bobby!"

"I closed up shop thirty minutes ago! It's time to get out of here. It's Friday, I'm hungry, and I'd like to see my family."

Tossing the rag aside and looking through his toolbox, Henry answered over his shoulder, "Go, already. We don't both have to be here all the time."

"Right. How's that going to look to everyone? Bobby and Henry, joint owners—"

"Henry and Bobby," Henry corrected the order of the names, pointing to the sign painted on the office's outside window.

Bobby dismissed his comment. "My point is that you're putting in way too many hours, while I'm cutting out as soon as it's closing time. That doesn't seem fair. I feel bad every time I leave you here. Plus, I know that if I don't push you out the door, it'll be hours before you drag yourself away."

Henry smiled. He believed Bobby and could only imagine how guilty he probably felt. Having only one arm, Bobby already felt inadequate, the weaker link in their partnership. When they had decided months ago

3

to branch out and try their hands at owning their own business, a small auto repair shop, Bobby had expressed his fear that he would be more of a hindrance than help to Henry. Henry, Olivia, and Catherine all had worked hard trying to convince him otherwise. But it was Catherine's no-nonsense words that finally had persuaded Bobby.

"Look at that flag display case, Bobby. You did that with one hand. You help keep this place from falling apart," Catherine had said, indicating her surroundings. "Plus, you're the only one, besides me, that can deal with Henry. If you won't do it for Olivia, your son, or Henry, then do it for me. I don't want to hear Henry complain for the next ten years about how you didn't open this venture with him. You always were a team, don't stop now."

Just the thought of Catherine made Henry seriously consider stopping his work on the mayor's car. But the fact that it was the mayor's car was all the more reason to finish it. The one thing he didn't want was the mayor's daughter, Susan, at his doorstep.

"Go on home. Tell Catherine that I'll be by soon to pick her up for dinner."

Defeat in his eyes, Bobby glared at him. "You're not—"

"You do remember whose car this is, right?"

"Absolutely."

"Bobby, I have to finish it. The sooner I get it fixed, then the sooner I can get it out of here. I don't want to give Susan any more reason to be here than necessary. And I don't want to give her father any other opportunities to blacklist Catherine."

Bobby nodded, understanding. "She still hasn't been able to find anything, has she? It's a good thing, then, that Michael gave her the job at the club. At least she's got that income."

Henry threw a tool in the toolbox in frustration. "Yes, she does have *that*."

"Obviously a sore subject." Seeing that Henry had taken a break from the car to vent, Bobby aimed to keep him from returning to the work.

"I don't know what frustrates me more: the fact that Susan is still so bitter about not 'winning' me that she's making Catherine suffer by blacklisting her or the fact that Catherine is being so stubborn and refusing my help. I can take care of her. I can make sure she doesn't have to work." He waved his hand around the shop. "I mean, that's the reason I wanted to do this whole thing! I want to be able to provide for her. That's why I'm putting in so many hours. I want to make as much money as possible to ..."

"You want to propose," Bobby said as the idea dawned on him. Henry's sheepish smile gave Bobby his answer. Bobby laughed as he continued, "That's no small task, considering the complex creature she is."

"The sooner I can get this place established, the sooner I can make money. The sooner the money comes in, the sooner I can propose. The sooner I get married to Catherine, the sooner I can completely get her out of Susan's clutches. She'll never need to work again. She can—"

"Do me and everyone else a favor. When you do finally propose to her, don't use that as a reason for it. She'll throw the ring in your face and kick you for good measure." He chuckled at the image. "Okay, I'm leaving. I'm going to go home, eat a hearty meal, kiss my son good night, and make love to my wife." He looked over his shoulder at the clock once more. "I'll see you tomorrow. Should I tell Catherine you won't be swinging by tonight? You and I both know it's already late. And if you stick around here until the car's fixed, it'll be too late to stop by."

He sighed, nodding. "Please. I'll phone her before she goes to bed. But you'd better give her a heads-up."

He waited until Bobby had left the shop and had locked the door behind him before he headed back to the waiting Plymouth in the garage. Another reason that he wanted to marry soon was also the reason that he was still here working late: he needed a distraction. Bobby's evening agenda still echoed in his ears.

I'm going to go home, eat a hearty meal, kiss my son good night, and make love to my wife. Henry shook his head, trying to erase the thoughts. The more time he spent with Catherine, the more it brought fighting, laughter, and unmistakably more desire. If he thought he had wanted her when they weren't yet a couple, that was nothing compared to how much he wanted her now. To be able to go home at the end of a long day to Catherine, his wife, and to be able to stay with her the entire night was becoming more enticing with each passing day.

The sound of the bells jingling on the doorknob brought him out of his daydreaming. The front door had opened and footsteps reached his ears before Henry could get out from underneath the car. "You should have made it home by now. Did you forget something, Bobby?" Henry asked, making his way into the shop.

"Yes, you." Catherine looked at him, a mischievous smile touching her eyes as she held up the spare set of keys Henry had given her. "So, you've got the mayor's car? Spending more time with something that totes Susan around … it's a good thing I'm not the jealous type."

Momentarily forgetting about the work he still needed to do on the car, he moved in to embrace her and give her a deep kiss. Catherine responded just as eagerly but was quick to pull away.

"As much as I love doing that, I'm not sure the whole town would enjoy the show." She nodded her head, indicating the open blinds on the windows.

"Very true. Don't go anywhere." As quickly as he could, he pulled down the shades and closed the blinds in the office.

"Wow, what moti—" Henry was back to her, covering her mouth with his own before she could finish. He held on to her for dear life, hunger in every inch of his body. When they finally broke free for a breath, Catherine finished, "—vation." She smiled and questioned him in between the kisses he continued to plant across her face and neck.

"Henry?"

"Mmm-hmm?"

"I thought you had something you were working on?"

He paused, his face still inches from her own. His eyes were intense, and the desire written in them left nothing to the imagination. "I *am* working on something." His whisper was husky.

Despite the time that they'd been together, Henry's touch still sent a wave of electricity through her. His whispered words tickling her ear were twice as hard to handle. "I meant *that*." Catherine leaned back, her head indicating the garage behind them. "That's the whole reason you're not coming to dinner tonight."

His eyes never left her face as he suddenly pulled her into the garage. "Tell you what; you can help me." A mischievous glint filled his eyes. "I need to make sure that the car is in tip-top shape before the mayor—"

"You mean Susan."

"Before the *mayor*—I'm not dealing with Susan at all—comes to get it.

6

You can help me make sure it's all in good shape."

Catherine decided to take the bait for a bit. "Okay, I'll play along for now. What do you need me to do?"

"Do you remember at the train station, before I left for war?"

"I try not to. Wasn't one of the better times in my life."

Henry instantly regretted bringing that day up. The memory of Caleb and his death was still too raw for them both. But he had already entered into the subject, and he couldn't back out now. He kissed her neck and earlobe, trying to soften the memories. "Do you remember, then, Susan's comment about how my truck would be safe with you?"

Catherine stilled, sensing where Henry was going with this topic. She didn't dare breathe but waited for him to continue.

The way she clenched his shirt at his waist answered his question. "What do you say we give her a little payback? Fog up the windows? Make sure the back seat is in prime working condition?" He found her lips as he spoke, dragging her even farther into the garage.

Not for the first time, Catherine felt a great wave of temptation. Although she'd much rather take a baseball bat to the car and set it on fire, the idea of sharing any back seat with Henry gave her a moment's hesitation in her normally ironclad resolve. She was experiencing so many new feelings and emotions with Henry. He was so much more advanced in this area than she was; in moments that he got bolder, she seemed to skid to a shy halt. As much as she dreamed about doing exactly what Henry suggested, she was too shy to do anything.

Henry sensed her stiffening up in his arms. He knew where this was going, or rather, not going. "Okay, maybe Susan's car is a bad idea. But Catherine, I'd take any car if you were there. You know that, right?" He turned her face up to his, searching her eyes. He saw the hunger there that so readily matched his own.

"I brought you dinner," Catherine said, suddenly very nervous. Just when she thought Henry's looks and her own feelings couldn't get any more intense, she had been proven wrong. "It'll get cold if you don't eat soon."

"It's probably better cold anyways." He held her there, cupping her face in his hands.

"No car." Her voice was a whisper.

"No car," he repeated. "Come home with me tonight for a while." It wasn't a question; it wasn't a plea.

Catherine's head started to swim, and she found herself clinging tighter to Henry to keep from falling. This was the first time since her long stay at the hospital that he had made this suggestion. She had wanted to then, and she wanted to even more now.

It would be so easy. But thoughts of Henry's notorious past filled her. He had experience. The only thing Catherine had experience in with men in her past was how to avoid getting killed. Henry was the first man to treat her well, and while she finally had realized he truly loved her and wanted to be with her, her fear of disappointing him in so many areas, particularly the more intimate ones, always left her feeling shy and insecure.

Henry could see the indecision and battle in her eyes. He knew her so well—better than she realized. He saw the debate raging within her. While he figured that she would eventually refuse, it was encouraging to see that she struggled with the refusal. In truth, he hadn't planned on asking her. But it was getting harder and harder to keep these emotions at bay. If nothing further happened, he wanted her to at least know what he was feeling.

"What are you thinking, Catherine?"

I don't want to disappoint you. I don't want to disappoint you.

"A compromise. How about instead of the back seat, we test out the radio."

Vowing not to let the conversation stray permanently, Henry cut her some slack. "What do you mean?"

"Dinner and dancing. How about you turn on the car radio and we get at least a good dance out of this? Then we can eat dinner."

Open to any excuse to keep Catherine in his embrace, he got the car radio going and pulled her into his arms as a slow song played. For a while, they danced in silence, swaying to the music.

Henry waited until Catherine tucked her head under his chin before revisiting the previous conversation. "So, will you? Come home with me tonight? You never answered my question."

Catherine closed her eyes, hoping her silence would be enough.

It was.

"It's okay, love." He leaned closer to whisper in her ear, even though they were the only two in the shop. "I just want you to know ... I want you."

Catherine kept her eyes closed, listening to Henry's heartbeat. "I know." It was all she dared say to him.

"Tell me what you're thinking, Catherine. And I don't mean about dinner, this dance, the mayor's car, or anything else that you can use to try and change the subject."

She couldn't help but laugh. "You've caught on."

"Because you do it so much." He forced her to stop and lifted her chin so that she could face him. "Talk to me. Nothing between us to separate us, remember?" He stroked her jawline. "And I promise, no matter what you say, I won't take it as permission to act on it, okay? I just want—*need*—to know what you're thinking."

Knowing she could never have the courage to say this to his face, she extricated herself from his embrace. "If I tell you, will you promise to leave it here? To just drop it and go into the shop with me and have dinner?"

"Absolutely." But his eyes told her something else entirely.

"I don't trust you'll do that. Let's bring things down a bit. Why don't we eat, then I'll tell you?"

"You're killing me, Catherine."

Only when they were both seated around the office desk and biting into their meal did Catherine open up. "I don't want to disappoint you," she whispered. She stared at the hamburger in her hands, focusing hard on the tomato that was sticking out of the side.

Henry chewed slowly and swallowed before setting his own food back down on the plate. He reached his hand across the table to grab her arm. "Catherine, set the food down." She silently obeyed. "Look at me."

That order was a bit harder to obey. "A bit embarrassed at the moment," she whispered as the color seeped into her cheeks.

He came over and twisted her chair to face him. "Catherine."

His tone sent the butterflies in her stomach aflutter once again. "You said you'd leave it alone once I told you."

"No, what I agreed to was dropping it, then having dinner. Technically, we've had dinner first, so that makes our prior agreement null and void."

"You took one bite. That's not dinner."

"You're changing the subject."

Catherine's embarrassment began to turn to anger. "You wanted to know, all right? That's what I'm thinking. You have experience in things that I don't. I'm tainted, but you're ..." She searched for a word.

"Seasoned?"

Catherine couldn't help but chuckle. "No, that's not quite the word I was looking for." She found the courage to face him. "Henry, each day I'm no less amazed that I'm with you. *Finally*, with you. And I'm just afraid that one day I'll wake up and find this is all a dream. You could have any other woman out there. You can have one that's so much more experienced in every aspect of life."

"At the risk of sounding like a complete jerk," he cringed, knowing that no matter how he worded it, it would still come out wrong, "everyone, each person, is different, Catherine. And that's the joy of it all, discovering each other. I don't compare other women with one another. How could I? Besides, being with you, it's the real thing. Nothing else, *no one else*, from my past matters."

"Only because I know what you're trying to say, I'll let that slide. But yes, you do kind of sound like a jerk. Good thing I know you so well."

The sound of Catherine's stomach growling brought Henry's mind back to the food. He grabbed her hand, kissing it. "Then forgive me. And as much as I'd love to sit here and show you how much you don't disappoint me, I think we both should eat."

Catherine was happy for any reason to change the subject. "Forgiven. Now eat up. I had to fight hard for these hamburgers. The diner was closing up when I got there. I had to run from Sal's."

"Run? You mean, you came straight from work?"

Realizing too late the mistake she had made, she nodded. "Um, yes. I called the house, and Bobby had just gotten in. When he said you wouldn't be coming over, I decided to drop by."

Anger tipped the edge of Henry's heart. "Catherine, how many hours did you put in today at the club?"

"They needed my help. It's not every day."

"How many?"

"Besides, they pay me overtime."

"*How* many?"

Catherine looked back down at her food. "Twelve."

Henry reached out and grabbed her hands, noticing the new blisters for the first time. "Twelve hours! Michael worked you twelve hours?!? He should know better. I'm going to have to talk with him."

"Oh no, you're not!" She jerked her hands away from him. "This is my job, Henry. *Mine*. You have no say in this. If I want to work twelve hours, then I'll work them. You can't stop me."

"Catherine, I just don't want to see you overworked."

"Says the man still working in his garage. How many hours did you put in today?"

"That's different. I'm doing this so you won't have to work." As soon as he said it, he regretted his words. By this point, Catherine was already on her feet. Henry cautiously rose up as well. "I didn't mean that."

"Yes, you did. You wouldn't have said it otherwise." She grabbed her bag and purposefully marched to the door. "You can have my burger too. I've suddenly lost my appetite."

"Will you be reasonable, Catherine?" Frustrated, Henry hurried after to her. "No, all right? I don't like you working there. It's long hours, it's hard work."

"So was my job at the factory."

"And I hated that too!"

"What would you have me do, Henry? I can't drive—"

"Legally."

"I don't have a car. I have no college education. I'm too hard to handle a delicate job. I can't type. I don't have any of the qualifications to be a secretary, nor do I have the patience. The only thing I can do is clean. And be your girlfriend. And I have to be known for something more than that."

"Look, I love you, Catherine. And I'm not going to stop being concerned about you. We're in this together, and if we want a life together, you need to let me be a part of it."

"Be a participant, yes. Be a dictator, no."

He sighed. "This isn't going to end well tonight, is it? Look, I'm sorry. I need to take my own advice. If I complain about you working so many hours, I shouldn't be doing the same thing." He grabbed her hand and pulled her to him. "Let's just call it a night, okay? Give me a few minutes, let me close up the shop, and then I'll take you home."

But Catherine was still fuming from his earlier words. "I think that tonight, you should just go on home, Henry. I have my bicycle. I think we both need to cool off and try again tomorrow. Good night."

Catherine left the shop as angrily as possible. After the door slammed shut, Henry let out a breath.

That woman. If her kisses don't drive me mad, her stubbornness will.

Still heeding his own advice, Henry decided to close the shop. Even if Catherine was already halfway home, he knew he'd follow her to be sure she arrived safely. But it would have been much easier if she would have just agreed to ride with him.

As he locked the door to the shop behind him and turned to head toward his truck, he stopped short at seeing Catherine's bicycle resting in the truck bed. The shadow inside told him that Catherine was there, waiting for him.

Cautiously, he came around to the passenger's side where the window was down. Catherine stared down at her hands, refusing to meet Henry's eyes.

"I'm sorry," she whispered.

"I thought you were going home alone."

"Change of plans."

"Flat tire?" Although Henry's frustration with Catherine was already fading, his pride kept him from offering his own apology just yet.

She shook her head. When she looked up, Henry saw the trace of tears in her eyes. "Flashback. Robert ..."

But she didn't need to finish. In the next moment, Henry had the door open and Catherine gathered into his arms. He held her close as her body shook with sobs. Knowing how quickly flashbacks could come, he understood all too well how easily they bring their victims to their knees.

Yet, here in this moment, none of that mattered. What mattered was that the woman he loved was hurting and now she was allowing him to protect her.

* * *

Susan glowered as she watched Henry hold Catherine in his arms outside of his truck. Because it was so late in the evening, it was dark enough that she could watch them without any fear of discovery as she sat in her car.

Banking on Henry remaining in his shop late to finish her father's car, Susan had donned her most tantalizing dress and had cheese and wine in tow to spend the evening luring Henry away from her most hated nemesis. But she had arrived only to discover that Catherine was already there, securely nestled in Henry's arms.

How she hated Catherine! Susan couldn't understand how things had ended up this way. She was definitely the type of woman Henry had always dated in the past. Susan understood *that* Henry, and Susan knew how to handle that man. Yet, after he came back from Europe, he had become untouchable. Nothing she had said or done could lure him to her. Instead, he had seemed to cleave to Catherine, the polar opposite of anything and everything feminine. *What does she possess that keeps him ensnared?* Susan bit her lower lip in frustration. Initially she had tried to convince herself that Henry was with Catherine because of being so close to Caleb and needing to grieve his death. Then, when some man from Catherine's past had nearly killed her, Susan had felt that Henry had remained out of guilt.

It definitely can't be because he loves her, can it? Smirking at the thought, she shook her head. *Of course not. She's a challenge for him, a conquest. That has to be it. Once he's succeeded in bedding her, he'll be through with her. This is, after all, Henry.*

As she watched them drive away toward Catherine's house, Susan slowly drove home. The wine and cheese would have to wait until her father's car was finished. Then she would pick up the car herself.

She smiled. "No war and certainly no woman can change who you are, Henry Bradley. You can't run from your past forever. And it looks like I'll have to remind you of that."

Two

Henry opened his eyes to the sound of the screen door opening. His hand instinctively found the knife under his pillow, his fingers curling around its handle. The soft knock on the door jerked him awake the rest of the way. The sun was only beginning to rise and peek through the bedroom curtains. He rose briskly, stealing a glance at the wristwatch on his nightstand. Six o'clock: it was too early for visitors.

The gentle knock came a second time, but now with a little more force. He put on a pair of slacks, grabbed his knife, and headed toward the living room.

"Who is it?" he called as he crossed the room, all traces of sleepiness now dissipated.

"Me."

He could barely hear the response, but it was enough. With a smile, he placed the knife on the nearest table and hurried to the door. His own personal sunshine waited there as he opened it.

"Hi, me."

Catherine smiled, sleepiness still puffing her eyelids. She stood there, a basket of food in her arms, waiting for an invitation to come inside. In the few seconds it took for Henry to take the basket from her and lead her inside, she felt warmth and color rise up her neck and build in her cheeks. Feeling bad about their fight and her flashback the previous night, Catherine had slept very little, wanting to apologize to Henry as soon as possible. But seeing him in his half-dressed state, she realized that she had come too early.

Henry's own thoughts whirled from Catherine's surprise visit. As he set the basket aside, he pulled her to him, wanting nothing more than to keep her in his arms. But he stopped, feeling her sudden hesitation.

"What is it? Is everything okay? Did you have another flashback?" He held one of her hands and cupped her cheek with the other, bringing her face up to look her in the eyes.

Seeing the concern written there, Catherine felt her blush deepen. "Um … n-no. I felt bad about our argument last night, and—"

"What argument? It's forgotten."

Catherine took a deep breath, trying hard to forget how close she was to him right now and how handsome he looked. "Yes, well, I still feel bad. About the flashback too." Her eyes fell on the discarded knife. "Which you apparently still struggle with too."

He quickly took the knife and slid it out of sight in the table's drawer as he replied, "The war created some habits that are hard to break. But let's focus on your early, but most welcome, visit."

"I just … I don't know. I know it was a late night for you since you took me home and made certain I was okay before coming home yourself. I knew you probably would be too tired and too rushed for breakfast this morning. And I know how much you like my pancakes, so I got up early and made some. They might be somewhat cold since I brought them on my bike, but I think they should still be okay. I mean, pancakes are good warm or cold, right? At least, that's—"

Henry smiled, relieved that she was okay but also sensing her unease. "You're rambling."

She looked up, startled and embarrassed. "Am I? Well, here, let me get it set out for you and then …"

She started to pull away to retrieve the basket from the table, but Henry wouldn't let her go. "Why are you rambling, Catherine?" He smiled, already knowing the answer.

"I, uh, suddenly realized that maybe I came too early. I obviously woke you up." She couldn't meet his gaze, and the redness deepened in her face.

"Six o'clock isn't too early. I should be up anyway. But I don't think that's it. Am I too frightful to look at in the morning?"

Catherine swallowed. "On the contrary, Henry. You look," she searched for the right word, "*inviting*."

Henry chuckled, a huskiness filling his voice. "Am I seducing you, Catherine?"

She glanced up. "Are you trying to?"

"I wasn't. But now I am," he replied, allowing himself to pretend, even for a moment. He kissed her hungrily and passionately. As his heart raced, he tightened his hands around her.

The telephone's ringing made them both jump.

"Let it ring," Henry said, reaching for Catherine again.

"No way!" She moved away as the phone continued to ring. "It's early; it may be important."

"It's early; it may be a wrong number."

"Answer it," she said, silently thankful for the interruption, and headed to the kitchen with the basket.

Taking one last lustful look at Catherine, he reluctantly obeyed. "Hello?"

"Hey, Henry, it's me."

"You'd better have a very good reason for calling me so early, Bobby."

Bobby laughed on the other side of the line. "Early? I take it Catherine made it over with breakfast, then."

"Again, you'd better have a good reason for interrupting."

"I won't be in today. Olivia has been feeling under the weather for the past few weeks, and I think I need to take her to the doctor. So I'm going to do that today."

"Liv's sick? I hadn't noticed." He saw Catherine come back from the kitchen, concern written on her face.

"I can take her to the doctor," Catherine volunteered.

Bobby was able to hear her through the phone. "No, it's okay. She'll be okay. Tell Catherine thanks, but we've got this. But if she's got the day off from the club, maybe she can help you out at the shop?"

"Don't worry about the shop. Just make sure Liv is okay, all right?"

While Bobby and Henry finished conversing, Henry saw Catherine slip away into his bedroom. He could no longer pay attention to what Bobby was saying and couldn't get off the phone quickly enough.

No sooner had he hung up the phone than he found Catherine back in the living room with a shirt in her hand. She held it out to him, her timid look stealing his breath.

16

He started to speak, but Catherine shook her head. "I think you should put this on first. It's safer that way."

Henry smiled at Catherine's obvious discomfort. "Okay, love." He slid his arms through the sleeves, and then, seizing her hands, he brought them to his chest. "You can help."

She scowled. "You're not a child. You can dress yourself." Then her eyes grew pleading. "*Please* dress yourself."

"Tell you what—I'll do all the buttons except for the top two. Safe enough?"

"Turn around when you do that." Henry didn't move. Catherine growled in frustration and turned her back to him.

"Do I bother you, Catherine? Do I make you uncomfortable? Tell me, and I'll stop," he said over her shoulder.

She shook her head. "No." She took a deep breath before continuing. "It's not you at all. It's me. I'm having problems with what *I'm* feeling. I think it's probably wrong to have such thoughts going through my head so much. I mean, I certainly can't act on them, even if I did have the courage … which I don't." Henry witnessed the stubborn determination that he knew so well come over her. He touched her shoulder to indicate he was dressed, and she turned back to face him. A new resolve filled her eyes when she looked up at him.

"I love you, Henry. I hope you understand that. But I can't. No matter how much I want to, I can't spend the night with you. I don't want to have any regrets with you. I have too many of them in my past."

Henry took her precious hands and held them to his chest. He loved her so much. But when she held her ground, held fast to her beliefs and principles, he loved her even more. He kissed her fingers, his lips light as feathers.

"I know. I've always known that, Catherine. And I'm not going to push anything. I want our relationship to be strong. I'm not going anywhere. I'm in this for the long haul, and I can wait. I *will* wait. I don't want to do anything that will compromise you. I know that I'm pretty vocal about what I'm feeling. And yes, a part of me wants to take you in my bedroom right now and—" Seeing her blush, he stopped short of explaining. "But that can wait. Yesterday … I need to apologize for that and for my behavior this morning

17

as well. Last night, Bobby had shared some of the joys of being married, and it made me think." He saw unease enter Catherine's eyes. Kissing her forehead, he led her to the kitchen and continued to talk.

"What I'm saying is that I'll never pressure you. I won't mention it again, okay, Catherine? I want you to know what I'm feeling, and knowing that you feel the same way, even if we can't act on it at the moment, well, that's more than enough for me."

She sat down across the table from him and placed a few pancakes on his plate. She was still skeptical. "So, you're not going to mention this anymore? You're not going to invite me to come home with you again, right?"

"I'm not perfect, Catherine. I may slip up. But know that even if I do say it, I've no intention of acting on it. We'll wait. But I need your strength in this. Believe me, from this side of the table, seeing your beautiful face every day is going to make that extremely difficult."

Catherine knew this was the best promise she was going to get out of him. She nodded. "You're stronger than you think, Henry. Now, enough talk about that. Liv is sick?"

He nodded, diving into the stack of pancakes now on his plate. "Yes. Bobby said she's been sick for a few weeks. Have you noticed anything?"

Catherine shook her head, lost in thought.

"Bobby appreciated your offer to take Liv, by the way, but he insisted on taking her himself. He made a great suggestion that if you're free today, you could come help me at the shop with paperwork. What do you think?"

She nodded. "Sure. I need to stop by the club for a few hours later this afternoon, but I can help you out until then." But her mind was still on Bobby. "Did he seem worried?"

"Not really, no." They were silent for a few moments, each lost in their own thoughts.

"Oh my goodness." Her voice was a whisper as an idea dawned on her.

Henry asked, "Catherine? Are you okay? You look like you've seen a ghost."

Brightness filled hers. "Don't you see, Henry? Think about it. She's been sick for a few weeks. I haven't noticed anything different, and I live with her. Bobby insisted on taking her to the doctor himself. Henry, Liv's pregnant!"

*   *   *

"Penny for your thoughts," Olivia said, squeezing Bobby's thigh as they drove back home to Catherine's place. They had just left the doctor's office and were still a bit dazed as the physician's news sunk in. "Are you all right?"

Bobby looked over at her, soaking in the warmth of her smile and wishing for the millionth time that he still had his left arm so that he could drive and hold Olivia at the same time. "Come here, you." He waited until she slid over in the seat next to him and laid her head on his shoulder before continuing. "I'm terrific. I'm ecstatic. I'm the luckiest person on earth. Why God continues to bless me is beyond me." He leaned over and kissed the top of Olivia's head. "I don't deserve any of this." He eyed her stomach. "And the best part is that I'll get to be here for the whole thing this time."

"That is the best part, isn't it?" Olivia chuckled, adding, "And I'm sure Catherine will agree I wasn't the best patient at times with my first pregnancy. But with you here, I'm sure this one will go much better."

Yet despite all of Bobby's happiness, a moment of sadness passed over his eyes. "I wish ..." He paused, searching for the right words.

"What? I don't know what more we could wish for."

"I won't be able to hold both of our children at the same time, Liv."

Olivia laughed, raising her head to kiss Bobby's cheek. "Oh, I have no doubt you'll find a way. You always do. I can't wait to tell Cat and Henry. They'll be so excited!"

Seizing this moment as an opportunity to broach a subject that had been gnawing at the back of his mind for weeks, Bobby kept his eyes focused on the road as he spoke. "Liv, they will be. But speaking of Henry and Cat, I'm thinking that we'll need to start considering other living arrangements."

Confusion clouded her eyes. "Why?"

"Liv, you're pregnant. We'll be bringing another child into the house. We have to consider Cat. This is her home."

"But she said we could stay there as long as we'd like. Don't you like living there?"

"Yes, I love it. But that's not the point. It's a lot to expect her to not mind us taking up more space. Besides, you know as much as I do that she and Henry are pretty much inseparable these days."

"It's great, isn't it?" Her eyes sparkled with enthusiasm.

"Focus, dear. While it's wonderful that things are working out for them, that's also my point: things *are* working out for them. I think—no, I *know*—that Henry has hopes of one day marrying Cat." He knew her so well, he could practically see the wheels turning in Olivia's mind. "And stop it right there, Liv!"

"What?"

Bobby tried to hold a stern look but couldn't. Olivia could widen her eyes in such an innocent manner that it was impossible to scold her. He sighed, trying his best. "Don't start thinking about all of us living together. That's not fair to them. We have to consider that, at some point, they may want to live at the farmhouse, just the two of them."

Olivia bit her lip, staring straight ahead and considering Bobby's point. "I see what you're saying, and I understand. I do. But we've got time. Because there's no way I'm going to let them marry while I'm pregnant! They're going to have to wait until after the pregnancy when I'm able to fit in a bridesmaid dress."

He couldn't help but chuckle at her logic. "Because their wedding is all about you."

She elbowed him gently, taking his teasing in stride. "Very funny, Bobby. But we women, even Cat, think like this from time to time. She'll wait; you'll see."

"Let's take it a day at a time and see how things stand with them, okay?"

"Fair enough. So ..." Her perkiness returned, her eyes dancing once again. "... when do we get to tell them the news?"

"Whenever you want to, dear. We can head over to the shop right now *or* wait and tell them tonight. I can call the shop to tell Henry he has to come to dinner tonight."

"You really want to wait until dinner?" She was eager to share the news with Catherine. Catherine had been there for her the first time when Olivia had been a sobbing mess on her doorstep. She couldn't wait to be able to share the news under much happier circumstances.

Bobby nodded, giving Olivia a wink. "Yes, I do. Caleb is with my parents, so we have the afternoon free. I want to go back to the house and spend the afternoon having our own private celebration, if that sounds good to you."

Olivia raised an eyebrow and smiled mischievously. "You don't have to twist my arm. Let's get back to the house, you make your phone call about dinner, and then you can show me just how excited you really are."

*   *   *

"Have you heard anything yet?" Henry asked, poking his head into the office. He wiped his oily hands as he came in.

Catherine smiled as she took in his appearance. While he worked at cleaning his hands, there was a large smudge of grease on his forehead that he seemed completely unaware of. She left the desk and met him halfway across the room. "Not yet, no. But I think if they do have news, good or not, they'd probably want to tell us in person, not over the phone. Come here." She grabbed the rag from his now clean hands and brought it up to his forehead. "You missed a spot."

Kissing the tip of her nose in appreciation, he smiled. "I could get used to this, you working here."

Catherine swatted him with the rag and returned to the desk. "We'd kill each other, eventually. Besides, I have a job. And as much as I like helping you out, I need the independence of earning my own money. You paying me, well, that'd be like getting an allowance."

"But only if you're good," he teased, sitting on the edge of the desk. "Can you do me a favor, though? The mayor's Plymouth is finished, and I need a call to be made to let him know."

He saw Catherine's eyes narrow slightly as her focus shifted from him to the entrance behind him. He could almost feel the coolness that came over her. "Looks like that won't be necessary." Her voice was a calm whisper.

Too calm.

Henry glanced over his shoulder to see Susan standing in the entranceway. As always, she was dressed to kill. For the smallest moment, he saw her icy glare at Catherine before she shielded it with a flirtatious smile at Henry.

"Henry!" Susan's focus shifted to him, ignoring Catherine entirely. "I was in the neighborhood, and I thought I'd stop in to check on Daddy's car." She held up a bottle of wine. "And, of course, to congratulate you on your new business endeavor. I haven't had the opportunity to do that yet."

21

"Glad to see you took my advice and went with the white wine," Catherine said with a smirk, recalling the time she knocked Susan's drink into her lap. "Were you ever able to get the red stain out of your dress?"

Susan's smiling demeanor faltered for a moment. She quickly replaced it with a smug look. "Henry," she began, her eyes never leaving Catherine, "I think it's very sweet and generous of you to let Catherine play house in your office. I understand she's had some difficulty finding work."

Catherine opened her mouth to reply, but Henry stopped her, placing his arm protectively around her shoulders. "Catherine's not had any trouble finding work. I don't know where you got that idea. And I simply asked her to come here today for selfish reasons. I miss her when she's not around."

The disgust in Susan's eyes couldn't be denied. "Yes, well, we all have our guilty pleasures, I guess. But seriously, Henry, you know that I have connections. I can get you as much business as you want coming into this garage. All you have to do is ask."

"Bobby and I are fine for the moment. But speaking of business," he tried to curtail the conversation away from Catherine, "I have your father's car all ready to go."

"Splendid." Her eyes were locked on Catherine's as she spoke. "Why don't you be a dear, Catherine, and have the car pulled around the front while Henry and I take care of the unfinished business."

Not on your life, Susan. Catherine smiled sweetly, her eyes large and innocent. "I don't work here, remember? And I don't have a legal driver's license. I'm not sure you want me to drive your father's car. I'm too likely to wreck it. Although that *would* create more business for you, wouldn't it, Henry?"

Knowing Catherine's temper all too well, he quickly kissed her on the forehead. "I'll move the car. And then we can draw up the paperwork." He hurried to his self-appointed task, not at all at ease with leaving the two women alone for long.

Susan waited until Henry left the office before dropping the smile completely. "You think you've won, don't you?"

Catherine fought hard against the anger that rose up easily around Susan. "I don't know what you mean, Susan."

"Yes, you do. Henry."

"Henry isn't a prize to be won. We love each other. There's no competition for him. He's not interested in you."

"How soon you forget the past, dearie. He was, indeed, interested in me until you came along with your sob story."

Catherine's voice was eerily calm as she replied, "Excuse me? My sob story?"

"Caleb's death, of course."

"How dare you imply that I used my brother's death to gain Henry's affections."

"I don't see any other reason why he would even put up with you. You're a prude, Catherine. So innocent, so childish. Why, I bet your first kiss was given to you by Henry." She laughed, a sneer in her eyes. "You know Henry's past, Cat. You know that he's been with *real* women ... women who know how to give him what he wants and what he *needs* as a man. I was one of those women, Cat, remember?" She came over and lifted Catherine's face with a manicured finger to look her square in the eyes. "You, Catherine, are just a plaything to him. *A conquest.* That's all. Once he's had you, he'll toss you aside."

"You have no clue what you're talking about."

"Don't I? I'm sure he's already expressed to you what his needs are. And yes, you may be able to keep him at bay for a while, but in the end, one of two things will happen."

Catherine found her fists clenching. "And that is?"

Unbeknownst to either woman, Henry reentered the shop and stood on the other side of the door connecting the garage to the office, listening in horror to what Susan was saying to Catherine.

"Well, you'll give in and give him what he wants. He'll compare you to others, to *me*, realize your inexperience isn't what can sustain him, and he'll leave. Or, still feeling guilt over Caleb, he'll keep you around in the daytime but will visit someone else in the night."

"That's enough!" Fury filled Henry as he charged into the office. He managed to get himself between Catherine and Susan before Catherine had the opportunity to lash out at Susan. Whether she would have, he didn't know, but he wasn't going to take a chance. He could feel Catherine behind him, leaning on him for support as her body shuddered in anger. "The Plymouth is out front; you can go now."

"But I still need to pay you." She lasciviously raked her eyes over him.

"The debt is with your father, not you. I'll send him his bill in the mail. Go, Susan."

She smiled, leaning forward to place the bottle of wine on the table next to them. Henry gently moved his right arm behind him, protecting Catherine and offering a silent attempt to calm her. When Susan stood back up, she stood on her tiptoes to whisper in Henry's ear but loud enough for Catherine to hear her.

"Let me know when you want to break into that bottle of wine, Henry. I know it's your favorite. And seeing as your pet doesn't touch the stuff … well, no one should drink alone, right?"

It took everything in Catherine not to reach over Henry and tear Susan's eyes out. The only thing that kept her grounded was the fear that anything she did to Susan would result in retaliation against Henry and his business. So instead, she turned her back to Henry and Susan, closing her eyes and trying hard to erase all of Susan's remarks from her memory.

"Go." Henry's voice was full of controlled anger, and even Susan realized she shouldn't push her luck. She smiled and, nodding her head, left silently.

Catherine tried hard to scrub Susan's words from her mind, so focused on the failing task that she heard neither Susan leave nor Henry close and lock the door behind her. She hated that Susan got under her skin so easily. But she hated even more that Susan understood her own insecurities. She knew that she was inexperienced, and she was petrified of disappointing Henry in every way. In the end, she was afraid she'd fail him.

Henry approached Catherine slowly, unsure of how his spitfire of a girlfriend would react. He knew she was angry. Her rage filled the entire office. That temper he knew and was used to dealing with. That temper lashed out and swung punches. But this silent, still being who stood with her back to him concerned him. While he had expected her to contain herself in Susan's presence, he thought she would come unglued as soon as Susan was gone. But she hadn't even moved.

When he reached her, Catherine's eyes were closed, and her hands were still gripped in tight fists. Slowly, he took her hands and brought the fists up to his chest. His touch caused her to immediately open her eyes.

"You can put the fists away now. She's gone." Henry smiled reassuringly, gently opening her fists and kissing each finger. Only then did he look in her eyes, hoping to find some of the storminess now calmed. If he expected anger, hatred, or wrath, he was disappointed. The only thing he could see in her eyes was deep sadness.

"Hey, love, are you okay?" He enfolded her in his arms.

"No." Her voice was muffled in his chest.

Normally he would feel Catherine cozying in and melting in his arms by this point. Now she stood rigid, distant. He held her out at arm's length, looking her straight in the eyes. "What are you thinking? You're not letting Susan's words get to you, are you?" Yet she didn't have to answer.

"She's right, you know." Her voice was a defeated whisper. "You're only going to be disappointed ..."

"Hey, hey, hey," he shushed her, enveloping her tightly in his arms. "Not true. And you know that. Don't even talk about such nonsense. I'm so in love with you, Catherine. And like I promised you this morning, I'm not going anywhere. Everything I did before, everything I was ... it's nothing. You have already given me so much; I only want *you* for the rest of my life, Catherine. Don't ever doubt that. Especially because of Susan. She's trying to break you."

"Yeah, well, it's working," she replied in despair.

"Catherine." This time his voice was strong, stern, and demanded her attention. She looked up, sensing the seriousness she would find on his face.

"Catherine, listen to me. Our relationship is about us. You. Me. No one else. Do you love me?"

She nodded, her throat closing and preventing her from speaking.

"Then tell me."

She swallowed back her tears. "I love you."

"You don't mean it."

"Yes I do!" Conviction filled her. "You know I've loved you since—"

"Yes, I know that." He smiled at successfully catching her in his trap. "But not because someone else told me that, but because you did. Because you show me that daily. I don't doubt your love for me for an instant. So I'm asking that you treat me the same. Don't doubt mine." He cupped her face, kissing her hungrily. "I mean, I think we've been through enough that we're strong enough to survive anything Susan can say or do. Don't you agree?" His voice was husky as he spoke.

Catherine could only nod, allowing Henry to kiss the fears away.

"I love you." His voice deepened as his kisses grew in intensity. He found his arms tightening around her.

"I—" But Henry wouldn't let her get a word in between the kisses. Finally, she pushed herself away. "I have to go to work!" A small smile tugged at the corner of her lips.

Henry grinned, pulling her back to him for one more kiss. "Okay. Do you need a ride?"

"No. I can manage."

"Do you need me to pick you up afterward?"

"I don't know what time I'll be finished. It could be late."

"Catherine." His voice held a gentle warning.

"No. We'll fight about this later, okay? But not now. Susan already did enough for today." She hugged him, giving him a quick kiss on his cheek before turning toward the door.

Henry reached for her hand to stop her from leaving. "Catherine, look at me," he gently demanded. He waited for her to return his gaze. "All's well, right? You're not going to let Susan's words …"

Catherine shook her head. "Of course not. I'll see you later." She gave his hand one more squeeze then left.

I'll give you credit for trying, Catherine, Henry thought. *You may be a great actress to everyone else, but you didn't convince me.*

He knew sadly enough that Susan's words had left a strand of doubt in Catherine. Susan had succeeded in exactly what she had set out to do. While Catherine had spoken the reassuring words he had wanted to hear, her eyes had told him something else entirely.

But don't worry, Catherine, I'll do whatever it takes to erase every ounce of doubt you have.

THREE

No sooner did Catherine step inside Sal's Club than she realized Susan was only the beginning of her day's problems. Her dance instructor, friend, and now employer sat alone in the far corner of the dance hall. Normally full of positive energy and enthusiasm, his slumped posture and indifference to her entrance brought immediate concern. Catherine approached him with caution, taking in his appearance. His clothes were rumpled, and a few days' beard covered his face. The near-emptied bottle and shot glass on the table explained the glassy look in his eyes.

Catherine had never seen Michael like this before, and she was unsure how to handle the situation. She seated herself next to him, and when he made no acknowledgment of her presence, finally whispered, "Rough day?"

For a moment, Catherine was certain he hadn't heard her. She sat still, unsure of whether to leave him alone or stay. The strong smell of alcohol on his breath convinced her to stay.

"She told me I needed to get away for a bit," he whispered, his eyes focused on some distant, invisible item. "She probably wasn't expecting me to do this." He slowly dragged the bottle from the table, studying its dwindling contents. Then suddenly, Michael hurled it across the room with as much force as possible. It shattered against the opposite wall. Before Catherine could react, the small shot glass joined the bottle across the room.

Catherine couldn't stop the surprised scream that came from her. But this brought Michael out of his momentary distress. He finally looked at Catherine, his eyes full of a pained apology, but didn't say a word. He collapsed once again in the chair next to her, clenching his fists as he did.

When Catherine finally found her voice, she was surprised at her calmness. "Michael, where's Patricia?"

He didn't answer her directly. "She said she knew you'd come by here at some point, so she was confident in sending me back for a while." He looked at her and smiled despite the obvious pain written on his face. "But she'd never think I'd wipe out a whole bottle by the time you got here."

Catherine felt confused and helpless. Michael was obviously struggling over something. Though she could never believe it, her only thought was that Patricia had left him.

"Michael, *where's* Patricia?"

He shook his head, his face crumpling in heartache. "With him. With *him!*" He rose to his feet and violently sent a chair across the room.

He reached for another one, but Catherine was quick to stop him. She grabbed his arm and pulled him away from the tables with all her strength. "Oh no, you don't! I'm not going to let you make a bigger mess for me to clean up by myself. Not a chance!"

But Michael wasn't to be dissuaded. Anger and heartbreak were etched in every inch of his face. He tried to free himself from her grip and grew frustrated at Catherine's determination.

"Let me go!" An unfamiliar anger reached Catherine's ears. Something was terribly wrong to put Michael in this state. Remembering briefly how he had helped her get over her depression of losing Caleb, she dug in her heels and held on to his arm with as much strength as she could muster.

"Michael, stop this! You're—"

"*Let me go!*" Before either of them realized it, Michael turned on Catherine and pushed her away from him with enough force to send her toppling to the floor. Her head flew back and hit the floor beneath her.

The cracking sound that resulted snapped Michael out of his stupor. He stared at his hands then at Catherine, who was holding her head and now scrambling to get as far away from him as possible. He couldn't blame her, and he immediately loathed himself for what he had done.

"Catherine." His voice was broken, hurt. "I'm … I'm sorry." He held his hand out to her. "Please, let me help you."

But Catherine was momentarily unable to respond. She knew that Michael, one of her dearest friends, stood before her. Yet all she could see was Robert's face, Robert's hand beckoning her toward him. She shook her head, pain searing throughout her skull. "No. Go away," she said, her voice a scared whisper. She touched the back of her head, and when she looked at her hand, blood colored her fingers.

"Oh, God, Catherine, I'm so sorry." The anger in Michael's voice was gone and replaced with deep remorse.

Dizziness clouded Catherine's vision. She shook her head in an effort to clear it, pain engulfing her once more. "Michael?" She heard his voice, but images of Robert swam before her eyes.

"Yes, love, it's me." She jerked involuntarily as she felt hands softly touch her. "Come on, let's have a look." Michael, despite his drunken state, had suddenly sobered up at the realization of causing Catherine harm.

"Don't touch me." Her voice was still a whispering plea as Michael knelt and scooted closer to her before easing her head to the ground.

"It's Michael, Cat. Albeit a very drunk Michael, but Michael all the same." The tenderness in his voice brought Catherine out of her small flashback.

She blinked hard as her eyes began to refocus on Michael's face. He was on the floor beside her, concern written in his still-glazed eyes.

But he wasn't so far gone that he couldn't see when recognition finally came back to Catherine's eyes. "There you are," he smiled sadly. "Welcome back. I'm sorry to have sent you down an unpleasant road from your past."

Shaken by the push Michael delivered, Catherine still struggled against the waves of dizziness overcoming her.

Michael. That was Michael. Robert isn't here anymore. Robert can't hurt you. You're with Michael; it's safe.

Using all her willpower to focus on these thoughts, she finally managed to whisper while still holding her head with her now-bloodied hand, "Why did you push me?"

Cursing silently to himself, Michael removed his dress shirt to press it against the back of her head. "Here." He coaxed her to her back, his shirt a pillow between her head and the floor. "I think you should probably have this looked at. You're going to need some stitches."

"Why did you push me?"

"Although I'm not in any shape to drive, we need to get you to the hospital." Unintentionally ignoring her question, his face crumpled in pain. The pain that had been evident when Catherine first arrived had returned.

"Michael ..." Catherine was starting to get sleepy and fought against what she feared was a concussion. "Get Patricia. She can—"

But Michael was shaking his head, momentarily lost in his own sorrow once more. "She's not here. She's—"

"Michael, I want to sleep for a bit. Get Patricia to help us."

Michael, realizing that Catherine showed symptoms of a concussion, immediately forced her to sit up. "Come on. I'll take you."

"No! You're drunk. Michael, where's Patricia?" She wanted to close her eyes so badly and sleep.

A long shadow passed over his face before he finally answered. "She's at the hospital, Cat. With Sal ..."

"Sal? Why is Sal ..."

"Cat, my uncle's dying."

* * *

"I was hoping you would keep him *out* of the hospital for a while, not give him reason to rush back over here." Patricia's voice filled the room as Catherine struggled to open her eyes. The sudden burst of light from the lamp Patricia had turned on caused her to recoil, wincing sharply.

Patricia saw the confusion on her face and couldn't help but feel for Catherine. A few hours earlier, Michael had burst through the emergency room, carrying Catherine in his arms. In his drunken state, he was honest about how Catherine had come to the club and found him inebriated. While some of the details were still fuzzy, he admitted to pushing her then calling a cab to deliver them to the hospital.

"How did I—?"

"Don't worry, Michael didn't drive you. He's stupid, but not *that* stupid. He called for a cab to bring you here."

Catherine struggled to sit up, but the dizziness prevented it. "Ugh. I'm so confused."

Patricia came up to her and placed a loving hand on her arm. "Let me explain. Sal suffered a stroke. Michael and I have been here the entire time. You saw the wreck that Michael was earlier today. Sal is it to him. We're losing Sal ..." Even Patricia started to choke up and paused momentarily. "Michael's taking it really hard. I knew you'd be working today at the club, so I sent Michael there, hoping you'd be able to distract him for a bit."

Catherine began to understand what had transpired. "I had no idea, Patricia. You both haven't been at the club when I was working the past few days. And when I got to the club this afternoon, Michael was already so drunk. He started throwing things around. I remember trying to stop him. Then ... I fell." Understanding the reason for Michael's raw emotions, she couldn't find fault with what had happened. She found herself wanting to protect him.

"You fell when he pushed you. Michael's a terrible drunk, dear. He confessed to everything. You passed out; you have a concussion, by the way. And a few stitches. Now he's with Sal, savoring every moment he still has with him."

"I'm sorry, Patricia. I had no idea."

"Of course not. How could you? We haven't said a word to anyone. Michael made some phone calls to secure enough staff coverage to keep the place going while we were here. But weekends are always busy. Either Michael or I will have to be available to work then, if Sal's still hanging on."

"What can I do to help?"

Patricia couldn't help but smile. "You're something, you know that? You're not upset about Michael pushing you, you're not concerned about being in a hospital bed, you're worried about what you can do to help."

"Sal was a lifesaver for me when Caleb left for Europe. He means the world to me, as do you and Michael. If I can do something to make this whole thing easier for you all, then I want to do it. What time is it? If it's not too late, I can still swing by the club and start cleaning."

"It's close to midnight, Cat."

"Then the cleaning will have to wait until tomorrow. But this weekend, I'm sure that Henry, Liv, Bobby, and I can help hold down the place for you."

"One thing at a time, dear. First, let's get you discharged, then we'll let Michael know you're okay. He'll grovel and beg for forgiveness, by the way. Then I can take you home, or we can call Henry."

"No one called Henry?" Dread filled Catherine. He wasn't going to be happy at all with what had happened. "He's going to be worried sick about

31

me. I should have been home hours ago, even if I did tell him I'd most likely be working late."

"No, I didn't call. And I wouldn't let Michael call either. I wanted you to have the first opportunity to take a swing at him before Henry found out. You and I both know that once Henry knows, Michael's in serious trouble."

"I'm sorry."

"I'm not. Michael deserves whatever Henry wants to do to him. And Michael knows that, too."

"It's true." A voice came from the doorway. Michael stood there looking as bad as he had at the club. Only now, his eyes were sober and clear. He entered with timid steps.

"Come here, you." Catherine held out her arms for Michael. He rushed forward, giving her a hard embrace.

"I'll go sit with Sal," Patricia whispered, making her exit.

"I'm so sorry, Cat," Michael apologized, gently touching the bandage wrapped around her head. "Are you okay?"

"I'm fine. It's forgiven. I'm the one who's sorry. Michael, I had no idea about Sal."

Michael waved a hand in dismissal. "What's going on with my uncle is no excuse for my behavior. I just wanted to drown in my own sorrows for a bit, and you wouldn't let me." He sat on the edge of the bed next to her. "You should hate me right now. I fear my actions triggered a flashback. You should definitely hate me."

"It's not happening."

"Well, at least Henry will hate me enough for the both of you."

"I need to call him. He's going to be worried. But don't worry, I won't tell him what really happened."

Michael shrugged. "Doesn't really matter what you tell him. He should be here any moment. I already called him and told him everything."

"Michael! You know how protective he is! He's going to kill you!"

He smiled. "Love, I do understand. Because I'm just as protective of you. Had Henry done this very same thing, I would want to know so I could properly kill him."

She shoved him off the bed. "Go. Get out of here. Go to Sal's room. I don't want you near me when he gets here."

The sound of someone entering the room made them both jump. But relief washed through them both at the sight of the doctor.

"I'm sorry. Am I interrupting? I wanted to check on you to see if we can get you discharged."

"That's ok," Catherine said. "My friend, Michael, was just leaving."

Dismissing him, Michael had no choice but to leave and head back to Sal's room.

As he turned the corner in the hall, he met Henry.

"Henry, the doctor is seeing her—" but he was unable to finish his sentence as Henry's fist connected with his face. The force of the hit spread stars across his vision, blinding him from seeing the second blow across his face. He tasted blood in his mouth, and understanding that a full onslaught was coming, Michael stood there, bracing himself.

But it didn't come. He opened his eyes, one good and one starting to swell, to see Henry taking a step back from him. Rage filled every part of his body, and his fists remained clenched, but Henry was making an attempt to calm himself.

"I deserved that."

"You deserve more than that." Henry started to come at Michael again but showed great restraint in stopping himself.

"Do you feel better?"

Henry came forward and struck another blow to Michael's stomach. "*Now* I feel better." He motioned down the hall that Michael had come from. "Is she down there?"

Struggling for breath, he nodded before finding his voice. "Yes. Right around the corner. The doctor is discharging her right now."

"You'd better hope so ... for your sake."

He nodded. "Listen, I'm in room 302 if she asks, okay?" Michael had no clue if this registered with Henry as he made his way to Catherine's room.

All the anger that Henry held toward Michael evaporated the moment he saw Catherine. Although she was in a much better state than the last time he saw her in a hospital bed, images of that nightmarish time instantly came to his mind. This hospital was a place that he had never wanted to see her in again. Seeing the bandage wrapped around her head intensified his urge to want to protect and take care of her.

Catherine sensed Henry there even before she looked up. Standing in the doorway, relief and concern showed in his eyes.

"It's not as bad as it looks," she tried to explain. She slid to the side of her bed, making room for Henry to sit next to her.

"I already saw Michael, so don't sugarcoat things." He lightly touched her bandage. "I'm going to go back out there and finish him off."

She grabbed his hand. "Don't you dare. Wait ... what do you mean, 'finish him off'? What did you do?" She looked down at the hand she held, noticing its slightly swollen state. "Henry?"

"He'll live. Although from what he told me, he shouldn't."

"Stop that right now. It's a small concussion and a few stitches, that's all."

"That's all? Catherine, he's supposed to be your *friend*!"

"And he still is." She tried frowning, but the effort hurt her head. She sighed and started to lean back, but Henry turned in the bed next to her and pulled her in his arms. "You don't understand what happened."

"No, love, I think I do. He told me everything over the phone. Everything. So don't try to defend him." He leaned in and kissed her lips. "Can I take you home?"

"Not yet. The doctor wants to keep me for the rest of the night for observation. But I should be free to go tomorrow morning. I need to go to the club to clean up the mess."

Catherine felt Henry stiffen underneath her. "Absolutely not. I don't want you going back there, Catherine. Not alone."

"Michael isn't going to hurt me, Henry."

"Says the woman with stitches in her head. Let's not argue about this. Not tonight anyway. Instead, can I hold you for a while until you go to sleep? Then I'll camp out in that inviting chair in the corner."

She begrudgingly smiled. "You know, you don't have to stay. I'm fine. You can go on home, get some rest, then pick me up in the morning."

"And miss the opportunity to spend the night with you?" His eyes held a teasing look in them. "Not a chance."

Susan's words from earlier in the day repeated in her mind.

The feel of Henry's hand lifting her chin to face him brought her out of her trance.

"I'm sorry, what?"

"I said I only meant to tease you." Henry looked at her, concerned. "What were you thinking about? You're a million miles away."

"Susan," she said before thinking, instantly regretting it.

"Like I told you before," he said, kissing her temple before tucking her in his arms again, "don't listen to a word that twisted woman says. She's full of lies. Besides, you need to rest."

"No, not yet."

"Then let's talk about something else, like what happened with Michael this afternoon."

She tried to squirm out of his grip, but he held onto her tightly. "Maybe I should rest."

"Not so fast." He grew more somber as he spoke. "While I was on the phone with Michael, threatening his life, he mentioned something." He searched for the right words. "He mentioned that, for a brief time, he thought you experienced a flashback of Robert."

Now Catherine didn't try to fight him. She cozied into his embrace, clinging to him and resting her head on his chest so that she wouldn't have to face him. "Maybe. I don't want to talk about it."

He kissed her gently on the top of her head. "Okay. I'm sorry that I wasn't there."

"You're here now."

"So, you'll let me stay?"

"Only for tonight." She lifted a hand and pointed to the corner. "But only if you're willing to sleep in that chair."

Henry smiled, grabbing her uplifted hand and kissing it before intertwining his fingers with hers. "Fair enough, but only after you've gone to sleep."

They were silent for a long time, savoring the closeness of each other. Henry felt Catherine start to nod off in his arms. "I love you, Catherine."

"I love you." Henry's heart soared as she tried to nestle in deeper in his embrace, grateful that she was all right.

"And Sal?"

Her question brought him out of his thoughts. "What's that, love?"

Her voice was heavy with sleepiness, but she asked again. "Sal. Did

Michael or Patricia say how he's doing?"

"I don't understand. What do you mean?"

"He's here at the hospital. That's why Michael was so upset. Didn't Michael explain that to you?"

"No."

She stifled a yawn. "Sal had a stroke, and they don't expect ..." Fatigue cut off the rest of her words as Catherine finally succumbed to sleep. But Henry had heard enough to catch their meaning, and it explained Michael's current state.

Although nothing will ever justify putting Catherine here, at least I understand what's going on now. As soon as Catherine was in a deep sleep, he would go to room 302 to see Michael and Sal, confident that the older man was a patient in that room.

But that could wait. For now, Henry held Catherine in his arms, finding delight in the thoughts of spending every evening like this. He wanted to protect Catherine always, for the rest of his life, for every second of every day. He wanted Catherine as his wife.

He smiled to himself as he thought back to Bobby and Olivia's wedding. Catherine had been so certain that such a happy ending would never come to her.

He looked forward to proving her wrong.

FOUR

Catherine woke the next morning to find her hospital room empty. She felt a twinge of sadness as she dressed in her street clothes from the previous day and signed the release papers that a nurse promptly brought to her.

Henry wasn't there. She fought hard to quash Susan's words inside her mind. *Nonsense. He had to get to work. I'm sure that's why he's not here. Catherine, don't go there. Put your faith in Henry, not Susan.*

A soft knock on her door interrupted her thoughts. "Good morning, sleeping beauty."

"You're still here." Catherine found herself beaming as Henry came in and planted a kiss on her forehead.

"I told you I would be."

"I know. I just saw the empty chair and thought you must have left for work." She noted the fatigue in his eyes.

"Not today." He seated himself on the edge of the bed and took her hands. "Are you feeling all right? Did the doctor release you?"

She nodded. "It looks like you had a rough night."

Henry gave her hand a squeeze and smiled, but it didn't reach his eyes. "You could say that. I paid Michael a visit after you went to sleep last night." He rubbed her hands as he spoke.

"How's Sal?" She already knew the answer before she had asked the question. It was written all over Henry's face.

He shook his head, taking her in his arms. A long moment of silence followed.

"And Michael?" She pulled out of the embrace, knowing personally the pain caused by losing family members. Catherine's heart broke for her dear friend.

"Patricia took him home a few hours ago. They're going to meet with the funeral home later this afternoon. Hopefully, they're both resting right now. The club is going to be closed until after the funeral and legal logistics get worked out."

"What do you mean?"

"Sal had a will. While everyone's pretty sure that it names Michael as his successor, Michael can't really operate it until we know for sure."

"I need to go there. To clean it up, at least. I don't want Michael to go in there and have to do it."

Henry obviously wasn't pleased with her line of thinking. Something flashed in his eyes as he sat there, still absently rubbing her hands. Eventually, he nodded. "I figured that's what you'd say, so I've asked Bobby to cover the shop for the day. I'll take you and help you clean up."

"I'm not sure that's such a good idea." She knew Henry wouldn't be happy with the mess that preceded Catherine being hospitalized.

"Probably not. But if you insist on cleaning, then I insist on coming with you." He stood up from the bed as he continued to speak, never letting go of her hands. "I wasn't joking last night when I said I didn't want you there alone."

Catherine found her anger flaring. "Michael is not a threat to me."

"Not sober, no. But until I see more of how Michael handles grief, I'm not taking a chance."

She pulled her hands from his. "So, we're back to this? Back to babysitting?"

Henry swiftly blocked the door, folding his arms across his chest. "If you're going to be a baby about it, then yes." The fire in his eyes matched hers. He wasn't going to back down from this argument. "Besides, with your concussion and stitches, I don't want you to overdo it."

"Because you think I will?"

"Because I know you will." He leaned down to her, so close that he could kiss her. A great part of him wanted to do that very thing. "Be happy I'm not taking you straight home to rest, as I'm sure your doctor would prefer."

"Most men trust their girlfriends to be able to handle their own health."

"And most women are eager for the opportunity to spend as much time as possible with their beaux. Any opportunity. Even if it's cleaning a club."

Frustration filled her. She knew Henry wasn't going to budge, and he was large enough to keep her from going to the club if he really wanted.

"Catherine, I'm not happy with Michael. I'm furious with him, actually. I think, all things considered, I'm being very gracious in even offering to take you there. And I think I'm being even more gracious in letting Patricia bring him over for dinner tonight."

"*What?*" Catherine's argumentative retort fell off at his last comment.

Still maintaining his determined pose, Henry was secretly pleased to see that he had caused Catherine to falter. "When I called Bobby this morning to let them know what happened, he and Liv wanted to do something as well. Patricia and Michael are in no position to be going through this alone. And seeing as we're their closest thing to family, even if I did give Michael a few bruises, I suggested to Liv that we have them over for dinner to—" Catherine suddenly grabbed his neck, silencing his words with a passionate kiss.

Now it was Catherine's turn to catch Henry off guard. Feeling the heat in her kiss, he momentarily forgot their discussion and instinctively wrapped his arms around her.

As abruptly as she had kissed him, Catherine just as quickly pulled back from him, her cheeks rosy and her eyes warm.

"What was that for? Don't get me wrong, I'll take another, but I thought we were arguing."

"That was for being so amazing." She stood on her tiptoes to kiss him again, biting at his lower lip at the end of the kiss.

"Oh, you can't do *that*," Henry protested in a husky voice, "and then stop." He dipped his head to receive another deep kiss, but Catherine smiled, turning her head to the side.

"Thank you for suggesting that dinner to Liv. I'm lucky to have you."

But Henry's mind was already elsewhere. "Yeah? Why don't you show me?"

Catherine nodded. "Fair enough. I won't argue with you when you take me to the club to help me clean. How's that for showing you my love?" And she impetuously grabbed his hand and led him out of the hospital room.

He had to chuckle despite himself. "Actually, knowing how argumentative you can be at times, that's probably more proof than any kiss."

But I'll still take those all the same ...

* * *

Susan's eyes narrowed in distaste as she took in the scene around her. Sal's funeral service had been a closed, private event for select family and friends in town. Needless to say, because Catherine was part of that intimate group, Susan wasn't. Her father, the mayor, didn't mind not being present at the funeral. He was a politician, after all, and the memorial/celebration service that the club had this evening for the public gave him enough of a spotlight. He didn't care about Sal, but he cared about publicity.

Not that Susan cared about Sal either. She had frequented his club, but she had rarely ever spoken to the man. What bothered her was seeing Catherine there in the midst of Sal's family. Catherine had hated the club and everything it represented up until Caleb, Henry, and Bobby had left for the war in Europe. Since then, she had weaseled her way into Sal's family and Henry's heart. While Susan had done everything she could to make sure that Catherine couldn't find work and would struggle, Sal had made sure his family protected her and kept her employed. Susan didn't have enough of a foothold on the club to keep Catherine from being employed there. Seeing Catherine now in the corner of the club, speaking with Sal's nephew while Henry kept her in his line of sight, was more than she could take.

Enjoy the throne while you can, princess. I'll knock you off soon enough.

Catherine, sensing a pair of eyes on her, looked away from Michael to find Susan staring at her with pure hatred.

Michael, following Catherine's gaze, sighed heavily, saying, "She doesn't ever let up, does she?"

Catherine shook her head and replied, "Only when she has Henry as her own. Then she'll stop."

"She'll be waiting for an eternity then," Henry commented, coming up and putting a possessive arm around Catherine's waist.

Henry's touch never got old for Catherine, and she found goose bumps covering her arms in response.

For a moment, Michael forgot about his uncle's passing and admired the couple in front of him. It was such an amazing journey that the two had taken to finally be together. More than once, it almost hadn't happened.

There was no denying their love for one another, and his black eye was further testament to that.

A crash from across the room drew all of their attentions. Someone had collided with a server, and several glasses now lay shattered on the floor.

Michael took a step in that direction, but Catherine stopped him. "I've got this. You try to take it easy, okay?" Before he could protest, she was already heading toward the accident.

Henry started to go and assist her, but Michael held him back. "She'll be back soon enough, Henry. In the meantime, I wanted to talk to you and apologize once more—"

"It's not *me* you owe the apology to."

"You're the one who still hasn't forgiven me." Michael turned his attention to Catherine across the room. "Cat, she's a remarkable woman. She has a way of drawing things out of us even if we're kicking and screaming the entire time. And she's so forgiving ..."

Henry looked over at Michael, particularly at the black eye that had only now started to fade. He had a powerful urge to blacken Michael's other eye to match, and it took great self-control to keep from doing that. "Listen, Michael, I know you're in a tough spot right now. I get that. And this time, I'm willing to forgive you for what you did." He lowered his voice so Michael had to strain to hear. "But I don't forget. And I don't trust Catherine to be alone with you at the moment." His eyes focused on Catherine as he spoke his next words. "But I trust Catherine, and if she trusts you, then I don't really have a choice now, do I?"

"Henry, I'd never—"

"No," he interrupted, "you won't. Rest assured, if you ever harm a single hair on her head again, there won't be anyone or anything to stand in my way of destroying you. Do I make myself clear?"

Michael nodded, a small smile coming to his lips. "I'm glad she has you, Henry. Whether or not she'll ever admit it, she needs you to watch out for her, protect her, and most importantly, love her. No one can doubt your love for her."

No one but me, Susan thought as she approached the men and heard Michael's last comment. Putting on her most mournful expression, she offered her hand to Michael. "I am so very sorry for your loss, Michael."

Guarded, Michael shared a wary look with Henry before responding, "Thank you. Uncle Sal was a great man and will be sorely missed."

"Absolutely. Therefore, I wanted to offer you my condolences and my services. As you take over this club, I'm confident that there are many changes you'd like to implement. Just know that I can help you finance any of them. If you need additional housekeeping staff, I can furnish that as well."

"I'm not sure this is the time and place to be discussing this, Susan," Henry interrupted curtly. "We're at Sal's memorial service, for heaven's sake."

But Michael knew enough about Susan's relationship with Catherine that he could easily read her and understand her motive. Susan wanted a foot in the door so she could push Catherine out of it. He held his hand up. "It's all right, Henry. I might as well address this now, right away." He focused his full attention on Susan as he continued, "We have yet to read my uncle's will, but should I inherit this place, I don't plan on changing a thing. Sal turned over most of the duties to me over a year ago, so I've pretty much been running things my own way for quite some time. And as far as any employees I have working for me, I value each of them and don't plan on letting *any* of them go." There was emphasis in his words, a silent warning to Susan that couldn't be denied.

She smiled sweetly, an innocent look in her eyes, and said, "Why, Michael, I didn't mean to insult you in any way. I only meant that if you were holding back any—"

"I'm not. At least, not in regards to this club."

"Well, it looks like someone didn't hold back on you, though," she said, indicating his black eye. "What happened?"

Michael cast Henry an appreciative look before replying, "I was properly put in my place for poor conduct." He glanced back at Henry and, seeing the opportunity for a truce, took advantage of it. "But Susan, let's be honest with one another, shall we? I know what you're here for and what you're implying with your suggestions. Let me say for the record that I have no intention whatsoever of letting Catherine go. She's a great employee and amazing friend. I'm not going to blacklist her. She will have a job at this club for as long as she wishes. So, you'll need to take your efforts and focus them elsewhere. They'll fall on deaf ears here." He noticed the appreciation in Henry's eyes.

Taken by surprise at Michael's bluntness, Susan started to respond. However, seeing that Catherine was making her way back to them, she averted her attention to Henry instead. *Fair enough, Michael. I'll focus my attention elsewhere.* She waited until Catherine was within earshot before speaking to Henry. "Well, Henry, as I said before, you know where I am when you decide to break into that bottle of wine. We can make an entire night out of it." She traced a fingernail down Henry's chest in passing. "I'll promise to make it worth your while."

Catching the tail end of Susan's words, anger flared inside Catherine. She knew Susan was trying to get an outburst from her, and it was working. Frustration set in. She was tired of this, tired of Susan. All she wanted was to be able to enjoy her relationship with Henry without any doubts, fears, struggles, and battles. She had overcome so much to be with Henry, and she still felt that she was fighting for him. Deep in her heart, she knew that Susan would never stop.

Suddenly, she felt tears stinging her eyes. Not wanting Susan to see how much her words had affected her, Catherine made a quick turn and headed for the kitchen to dispose of the rags that she held with a death grip. Once in the confines of the kitchen, hidden from the eyes of the guests, she took a deep breath and silently screamed a retort to Susan. As the words came to her mind, the tears left her eyes. She collapsed in a chair in the corner, dropping her head in her hands in weariness.

How can I compete? How on earth can I keep fighting when I have such a strong enemy?

Lost in her thoughts, Catherine didn't hear Henry slip into the kitchen. He held off going directly to her, taking in the defeated image in front of him. He knew the moment he saw Catherine turn to the kitchen, glimpsing the fire in her eyes, that she had heard what Susan had offered him. She was already behind the kitchen doors before Henry had given his curt refusal and Michael had ushered Susan away. Susan's words a few days back and her invitation this evening were getting to Catherine. Although Catherine was tough in many ways, she had her weaknesses as well. Few things brought Catherine to her knees and left her shaken in her confidence. As much as Henry was her strength, he was also her weakness.

He approached her without a word and sat on the floor in front of her. He waited until she looked down at him with tear-filled eyes before saying, "Hi."

"I hate her." Her voice was a whisper as she angrily brushed away a tear.

"No, you don't, not really." He pulled her down on his lap. "It's not in your nature to hate." He wiped at the tears on her cheeks. "Don't let her get to you, Catherine."

"That's easy for you to say. You're not the one constantly being threatened by someone else. You don't have someone trying to steal me away. This is easy for you; no one wants me. But you, on the other hand—I feel like I'm constantly fighting for you." She shed a new wave of tears. "I'm tired of that feeling."

Henry took her face and lifted it to face him. "There is no threat, Catherine. There is no need for a fight. I'm yours. I will always be yours." He kissed her tenderly. "And don't think for a second that you don't drive me absolutely crazy." His voice took on a husky tone. "I've already expressed to you how much I want you—that's no secret. But what I don't think I've shared with you is my constant prayer that you'll always be with me. You're a rare find, Catherine, and I'm fearful that one day, some man will come who is so much more deserving of you than I am. I'm scared he'll sweep you off your feet and take you away from me."

"You think my heart is that easily persuaded? I've given it to you. It's always been yours."

"Then don't doubt my feelings for you, either. Put your trust in me, Catherine. We're together in this, and we're not going to let anyone separate us."

Marry me, Catherine. Marry me today. Let me show you for the rest of my life how committed I am. But rather than express what he truly wished for, he simply asked, "Deal?"

Calm and reassured, she cozied into his arms and replied, "Deal."

* * *

A few days later, Catherine, Henry, Bobby, Olivia, their son Caleb, Michael, and Patricia all sat around a large table at Sophie's, their favored Italian restaurant. With Sophie's holding so much history for them all, Catherine felt it only appropriate to go there after the reading of Sal's will. Despite the sadness and mourning of Sal's passing, a bittersweet joy was felt by those around the table. Now that it was official that Michael was the owner of the dance club, it seemed everyone could breathe a little easier and start to rebuild their lives and move forward.

"Congratulations again, Michael," Bobby said while jostling Caleb on his lap. "When do you plan on reopening the place?"

"Next weekend. I want to make sure everything's in place legally before I start operating again. I don't want anyone, particularly the mayor, finding reason to shut me down."

Guilt hit Catherine in her stomach. Michael was no longer in Susan's favor, and that with just a word, she could see to it that Michael's life would be riddled with problems. While Catherine knew that Michael could take care of himself, she couldn't help blaming herself for the potential problems he might face. She didn't want anyone else to suffer because of her. As much as she needed that job at the club, Catherine knew that her being there would only hinder Michael.

"You should let me go," Catherine said, immediately quieting the entire table. Everyone turned to Catherine, surprised by her comment. But she continued speaking before she lost her nerve. "Yes, Michael. You should lay me off, let me go, fire me. Susan will be sure to leave you alone if you do."

"Nonsense," Patricia answered before anyone else. "We can handle Susan. I don't have this red hair for nothing, you know. Whatever that woman wants to dish out, I can serve it right back to her on a silver platter … with garnish."

While Henry was secretly thrilled with the idea of Catherine no longer putting in long hours at the club, he was equally humbled by her act of love. She was willing to sacrifice her own necessities and income for the sake of helping her friend. His heart swelled for her, and he realized all over again how lucky he was to have her as his own.

"I thought you liked working there," Michael said to Catherine, interrupting Henry's thoughts.

"I do. I don't want to see you with any type of hurdles so early in the game. I mean, it's bad enough I'm in constant fear that she'll somehow manage to shut down Henry and Bobby's shop—"

"Stop it right there, Cat," Bobby protested. "You don't have to worry about us or Michael. We are all so amazingly handsome that even if the male customers are driven away by Susan, we won't ever have to worry about losing the female ones." He winked at her and raised an eyebrow to everyone else. "Am I wrong? Who at this table is going to argue with that?"

Bobby had succeeded in lightening the mood as they all laughed and started to tease one another. But without drawing attention to it, Michael reached under the table and squeezed Catherine's hand beside him.

"I'm not letting you leave, Catherine. Don't entertain that thought a minute longer," he whispered so only Catherine could hear him. She nodded, appreciation and sadness mingling in her eyes.

When she turned to face Henry, she found his eyes searching hers. "I love you," he whispered.

Before Catherine got the opportunity to respond, Olivia took over the reins of the conversation. "All right. Well, since we're here trying to celebrate as much as possible despite our loss, I think Bobby and I can offer something else to lift everyone's spirits." She winked over at her husband, waiting for his nod of approval.

"We're going to have another baby!"

Congratulatory exclamations filled the air as everyone's words stumbled over one another's. Henry, remembering clearly the pain Bobby had suffered in Europe while Olivia went through her pregnancy without him, leaned over and clapped Bobby on the shoulder. He wanted to say something, anything, but words escaped him. He recalled when Bobby told him he would be a father the first time, when Caleb was still with them. Life was going on now, moving forward without his best friend and Catherine's brother. As happy as he was for everyone, his heart ached in this moment.

"I know, Henry," Bobby said, reading Henry's thoughts and understanding all too well the inner suffering he was experiencing. They simply shook hands as a deep understanding passed between them.

"So many changes."

Henry turned to Catherine as she whispered that more to herself than to the others. He could see that she, too, was thinking about her brother. He put his arm around her, kissing her temple. "I miss him too," he whispered in her ear.

Tears sprang to Catherine's eyes. She locked eyes with Henry, grateful that he understood. Blinking away the tears, she nodded, wanting nothing more than to be alone with Henry so she could fully allow herself to miss her brother. But for now, Olivia and Bobby needed her smile more than she needed her private time for tears.

"Congratulations, you two," Catherine said.

"Now, Catherine," Bobby began, "I know that this may be a burden on you."

"On me? How?"

"Another person would be in your home. It's a lot to ask you to be so flexible with all of that. So, I want you to know that I'm going to start looking in town for a place—"

"Nonsense," Catherine interrupted. "You can stay at the house. You don't have to look anywhere else. We've got nine months or so to figure out any changes we need to make to the place to accommodate the newest member of your family."

"Are you sure, Cat?" Bobby tried to keep his hope at bay.

She nodded.

Olivia squealed in delight. "See, Bobby? I *told* you." As Olivia immersed herself in conversation about the baby and the necessary planning, a moment of envy came over Catherine.

Any changes made in my home was supposed to be for my child ...

Ashamed at herself, Catherine had to admit that it was sometimes hard to watch her own dreams lived out in her home but by someone else.

FIVE

"So, are you ready for the reopening?" Catherine asked as she scrubbed the counter one more time, glancing up momentarily at Michael and Patricia as they worked on giving the dance floor one final cleaning. From where she stood, she could see the concentrated look on Patricia's face as she knelt on her hands and knees rubbing out scuff marks only she could see. Michael stood beside his wife with his arms crossed in obvious frustration. It was evident that the couple was fighting, and Catherine hoped her question would succeed in diffusing the tension.

"This place has been in great shape for days now," Michael replied, never taking his eyes from Patricia. "You ladies have done a terrific job. The place is spotless. *Spotless*." He aimed his words at his wife, but she blatantly ignored him. "Seriously, Patricia, you can stop now. The floor looks great."

"I'll stop when she does," Patricia responded, nodding her head in Catherine's direction. "You've worked her like a horse. I'm merely helping."

"Yes, but I think—"

Patricia sprung to her feet and turned on Michael. Wielding a rag in her hand, she hurled it at him and stomped her foot. "Don't you even go there, Michael," she interrupted. "It's not fair to be working Catherine so much and not expect me to help. So, if you want me to stop, send her home. At this rate, our Cinderella will be too tired for the ball. If you keep her here, then you're telling me that you need help." She crossed her arms, stubbornness written across her face. "*Decide*."

Throwing his hands up in frustration, he strode toward Catherine. "Lucky for you, I love you, you waspish woman," he threw back over his shoulder to Patricia. Without easing his stride, he seized Catherine's hand and ushered her to the door.

Completely at a loss over their argument over her, Catherine struggled to find something to say. "Um, but I still have—"

"Not you too, Cat," Michael interrupted between gritted teeth. "You're done for the evening."

"But my shift—"

"I'll pay you for the full shift. But I need you to go *now*."

"Take her home, you oaf," Patricia called after them as they approached the club's front door.

Michael stopped. With his grip still on Catherine, he turned to his wife. "If I take her home, you'll continue to work. You won't stop until I get back. Not happening. Nice try, love." He turned his attention to Catherine. "I'm sorry, but are you okay with getting home on your own tonight?"

She nodded, still trying to make sense of everything. "I have my bicycle. Or I can call Henry to come get me."

Michael shook his head, his eyes still glued on Patricia. "If you stay to wait, you'll work, and then *she'll* work," he said with enough volume for his wife to hear.

Catherine heard Patricia's farewell as Michael escorted her out of the club. Once outside, Michael let out a string of curses aimed at his wife as he released his grip on Catherine. She was silent for a moment before asking, "Do I even want to know?"

Heaviness seemed to press on Michael as he ran a hand through his hair. "I'm not supposed to say anything," he responded.

"Why won't you let Patricia work?"

"I will. I *do*. I just don't want her to overdo it."

"Um, she was my instructor part of the time during our dance lessons, and I don't think cleaning a floor is going to overdo it for her. She's a strong woman. Besides, I've cleaned that floor many times. I can vouch for the lightness of the work."

But Michael's focus was on the closed door behind him and the woman on the other side. Concern etched every corner of his face. Only when Catherine touched his arm did he drag his eyes away to look at her. "I'm sorry, what did you say?" he asked.

Catherine rarely saw Michael this distracted, and it made her uneasy. "Michael, is Patricia okay? Is something wrong?"

Something flashed in his eyes, and a quick smile came to his lips. "No, she's fine," he said as the smile disappeared. "I don't want her working so much."

"Again, that's not too difficult a job. Besides, she's always worked beside me at the club."

"Well, maybe I should take Henry up on his suggestion that I give you easier duties. Then maybe Patricia will concede." He gave Catherine's hand a squeeze as he continued, "Thanks for leaving early tonight. Are you sure you're okay getting home?"

But Catherine wasn't listening. She was still stuck on his previous remark that Henry had suggested to Michael to lessen her workload. Her employment at the club was a continual source of disagreement between the two of them. While Catherine loved being there every day at a place that reminded her so much of Caleb, Henry apparently only remembered how she had once almost worked herself to death to distract herself from her brother's passing. While she eventually had worked through the depression associated with her loss, Henry obviously wanted to make sure that she never revisited that path again. Her employment was their main cause of conflict.

And now he's gone behind my back and suggested to Michael that my duties be lightened? What right does he have? She shook her head as she felt her frays of patience snap. As much as she loved Henry, she wouldn't let him control her.

"Henry asked you to lighten my duties?" she asked, not trying to hide the anger and disbelief in her voice.

"Ah, now I've done it." Michael answered. He gave one last look at the club door before focusing on Catherine. He gently held her shoulders as he faced her. "Henry—"

"Did he or *didn't* he?" Catherine demanded but continued before he had a chance to reply. "Michael, you know I'm strong! I can do this work. Henry had no right to—"

"Henry loves you, Cat," Michael interrupted her in a calm voice. He reached down and took her hands to inspect them. He traced the blisters on her hands before speaking again. "Wow. I *have* been working you too much."

Catherine jerked her hands free from his grip. "Not you too, Michael. You know me."

Michael smiled as he replied, "I do. You *are* strong, love, very strong. And you're a strong leader too. Did you know that? People follow you. Patricia follows you. And while you can be strong right now, there may come a time when you won't be. Or when those who follow you aren't able to be." Confusion wrinkled her brow, and Michael smiled as he kissed her forehead.

"I'll get weak if I stop working."

"Or you could become weak for other reasons."

"Michael! I have no idea what you're talking about!" She pushed away from him, allowing her anger at Henry to be redirected at Michael. "First, you insist on keeping me because you need my work. You work me long shifts because, let's face it, the changes you've made to this place require more maintenance. You've always stood up for me when Henry's disapproved of my work. You've always allowed Patricia to help. Now you're siding with Henry, you're asking me to leave before my shifts are over, and you're forbidding Patricia from working with me. What do you want? Make up your mind!"

Michael looked uncomfortably back at the door before answering, "Perspectives change."

"What type of answer is that? Michael, what's gotten into you?" she asked, tiring of his cryptic responses.

"Do you remember the announcement Bobby and Liv made at Sophie's?" He didn't meet her eyes as he spoke.

"About them ..." The realization of what Michael implied suddenly dawned on her. "Oh my goodness. Patricia's pregnant?"

Michael didn't answer, but when he finally met Catherine's eyes, she saw his answer written there. Finally, although there was no one else around, he whispered, "I'm not supposed to say anything. But something like that *would* change one's perspective, wouldn't it?"

She pulled Michael into a strong hug to congratulate him. "Yes, I guess that would change things," she said with a smile. "How are you?"

"Besides being overwhelmed, scared out of my mind, and worried beyond belief? I'm fine."

"I don't understand, Michael. Aren't you happy about this?"

His features softened as he answered, "Yes, we're ecstatic. But Catherine, Patricia was never supposed to get pregnant. Earlier in our marriage, we learned that it would probably never happen. And if it did … let's just say, she's at a high risk for problems. We've always been so careful."

Catherine didn't want to pry, but she wanted to offer comfort and reassurance at the same time. "Michael, every pregnancy has risks. But if you're both happy about it, enjoy what God's given to you. I mean, you're going to be a *father*, Michael. How great is that?"

Despite the worry on his face, Michael broke out in a smile. "I know, and I am excited," he explained. "But I don't want a child if Patricia is the cost. I don't want to lose her."

Catherine's heart warmed at Michael's profession of love for his wife. Now she understood why he was so concerned about her working too much. "You want nothing more than to take care of her, don't you?" She hadn't realized she had spoken her thoughts out loud until she saw Michael nod in agreement.

"Yes. Kind of like the way Henry feels about you. I think your hospitalization after Robert … I think that was what changed his perspective. He only wants to protect you."

The mention of Henry's name brought back the anger she had been feeling moments earlier. "Yes, well, that doesn't give him the right to talk to you about my work. I'm not pregnant."

"He never really talked to me directly, Cat."

"No, he's just made it known to everyone how he feels." Rolling her bicycle away from the side of the building, Catherine continued, "Michael, I know you love Patricia and you want what's best for her, but here's some free advice. Let *her* decide what's best for her. Then support her, even if you don't agree with her. That way she'll never resent you for anything." She straddled the bicycle and placed a foot on the pedal. "I'll respect your wishes and stay away until tomorrow night so you don't have to fight with Patricia about working. I'll see you at the reopening, okay?"

"Do I get a dance?"

"Naturally."

"Good. And Cat, I know you're upset with Henry, but go easy on him, okay? He wants you to be safe and happy. Almost losing you nearly killed him."

Catherine wanted nothing to do with the direction this conversation was taking. She hated thinking about her time in the hospital. Inevitably, the cause of her hospital stay would resurface, and Robert would be there. Even in death, he was still able to sends chills of fear down her spine. While her body had healed from that horrific night, her mind hadn't. Her flashbacks occurred more often than she wanted people, especially Henry, to know. She hid them as best as she could, but conversations about that night were easy triggers for them.

Even now, she could feel Robert's hands tightening around her throat as she thought of him.

"Catherine!" Michael gently shook her arm, bringing her back to the present.

"I'm sorry, what was that?"

The concerned look on Michael's face was now aimed at Catherine rather than his wife. He gave her a long, serious look before saying, "You're still having a hard time with it all, aren't you?"

"Well, talking about it certainly doesn't help," she replied a bit defensively. Even as she spoke to Michael, Robert's face clouded her vision. She shook her head as she tried to clear the image. "I'll see you at the grand reopening, then?" she said, signaling her eagerness for departure.

However, Michael's hand reached out, grabbing the bicycle by the handlebar to stop her. "Catherine, are you all right?"

By now, Robert's image had gained ahold of Catherine's thoughts. Like outrunning an impending storm, Catherine knew she needed to get home as quickly as possible before the flashback completely consumed her. She saw Michael's face only briefly before Robert's took over.

"Yes, I'm going home. I'll see you later, okay?"

Michael sensed the change coming over Catherine. Although she was here talking to him, she seemed to be miles away. He feared that he had sent her traveling back in time to that nightmarish evening. While he had been eager for her to leave earlier, Michael now felt the importance of keeping her here long enough for Henry to come by to get her. "Why don't you stay for a bit, Cat? Let me call Henry to come take you home."

"You told me that wasn't an option. I need to go home. I need to go home." Catherine didn't even look at him as she answered.

Get home. Home is safe. Get home. He can't hurt you anymore.

Michael gently placed a hand on her shoulder. "Come back inside, Cat," he said with a gentle plea in his voice. But as reassuring as Michael was trying to be, Catherine only felt Robert's hand on her, trying to restrain her. His greedy hands were suddenly all over her, working their way back up to her throat.

Get away. Break free.

"Let go!" Catherine screamed. Michael instantly pulled back as though burned. Still envisioning Robert all around her, Catherine began pedaling the moment she felt the release of her shoulder.

Get home, Cat. Get home. He can't hurt you there.

But that's exactly where I did *hurt you,* Robert's voice whispered in her head.

With her home now a threat to her as well, Catherine pedaled as hard as she could to outrun the memories. Yet they remained on her heels. While the memories of Robert clouded her vision, Catherine fought frantically to keep herself grounded in the present. She had to find a safe place to hide. This thought she repeated in her mind. But where would she be safe from Robert's nightmare?

Henry. The one word, one name, was a beacon to her distressed soul. Keeping Henry foremost in her thoughts while thoughts of Robert chased close behind, Catherine struggled every bit of the way as she pedaled to Henry's house. She knew that once she was there, she'd be safe.

Robert can't touch me there.

* * *

"We're closed!" Henry called out from the garage as the office phone rang in the other room. "Don't answer it, Bobby."

"Wow, what a change of tune for you. Not working late this evening?" Bobby asked, allowing the phone to ring as he locked the front door.

Grabbing a rag and wiping his hands, Henry made his way to the office as he answered, "Not tonight. I want to spend the evening with Catherine and do something nice for her. I've been spending so much time here; I think I've neglected her a bit. And with the reopening of Sal's approaching, I know I'll have to share her with other people once we're there."

And I want to spend as much time with her creating good memories for her so she doesn't have to constantly watch you two lovebirds, Henry added silently. Ever since she had confessed to him that it was sometimes difficult to see Olivia and Bobby's blissful life unfold in her home, Henry had made it a point to give Catherine as many distractions as possible. Not that he minded. He loved spending time with her, and he had recently started to realize that by putting in so much time at the shop to build their future, he had been neglecting their present.

By this point, the phone had stopped ringing only to begin anew. "Persistent customer," Henry joked as he continued to ignore the phone. "They'll just have to wait until Monday."

"What if it's Liv or Cat?" Bobby asked as the ringing ceased.

Before the phone could start ringing again, Henry picked it up and let the receiver swing freely on the wall. "That should fix it. If it was Liv or Catherine, we're headed there anyway, right? We'll get there soon enough."

"You really are checked out for the weekend, aren't you?" Henry's carefree attitude was contagious, and Bobby found his concern over the missed calls fading.

"Absolutely. Race you there?" Henry challenged as the two headed to their vehicles.

"Just like old times, eh? You're on!"

* * *

Michael cursed after his second attempt to reach Henry at his shop failed. Since Catherine had left the club in an obvious state of distress, Michael had been trying to reach Henry. He didn't dare leave his wife, nor did he want to mention anything to her that would upset her.

"Do you plan on telling me why you're glued to the telephone?" Patricia asked as she came up behind him. "Or do you want me to eavesdrop?"

Michael turned and saw how quickly Patricia's look of curiosity changed to concern. When he didn't answer but rather redialed Henry's number once more, Patricia watched his fingers closely.

"You're dialing Henry's shop." It wasn't a question.

"Do you have everyone's number memorized?" Frustration laced his words as a busy signal sounded in his ear.

He didn't have to look at Patricia to feel her cross her arms and frown behind him. "Why are you trying to call Henry? What happened?" she demanded.

"I said something to Catherine that caused her to leave in a state of ... upset."

"Upset? And you're trying to reach her to apologize?"

"I'm trying to reach Henry. And I'm wasting time answering your questions."

"Michael, spit it out. I know you. You're frantic." He felt a reassuring hand touch his shoulder. "Calm down and tell me what happened."

Her touch soothed him, and Michael immediately felt a wave of calm descend on him. But it was only when Patricia took the phone from his hand that he answered, "I think Catherine was beginning to have a flashback from that night."

"You're sure?"

"No. But the look in her eye right before she screamed at me to let her go ... she had that same look the night I knocked her down. For a brief moment, she thought I was Robert."

"Did she call you Robert?"

Patricia's reasonable question helped Michael regain control of his emotions. "No, it's just a hunch. She's headed home, but I wanted to give Henry a heads-up. He's able to calm her down when no one else can, and I wanted to let him know what he was walking into."

"If she's headed home, why don't you call the farmhouse? Maybe Henry's already there, or you could at least talk to Olivia and let her know."

Glancing at the wall clock, he nodded. "They're probably all already there."

Patricia handed the phone back to him. "Then call to make sure she got there all right."

While Michael flashed his wife a warm smile and dialed the McKinney residence, something deep inside told him that the evening's earlier events wouldn't be so easily swept away and forgotten.

The telephone rang several times before Olivia answered. After his greeting, Olivia apologized for the delay in answering. "Cat only has one phone, you know. So when you're across the house, it takes a while. What can I do for you?"

"Is Catherine there?" If his question wasn't short enough, his tone conveyed that something was wrong.

Olivia immediately sensed it. "No, Michael. I assumed she was working late at the club."

"I let her off early. If she's not there already, she should be there soon."

"Do you want me to have her call you when she gets in?"

"Yes, please. I'd appreciate it."

Olivia began to finish the call when she abruptly changed course. "Oh, wait, Michael, I see Bobby and Henry coming, racing like two schoolboys. But I'm sure they saw Catherine on her way in. Henry probably picked her up. Give me a minute, will you?"

Relief flooded Michael at the mention of Henry being there. No doubt he would have seen Catherine and was with her already. So when Henry's deep voice, not Catherine's, came through the phone, Michael was taken by surprise.

"Michael, it's Henry. Liv said something about you looking for Catherine?"

"Um, yes, I let her off early tonight. She was headed home."

"You should have let me know. I would've come to get her. I'll head out there now if she just left."

Ice gripped Michael's heart as dread laced his next words. "I did call the shop, but no one answered. Henry, Catherine left a while back. You should have met her on your way there."

But Henry had yet to pick up on Michael's tone of concern. "She must have stopped by the store or something on her way in. I didn't see her."

"Henry, you need to find her."

Now Henry heard the worry in Michael's tone. "Michael, did something happen?"

"Henry, I think that she left here in the middle of having a flashback. She—"

But Michael didn't get to finish his sentence. Henry had dropped the phone and rushed out the door.

Henry hit his steering wheel in frustration as a third cruise through town rendered the same results: no sign of Catherine. He knew her routine well and had made sure to drive by all the places in town that she might have visited on her way home. He couldn't find her anywhere, and the lateness of the evening reinforced his need to find her. Trying to keep his mind from going wild and digging up the memories of how he had failed to protect her once before, Henry mentally went through the options of her whereabouts to distract from his rising fear.

He could go back to Catherine's house and see if by some chance he had missed her. He swiftly dismissed this idea. Based on all the routes he had taken on his search, there was no way she could have slipped by his watchful eye.

He could go to the club and get the full story from Michael. But knowing he was still upset with Michael over the events that led to her *last* flashback, he didn't trust his self-restraint enough to believe that he wouldn't pummel Michael. Plus, he reasoned, Catherine was trying to get away from the club, not find solace there.

Solace. Sanctuary. From his own horrific nightmares from the war, Henry knew that Catherine would most likely be searching for these things if she had experienced a flashback. But where would Catherine go, if not home, to find this? He thought back to the night when he had found her in his truck after their argument in his shop. His truck would be a haven for her.

Or maybe the haven is me, Henry realized as he continued scanning the streets. *Maybe she's trying to find me.* With that thought foremost in his mind, he considered going to the shop once more for a look around but decided instead to head to the one place he had yet to visit: his home. At least if she wasn't there, he could telephone both Olivia and Michael to figure out his next move.

By the time Henry got to his house on the far east side of town, the chill of early autumn conquered every inch of air. His house was a modest ranch, its white porch the only point of interest on the faded blue house. The house had always been enough for Henry until Catherine's happiness had consumed his entire being. Now he wanted to be able to provide a nice home for her, to one day live with her in a nice brick home on the opposite side of town. As much as he loved Catherine's farm and the memories associated with the place, Henry hoped to have a home built for Catherine for them to make memories in together. He wanted their future home to be one that was new for both of them.

Looking at his slightly run-down house as it came into view, he knew this was not the place where he wanted his future family to live. While his neighbors were relatively decent people, he still lived in an area where you had to lock your doors at night to be on the safe side.

Pulling into the driveway, his headlights reflected off silver handlebars, and relief immediately filled Henry as he realized Catherine's bicycle rested against the side of his house. She was here. She *did* find her safe haven in him. Barely taking time to put the truck in park and turn off the engine, he bolted from the truck and scanned the porch for her.

"Catherine? Honey?" Henry called out. Although every part of him wanted to rush the porch in search of her, Henry knew from his own flashback experiences that he needed to proceed with caution. He didn't want to make a bad situation any worse. After he cleared the bushes in front of his porch and took the first step on the stairs, his eyes caught the dark shadows of a lump in the corner. Even in the dim light, he knew it was Catherine.

Catherine sat huddled on the side of the porch most hidden by the bushes. Although it was now dark, the whites in her eyes were bright enough that Henry could see she was focused on something in front of her. She stared at nothing, but he knew she was imagining the demon from her past. Her arms were crossed, and her hands held death grips on her sleeves. Her knees were drawn up to her chest, and her body shivered. Whether it was from the fear of the image only she could see, the cold night air, or a combination of both, Henry could only guess.

Henry took off his jacket and, as though approaching a wounded animal, held his arms out, palms up, in a nonthreatening gesture. He took small steps toward her, determined not to make any sudden movements that would scare her. Yet she didn't even acknowledge his presence as he drew closer. "Catherine, sweetheart, can you hear me?" he whispered. "It's me, Henry."

Catherine's eyes blinked but otherwise remained focused straight ahead of her.

By this point, Henry was almost to Catherine. Rather than standing above her, he knelt down and crawled the last few feet that separated them. "Catherine, it's Henry. I'm going to sit beside you, okay? That's all I'm going to do. Just sit. I won't hurt you." He stopped and waited for a reply. When none came, he painstakingly turned and sat down next to her, careful not to come between her and the images on which she focused. He placed his jacket on his other side, and as much as he wanted her in his arms, he made sure that he didn't brush up against her.

He settled himself in, fully prepared to sit with her the whole night if need be, to ride through this flashback with her. While she silently relived horrors, the evening's chill began to blanket Henry so that he, too, grew cold. He reached for his jacket, but rather than put it back on, he slowly unfolded it. "Catherine, honey, I know you're probably freezing by now. I'm going to put my jacket over you, okay? It's only meant to keep you warm. It's not going to hurt you. It's only material. I'm Henry, Catherine. I'm only going to cover you up." He spoke in as soothing a voice as possible as he gradually wrapped Catherine in his jacket.

She remained unresponsive for a few more minutes. Then, like a swimmer underwater for too long, her body jerked as she inhaled deeply. Her legs kicked out unexpectedly in self-defense, but her hands seized Henry's jacket before it slipped off her. Closing her eyes, Catherine lifted the jacket up to her face, inhaling Henry's lingering scent.

"Henry?" her voice sounded frightened and timid in the night's silence.

"I'm here. I'm right beside you."

She turned toward his voice. Then, finally, she was back.

"Henry." Recognition filled her voice as she allowed him to enfold her trembling body into his arms. In one swift motion, he was on his feet with her in his arms to carry her inside. "It was you. I smelled your scent. You brought me back. But how did I—" she asked, her voice never rising above a whisper.

"Shh," Henry hushed as he unlocked the door while still holding Catherine. "Let's get you warmed up first, okay? Then we can figure it all out."

She nodded, her grip tightening around his neck as she buried her face in his shoulder.

Henry headed straight for his bedroom at the back of the house after shutting the front door behind him. Without either of them saying a word, he placed her on his bed and dragged a chair from across the room to sit by her. He rubbed her chilled arms, allowing her to fully come back to the present, before speaking.

"Welcome back, Catherine."

"How long have I been …?" She grabbed his hand to stop his comforting touch, forcing him to look her in the eyes.

"I honestly don't know. When I got to your place, Michael was on the phone in a frenzy trying to find you. I swept through town a few times before ultimately finding you on my porch."

Catherine released his hand and stared down at her lap, a frown carved into her face. "What time is it now?"

"Near midnight."

She dropped her head in her hands and took a deep breath. "That was a long one then." Embarrassment and guilt filled her. If men like Henry could handle the nightmares of war, why couldn't she handle the measly situation she had survived?

"I should go," she said, suddenly rising to her feet. "Liv is probably worried about me. Michael too."

"Whoa." Henry rose and grabbed her arm to keep her from taking another step. He held both of her shoulders and gently sat her back onto the bed. "You're not going anywhere tonight. You came here because it was safe, even in your subconscious mind. You're staying here until the morning. I'll call Liv and Michael and let them both know you're okay." He kissed her forehead. "But you need to rest."

"I can rest at home," she protested.

"No. I know who is in your flashbacks. You need an evening free from the farm," he explained as he reached behind her and pulled back the covers and gently removed her shoes one at a time. "Tomorrow, in broad daylight, we can talk about all of this. But for now, you'll sleep. I'll be in the living room sleeping on the couch if you need me." He lifted her feet up in bed and tucked the covers around her before she could protest further. Only when she was nestled in did he offer a quick smile. "I'm going to go telephone Liv and Michael. Then I'll bring you a small snack before you go to sleep, okay?"

When Henry returned several minutes later, he hoped to find Catherine asleep, the worries of the evening behind her. Instead, he found her sitting up in bed, her eyes on the door, awaiting his return. She immediately asked him, "Did you call them?"

He nodded, placing a tray of food on the nightstand beside her. "Yes.

Everyone is relieved to know you're okay. They all want you to get some rest and will see you tomorrow."

Unable to meet his eyes, Catherine began picking at the blanket that covered her. "I'm really sorry about all of this, Henry. I don't mean to be an inconvenience."

Henry sat back down in the chair next to the bed and took her hands in his before speaking. "Don't. You have no need to apologize. And I mean it when I say that this can all wait until tomorrow. I want you to sleep now. Well, eat first and then sleep."

"Thanks for pulling me out of it." She kept her focus on the blanket.

"I'm glad I have an odor strong enough to work magic," he teased. When he saw her lips curl in a small smile, his own smile broadened.

"Well, that's part of you that I have memorized, you know." Her voice was still soft as she accepted an apple from Henry, but she didn't bring it to her lips. "When you all were in Europe, I spent many nights in your truck, wearing your jacket and praying for your safe return. Even if you dragged that jacket through all the elements of nature, I'd still be able to find a trace of you lingering. It's always been a lifeline for me, you know."

"I don't know whether to be flattered or mortified."

She looked up at him, her eyes wide in the soft light the nightstand lamp provided. "You can be flattered this once, but don't let it go to your head."

Henry chuckled, and relief loosened the concern that had gripped his heart. Her teasing told him she would be okay, even as she placed the uneaten apple back on the tray, signaling that she wouldn't be eating tonight. "Well, I'll tell you what. Since it seems to be so helpful to you, why don't you keep it for now? Just until you don't need it anymore."

Or until I can be with you full-time so you won't ever need a reminder of me again.

"You may never get it back then."

Henry leaned over and gently kissed her before replying, "Something tells me that I will. Now, I'm going to leave you to rest, okay?" He waited for her nod of affirmation before turning off the lamp. From the darkness, he told her, "I'll be in the next room if you need me. Good night, Catherine. I love you."

Now that the flashback had passed, Catherine's discussion with Michael resurfaced. She knew she was supposed to be angry with Henry. Earlier, she had had every intention of putting him in his place for his suggestions to Michael about her work schedule. But in light of what he had done for her tonight, she couldn't find it in her heart to harbor those negative feelings. The only thing Catherine needed was her lifeline.

He was at the door when he heard Catherine call out, "Henry."

He stopped with his back still to her. Walking away from her was one of the hardest things he'd done tonight, and lingering in the doorway at her request made it even more difficult. The fact that Catherine was in his bed erased all the other unpleasant events of the evening. "Yes?" He didn't turn to face her. He didn't dare.

"Please ... I do need you." Her voice wavered a moment, betraying her nervousness.

Henry held his breath and turned slowly to face her. "Catherine?"

"Please, at least until I'm asleep ... can you stay with me?" she asked shyly. "Just until I fall asleep," she continued, more to herself than Henry. "But only if you want ..."

"I want," he whispered, suddenly close enough to speak in her ear, refrained desire dripping from the two words. He lay on the bed next to her, making sure he stayed completely above the covers, and wrapped her in his arms.

"Just until I—"

"I know, until you fall asleep," he whispered, a part of him wanting to keep her awake for the rest of the night. He settled for a sweet kiss on her forehead. "Sweet dreams, sweetheart."

To his surprise and utmost delight, Catherine reached out in the dark to find his lips with her own. The kiss left him hungry, and he found that his hold on Catherine involuntarily tightened. Her next words sent sensations through him that he knew meant sleep would not come for him this night.

"Don't worry," she replied in a tone that, even in its fatigue, lured Henry in deeper. She settled into the security of his arms. "I will."

Six

Susan sat at the diner's corner booth, brooding over her second cup of morning coffee. Tonight was the reopening of Sal's, or of the club formerly known as Sal's. She'd heard that Michael, as the new owner, was debating on whether to change the name, but she didn't really care. She had a beautiful, flirtatious dress for the evening's event waiting for her when she got home. She knew exactly how she'd wear her hair and makeup. But what frustrated her was that she'd be going without the most handsome man in town by her side. Instead, Henry would be going with Catherine. Just the thought of Catherine brought out the deepest hatred inside her. Susan always got what she wanted. *Always.*

I certainly won't lose anything or anyone to a country bumpkin like Catherine. You may have won the battle, little shrew, but you most certainly haven't won the war for Henry. Indeed, Susan was convinced that there had to be a crack somewhere in their relationship that could divide them. She only had to figure out what it was.

"Good morning, Henry! You're out quite early for a Saturday morning," the server at the counter called, interrupting Susan's thoughts. She looked up, a smile spreading across her face as Henry stood at the counter. It *was* early for him to be out. She knew him well enough to know he was a night owl. But what pleased her even more was that he was alone. She cast a fleeting glance out the window and spotted Henry's truck parked across the street. The cabin was empty. Catherine was nowhere in sight.

Never one to neglect an opportunity, Susan left her seat and approached Henry as he placed his order. Ignoring that he ordered two of everything, she hopped up on the stool beside him. "Good morning, Henry," she cooed.

Henry had seen Susan coming from the corner of his eye and wished he had hit the bakery across town rather than coming to this diner. As much as he wanted to ignore her, he knew he couldn't be as rude as he wanted to be—not in public. Biting back a smart retort, he didn't even look at her as he replied, "Good morning, Susan."

"He's right," Susan said as she indicated the server putting together Henry's order. "It *is* early for you. The dance isn't until this evening. I figured that you'd be home resting up."

A secretive smile spread across Henry's face. "That's a great idea. I think I'll do that as soon as I leave here."

Ignoring his smile, Susan continued, "Tonight's dance is the talk of the town. Everybody is going to be there." She coyly touched his shoulder. "I'd be willing to change my plans if you wanted me to make an appearance with you. It'd be good publicity, you know. It would drum up business for you."

"My good work ethic will drum up enough business for me, Susan, so you don't need to change your plans. Besides, I'll have Catherine with me. That's all I want and need."

"For now," Susan replied slyly. Frustrated with Henry, she tried to keep the edge out of her voice. "But you'll grow tired of her Henry, just like all the others. And I'll be here when you're ready for something more."

"Not this time, Susan," Henry responded as he shook his head, paying the server after he handed him his order. "This time, I've found what I want, and I don't have any plans of moving on. She's it for me. The sooner you figure that out, Susan, the less of a fool you'll appear to be."

She narrowed her eyes, silently noting that Henry held two cups in his hands along with the bag of food. He'd be sharing his breakfast with Catherine, no doubt. "No, Henry, you mark my words. The sooner you figure out that Catherine isn't right for you, the less of a fool *you'll* be."

Henry glared at Susan, again wondering what he had ever seen in her. "Then I guess I'll die a fool," he replied seriously. Without another word, Henry left Susan alone at the counter.

Embarrassment and anger raged inside her. She watched Henry put his breakfast inside his truck, and her mouth fell agape when she saw him abruptly turn and step into Zachariah's Unique Glass Shop, the local glassware and jewelry store.

"No. Surely he's not thinking …" she said aloud in disbelief. *Marry Catherine? Had Henry gone insane?*

"Whatever he's thinking, he's been thinking on it for the past several Saturdays."

"Excuse me?" Irritation filled Susan as she addressed the busboy cleaning a table near her.

The boy timidly shrunk back at Susan's forceful manner. "I'm sorry. It's none of my business. Pardon me," he mumbled, stepping back hesitantly.

"Well, now that you've said it, you might as well finish it. What do you mean?" She jerked her thumb out the window toward the jewelry shop and asked, "Henry … what business does he have with Zachariah?"

The boy glanced past Susan's shoulder to the shop across the street but didn't say a word, obviously afraid to speak further.

"Elaborate, please." While her words were polite, the iciness in her eyes displayed no patience.

"I only meant that I've seen him go in there for the past several Saturdays now."

"Do you know why?"

Confusion lit the boy's eyes before he answered, "To buy jewelry? Or maybe a vase?"

"And tell me, has he ever come out with a purchase?"

"Um, not that I can recall. Every Friday, new shipments come in, so I assumed he went to look at the new items. Window-shopping. Haven't you ever—"

"No," Susan interrupted him. "I've never had the need for it." An idea dawned on her, and she quickly reached in her purse to find her wallet. "What's your name?" she asked as she fumbled through her money.

"Todd, ma'am."

"Well, Todd, I'm going to give you the opportunity to earn a little extra money." She discreetly slid the money across the table to the lad. "Take it. That's for the information you've already provided me."

"But I only said what was obvious," he said, shaking his head and refusing the money.

"But this is also for what you're *going* to do for me." She nudged it back toward him and explained, "You're going to find out why Henry's visiting the store every Saturday. If he is more than window-shopping, I want to know what he's in search of. Do you understand?"

"You want to see if he's buying an engagement ring?"

Does everyone know about Henry and Catherine? Susan forced a bitter smile to her face and replied, "Exactly. You get me the information I need, and I'll double what I just gave you."

Todd's eyes widened as he did the math in his head. "Yes, ma'am," he agreed, unable to walk away from the large sum of money.

Satisfied that she now had a loyal spy, Susan smiled. She felt in control again, knowing that she had someone looking into Henry's business for her. As thoughts began to formulate in her mind, she realized that none of this had anything to do with getting Henry, but it had everything to do with bringing down Catherine.

"Find out what I need to know by the end of the night, and I'll triple it."

* * *

The sound of keys jingling in the doorknob caused Catherine to awaken. When she first opened her eyes and observed her surroundings, she felt disoriented. She was supposed to be in her bed, her room across the hallway from her late brother's.

And I'm definitely not supposed to still be wearing my clothes from the previous day. Catherine sat up in bed, yesterday's sweat and dirt still clinging to her. In a somewhat groggy state, she focused on the picture resting on the nightstand next to her. The photo of her brought most of the previous evening's events crashing down on her. She was in Henry's home, *in Henry's bed ...*

The flashback. Everything came rushing back to her, and by the time Henry stood in the bedroom doorway, she had nearly everything pieced together. She was at the club when the flashback had started. She had no idea how long it had lasted or how she had managed to get herself to Henry's.

"My bike," she whispered out loud, still trying to figure out the puzzle of her transportation.

"Don't worry, it's safe," Henry offered as he stepped into the room. "Good morning. Are you feeling better?"

She looked at him, a self-conscious crimson covering her neck and cheeks. "Better? I'm sorry, I must look terrible. And smell even worse."

He smiled, sitting down in the chair across from her, and said, "You being here is more important than any of that. I didn't know if you'd be hungry. And seeing as this house isn't really equipped for morning guests, I ran into town to get you something. I thought it'd be too much to ask you, my guest, to make me pancakes." He gave her a wink, reaching out to grab her hand and lace his fingers with hers.

She returned his smile with a meek one. She knew she owed him her appreciation, an explanation, and clarification but didn't know where to begin. She was silent a little longer before finding her voice. "My bike?"

"I went out last night after you went to sleep and put it in my shed. It's not out there for everyone to see and give reason to create a scandalous rumor."

"Oh, Henry, I didn't mean it that way." For once, people's perception of her at Henry's was the furthest thing from her mind.

"I know. But I can see the confusion written on your face. And once you get everything figured out and have time to focus on that aspect, I want you to know that I've already taken care of it. I won't have anyone seeing you in a negative light."

His thoughtfulness shook her to the core. *I don't deserve this man.*

His gentle prodding broke through her train of thoughts. "Catherine, honey, are you up to talking about it?" he asked.

She shook her head and responded, "Doesn't really matter if I am, does it? I need to figure it out, I guess."

"Come on, let's go to the kitchen and sit down to breakfast. That'll help clear your head. And I'll start, if that makes it easier."

"I don't see how it can hurt."

Lifting her to her feet, he planted a kiss on her nose before leading her to the kitchen, diving into what he knew. "Michael called at the farm last night looking for you. He said that he let you out early, but when you left, you screamed at him and rode off. I instantly started looking for you when I found out. It took a bit of time to find you, and it was only because I had run out of all other options. I never really expected you to be here. But when I got here, there you were, sitting in a corner of the porch. You didn't snap out of it right away, not until you had my jacket around you."

"I remember everything from that point on. It's everything else that's a little unclear." She chewed on her lip nervously as she forced herself to recall all that she could of the previous night's events.

Henry sat across the table in complete silence, patiently waiting for Catherine to figure this out on her own. He opened the bag from the diner and pulled out a muffin for each of them.

He handed Catherine hers, but she didn't acknowledge the act as she began again, thinking out loud, "I remember leaving the club last night pretty upset. *At you.*"

As Catherine recalled this, the anger he knew too well flashed across her blue eyes. "At me?" he asked. "What did I do?"

"I'll get back to that, I'm sure. I think the more important question to ask is how I got here. I remember the flashback coming on, and I had been focused on you and getting to you before I lost all sense of where I was. When I snapped out of it, I was here." She shook her head as though the movement would clear her jumbled thoughts.

"Do you remember, when you focused on me, what was going through your head?"

"Besides Robert?" She involuntarily shuddered at even mentioning his name. Henry gently reached for her hand to offer comfort.

"Yes," he encouraged. "I know this is difficult, but if we can figure out any clues to this whole process, maybe that'll help in the future."

Catherine groaned inwardly. She didn't like the idea of future flashbacks. Realizing that she had no memory of getting to Henry's house made her fear them even more. What if she had a flashback in a place that she wasn't familiar with? Would she be putting herself in danger? What if she couldn't reach Henry? "The last thing I remember was telling myself to find you, that getting to you would be my haven. Robert couldn't hurt me if I was with you. And when I came out of it, your scent was all around me."

While Henry's heart soared at hearing this, his mind analyzed her words. He leaned over and grabbed her chair, drawing her to him. In one swift motion, he had her sitting on his lap in his arms. Pushing a few wild strands of hair behind her ear, he took her chin in his hand and turned her face to him. "Always let me be your safe haven, Catherine. Anytime Robert resurfaces or any other evil from your past, present, or future, know that I will always be here. Focus on me, and no matter what, will yourself to come back to me. So long as you believe in me, I'll always find you and bring you back home."

Home. The word that should normally offer comfort left a cavity in Catherine. Henry was her home. The fact that he was her beacon while she was lost within the nightmares of her mind *was* comforting, but in truth, she still wanted to depend only on herself for overcoming the flashbacks. Time on her own over the last few years had left her with an independence few women her age had. She was so used to relying on herself that dependence on someone else for anything was hard to acknowledge. As much as she loved Henry, it bothered her that she wasn't strong enough to free herself from the flashback.

She was even more disappointed that she lacked the strength of mind to keep from revisiting her nightmarish past. Henry, who had endured the horrors of war, seemed to handle his ghosts a lot easier than she could. Heaviness filled her as she remembered Susan's taunting. Henry was her beacon and offered her security. What could Catherine ever offer him? She had a farm, but her friends currently inhabited that with her. She had a job that barely covered her meager living expenses, and she was fairly certain how Henry felt about her work. Finally, even while he held her in his arms and offered her physical comfort, she lacked the experience to offer him the type of physical comfort he needed. Even if they were one day married, she knew she could never compete with the years of experience he had with other women … *with Susan.* A wave of jealousy flamed within her. But before she was able to travel any farther down that path, Henry interrupted her thoughts.

"Catherine?"

She blinked and gazed into a pair of eyes that deeply searched hers. "Yes?"

"Do you promise?" He had held his breath when she didn't respond at first, afraid that she was once again being visited by Robert's memory.

"Promise you what? I'm sorry, I was thinking on something else."

"Promise me that you'll always believe in me and let me find you … no matter how far away you are."

The tightening of his arms around her told her how serious this promise was to him. "Henry, I hope at some point to be able to—"

"You'd do the same for me, right?" he interrupted. "You *have* done the same for me." He didn't have to explain what he was referring to. She still blushed every time she remembered posing as his fiancée in order to get information about him when he was MIA. For Henry, discovering what Catherine had done had allowed his hope of a life with Catherine to blossom. In that moment, he started to believe that her affections matched his own. Now, when she nodded, Henry pulled both of them to their feet. He cradled her face in his hands and added, "Then let me be there for you."

"Okay," her voice was a whisper. "I promise."

As he started to reach down for a kiss, she turned away suddenly, her hand protectively covering her mouth. He gave her an inquisitive look so she explained, "Morning breath. I'm in desperate need of toothpaste, shampoo, a shower ..." As she spoke, she wiggled out of his embrace.

Henry chuckled at her self-consciousness as he pulled her back into his embrace. "I'm loving the view from here, seeing you first thing in the morning. I could get used to this." Before she could find the opportunity to argue, his mouth covered hers with a hunger that no amount of food would satisfy.

He loved having her here, loved that she needed him. Knowing that he was able to bring her back from flashbacks served as an additional reason for keeping her near him. Not that he needed another reason, and he actually hoped she'd never have another flashback. Although he had left her to hide her bicycle after she had gone to sleep, he had returned to her side and watched her sleep until leaving to get them breakfast earlier this morning.

As much as he hated the reason for her presence in his home, he had loved every minute of having her here, and he wanted more mornings like this. Indeed, he wanted to be the first one to see her in the morning and the last to see her at night.

Every Saturday for the past month, Henry had visited the local jeweler to see the newest arrivals. The jeweler was an old acquaintance of Henry's from when Henry had used Zachariah's services to purchase a replacement vase for Catherine. Familiar with the reason for Henry's frequent visits, Zachariah tried to keep an eye out for the perfect engagement ring. Henry finally had found it on this morning's visit. He made the purchase immediately and asked Zachariah to keep it until he could get a better idea of

Catherine's ring size. Henry thought it would take longer to find the perfect ring for Catherine, so he had figured that he'd have plenty of time to find out her size. Now that he had the ring purchased, he wanted more than anything to give it to her, to see it displayed on her hand, announcing to the world that she was his. Yet he wasn't about to give it to her in the wrong size.

Catherine's been through so much ... she deserves something perfect. I'm not about to give her a ring that isn't the perfect fit.

Catherine broke free of his hold, bringing Henry out of his reverie. "Seriously, Henry, I feel disgusting," she was saying. "Can you please take me home so I can shower and change? Especially since we're going to the club tonight for Michael's reopening."

"You could shower here," he suggested.

"I don't have any other clothes with me," she argued, swatting at him as she took in his devilish look. "No, Henry! Take me home, please."

He held up his hands in defeat, smiling. He kept the smile on his face as he said his next words, not knowing how she would take them. "Catherine, maybe you should keep an extra set of clothes here, just in case ..." Despite his light tone, he was being completely serious, and it honestly wasn't for the reason of sharing a bed with her.

Catherine's eyes flashed, and Henry knew instantly that she took offense at what he had said. "Just in case what, Henry? That would make it easier for you to try and keep me here at night, wouldn't it?"

Seeing that Catherine thought he was implying a more intimate reason, he shook his head in frustration. "No, Catherine. I told you before that I wouldn't ask you to stay with me like that, not in that way. I know you're uncomfortable with it, and I won't compromise you. I only meant in case you have another flashback."

"You mean in case I can't overcome this?"

The hurt in Catherine's eyes tore at his heart. He hugged her fiercely and said, "You will overcome this, Catherine. But trust me, it may take a while. Or it may never happen again. But knowing that you have something here, well, it means you're preparing for the situation. I find that if you prepare, it's easier to fight. If the war taught me anything, it's that preparation makes the battles easier to win."

But unfortunately, there's still the fight, he silently added. Still seeing indecision in her eyes, he continued, "At least think about it, okay? But for now, I'll take you home." He laced his fingers with hers, already making up his mind that her decision didn't matter. He would buy her some clothes to keep here. If a repeat of last night never happened again, she'd be none the wiser.

"I'll think about it," Catherine answered, already determined not to give any excuse for staying here. With clothes here, it would be too easy to stay, regardless of whether she had a flashback. Having a set of clothes would make things too easy and weaken any resolve she still had. Even now, her desire to go home to a house filled with people waned as she soaked up the cozy quietness that surrounded them. Here, it was just the two of them. How often did they have time alone from everyone else? It was seldom. There was always someone else around. Usually, she didn't mind. But this morning, with no one around to serve as a distraction, her resolve was weak. She prayed that Henry couldn't pick up on that. It would only take a small nudge to send her down a path she'd regret later.

Henry saw her mind whirring as she looked around the room. He realized that even though she wanted to leave and needed to go home, she was reluctant to as well. If she wanted to stay, then he wasn't about to hurry her out the door.

"If I told you that I had an extra, unused toothbrush, would you be willing to use it and stay for at least part of the morning with me?" he asked. "I promise to have you back to your house by noon. That's plenty of time to get ready for tonight, right?"

Catherine opened her mouth to reply that she needed to help tidy up the club, but suddenly remembered that Michael had asked her to stay away for Patricia's sake. That was the only excuse that she had, and as she saw it crumble before her eyes, she found herself nodding before she could think of another reason to leave.

Truth is, you're a couple. Why are you looking for reasons not to be with him?

A timid smile touched her lips as she watched Henry nearly trip over his feet to get to the bathroom. While the action was endearing, it also made a wave of guilt pass through Catherine. But it was only after she brushed her teeth and found Henry waiting eagerly outside the bathroom for her that she laid the guilt at his feet.

"I'm sorry, Henry. This has made me realize that even if I'm not comfortable with certain ... levels of intimacy, that doesn't mean I should be avoiding time alone with you altogether. I've neglected private time with you that we both apparently needed. I—"

Henry's impatience won out as he pulled her into an embrace and smothered her neck with kisses. "Tell you what," his husky voice whispered in her ear, sending pleasant shivers through her, "you can spend the rest of the morning making it up to me. It's a much better use of your time than apologizing." Catherine never got the opportunity to protest.

SEVEN

Todd busily wiped down the table closest to Zachariah Hastings, the glass shop owner, as he sat in a booth savoring the two pieces of apple pie he had ordered before heading home for the evening. Todd couldn't believe his fortune. He wouldn't have to travel to the store and feign interest in the merchandise to get the information he needed. If he could only keep Mr. Hastings here long enough to learn about Henry Bradley's visits, it would be the easiest money he'd ever earned. Susan's promise of tripling the total sum encouraged Todd to gain as much information as possible tonight.

He waited until Mr. Hastings had finished the pie and placed his fork on the plate before speaking to him. "Did you enjoy your pie, Mr. Hastings?"

"Immensely," the older man replied, rubbing his stomach in appreciation.

He looked over his shoulder to make sure his boss didn't see him in idle conversation before continuing, "Two pieces today. You must be celebrating."

Mr. Hastings grinned broadly, his mustache partially covering his smile. "Is it that obvious? Well, no matter. Yes, indeed. And I plan to take the missus out for a fine dinner this evening. Not," he quickly caught himself, "that this isn't a fine place to eat. It's just that—"

"It's okay, Mr. Hastings. I understand. You want to take her somewhere she can get dressed up for."

"Precisely, my boy. Precisely."

"You could always take her to Sal's. I hear they're having a reopening tonight."

"Oh no, I couldn't!" His eyes shown mischievously as he spoke. "That'd be too much of a risk."

"Risk, Mr. Hastings? I don't understand."

It was obvious that Mr. Hastings was busting at the seams to share some sort of news. Todd hoped it was the news he needed. "Can you keep a secret, lad?" he asked, not waiting for Todd to respond before tugging him into the booth. Draping a friendly arm around him, Mr. Hastings spoke in a hushed voice, "Mr. Henry Bradley is known throughout town for his dancing, you know."

"Yes sir, he is. Although I've never had the opportunity to see him dance."

"It's a site to behold. But at any rate, he'll be there tonight, you see."

"No, Mr. Hastings, I don't see. What does that have to do with you not being able to take your wife there?"

"Do you also know that Mr. Bradley is seeing Ms. Catherine McKinney?" Todd nodded, feeling that a verbal response would only delay the information he was trying to obtain. "Well, then, she'll naturally be there as well," the man continued. "A beautiful, independent woman, that's Ms. McKinney." He patted Todd's shoulder, as if that explained everything.

"I'm sorry, Mr. Hastings, I still don't understand."

"What? Oh, I suppose not. You weren't there, after all. Well recently—this morning, in fact—Mr. Bradley became a very valued customer of mine." He gave Todd a wink and leaned in closer. "Mr. Bradley purchased a very, very expensive gift for Ms. McKinney. Not a vase like last time," he whispered, chuckling to himself. "I told him he'd be a repeat customer."

"Expensive?" Todd asked, trying to follow the man's thoughts.

"Well, expensive enough for me to want to take my wife out and celebrate! But this gift is a surprise for Ms. McKinney. So, you see, I can't go to the club tonight. I don't want to take the chance of ruining the surprise and congratulating her prematurely!"

Todd understood now what Mr. Hastings was implying, but he feared the wrath of Susan, so he wanted verbal clarification. "Do you mean that—"

"An engagement ring, young man. Henry Bradley is going to propose to Catherine McKinney! And I can't be happier for them. She's suffered quite a bit of heartache over the past several years. She deserves this happiness!"

"That's swell, Mr. Hastings. Do you know when?"

He shook his head, a smile still plastered on his face as he answered,

"I still have the ring. He's got some planning to do beforehand. But what a celebration that will create!"

Feeling that Todd had enough information to earn his triple pay for the evening, he let Mr. Hastings ramble on a bit longer before apologizing that he needed to get back to work.

An hour later, Todd headed home to prepare for the evening. He wasn't old enough to get into the club through the front door, so he'd have to come up with another way to give the mayor's daughter the information she had requested. He did feel a bit guilty. He had always liked Henry. When he came in for breakfast, Henry was pleasant, tipped well, and always asked about Todd's family. Todd was truly happy for him and Catherine. Susan, on the other hand, was difficult to handle. Everyone knew that crossing paths with Susan was like receiving a death sentence. The way that Susan blackballed Catherine was proof enough of that. Todd didn't like that he had been snared by Susan's trap. However, he needed the money. So as he hurried home, he formulated a plan. He would give Susan the information she needed, but only enough to get his payment. He'd withhold as much as possible. He'd then talk to Henry and let him know what was happening. He only hoped that he didn't create an even bigger disaster by trying to help.

* * *

Catherine could hear little Caleb's squeals of delight as Bobby chased his son down the hall outside her bedroom. While Caleb believed the chase was a game, it was obvious to anyone who looked at Bobby's flustered face that it was anything but. Although the aftereffects from last night still lingered, she found herself smiling at the two of them.

"Come on, Caleb. If I don't have you ready for your grandparents, your Momma's going to kill me!"

But Caleb seemed unaffected by this threat to his father's life. He continued to run about the hallways, managing to escape his father's arm swipes each time. Yet his squeals turned to near uncontrollable frenzy when Henry's voice drifted up from the lower floor of the farmhouse.

"Hello!" Henry shut the door behind him before asking, "Is everyone ready, or is it still the same madhouse that it was when I left earlier today?" He smiled warmly as Caleb came hurtling down the stairs as fast as his chubby little legs would carry him. He ran and jumped into Henry's arms as Bobby pulled up behind him, wiping his sweaty brow.

"Good! You hang on to him for a while. That little man has been running me ragged all afternoon," Bobby explained as he stole a glance up the stairs before continuing, "Olivia is going to have my hide if I'm not ready soon. You don't mind, do you? Until Catherine's finished, at least?"

Henry shook his head, already wrestling with Bobby's son after tossing him on the couch. "Take your time. But the moment Catherine's ready, we're gone."

"I'm almost ready!" Catherine called down from her bedroom door.

"You had to choose the most practical girl in town, didn't you?" Bobby asked Henry but aimed the question up the stairs to Catherine. "Come on, Cat. Give me a fighting chance, will you?" He started to head back up the stairs but stopped as Henry quickly grabbed his arm and motioned him to follow him into the kitchen.

Hearing the men move into the kitchen, Catherine didn't bother giving a response. Instead, she beheld her image once more in her bedroom mirror. The dress she wore was the one that her brother, Caleb, had bought for her what felt like a lifetime ago. Having only been able to bring herself to wear it a few times since his death, Catherine found that this time was no easier than the first time she wore it. She felt her throat constrict as memories of his carefree spirit came to mind. He loved to dance, and he would have loved going out with all of them tonight. Catherine refused to let her mind wander to the last time the club had a big event: the tribute to her brother. The dance itself had been a success, but discovering Robert in her home afterward had placed a stain on the memory that would never go away.

Don't you dare go down that path, Catherine silently scolded herself. With the most recent flashback fresh in her mind, she wanted to avoid another one at any cost. Looking around her room franticly, her eyes fell on Henry's jacket lying on her bed. In desperation, Catherine grabbed the jacket and held it in her clutches. She kept her focus on Henry, on the image of his face, and on the smell of his cologne. She stood that way for a while, and when the threat of a flashback finally passed, Catherine returned the jacket to her bed.

"How has she been since I left?" Henry asked Bobby as soon as the kitchen door swung closed behind them.

"Okay, Henry. A bit quiet, perhaps, but okay. We learned a long time ago not to pry or press her for anything. As much as Liv wants to talk to her, I have to brag that she's been resisting. That's a big thing for my wife."

"Give Liv some credit, Bobby. She knows when she can pry and when she shouldn't. This is a 'shouldn't' time. But I'm glad to hear that she's doing okay. I'd be lying if I said I wasn't a little bit concerned about tonight, though."

Bobby worked on his tie as he listened to Henry. It was difficult with one hand, but he'd had enough practice to do a fair job. Olivia would come behind him later and polish it up if need be. "Why?" he asked. "You and Cat have been to the club several times since ..." He found that he didn't want to finish the sentence. The night when Robert almost killed Catherine still haunted them all.

Yet he didn't have to. "Yes, but she had a flashback about that evening last night, Bobby," Henry explained. "And this evening, even though it's an official reopening, well, we both know that some sort of tribute will be given to Sal. Michael's too classy to do it any other way."

"I guess so."

"I'm going to have to keep an extra eye on her tonight, that's all. And if we cut out early, you'll know the reason."

A roguish smile spread across Bobby's face as he posed a question. "If you cut out early, will you head here or back to your place? She seemed to do well there last night, if I'm not mistaken."

"You're worse than Liv, you know that? Didn't you learn anything from the last time you made assumptions about us?" Henry shook his head, hating that he had likewise given thought about what should happen if they needed to leave early. But he didn't want to admit that to Bobby. "Let's hope it doesn't come to that."

Bobby grinned but nodded. "Indeed. So, if that's all you need, can I go get ready now? My time is valuable when you're watching Caleb."

Now entertaining the young boy by jostling him on his knee, Henry shook his head. "Not yet. That's not the real reason I dragged you in here," Henry replied. He arched a doubting eyebrow at Bobby before continuing, "I did have a small favor to ask you. But seeing as you're worse than Liv, I may need to ask her instead. And I really don't want Liv involved in this."

Bobby was instantly intrigued. The fact that there was something that Henry wanted only him to know about made him feel good. While the four of them had a great, open friendship, he still appreciated that some things needed to be kept between the men. He stopped messing with his tie and sat down at the table.

"I thought you said your time was valuable."

"Especially when it involves something secretive," Bobby nodded. "There's not much that I can do, so the fact that you're asking me to do anything at all, well, of course, I'm curious."

"Not a word to Liv."

"Oh, this must really be good."

"Bobby, I'm serious. Not a word."

Hearing the threat in Henry's words, Bobby realized that the topic of conversation had to be Catherine. He looked over his shoulder to make sure no one lurked there before turning back to Henry. "This is about Cat, isn't it?" he asked.

"I'm not saying another word until you promise to keep quiet." As Bobby held up his hand to make a silent oath, Henry continued, "I don't want this getting back to Catherine before I'm ready."

"You bought her a ring." Bobby's voice dropped to a mere whisper as he made his prediction.

When Henry nodded, the two men exchanged deep smiles.

"Finally. After all this time, Henry. It was always supposed to happen, you know. Caleb saw it long ago."

Henry knew that Bobby was referring to the letter Catherine's brother had left for him after his death overseas. He had begged Henry to consider Catherine. But the irony of it all was that Henry had fallen in love with her before reading Caleb's request. He was only sorry that Caleb wouldn't see their happy ending.

"Do you have it with you?" Bobby interrupted his thoughts.

"No, that's what I need your help on. It's still at the shop, but I don't want to pick it up until it's perfect. I want to make sure it fits before I give it to Catherine."

Confusion furrowed Bobby's brow. "Are you sure you don't want Liv involved?" he asked.

"Definitely not. I need you to somehow find out Catherine's ring size. I want this to be a complete surprise, or I'd ask her myself."

"Does Catherine even own a piece of jewelry?" Bobby asked more to himself than to Henry.

"I don't know. But her mother did. Lots of it. I've seen Catherine wear some pieces from time to time." He waited for Bobby to make the connection and, when it seemed that he wasn't going to, added, "What room are you and Liv staying in?"

"Catherine's parents' room ..." As it dawned on him, a smile emerged from his face. "I think there are still some things of her mom's in the closet. I can definitely look around and see what I can uncover. But you know that Liv is going to ask why I'm snooping."

Henry acknowledged Bobby's concern. "I thought about that. I'm going to tell Catherine that you want to surprise Liv with a home-cooked meal tomorrow, so she needs to get Liv out of the house. You'll have the place to yourself then."

"Great. While that helps *you* out, it puts me in a bind."

"How?"

"Now I've got to come up with something to surprise my wife for dinner. Everyone knows I can't cook!"

Henry laughed at the desperate look on Bobby's face and said, "Tell you what, you help me with that ring size, and I'll make sure that Liv has a romantic meal to come home to tomorrow night. Deal?"

Bobby gave one last frustrated tug at his tie as he scowled at his best friend. "I want you here the second Catherine leaves with her, okay? Come ready to cook. She loves Italian." Yet even as he tried to be firm with Henry, a smile surfaced as he added, "But seriously, should I congratulate you now or later?"

"Wait until it's official. Then you can congratulate us together."

* * *

Every night that Michael's uncle had opened up Sal's for dancing, he had stood at the door and greeted the customers. Sal had had a sharp memory, retaining information about each person that had graced his club. He had known everything about everyone. Sal had made it a point to learn each person's unique traits, and the public had loved him for that. As Michael now stood in the place that Sal had occupied for years, he felt a knot form in his throat. He strived to fill the large shoes left behind. For the past several months, Sal had groomed Michael to take over, as if he had known he didn't have much more time. Michael understood the importance of knowing the people that kept the club in business. But he didn't know nearly as much as Sal did.

Yes, but Uncle spent several years cultivating these relationships. I can't get there overnight. Although Michael appeared to have complete confidence in what he was doing, Patricia, who stood beside him greeting the dancers, could see right through the façade. The only indication that she sensed his uncertainty was the occasional hand squeeze and wink that she gave him while working her magic to charm the patrons.

While she greeted the couple with whom Michael had just finished speaking, he saw her slightly avert her gaze and nod in the direction at the end of the line. Michael looked to where she indicated and felt relief flow through him at the sight of Henry and Catherine. To anyone else, they looked like a very connected couple, but Michael quickly discerned that they were a bit off from their normal disposition. Henry's arm snaked around Catherine's waist a little bit tighter than usual, as though he could be a physical barrier to protect her from anything the world threw at her. And Catherine, the independent woman who normally shied away from such public affection, seemed practically glued to Henry's arm. With her free hand, she gripped Henry's jacket with a strength that whitened her knuckles.

Although Henry had phoned him earlier to let him know that Catherine was okay, it was clear that last night's ordeal was not completely out of her system.

"Henry, darling!" Patricia cut through his thoughtful observation as she crossed past Michael to reach the couple before him. "You look incredibly handsome. If I wasn't already married and you weren't spoken for ..." She smiled, tsk-tsking at the same time. "But no matter. For now, I'm going to enjoy your charms. I insist you walk me in so that I can show you to your table."

"Catherine and I shouldn't have a problem locating it," Henry replied, finding his protectiveness take over at the thought of leaving Catherine alone, if only briefly.

"Nonsense," Patricia replied matter-of-factly. "Michael will be escorting Catherine in soon enough, but he owes her an apology. And since we both know how you two will be inseparable on the dance floor, he better make good on his apology while he has the chance." She gave Catherine's hand a reassuring squeeze as she disentangled it from Henry's arm.

The second she was free, Michael seized Catherine in his arms, giving her a crushing hug. Patricia was already walking away with Henry when Michael whispered in Catherine's ear, "She's right, you know. I do owe you an apology."

Catherine pulled back, an embarrassing sadness written in her eyes. "No," she began, "it's I who owe you the apology. I'm sorry I screamed at you yesterday and fled. I'm sure that I had you really worried. I should have more control over … *things*."

"Ah, love, you have nothing to apologize for. But if it'll make you feel better, all is forgiven. I, however, seem to be a bad luck charm for you."

"What? Michael, you're anything but bad luck."

He raised a skeptical brow and responded, "Sure. I just happen to be the source that has triggered your last two episodes."

She shook her head and held up Henry's jacket, explaining, "Well, there's no fear of it tonight. This is what brought me out of it last night: my own security blanket."

"And not the man himself?"

Catherine's gaze fell on Henry as he escorted Patricia inside the club. "He is my security, Michael," she whispered. "And that's a dangerous thing. He can't be with me all the time. Besides, I've got to get this thing fixed on my own. He's not going to want someone broken that he has to constantly repair."

She started to head inside, but Michael stopped her. "He said that?" He gave her a doubting look, hoping that she'd realize how foolish she sounded. "Judging from the way he's sticking to you, I think it's probably quite the opposite. He seems to be hanging on to you as tightly as he can. He's definitely not going anywhere." He ushered her through the door, leaning in like a conspirator as he spoke. "Has he ever mentioned marriage?"

"And *that* brings our conversation to an abrupt end," Catherine said with enough force to cause Michael to *almost* regret his question.

He smiled as they approached the table and saw Henry still standing, waiting for her. "Well, maybe with you, but I'm betting Henry wouldn't be opposed to the conversation," he commented with a wry smile. By this point, they had reached the table and his comments were loud enough for Henry to hear.

"And what conversation is that?" Henry asked, immediately sliding in to gain possession of Catherine once more. Henry watched as Catherine silenced Michael with a look that he himself had received numerous times. Whatever they had been talking about must have been serious, despite Michael's carefree smile.

"It's nothing," Catherine lied, shaking her head and taking the seat that Henry held out for her.

"I know that's not true," Henry answered as he sat down next to her. He grabbed her hand and rubbed his thumb over her knuckles. He waited until Michael had whisked Patricia away in anticipation of making his opening remarks before saying anything else. "You can let go of the jacket, you know," he said, indicating her left hand that still gripped it. "You can hang on to me instead. It might be difficult to dance out there with it in your hand."

Seizing the opportunity to avoid telling him what she and Michael had been discussing, Catherine smiled. "Michael said as much, about not needing the jacket since you're here," she said.

"Sounds like Michael knows what he's talking about. I'll have to remember to thank him for being on my side."

Any additional private conversation the two may have shared ceased as Olivia and Bobby arrived and took their places at the table. The conversation instantly turned more casual, and Catherine felt a wave of relief as they fell into their familiar routine. Henry continued to hold her hand on his knee under the table, squeezing it on occasion or caressing it with his thumb.

As always, Henry's touch sent sensations throughout her, and Catherine gave a small shudder. Henry, realizing he was the cause, smiled inwardly, and he began to massage her hand with his.

While she listened to Olivia's easy chatter, she threw Henry a scolding look, trying to disengage her hand from his. But the hunger in her eyes told him that this wasn't what she really wanted. So he held on tighter.

"I want to thank you all for coming out tonight." Michael's voice cut through conversations throughout the club. "As you all are aware, my Uncle

Sal established this club several years ago. His sweat and tears went into it, and he loved this place with everything in him. Seeing so many familiar faces, it's easy to see that this place holds many great memories for you all as well. It is my deepest prayer that I'll be able to continue Sal's legacy. He left enormous shoes that I can never fill. However, through hard work and everyone's support, I hope to at least pay tribute to my uncle every day for the rest of my life by keeping this club as dear to my heart as it was to his." Michael was humbled as he observed the crowd and took in the large number of patrons listening to his words. Emotions fought to overtake him, and he realized that he only had a small amount of strength left to complete his speech. Taking a deep breath, he concluded, "So without further ado, let's make this a night that would make Sal proud. The dance floor is officially open!"

With that, the band filled the club with a lively tune before Michael was even off the dance floor. As he approached his friends' table, Patricia rose from her seat. She hastily wiped at her eyes before grabbing Michael's hand. "Come on, darling, no time for sadness," she said as she led him back toward the dance floor. "We've got an evening full of dancing ahead of us."

He hesitated a moment, looking at her with concerned eyes. "Are you sure?" he asked.

"Oh, for pity's sake, yes! I won't overdo it, I promise!" she exclaimed as she rolled her eyes and gave his hand a hard tug. "If you won't come, I'll go find another partner." Michael needed no more encouragement. He threw the rest of the group a smile and followed his wife out to the dance floor.

Olivia and Bobby soon followed, leaving Catherine and Henry alone at the table. "Are you all right?" she asked, knowing they were both thinking about Caleb's tribute.

Henry nodded and simply replied, "Yes." Rising to his feet, he drew her up with him and smiled. Before she knew it, he had her pressed against him, nuzzling her neck. His voice was husky as he whispered in her ear, "Tonight will be different, sweetheart. Tonight, I'm going to seduce you on the dance floor. I'm not going to let another man touch you. And I'm going to let my imagination run wild and enjoy every minute of it."

Heat filled Catherine's face, and she was glad the dim lighting would conceal it. While his words set her pulse racing, she knew encouraging him would only weaken her own resolve. "Henry, stop," she said, hating how unconvincing she sounded.

He leaned in and kissed her hungrily on the lips, then pulled back, smiling. "Nope," he replied. "This is the one place where we can get away with it. People may roll their eyes, but they won't be whispering about our dancing tomorrow. And I know the type of dancing that you're capable of, Catherine." He leaned in again, and Catherine found herself holding her breath, both wanting and not wanting to stop him. The suggestive words in her ear sent many more sensations through her spine, and she found that she instinctively clung to his shirt to keep from collapsing as he whispered, "It's with great anticipation that I look forward to you seducing me."

Susan feigned interest in the conversation at her table. She even smiled flirtatiously at her date as he offered to bring her a drink from the bar. Yet the moment he was out of sight and the conversation didn't require her opinion, Susan focused her full attention once again on the couple dancing out on the floor.

Henry and Catherine's dancing was impressive, and Catherine's progress only gave Susan more reason to hate her. The two collected admiration from everyone else on the dance floor as couples politely gave way to let the two have more room to maneuver. Susan remembered all too well the times when people had given way to her and Henry's dancing. While Henry's moves were exact and well-practiced, Susan wasn't blind to the look he had in his eyes for his partner. While to most they appeared to be just dancing, Susan knew that the way Henry looked at Catherine was anything but innocent.

It was obvious that Henry was in love with Catherine. As the music changed to a slow song, Henry held Catherine closer, whispering in her ear and gently stealing kisses, and Susan knew Catherine wasn't a passing fancy. Susan had never been on the receiving end of such intimate looks from him. Although she and other girls may have been intimate with him in the past, it never reached his eyes. He was displaying emotions she had never seen before from him, not with her nor any other woman. He was giving his heart and soul to Catherine.

Susan reluctantly shifted her focus to Catherine to find the same emotions mirrored on her face. She clung to Henry as though he were her lifeline, closing her eyes and savoring every kiss he gifted her. For them, no one else existed. There could be one thousand couples on the dance floor, and they wouldn't notice that they weren't alone.

"They're gorgeous together, aren't they?" a voice came from over her shoulder. She started and turned to find Michael stooped to meet her at eye level.

"Excuse me?"

He smiled at her as he helped himself to the vacant chair next to her. While his voice was friendly, there was an undeniable warning in his eyes as he continued, "My friends, Catherine and Henry. They're great together, don't you think?"

Susan sniffed and gave him a flippant look before responding, "Your dance lessons with her seem to have helped her, yes. She's not making a complete fool of herself out there."

"You and I both know that wasn't what I was referring to."

Anger filled Susan at Michael's insinuation. She leaned in and hissed in his ear, "They're not going to make it. Henry's too wild. Catherine's too tame. Oil and water don't mix, my friend."

"Stay away from them, dear."

"Are you threatening me? Do you realize the power I have?"

Michael's gaze focused on Henry and Catherine as he replied, "I realize the power you *think* you have, yes. But as far as actually having any ... you don't have anything that can separate those two. You're not strong enough. Whatever you try to throw at them, they'll be stronger." He gave her a wink as he rose to his feet. "So, you should save yourself the time trying." He walked away before she had the opportunity to respond.

Susan sat brooding over his words. He was right; Henry and Catherine's relationship was strong. But it wasn't airtight. No relationship was. They all had a weakness, but Michael had confirmed to her that their weakness would be more difficult to find.

But it's there all the same. If it wasn't, Michael wouldn't have felt the need to try and discourage me. There's a crack there.

Suddenly feeling encouraged rather than thwarted by her exchange with Michael, Susan excused herself from the table to go and refresh herself in the ladies' room before taking a quick cigarette break outside. She felt someone following her, so she wasn't surprised to have company once she was outside of the club.

"Good evening, ma'am," Todd spoke hesitantly as his eyes darted from side to side.

"I have to applaud you for finding a way to sneak in there. You're underage, aren't you?"

"For three times the pay, I can find a way easily enough."

Although she was eager to hear what news he had, she didn't want to appear desperate. "Well? What did you find out?" she asked.

"No offense, ma'am, but I'd like my pay first."

"No offense, *boy*, but I want to make sure the information you have is worth the pay."

He swallowed but bravely replied, "I reckon that seeing as I have the information you need, I have the upper hand in this. Besides, you didn't say anything about the quality of the information earlier today."

Susan smiled smugly at the teenager. He was sly; she had to give him credit. He might be a more useful ally than she originally thought. "You're good, kid," she complimented as she reached in her purse and pulled out his payment. "Fair enough. It'd better be worth it."

Only when Todd had the money safely in his own pocket did he nod in response. "It is. Henry—Mr. Bradley—did buy an engagement ring for Ms. McKinney."

Susan had to fight to keep her anger at bay because Todd didn't seem to be finished with his information. "Is that all?" she demanded. "Do you know when he plans to propose to this fuddy-duddy?"

Susan's words confirmed to Todd that she was up to no good. He felt relieved with his decision to enlighten Henry at the first opportunity. He only hoped that the next bit of information would be enough to keep her at bay long enough for Henry to take whatever steps necessary to thwart any plans that Susan had against him. "No, ma'am," he answered, "but I do know that he doesn't have the ring yet. It's still at the jewelers. I figure that he must not have been able to pay for it all at once." The last part was a lie, but he hoped Susan didn't notice.

She didn't. Already, Todd was forgotten as the wheels in her head turned to formulate a plan. *The ring is still at the jewelers. Then I have a little time.*

She remembered Todd standing there. She smiled sweetly as she said, "Thank you. This information is exactly what I needed. I'll match the pay I just gave you if you keep an eye out and inform me the instant Henry has that ring in his possession."

Although Todd knew that it was wrong, the need for the extra cash tempted him once again. He nodded in agreement.

"Perfect. Now, get out of here. I don't want to raise any suspicion by conversing with a minor outside a club."

Disappointment filled Todd as he realized he'd need to find another opportunity to speak with Henry. He nodded, obeying Susan and making plans to visit Henry at his shop first thing Monday morning.

Susan reentered the club and paused near the entrance, eavesdropping on a conversation that caught her interest.

"Henry's got a tight leash on her, that's for sure," one man commented while finishing his drink.

"I can't believe he's been with her for so long. Isn't he the 'love them and leave them' type?" another man responded.

"Yes, absolutely. He was always my idol in that regard. How many do you think he's actually had?"

"Probably more than he can remember. He was pretty wasted on some nights, I'm sure."

Susan's lips curled up in a devilish grin as an idea took root: Henry *did* have many conquests in his past.

And no matter how hard you run, you can't outrun your past.

EIGHT

As Todd stood outside Henry and Bobby's auto shop, he gave one final look around him before gaining the courage to complete his self-appointed mission. He was terrified of Susan Thompson, and he didn't particularly relish the idea of doing anything that would make her a certain enemy. But his respect for Henry was greater than his fear of Susan. While he needed the money that Susan was paying him, he knew it would burn a hole in his pocket if he didn't at least let Henry know about all of Susan's questions. Praying that no one took notice, he practically ran through the shop's front door.

*   *   *

"I still can't believe you pulled it off," Henry admired, holding a ring in his hand. "Not only did you find one of Catherine's mother's rings, you found her wedding ring." He shook his head as he replaced it for the hundredth time in his pants pocket.

"Give me *some* credit, Henry," Bobby replied proudly. "I was a soldier, remember? I can carry out missions easily enough."

"And Liv has no clue?"

"Not a one. She loved the Italian dinner, by the way, so you'll have to cook another one again for us sometime soon." He wiped his hands clean as he indicated the ring, now safely tucked away, with a tilt of his head. "So now what? You have her mother's ring. How does that help you?"

"You struck gold, my friend. After Catherine's parents passed away, Caleb used to say how concerned he was about Catherine. He'd find her at random times of the day tucked away in their parents' room. She'd be curled up in her father's shirt, wearing her mother's wedding ring, doing anything she could to hang on to them."

"Okay, if this is supposed to be a good story, it's not working."

"This wedding band is the one piece of jewelry I know for a fact that she's worn. So, don't you see? I now hold in my possession the last thing needed to make Catherine's ring perfect."

"I get it," Bobby said as the bell to the front door announced a customer. "But it's still not a happy backstory." He headed to the front office while Henry, with a deeper smile on his face, resumed his labor on the automobile in front of him.

"Did we place a lunch order that we forgot to pick up from the diner?" Henry heard Bobby ask the person who had entered the shop. "Goodness, lad, you're pale as a ghost. Sit down for a spell."

"Is Mr. Bradley in today?" the youthful voice barely reached back to the garage, but it was loud enough to pique Henry's interest. Grabbing the nearest rag to wipe his hands, he joined Bobby in the office.

"I am," Henry answered the question as he stood in the doorway between the garage and the office. "What can I do for you, son?"

Relief filled Todd at seeing Henry's face. "Um, hello, sir. I was wondering if I might take a few moments of your time to speak with you."

Henry recognized Todd from the diner. "You're Todd, right?"

"Yessir."

Henry indicated Todd's clothes and asked, "Are you still on the clock?"

"Oh no. I got off of work and hurried over here as fast as I could to talk to you."

"As fast as you could? Is everything all right?"

Todd cast a sidelong glance at Bobby, obviously reluctant to speak in front of him. "Begging your pardon, Mr. Bradley, but what I have to say is for your ears only."

If Henry wasn't so intrigued by Todd's cryptic appearance in his shop, he would have laughed at Bobby's displeasure as he grumbled his way back to the garage. Only after Bobby was safely tucked away in the garage with the door closed did Henry see Todd relax slightly.

"It's okay, Todd. Bobby's my partner. You could have said anything in front of him."

"I'd rather let you be the judge of what your friend has the privilege to know, sir." Over the next several minutes, Todd explained to Henry about Susan's interest in his engagement ring to Catherine and about his continued pay for reporting to her everything he discovered.

When he was finally finished, Henry was glad Todd had wanted Bobby removed from the conversation. Henry sat at his desk, his anger at Susan bursting at the seams.

"That little—" He almost cursed, but Todd stopped him.

"Please, sir, I just wanted to warn you about everything. I need the money, you see, so I plan to let her know when you do have the ring in your possession. Besides, she's not really someone you can say 'no' to. But she's planning something. And I thought that maybe if you knew this, you might be able to stop her. I think really highly of you, and I would feel bad if she did something hurtful to you or Ms. McKinney."

Henry pushed his thoughts aside as he regarded Todd. As much as he wanted to take action immediately, he knew by the scared look on Todd's face that anything along those lines would probably send the poor lad over the edge. Instead, he gave the boy a warm smile and squeezed his shoulder reassuringly as he said, "I appreciate you telling me, Todd. You're right; Susan is a force that you shouldn't toy with, and I'm sorry that she somehow snagged you in her scheme. But thank you for being decent enough to come and inform me. I want you to report to her and, by all means, take her money."

Todd couldn't help but laugh at Henry's last order.

"And I'll even help you. I'll let you know exactly when I have it in my possession. And once I propose—"

"You won't have to tell me that, sir. This town is small enough that word of the engagement will get to her before I ever could."

Henry thanked Todd for his honesty and his time before seeing him to the door. Only when Todd was halfway across the street did he allow his full anger to finally surface. "You can come out now," he called out to the garage. Bobby was already in the doorway.

"Do I even want to know?" Bobby asked, seeing the ire on his partner's face as Henry slammed his fist down on the office desk.

Henry took a few deep breaths before responding, "Susan Thompson. She's paying Todd to follow me."

Puzzlement touched Bobby's brow as he asked, "Why on earth would she do that? She's never thought twice about coming up to you before."

Henry bit his lip, speaking thoughtfully, "She knows about the ring. She wants to know when I pick it up."

"You don't think she's plotting something, do you? Oh, wait, never mind. This is Susan. Of course she is."

"She hates Catherine that much."

"So what are you going to do? Are you going to confront her?"

Henry shook his head. "Heavens, no," he said. "That will only make things worse. I may have to eventually thank her, though."

"Thank her?"

Henry nodded as a mischievous smile crept across his face. "She's forcing my hand," he explained. "I'll simply have to offer it to Catherine sooner than I had originally planned."

* * *

Over the next few days, Henry worked swiftly to set his plans for proposing to Catherine in motion. After Todd's visit, he had fought the urge to go to Zachariah's shop right away to compare Catherine's engagement ring with her mother's wedding band. Once he did go, Henry felt that things were finally working in his favor upon discovering that the ring sizes were the same and that he could leave that day with the engagement ring in hand. Deciding to hold off to keep Susan in the dark for as long as possible, he asked Zachariah to keep the ring for a bit longer.

With that part of his plan completed, he next called upon Bobby for help. To further prevent Susan from thwarting his plans and to keep Catherine in the dark about the proposal, Henry asked Bobby to convince Olivia they should go on a weekend getaway with him and Catherine for a small retreat.

"You know, we don't have to go at all, Henry," Bobby suggested as they closed the shop for the day.

"Yes, you do," Henry replied. "Catherine won't go away with me on a weekend trip without someone there—"

"To chaperone?"

Henry shrugged and said, "Call it what you want. If you're both there, she'll go. Leave little Caleb with your parents."

"Done," Bobby said eagerly, relishing the idea of alone time with his wife. Then he added as an afterthought, "Not that I don't love my son."

"No need to explain. We'll close the shop Friday through Monday, giving us a long weekend for our trip."

"Can we afford to be closed that long?"

Henry nodded as he replied, "Customers have to understand that we need vacations too."

"Where are we vacationing, by the way?"

"The beach. I already called and booked a beach house large enough to accommodate all of us."

"The beach?" Bobby asked with unease. "Don't you think we've seen our share of cursed beaches in Europe?"

Without warning, Henry's mind reeled back to his time in France, zeroing in on the memory of when Caleb's life had been taken and Bobby had lost an arm. He shook his head as the flashback fought to gain control.

But his love for Catherine was stronger, and it prevailed.

He took a long look at Bobby, understanding all too well the emotions his friend was feeling. "All the more reason for us to go," he explained. "We need a few good memories on a beach to erase some of the horrid ones."

"It's going to take more than one weekend," Bobby countered seriously.

"It's a start, at least. Think about it, Bobby. I know it's a lot to ask. Know that I wouldn't if I didn't need your help on this. I really want to propose to Catherine on the beach, but she'll never come alone with me."

Bobby nodded after a short time. "We'll come, but on the condition that I can let Liv know your plans. Not that she'll need any convincing to go on the trip, but she'll certainly need a good reason since she knows, having been awoken by my nightmares, that beaches aren't my favorite places."

"Fair enough. Now go home and explain everything to Liv. You'll have a bit of time since I'll be picking Catherine up from work tonight."

"There lays your biggest challenge," Bobby said matter-of-factly. "Catherine's inseparable from that club on Fridays and Saturdays—not to mention how much Michael needs her those days. How on earth are you going to get her away from there for an entire weekend?"

"By calling in favors," Henry said confidently as he followed Bobby out of the shop and locked the doors behind him. "Michael works her too hard, we all know that. Plus, he knows I'm not happy he's *twice* triggered Catherine's flashbacks. He'll let her have the time off. I'll see to that."

Henry knew as soon as he saw Catherine leaving the club that she was furious with him. After leaving the shop, Henry had gone home and telephoned Michael in order to have a private conversation with him before picking up Catherine at the end of her shift. Although Michael may have been initially reluctant to give Catherine time off, he had agreed with Henry that she both needed it and had earned it. When Henry had explained his intentions to propose to Catherine, Michael had offered to give her the entire week off.

"Good evening, beautiful," Henry greeted her as she stormed toward his parked truck. He held out his arms for an embrace as she neared.

"Don't come near me, Henry Bradley," she hissed, deliberately dodging his welcoming arms and going to the passenger side of the truck. She opened the door, got inside, and slammed it shut before Henry could respond. But he recovered soon enough, calmly walking to the passenger's side and reopening the door.

Catherine stared straight ahead, focusing on the club's brick walls before her. She sat with her arms crossed and fists balled, refusing to acknowledge Henry.

"Rough day?" he asked as he gently rubbed her arm.

"Just drive," she ordered, jerking away as though his touch burned her.

"No, I don't think so."

She turned to him, fire in her eyes. "Excuse me?"

"No, I don't think I'll take you home just yet. You see, I never want you sitting this far from me. So, unless you're willing to sit next to me while in an obvious fury, then I say we hash it out right now and be done with it. So, do you want to tell me what this is about, or should I guess?"

"Why on earth did you speak to Michael without first talking to me?" she yelled, ready to dive into the argument. "I'm my own person, Henry. I don't need to answer to you or to anyone else for that matter. If I want to work, I should have the right to determine how many hours I can handle. I don't need you to determine that for me."

"I agree," Henry said simply. Although he wasn't crazy about her choice to work so many hours, he did respect that the decision was hers.

"Then why did you call Michael?" Catherine demanded as frustration forced tears to her eyes.

"He didn't tell you why?"

"He said that you called and wanted me to be free on Friday and Saturday. So he gave me the weekend off. When I argued with him, he forced a week's absence on me. I needed those hours, Henry."

"You need time off more than you need money. I want to take you away for the weekend."

His words stopped her, and confusion took over. "You what?"

"I want to take you on a trip. So, I needed you to have the time off. We only need a couple of days, but I'm glad he gave you the entire week."

"Are you serious?"

"Entirely."

"Henry, absolutely not. You know that I won't do anything that—"

"Which is why Bobby and Liv are coming with us," Henry interrupted. Catherine, her mouth open to argue, fell quiet. He continued with his explanation while he had the opportunity. "I knew that you wouldn't be comfortable going without a chaperone, so I asked Bobby and Liv to join us. We'll all be sharing a place, and you can have your own room if you want."

Forgetting about her anger over Michael granting her time off, she raised a skeptical eyebrow. "Where are you planning on taking us?"

With Catherine now focusing on the trip's location, Henry knew that he had nearly won her over. "The beach," he answered.

"The beach? Henry, are you crazy? It's such a drive."

"Nonsense. It's already been taken care of."

"I don't know about this, Henry." Her tone softened, and Henry took this as an opportunity to reach in and turn her to face him. She didn't fight him, which encouraged him further.

"Catherine, sweetheart, listen to me." He drew her hands to his lips and kissed them softly as he said, "We need to do this. Bobby and I need to put some pleasant beach memories between us and the nightmarish ones that imprison our minds."

Guilt washed over Catherine as she realized this trip was more about healing Bobby and Henry than anything else. Her heart broke as she realized the men still harbored nightmares that would most likely never go away.

And here I am upset that they even thought to bring me along in their healing process! With this realization, a change washed over her. Suddenly she wrapped her arms around his neck and leaned her forehead against his.

"Catherine?"

"I'm so sorry," she whispered. "I didn't realize ... I'm so selfish, thinking about all my problems while you and Bobby need healing too. Of course I'll go with you. We can leave as soon as you all want to." She leaned in and kissed him, taking him by surprise.

Quickly enough, his own arms wrapped around her waist, pulling her against him. He knew it was wrong to let her believe that the trip was solely for his and Bobby's mental recovery. But because it had rendered her compliance so easily, he hesitated to correct her.

Besides, it is a trip of healing for Catherine too. She's gone through so much pain and hurt, she needs to get her happy ending. And I can't wait to be the one who gives it to her.

NINE

It wasn't until Henry and Catherine were an hour outside of town that Henry allowed himself to relax. With Bobby and Olivia following close behind, anyone who saw them leave town would know they were traveling together. First thing that morning, Henry had picked up the engagement ring for Catherine, knowing Todd would report this to Susan as promised. Shortly thereafter, before the couples left town, Henry had made a point to stop at the diner where Todd worked so he could further report to Susan that the four were together, buying breakfast and lunch items and speaking of their plans to spend the weekend together. While Henry knew that Susan couldn't really do anything about his decision to propose to Catherine, he still didn't want to run into her before leaving town and risk her tainting his plans.

Besides, even though he was confident that Catherine would accept his proposal, he was still nervous. Proposing was a big step for anyone, especially for someone who had always sworn they'd never get married. Henry reflected, realizing as he left town that he was also leaving behind the shell of a person he used to be. He could hardly contain his excitement when he thought about coming back in a few days and announcing to everyone that Catherine would soon be his wife.

She'll truly be mine. It's almost too much to believe that we'll finally be connected for life.

Meanwhile, Catherine cozied up next to Henry, noticing how his whole body seemed to relax after being on the road for a while. Since he didn't say anything, she could only imagine where his thoughts strayed when his grip instantly tightened around her. Ever since he had suggested to Catherine the need to have a pleasant beach memory to help erase some of the horrors he and Bobby had experienced in Europe, her thoughts had been focused on the men's need to heal.

He's worried about this trip. With both he and Bobby being there, is this going to be too much for them to handle? Will they even allow themselves to heal while in the presence of others?

"Penny for your thoughts," Henry whispered. He recognized the look of concern on her face and wanted to make sure a carefree smile replaced it as soon as possible. He withdrew his arm from around her to grab her hand and kiss it.

"Are you okay?" she asked, squeezing the hand that now held hers up to his lips.

"Never better."

"Really? I mean, ever since you mentioned the need to have good memories at a beach, I can't help but be ..."

Realizing that Catherine still dwelled on the excuse he had given her to gain her cooperation for the trip, he hurried to stop her before guilt at misleading her seeped into his thoughts. "Don't worry yourself, sweetheart. The purpose behind making a good memory is so we don't dwell on a bad one. So," he continued, pulling her to him and planting a kiss behind her ear before focusing his attention back on driving, "no more negative thoughts. Don't think about any of that stuff. Your job is to help me forget. So, you're only allowed to please me this weekend."

Catherine knew a dismissal when she heard one. Deciding still to maintain a watchful eye on Henry for any flashbacks, she gave him a warm smile and snuggled into his arm. "Okay, fair enough," she agreed. "I promise to be on my best behavior."

"I was actually hoping for the opposite," he said, winking. "I plan on some private dancing on the beach so you can seduce me all over again. I'm still reeling from Saturday night." He watched with pleasure as Catherine blushed.

"Thank goodness Bobby and Liv will be here to see you behave yourself," Catherine said softly as she tried to regain her composure.

Henry drew her in even closer. When she was close enough, he nibbled on her ear and teased, "They won't be around *all* the time."

Catherine nearly jumped out of her skin from his touch as she exclaimed, "Henry!"

Although Henry knew he'd get a reaction out of her, he wasn't quite prepared for one so strong. His truck veered off the road for a minute before he regained control. In the meantime, Catherine freed herself from his grip and scooted to the far side.

"Focus on driving," she ordered as her heart raced.

"You startled me," he replied, a smile playing at his lips.

She gaped at him in disbelief. "I startled *you*?"

"Clearly you're not used to that, so I'll have to make it a more common practice."

"Henry Bradley, behave yourself!" she said as she swatted at his outreached hand as he attempted to bring her back across the seat.

"Come on, Catherine, come back over here."

"Absolutely not! You should have ridden with Bobby," she argued, her voice softening as Henry managed to seize her hand and administer a one-handed massage to it.

Although Henry heard her protestation, he pulled her toward him, knowing this time she wouldn't fight him. "Bobby wouldn't enjoy this as much."

"Bobby and Liv are going to think you're drunk." It was the only argument Catherine could come up with as her body reeled from Henry's touch. She closed her eyes, fighting to keep control of her desire.

Her struggle encouraged Henry, knowing he was affecting her the same way she affected him. While it caused his heart to soar, it also made it difficult not to propose immediately to her. With a few hours still of travel before they'd reach the beach house, he had to acknowledge the need for restraint.

"Okay, I'll behave," he said somberly, but with a teasing look lingering in his eyes. "I can't have them thinking that. They'll make us stop and demand that you ride with them."

She arched an eyebrow as she responded, "Maybe I should."

"I'll behave! I'll behave!"

Catherine laughed as his protests lessened the intensity of the moment, and she began to feel the mood slide back to what was normal and safe for her. What she had just experienced with Henry had left her shaken, and she wasn't ready to admit to him how much.

But she was fairly certain that he already knew, and she was even more certain that he'd duplicate it at the next opportunity.

"Goodness!" Liv exclaimed as she saw Henry's truck momentarily swerve off the road before being righted again. "Is Henry all right?"

Bobby chuckled as he focused on his friends traveling ahead of them. Although they weren't close enough to see anything in detail, he was able to see Catherine suddenly scoot across the seat far from Henry. "I'm sure he's fine, Liv."

"Do you think he's tired? Maybe we should all stop for a quick break—"

"Will you listen to yourself, woman?" Bobby asked, surprised by his wife's moment of naivete. "Think about it. Henry has an engagement ring burning in his pocket. If he's anything like I was, he's wanting it on Catherine's finger as soon as possible. Plus, this is the first time she's agreed to go away with him on a trip."

"Under the belief that this is some sort of therapy trip for you both and that we'll be with them the entire time!" she countered. Although Olivia was ecstatic about Henry's plans to propose, she also knew Catherine well enough to know that his plans carried a few snags. "She's going to flip when she finds out we may not be around the entire time. In fact, we may need to—"

"You think any of that will matter once he proposes?"

Now it was Olivia's turn to shake her head at her husband's lack of understanding. "And this question comes from the man who got his fiancée pregnant the night he proposed," she reminded him. She gave him a quick kiss on his cheek to reassure him that she didn't harbor any bad feelings about that night.

"You actually think Catherine will think about us and our—" he paused, not quite knowing how to label it, "the moment she accepts Henry's offer?" He shook his head. "Women are crazy. Your minds are too complex."

"You obviously don't know Catherine as well as you claim. The same goes for Henry. But he's convinced there won't be any issues. That's wishful thinking. But at any rate, that doesn't explain Henry's reckless driving."

"Absolutely, it does! He's probably having a hard time keeping his hands on the steering wheel. I know how hard it is for me with you right next to me. I guess having only one arm is a blessing in this case; it *has* to stay on the wheel."

Olivia smiled as she watched Catherine scoot over next to Henry once again in the truck. She supposed Bobby was right in what was transpiring between their two friends. However, she silently prayed that Henry's proposal would go well. When Bobby had told her the plans, he practically had to sit on her to prevent her from rushing to spill the beans to Catherine. Even now, she was under strict instructions from both men to say little to Catherine, as they feared she'd let the secret slip.

"We'll at least get to stay around long enough for her to show us the ring and everything, right? We have to at least be allowed to stay for that before we go exploring the area on our own. I really believe Catherine will want us there for the entire weekend."

"This is Henry's show, Liv. We'll stick around as long as he wants us to, and we'll leave them alone as soon as he tells us. It's my guess that we'll stay tonight, but I already volunteered for us to leave sometime on Saturday."

"If that's the case, then Henry's thinking a little bit anyway. This would give Catherine enough time to be comfortable with the four of us staying together before you make us abandon her. If we left at the very beginning, showing we had no intention of spending the weekend with them, he wouldn't get the opportunity to propose. Besides, things may still go south when she learns we've left."

"We're not abandoning her, Liv! Don't make it sound like Henry's a monster or something. And give the man some credit. He knows Catherine well enough to know what she's comfortable with. He stayed at her place while we were on our honeymoon. He wants to give her the perfect marriage proposal. He's not going to do something to jeopardize that."

Olivia nodded in agreement, a satisfied smile on her face. "He wouldn't, would he?" she relented. "And I can't tell you how happy I am that they're finally at this point. I'm bursting with happiness for them."

Olivia's enthusiasm was contagious, and Bobby found himself feeling giddy as well. He reflected on the hardships Henry and Catherine had faced in their pasts: losing Caleb in Europe, Henry going MIA in Germany,

Catherine's ex-boyfriend Robert nearly killing her. There were so many hurdles that they had overcome together.

Yes, Bobby agreed, *if anyone has earned their happily ever after, it's those two.*

*   *   *

As Henry watched Catherine standing on the beach, facing the ocean's waves as the sun began to set, he knew without a doubt that he had made the right decision. While the weekend getaway was proving to be everything he had hoped it would be, the decision to make this trip wasn't the one on his mind.

He was right in choosing *Catherine.*

Not wanting to create any discomfort upon their arrival earlier in the day, Henry had volunteered right away to sleep on the couch when the beach house revealed only two bedrooms. After taking a quick inventory of the house's kitchen, the four had headed to the local market to pick up enough food essentials to get them through the weekend. Then, having spotted a local Italian restaurant, Olivia and Bobby had opted to go there for dinner while Henry had volunteered to take the food back to the beach house and share a picnic dinner with Catherine. While his plans didn't include proposing on the first night, he still planned on as much romance as possible.

Stepping off the porch with a basket of food in hand, he headed toward Catherine, marveling at how much his life had changed. Before going to Europe to fight alongside Bobby and Caleb, he would have never guessed that he would be so hopelessly in love with Caleb's firecracker sister and dreaming about spending the rest of his life with her. Catherine's ex, Robert, had nearly robbed him of this dream, a dream he hadn't fully realized until it was almost too late.

A sudden wave of possessiveness coursed through Henry as the thoughts of missed opportunities filtered through his mind. Giving the engagement ring in his pocket another reassuring touch, he came up softly behind Catherine, placing a gentle kiss on her exposed neck and smiling at her shivered reaction. He stood beside her, watching the ocean and holding her hand tightly in his.

"Care to share what's on your mind?" he asked.

"It's beautiful here," she whispered, her eyes set on the scene before her. "I could stand here all night, lost in the hypnotizing waves that seem to extend to forever."

"Not quite like the river at home, is it?"

"The river has its own beauty. It's safe and harbors some of my favorite memories. But this," she said as she held out her free hand to the ocean as she struggled to put her thoughts into words. "This is—"

"Beautiful. And dangerous. The ocean has an edge to it that the river never will."

As Henry spoke, Catherine immediately regretted sharing her awe with him. While the ocean triggered a serenity in Catherine, she could only imagine the nightmares it resurrected in Henry. She turned to him, saying, "Henry, I'm sorry, I wasn't thinking. Should we go into the house?"

"Why are you apologizing? I'm here because I want to be." He held up the basket as he continued, "Besides, we're not going anywhere yet. There are grapes in here, my dear. I plan to lie on this beach with my head in your lap, letting you feed me while we stay warm by a campfire. I guarantee *that* will erase any bad campfire memories I might have from Europe." Giving her a wickedly mischievous smile, he tugged her hand and led her down the shore to the remains of a campfire location used by previous houseguests.

"You're incorrigible," Catherine said, although still allowing him to lead her down the shore. Despite the smile she returned to him, she found herself asking, almost in desperation, "Seriously, Henry, how do you do it? You're in a place that could and should trigger flashbacks. And yet you can tease me and joke with Bobby and Liv. How do you do it?"

She didn't want to admit, even to herself, how much she envied him. He was so in control of his emotions. While she lived in constant fear of losing herself to her nightmares, Henry seemed carefree and fearless.

Henry waited until he had a small bonfire going before he answered her questions. "Catherine, don't be fooled. I have my battles. And my flashbacks come. But they come at night when I'm asleep."

She allowed him to pull her down next to him and wrap his arms around her as the evening chill settled over them. "And that's it?" she asked in disbelief. "You never have them when you're awake?"

"Not anymore. See, I found a talisman that keeps them at bay during the day: you. They only come when you're not around." He drew her near to him, whispering in her ear, "You're what kept me alive over there. After losing Caleb and when Bobby returned home, I found myself quite alone. But when I'd look at your photo or reread your letters, I found home. You kept all but one of my nightmares away while I fought in the war."

His lips brushed her ear as he spoke, and Catherine found that his voice paralyzed her. "All but one?"

He tightened his grip on her, the serious subject chasing away any lightheartedness he had felt earlier. "The one about not getting the chance to tell you how I feel," Henry explained. "I lived in constant fear of never getting that opportunity once I knew *how* I felt. That nightmare consumed my thoughts day and night. It only disappeared after nearly losing you at the train station when you planned to leave."

Although the sun was setting and the beach was emptying of its day visitors, Catherine prayed the darkness would hide her blush of embarrassment. "Ah, yes, the train station. Where you finally healed my stubborn blindness," she said with a small smile.

"I won't argue with that," Henry agreed.

She jabbed him playfully in the stomach with her elbow. "And now, you're nightmare-free while you're awake."

"Oh, I never said that, darling. I have my fears that visit me during the day. But my flashbacks of Europe only come at night. The moment I wake up and think of you, they disappear. Every time."

"And during the day? What nightmares are those?"

That I'll lose you. That one day, you'll slide through my fingers like sand.

"That this night will end before I've been fed any grapes!" he replied, bringing lightheartedness back to the conversation. Before Catherine had time to respond, Henry placed his head in her lap.

Catherine shook her head, smiling. She knew Henry well enough to know when a conversation was over. If she tried to pry information from him, he'd clam up and refuse to talk about it, so she let him change the subject.

Besides, this trip isn't about me anyway. It's about Bobby's and Henry's demons, not mine.

She couldn't help but chuckle when she saw a handful of grapes come up to her at eye level. "Can we begin now? I'm getting hungry."

"You're lucky I don't shove them down your throat," she threatened as she placed a grape in his mouth.

"If it gives me this view," he said, raising his hand to touch her cheek gently, "then it's worth the risk. Your face is more beautiful than any star-filled night."

Catherine rolled her eyes but smiled appreciatively as she continued to feed him. "Good thing that I'm with you for your dancing. Your dance moves are a whole lot smoother," she teased.

"My dancing isn't the only reason you're with me, is it?" Henry asked as he sat up and quickly enveloped her in his arms. The movement took Catherine by surprise, and she found her heart racing as his arms tightened around her waist and his voice tickled her ears. "Surely I'm smooth in other areas too?" His lips curled in a smile as he felt goose bumps rise on her neck beneath his kisses.

"Yes," Catherine struggled to respond. "And while that may be one of the perks, being in love with my best friend is the real reason you've been able to keep me around. Plus, the fact that I can throw a hammer at you without you taking it personally ... that definitely doesn't hurt anything."

Henry heard Bobby approaching long before his friend made it to the beach house's porch. *I guess there are some things that no amount of time can erase,* Henry thought, as he waited for Bobby to get closer. He had told a partial lie to Catherine earlier when he said that thoughts of Europe never entered his mind during the waking hours. Now, sitting on the porch and listening to the familiar sound of the waves, France was foremost in his thoughts.

"You never were stealth," Henry said quietly as Bobby entered the porch.

"Couldn't sleep either?" Bobby asked as he handed him a cup of coffee and sat down next to him.

Arching an eyebrow, Henry looked at the mug and then at Bobby. "Coffee?" he asked. "It's too late at night for coffee. And with the memories I'm entertaining, I think something stronger is in order."

Bobby gazed out at the ocean as he took a drink from his own mug. "Trust me, it's strong enough. Just be sure not to let Liv take a sniff of it. I'll be sleeping on the couch for the next week."

They sat in companionable silence for a while, both men lost in their memories of war that the ocean brought crashing down on them.

"This is harder than I thought," Bobby said out of nowhere, still focused on the invisible horizon, swallowed by the darkness of night. Not wanting to interrupt Bobby, Henry sat there, waiting for him to continue. "I mean, we're not even on French soil."

"The ocean sounds the same no matter what part of the world you're in, Bobby. If it makes you feel any better, I'm right there with you."

"I kept busy enough during the day, but lying in that bed with the ocean right outside my window ... I don't understand how Liv can sleep through it. It's so loud. So—" He struggled for the right words to describe how smothered he felt by the waves then asked suddenly, "When do you need us to leave?"

While anyone else would have taken that as an abrupt change of subject, Henry understood what Bobby was asking. *He wants to leave. He's having a hard time.*

"I was doing some research while in town," Bobby continued. "There are some fancy, historic hotels not far from here. Liv's never stayed in a hotel that looks like a mansion from the 1800s, and I think it'd be nice to treat her since they're so close, you know? We certainly don't have to stay here and invade your time with Catherine."

"Why don't you two head up there tomorrow after breakfast? I agree that if she's always wanted to go, you shouldn't miss this opportunity."

Bobby nodded, the two resuming their silence for a while before he found his voice. "Thank you, Henry. I'm sorry I—"

"Why are you apologizing? You came up here knowing that I'd most likely kick you out before the end of the weekend. So, I'm kicking you out tomorrow morning rather than later."

Bobby nodded, thankful that the dark concealed the tears in his eyes. He appreciated that he didn't have to explain things to Henry. He understood. Henry always understood.

* * *

When Catherine woke the following morning, nothing seemed out of order. Bobby and Olivia, Henry explained when she found him alone in the kitchen, were taking advantage of sleeping in without their son here to wake them at the first sign of daylight. Glad to see that their friends were seizing the opportunity to rest, Catherine was only slightly disappointed at missing them and readily agreed to Henry's suggestion that they take breakfast away from the house.

Henry knew that Bobby and Olivia would be leaving sometime during the morning, so he wanted to make certain they had plenty of time to pack their things and leave. If he and Catherine came back while they were in the middle of leaving, things would unravel quickly and his romantic proposal to Catherine would be in jeopardy. He fully believed that once he proposed, everything would fall into place. But he wanted the opportunity to get to that point. He also didn't want to take her to town and run the risk of bumping into the two as they left. So when Catherine suggested that they take breakfast and lunch out on the trails in the woods that connected to the southern part of the beach, Henry was more than willing to go.

Between the two meals and stopping several times to steal kisses from her behind trees and off the pathway, Henry led Catherine on a rigorous hike.

When they reached a summit that held a breathtaking view, he squeezed her hand encouragingly as he led her to a rock to rest. "I'm sorry. I hope I didn't wear you out."

Wiping the sweat from her brow, Catherine shook her head as she took in the majestic view of the ocean down below. "It was worth it to see this view. Besides, it seems I'm not the only one who's a bit winded." She glanced at him from the corner of her eye, secretly pleased to see that Henry seemed as fatigued as she did. He fought hard to hide his own labored breathing and, ever the gentleman, stood while she took the only rock large enough to rest on.

"Come here," she said, motioning Henry to join her. "I'd much rather rest on you than on the rock. You can have this spot."

Henry smiled as he took a seat and pulled Catherine onto his knee. For a long while, the two were silent as they took in the view.

"It's beautiful here. Quiet and peaceful. You can enjoy the view of the ocean without hearing its waves," he explained. Catherine allowed Henry to snuggle against her as he spoke.

"You have a hard time with those waves, don't you?" she asked. She didn't need to look over her shoulder to know what was written on his face.

"Not now. Not like this."

"But you did last night. You and Bobby. I heard you two on the porch until late in the night."

For a moment, Henry was fearful that she had overheard their conversation. "Eavesdropping, were you?"

She shook her head, lacing the fingers that snaked around her waist with her own. "No, you know me better than that, Henry. You and Bobby have demons that I'll never understand. I'm not going to act like I can fix those problems. I trust that you know how to handle them better than I do. I'm here when you need me, but I don't force myself into places I'm not invited."

"I'm sorry if we kept you up."

Catherine turned from the view to kiss Henry soundly on the lips. "Not at all," she replied. "Your mumbling voice outside a window is the most soothing sound to me."

"Okay, I'm not too sure how to take that," he said, turning her in his lap so that she faced him. "But I eagerly await your explanation because I'm not *that* boring."

Catherine found herself unable to respond. A part of her needed to get off his lap for fear their public display of affection might be seen. She didn't want to offend anyone, so she started to pull free from his embrace.

Sensing what Catherine was trying to do, Henry held her tighter, rising to his feet and making his way to a large boulder. There, he pinned her to the rock. "Not yet, sweetheart. You owe me an explanation, *and then* I'll let you go."

"And if I refuse?"

"Then I'll show you just how *not* boring I can be."

Her words came out rushed, hoping they would serve. "I only meant that after my parents died, you spent a lot of time on our front porch comforting Caleb. While I couldn't make out the conversations, I went to sleep so many nights with your muffled voice reaching my bedroom window. Even when you thought you weren't helping me heal, you were. Your voice calmed me. And last night was no different."

While Henry had been teasing, Catherine's heartfelt answer sobered him immediately. He didn't know if she realized the guilt that still haunted him over not being there for her during that time in her life, but her words were the balm that he needed to heal that heartache.

Catherine started to open her mouth to comment further, but Henry silenced her with a hungry kiss. He wouldn't allow this day to end without his proposal to her. As that thought sped through his mind along with the realization that Bobby and Olivia were by now in the next town over, he suddenly wanted to be back at the beach house.

With renewed energy, he leaned back and stood up. "Are you ready to go back? I think I've caught my second wind. If we hurry, we'll be back before dinner."

She couldn't hide her surprise. Catherine had been certain that Henry's thoughts were ones of secluding her, not sharing her. "Was my answer that much of a mood killer?" she couldn't help but ask.

Henry held her face in both of his hands as he planted another kiss on her lips. "On the contrary, it invigorated me."

"Well, I'm glad one of us has their second wind. If you want to hurry back, you're going to have to carry … ME!" Catherine squealed as Henry lifted her onto his back and started to descend the trail rapidly.

"Henry, I was only kidding!"

But he wasn't listening. Tightening his grip on her, he threw instructions over his shoulder. "When we get back, I want you to take a long nap. I've got a full evening planned, and you're going to need all your energy." By now, he was practically running down the trail's path.

"*Henry?*"

"I've just thought of a way to enjoy the waves, Catherine. And by the end of the night, they'll hopefully be music to my ears."

*　*　*

A sense of relief filled Bobby as the beach house disappeared from his rearview mirror. Happy to be leaving the vacation spot behind him, he could care less where they went so long as the ocean's sounds didn't reach them. Being at the beach house for one night had nearly unraveled him, and it took everything in him to make it through the night without breaking down into hysterical sobbing. He hated the sound of the ocean more than anyone—with good reason.

After the battle that had cost him his best friend and his own arm, Bobby had spent time recovering in a French hospital. Delirious from the pain of both losses, he had slipped in and out of consciousness in that hospital bed. Even now, he couldn't recall much about the place, but the one thing he couldn't forget was the sound of the nearby ocean through the hospital windows. He had grown to hate the sound. It served as a constant reminder of where he was and what he had lost.

How Henry could make plans to propose to Catherine on a beach, he couldn't understand. From the moment they had arrived, his mind had been back in France. Even if Henry was trying to create an amazing memory to replace his old ones, Bobby knew that there were some memories that could never be replaced.

"Bobby, are you all right?" Olivia asked softly from the car seat next to him. "You've been awfully distracted since we arrived yesterday."

Olivia's voice brought him back to the present, and as the last remnants of the town vanished in his rearview mirror, he found it much easier to smile. "I'm fine, dear," he replied. "I'm ready to begin *our* little vacation. I'm glad Henry let us go so early in the day. We still have time to do something on our own before going back home."

Olivia knew there was more to what Bobby had been thinking about but decided she'd be most helpful by playing along for the time being. *I'll let you think you've fooled me for now, Bobby, but at some point, you're going to have to address at least some of the demons from your past.*

* * *

When Catherine awoke later that evening, she had no clue how long she had napped. Judging by the darkness outside her bedroom window and the hunger pains in her stomach, at least a few hours had passed. As she sat up in bed, a smile sprang to her lips when she saw a single rose and note waiting for her on her nightstand.

I wasn't sure what you brought with you, so I took the liberty of going into town to pick up a few items that you'll need for tonight. What I'd like for you to wear is hanging in the bathroom. No shoes required. Go enjoy the bubbles and then meet me outside for dinner. But don't keep me waiting too long ...

Giddiness filled her as she took in the rose's scent and headed toward the bathroom. Henry had a romantic evening planned, of that she had no doubt as she took in the scene around her. Rose petals littered the bathroom floor surrounding the claw-foot bathtub. Nestled in every nook and cranny, candles provided the only light Catherine would need. Visible heat rose from the water-filled tub. Petals floated on the water's surface as well, and various scented soaps rested on a stand nearby. The atmosphere was inviting, and Catherine needed no additional encouragement to soak in the relaxing waters.

Only when she was in the bathtub did she notice the dress hanging on the back of the door. A simple, soft pink beach dress waited for her. Its organza material made the dress flow. While the dress appeared more daring than her usual taste in clothes, Catherine knew Henry would never ask her to wear anything that made her uncomfortable. A box rested on a small stand next to the dress. Too small to be a shoebox, Catherine's curiosity was piqued. From the bathtub, she reached out and just barely caught the box in between her fingers.

She opened it to find another letter from Henry resting on top of tissue paper. A blush slowly crept up her neck as she read the small note.

Don't blush too much, Catherine. This perfume holds a scent that traveled with me throughout France. I always dreamed of smelling it on you – from when I first started to realize I loved you while I was in France. Make that dream come true for me tonight.

She pulled back the tissue paper to reveal a small bottle of French perfume. She didn't know where he had managed to find this fragrance, but the instructions listed in the note on where to apply it told her his plans to be near her neck for much of the evening.

A blush crept up her face at the idea of Henry nuzzling her neck. She took in the scene and hoped Olivia wouldn't tease her too much once she saw what Henry had done to the bathroom. If she took time to clean up the rose petals, Henry would notice she'd been in there too long.

Henry could barely contain his longing as he saw Catherine leave the house, gliding along the beach toward him. He stood next to a small open fire that provided enough warmth to the nearby blanket where they would share their dinner. Two covered plates hid pasta, and a bowl of fruit sat in the center of the blanket to complete the simple meal. Two empty wine glasses rested next to a bucket of chilled champagne. Rose petals littered the beach in a trail that led from the house to where he stood waiting for her. He was glad the wind was calm enough not to blow them all away.

Even from a distance, Henry felt his blood race as he took in Catherine's beauty. The dress he bought for her was perfect. It flowed freely as the ocean's gentle winds caused the skirt to billow across her bare legs. As she came closer, Henry's mouth tugged in a smile as he noted how the pink shade complemented her skin.

Catherine's heart skipped a beat as Henry came up the shoreline to meet her. He, too, was barefoot. Sporting a white cotton shirt left mostly unbuttoned and sleeves rolled up and contrasting with dark khaki pants, Henry's handsomeness stopped Catherine in her tracks. The all-too-familiar hunger filled her soul entirely as Henry reached her. Without a word, he slipped an arm around her waist.

Softly, he kissed her jawline, and Catherine involuntarily trembled at his touch. "You," he said huskily, "look amazing." He deeply inhaled the skin right below her ear, which brought a timid smile to her lips. "And this perfume is better on you than I had imagined."

The mix of Henry's cologne and natural body scent heightened Catherine's attraction to him. She found herself gripping his sleeves and opening her neck to a deeper caress from Henry's lips. "You, too," she finally managed to whisper. "And thank you for the dress."

He forced himself away from her alluring neck to look her in the eyes. "Believe me when I say that I'm appreciating the gift much more than you."

The two stood in silence for a moment, so much more in their eyes than they could vocalize. Finally, Catherine asked, "Did you buy the flower shop out of roses?"

The teasing lightened the atmosphere of some of its intensity. Henry laughed and grabbed her hand, leading her to the blanket. "Just about. Is it too much?"

"Not at all. Did Bobby and Liv see any of this before going to dinner? I feel bad I haven't seen them all day."

Henry knew Catherine would find out eventually about their friends' departure, but he had hoped it would have been later in the evening or the next day. "They didn't see it, Catherine. They're not here."

"I know they're not here, Henry," Catherine said as she seated herself in front of a plate. "When I woke up, they were already gone to dinner."

"No, sweetheart, they're not here anymore." He held out his hand and slowly pulled her to her feet, letting his words sink in before continuing, "They left this morning while we were hiking."

"They left? You mean ..."

"Not just for a meal, they *left*."

Concern for her friends mixed with concern over her new predicament. At first, she pushed her own situation aside to focus on Bobby and Olivia. "Are they okay?" she asked. "Is it Bobby? Was this too much for him to handle? Where did they go?"

"Shh." Henry placed a finger on her lips to silence her. "They're fine. I believe they're heading to some fancy historic hotel before going home. They'll be there when we get back."

"When we get back? You mean—"

"We're staying," Henry interrupted confidently. He held her in his arms. "Just you and me."

"But Bobby—"

"He's fine, Catherine. It was never their plan to stay here for the entire weekend anyway." He saw a change in her eyes as suspicion settled in them.

Here goes nothing.

"What do you mean, never in their plan?" Confusion poured over her like cold water, and she tried to step out of Henry's embrace. "What are you talking about?"

Henry kept a firm grip on her, holding her close as he tried to explain, "Catherine, I knew you'd never come with me on your own, not if it was just the two of us. Even though the house has separate bedrooms, you would never have agreed."

This time Catherine did manage to pull herself free from Henry. "You're right about that. As much as I may want to, it's not right." Anger and embarrassment flushed her cheeks as she spoke. "So you're telling me the three of you planned this, knowing Liv and Bobby would leave the two of us here alone?"

"Yes." There was no apology in his response. There was no remorse in his eyes.

She crossed her arms defensively and, in doing so, remembered the flowing dress she wore. Her eyes brimming with tears, she angrily choked out, "You brought me here hoping—"

Henry saw the path Catherine's thoughts were taking and hurried to dispel them. "Catherine ..."

Okay, maybe Liv was right about this. I didn't think this part through very well.

"No! You brought me here hoping for ... you *promised* me that you wouldn't pressure me, Henry! You promised!" Her words came out in sobs, and she turned away from him, hurt and furious. She dropped to her knees, willing away the memories of Robert and his attempts to force her.

The heartache he heard in her voice seared his heart. Quickly, he dropped down behind her and tried to take her in his arms. "Catherine, it's not like that."

But she wouldn't have any of it. "Don't touch me, Henry! I can't believe I was such a fool. And I can't believe Liv and Bobby went along with your plan. Did they know *this* is what you had in mind?"

"What you're thinking, it's not what I had in mind, Catherine." He moved over so he was facing her as they knelt in the sand. "They know my plan and are in full support of it." *It's just the execution of it that I should have thought through a bit more.*

"I don't see how they could be."

"Will you at least listen to me? Then you can judge them, and me, accordingly."

She refused to meet his eyes. "You need to take me home," she finally managed to whisper. "I'll be up at the house, packing my things." She started to rise to her feet.

Henry grabbed her arm to stop her. "No, Catherine, we're not going anywhere." His voice was firm as he spoke. "I want you to sit down and listen to what I have to say. After that, and only after that, will I take you wherever you want to go. But I insist on speaking with you first."

Catherine could hear the hurt, frustration, and determination in his voice. Despite her own feelings, she was curious to hear what he had to say. Finally, she nodded.

"I didn't lie to you, Catherine. I was telling you the truth when I said that coming here would be good therapy for me. I thought it would help Bobby, too, but I was mistaken in that. We both have terrible memories of the ocean. So I wanted you to come here with me. I wanted to create a new set of memories on a beach to help erase the nightmarish ones from Europe. And I don't feel that is wrong of me to wish for such things. And do you know what the best memory I could possibly create with you on this beach is?" He stood and gently pulled her to her feet as his heart beat wildly. "The best memory would be you agreeing to marry me."

It took only a beat for Catherine to understand Henry's words. In that instant, her world fell off its axis as Henry dropped to one knee and asked, "Catherine McKinney, will you do me the honor of becoming my wife? Marry me."

Tears blinded her vision. For years, Catherine had dreamed of marrying Henry and had always believed the dream to be out of reach. Up until this moment, even since becoming a couple, she still found she held her breath on the idea. Now, seeing him kneel before her with a ring in his now-open palm, she was amazed to find her dream becoming a reality. It was too good to be true.

Henry saw a wave of emotions tear through her eyes as he knelt before Catherine. The ring seemed to burn a hole in his hand, and he desperately wanted to put it on her finger. He waited for her response, his whole life on hold.

"You're serious? You really want me? As your wife?" Her voice was full of disbelief.

"I've never been more certain of anything. The only question, Catherine, is whether this is what you want." He rose to his feet, the ring still lying in his open hand. "Will you have me?"

When Catherine tore her eyes away from the ring and peered into Henry's face, unshed tears filled his eyes as well.

Only when a small, timid smile touched her lips did Henry find the ability to breathe.

"Yes," Catherine whispered, her response mingling with the ocean sounds. "I want nothing more than to be your wife."

As Henry swept Catherine up in his arms, the crashing of the waves became music to his ears.

TEN

Henry silently watched from the corner of his eye as the glow on Catherine's face began to wane the closer they drove to town and despite the early dawn's sunrays touching her face. After Catherine had accepted his proposal, the two had spent the rest of the evening in bliss ... as much as was allowed, that is, before Catherine had insisted on driving back home that same night. And as much as he hated to admit it, Catherine had been right insisting they not remain at the beach house, despite the late hour. As hard as it had been, he had taken great efforts to show restraint, trying to ignore the temptation of the two of them being alone at the beach house. He wasn't sure how well Catherine had slept on the drive home, alternating his shoulder and the passenger window as a pillow. When she'd sit close enough that Henry could easily hold her hand, the feel of her engagement ring only confirmed his desire for a short engagement.

Now, after driving through the night, they were almost home. Part of Henry wanted to continue driving forever so he wouldn't have to let Catherine out of his sight. He liked the time they'd spent together alone, even if it was short-lived. With Bobby and Olivia living at Catherine's home, time alone wasn't a common event. Yet soon enough, that would no longer be a problem.

Is that what she's thinking about? he couldn't help but wonder as he watched her mindlessly toy with the engagement ring. He couldn't resist the urge to reach over and take her hand in his. He kissed her palm before confessing, "I love seeing that ring on your finger."

Catherine smiled and gave his hand a reassuring squeeze as she replied, "Me too."

"Then why do you look like you're a thousand miles away? What's on

118

your mind? You're not regretting your decision, are you?"

"Not at all," Catherine quickly responded as she slid across the seat to cozy up to Henry. Not knowing how Henry would respond, she was careful in choosing her next words. "But I was thinking over our new status and how everyone will react."

"They'll tell me it's about time I got my act together and asked. I know they'll be thrilled. Liv will probably drive us crazy wanting to help plan the wedding."

Catherine felt a wave of relief pass over her as Henry brought up the topic she had wanted to discuss but didn't know how to broach. "Actually, I was thinking about that."

"Our wedding?" Henry couldn't stop the smile from spreading across his face. He remembered all too well the sadness Catherine had displayed at Olivia and Bobby's wedding when she had believed she'd never have one of her own. "Don't worry about a thing there, Catherine. We're going all out."

"Why not just elope?" she asked suddenly, finding it difficult to meet his eyes. She hoped he would go with the idea and not ask for her reason behind the suggestion.

She should have known better.

She cringed inwardly as Henry slowed the truck and pulled over to the shoulder of the road. In the distance, she could make out the outline of the town's welcome sign. She focused hard on the sign as her suggestion met with uncomfortable silence. She didn't want to face Henry, already feeling his intense gaze on her. Yet as the silence between then lengthened, she knew this was exactly what he wanted her to do.

Finally, she dared to look up at him.

"Are you going to tell me where that came from?" Henry asked with an unreadable look in his eyes. The look made Catherine want to squirm away, and she began to turn her head from him. His hand, gentle yet quick, came up to capture her chin, forcing her to turn back to him. "Catherine, what are you worried about? Do you think I'll change my mind?"

"No," she reassured him as she reached up to hold the hand that caressed her chin, lacing her fingers in his. "That's not it at all."

Relief filled his eyes. He was thankful that Catherine was finally as confident in their relationship as he was. Yet there was still something in her eyes that told Henry her concerns were deeper. With his free hand, he turned off the ignition and said, "Then you're going to have to help me understand. Because the look I'm seeing right now … it wasn't anywhere to be seen last night. You're taking me a little by surprise. Please, talk to me."

Catherine felt her stomach churn at Henry's concerned expression. He deserved to know her worries and the fears that were intensifying the closer they got to town. *But how do I tell him that I'm worried about Liv and Bobby? Do I kick them out of my home? Do I let them stay and I move out? Do I have the strength to leave the only place that connects me with my family? Do I have the strength to be Henry's wife? How can I tell him that I'm afraid of Susan's retaliation? It's guaranteed. But he doesn't know that. And if I do survive that vixen, will he regret his decision to marry me once we're married and I'm not able to satisfy him? And finally, I don't have the money to afford a big wedding. A year ago, maybe. But losing my factory job and Susan making sure I don't find another one has left my pockets empty. Michael overpays me as it is, and I can't keep taking his charity pay forever. And with Caleb gone, I have no one to give me away.*

Though all these fears preyed on her mind, she found she was too afraid to voice them. "I have to say, Henry, you're taking me by surprise too," she finally managed to say.

He hadn't been expecting those words. "*Me?* How?"

Here goes nothing, Catherine thought as she held on to what little nerve she still had. "Well, seeing as how you're always so eager to get your hands on me and keep them there," she replied, trying to conjure up her most seductive look, "I assumed you'd want to wed me as soon as possible."

She barely got the words out before Henry had her in his arms and pinned against the seat. His lips covered hers before she could even let out an exclamation of surprise. It briefly robbed her of any rational thought as she found her arms circling his neck, clinging to him as she returned his kisses with as much intensity.

While her own desires matched his, she couldn't help but feel a small bit of guilt as she thought, *Let him think that's all it is. Surely he'll be on board with an elopement since I presented it to him* this *way.*

As Catherine's heart raced and she tried to recover her lost breath, Henry moved away from her face and kissed below her ear.

"Now it's you surprising me again," Henry huskily whispered in her ear as his hands lightly traced patterns in her lower back. "I definitely reached a point that you'd normally stop me in broad daylight. You'd say something about someone seeing us and believing we're broken down, or anything else to wiggle out of this situation. I mean, that's why we drove back in the middle of the night. If you wanted to elope, you should have told me when we were at the beach. We could have easily made that happen and spent the weekend there. No, this is sudden." He began to knead her lower back with his fingertips.

"M-maybe I'm tired of fighting it." She prayed he didn't hear the tremor in her voice.

"As much as I've longed to hear those words," he kept his lips close to her ear, tickling her as he spoke, "I don't believe them. I think you're trying to distract me." He sighed as a tremor went through him.

"From what?"

"Why don't you tell me? Before I take you at your word and embarrass any driver that might stop to try to offer their assistance." He slid away with obvious reluctance, allowing Catherine to sit back up in the seat.

Catherine sat in silence as she tried to collect her thoughts. Finally, she said, "I'm worried about my living situation with Liv and Bobby."

"That has nothing to do with this, Catherine. I understand your concern, and this is a topic to be hashed out, but an elopement would only rush things, so you can't give that as a reason." He looked at her with gentle but knowing eyes. "Nice effort, though. Try again."

Frustration swelled inside Catherine. She hated that even though he acknowledged her concern, he could also dismiss it so quickly. *Because he knows you better than you know yourself. Just tell him.*

"We're not going anywhere until you tell me what's really bothering you," Henry said as if reading her thoughts.

"Fine." She took a deep breath and blurted, "It's Susan. I'm not looking forward to the repercussions from her."

"And you think eloping will keep her from being upset?" A frown touched Henry's brow. "Catherine, you're not the type of person to let fear of someone else dictate your actions. Susan can't touch you. She can't hurt you. There's certainly not a thing she can do to destroy what we have. You can't let her rob you of your happiness." He lifted her chin to face him. "Where's my fighter?"

"She knows what buttons to push on me, Henry. She knows my insecurities about being able to—" Catherine's throat went dry, and she hoped she wouldn't have to say the words.

"To what, Catherine?" He knew what she was alluding to but forced her to vocalize it.

"To please you ... in every way." Her voice was barely a whisper, and although Henry had forced her to face him, she closed her eyes as she spoke. When she finally did open her eyes, she expected to see any reaction but the one that he had.

Henry's jaw clenched, and anger smoldered in his eyes. "She really shattered your self-confidence, didn't she?" he asked. Seeing unease flash in Catherine's eyes, he drew her into his lap as he slid from behind the steering wheel. "Don't think for one minute that my anger is directed at you. It's not. It's all for Susan. If she were a man, a simple fistfight would keep her away from you. But it's hard to threaten the mayor's daughter." He rested his cheek on her neck and took in her faint perfume scent. "I know you have concerns, but I wish you could see yourself the way that I see you. If you could, you'd never worry about this again."

"Henry."

She tried to squirm out of his grip, slightly embarrassed by their conversation. Henry tightened his hold on her, kissing her neck. "Make no mistake, Catherine, there isn't anything or anyone who will ever be able to quench my desire for you except you. But again, this isn't something that would prompt the need for elopement, at least not for the Catherine I know. While *I* may prefer an elopement for this reason, that's not you. So, try again."

"You don't fight fair."

Henry continued to hold her in his arms, nuzzling her neck. "I never claimed to."

"Promise not to get angry?"

"Do you ever make that promise when I ask it of you?"

Catherine had to smile despite herself. "No," she muttered.

"Then you know my answer."

Catherine tried to figure out the best way to explain her financial situation without upsetting Henry. She knew how much it bothered him that she never accepted his monetary support. "I don't have the money for a large wedding, Henry," she finally admitted. "A year ago, maybe, but times have been hard."

"And there it is," Henry said as he pulled back to look Catherine in the eyes. "There's the heart of it. This is one I'll believe." With serious eyes, he offered, "We do have enough for this wedding, for *our* wedding."

"Henry—"

"Don't start, Catherine. Don't you dare."

"Henry, I can't let you pay for this. The bride's family pays for the wedding. It's tradition."

He didn't even try to hold back his laughter, which filled the cab of the truck. "Tradition? You're a traditionalist on some things, I'll give you credit for that. But on something like this? The woman who wants to work independently and doesn't take lip from any man wants to follow tradition?" His smile remained on his face, but his eyes grew more serious. "No" he answered, "not on this. This is my wedding too. We're supposed to share our lives together, share everything. You won't let me help you financially right now, but it starts with our wedding."

Judging by his no-nonsense tone, Catherine decided this would be an uphill battle she most likely wouldn't win. "You don't have to do this. I don't need a big wedding."

"Yes, Catherine, you do. You need this more than anyone I can think of. And I'm so thankful I'm the one who gets to share this with you. After everything you've been through and the dreams that've been dashed, you deserve to have this one dream come true."

"My dream has come true, Henry. I have you."

Hearing the sincerity of her words, he fell in love with her all over again. Catherine never asked for anything else, and she never expected anything more. Yet she deserved more than what he could ever offer to her.

He leaned his head in to rest his forehead against hers. "You always will, sweetheart. And my dream is to see you dressed all in white, walking down an aisle to me, *for* me. From the moment in Europe when I realized I couldn't live without you, that's been my dream. Don't rob me of it because of money. I will pay anything to make that dream happen."

The raw emotion in Henry's voice silenced any other argument she could give. When she gave a reluctant nod, Henry's face lit up as he realized he'd won the argument.

"Fine, but I insist that I at least pay for my own dress," she countered.

"Deal." He sealed the agreement with another kiss before asking, "Are you ready to go tell the world now?"

She answered by planting a soft kiss on his forehead and sliding back over to the passenger's seat. She waited until they were back on the road before asking, "So, in your dreams, when you see me coming down the aisle, who's giving me away?"

Henry understood the pain in Catherine's question. Had she started with that as her argument, he probably would have ceded to eloping. Yet now that she had agreed to an actual wedding, the image he had conjured up in his mind of her dressed in white couldn't be erased. He didn't want to give up on that. He thought carefully before responding, "Catherine, I only have eyes for you. In my dreams, it's always only ever been you." He took a deep breath and added, "But I know how hard that might be."

"Walking down the aisle alone, it's a screaming reminder."

"Although no one can replace your brother, you've told me on more than one occasion you have a brotherly friendship with Michael."

As soon as Henry had mentioned the name, Catherine knew the suggestion was the right one. Michael *was* like a brother to her, and he had helped her get through a very rough time in her life after she had lost Caleb. She couldn't think of anyone better to stand up for her and give her away to Henry. Taking great efforts to contain her excitement, she asked, "Are you sure? Michael hasn't always been your favorite person."

"That was when I thought he was stealing you from me. And I'm sure that there were times when I wasn't his favorite person either." His mind drifted back to when Michael had punched him at the hospital after learning that Robert had nearly killed Catherine. "The truth is that Michael loves you fiercely, and that's impossible to deny."

"Thank you. That's a great suggestion, and I can't wait to ask him."

"Besides," he threw her a smirk, "he'll be handing you to *me*. That's the best part. No matter who's there, I'm the one who gets you in the end."

Eleven

As Susan sat on her front porch with a morning cup of coffee, she glared at the newspaper now resting on her knees. The photograph of Henry, his face beaming in happiness, mockingly stared back at her as his arm draped possessively around a timid-looking but equally happy Catherine. "Really? 'Hometown Hero Finds His Happy Ending,'" she read the headline out loud as a bitter taste filled her mouth.

When she had discovered Bobby, Olivia, Henry, and Catherine had taken a weekend trip out of town, she had known that Henry and Catherine would return engaged. Even if she hadn't known, the news of the engagement spread so quickly that she wouldn't have been left in the dark for long.

And now they're on the front page of the local paper ... that sure didn't take long. It's only been a week! Before she could dwell on it anymore, she crumpled the paper and threw it across the porch, furious that it seemed Catherine had truly won in the end. Susan knew that it wasn't so much that she didn't have Henry for herself; there were so many other handsome men that could easily occupy her time. It was the fact that she had lost Henry to *Catherine*, the plainest, most uncivilized woman in town, that really bothered her.

I never lose, especially to the likes of someone like Catherine. While she sat there brooding over her hatred for Catherine, a resolve reawakened inside her. She couldn't let Catherine win. She *wouldn't* let her win. Suddenly, with as much energy as she had used to toss the paper, she retrieved it from the corner of the porch.

A small smile crept from the corners of her mouth as she read the article.

Their plans were for an early autumn wedding. While that didn't give Susan a lot of time to work with, it would be enough to at least cause the wedding to be delayed long enough for her to do enough damage to eventually get it canceled altogether. She found her mood brightening as she hurried inside to finish getting ready.

While she and Olivia weren't nearly as close of friends as they had been, Susan still knew Olivia would want to go shopping with Catherine the first chance she got. If she wouldn't be looking for a bridesmaid dress for herself, she'd most certainly be there to help pick out Catherine's wedding dress. There were two bridal shops in town, so learning when they showed up at them would be easy enough.

Besides, she thought with a smug smile, *a bride could use all the feedback on dresses that she can get. And this way, I'll get to congratulate her personally.*

*   *   *

Catherine didn't know what to expect when she stepped into Michael's club on her first day back to work, a week after becoming engaged. She had hoped to be able to share the news with Michael in person, but with Olivia immediately pulling her into a whirlwind of wedding plans, getting to the club before her scheduled shift had become impossible. Then, when she had seen their engagement had made the newspaper that morning, she knew Michael would know about it before she got to work.

He'll either knock me down at the door with a hug or give me the cold shoulder, she thought as she approached the club. When no one greeted her at the door, she knew Michael was going with the latter. Yet when she found him at a table near the dance floor, patiently waiting for her, she didn't see anger in his face.

She groaned inwardly as she saw her face on the newspaper sitting on the table between his elbows.

"Hi," she greeted him somewhat timidly.

"How was your week off?" he asked nonchalantly, leaning back in his chair and picking up the newspaper, rifling through its pages.

"Um ..."

"Mine was pretty quiet, nothing worth making headlines. What about you?" He kept his face buried between the pages, preventing Catherine from reading his face to discern his emotion.

She sat at the empty chair beside him. "Oh, nothing too scandalous."

Michael lowered the paper, raising an eyebrow as he asked, "Oh, no?"

She saw the gleam in his eye and knew then that he wasn't upset with her. She flicked her fingers to the page of the newspaper with her photograph and asked, "You're not mad, are you? I wanted to come tell you right away, but Olivia—"

He calmly laid the paper off to the side. "I'll admit that I was hurt finding out this way. But my darling wife, who congratulates you, by the way, reminded me of how her time had been monopolized when we were first engaged." He tapped the newspaper page as he continued, "Besides, seeing the happiness on your face, a happiness that you've fought so hard for, easily quashed any selfish hurt I might have been harboring."

Catching Catherine off guard, Michael swiftly picked her up, enveloping her in a strong hug. "And I couldn't be happier for you," he whispered in her ear as his voice faltered with emotion.

Catherine couldn't hold back the tears that surfaced with his kind words. She buried her face in his shoulder as the memories of their friendship journeyed through her mind. Michael had known about her love for Henry long before anyone else, and he had done everything in his power to help her win Henry's love. He knew every heartbreak and fear she had experienced during the process, so she knew he'd understand her happiness better than anyone.

"We did it," she said, her voice still muffled in his shoulder. "It seems almost too good to be true."

Michael stood tall and lightly tapped her nose with his index finger. "*You* did it. And every bit of it's true. You're not dreaming." He reached out and grabbed her hand, kissing it before leading her away from the table. "Now come on, we've got a lot of work to do before that autumn wedding."

"What are you talking about?" she asked as they crossed the dance floor. A wave of nostalgia passed over her as she remembered their countless nights of dance lessons. "We're not having a big wedding, Michael. It'll be simple—"

"I'm not talking about the wedding, love. I'm talking about the dancing," he interrupted. "We've got to find the perfect dance moves for your first dance as husband and wife." He dropped her hand as they reached the record player set up on a table against the far wall. He began filtering through the records, his mind already focused on the task.

"Then you'll have to do twice as much work," Catherine responded as he stood with his back to her. "Because I'll need music for a song that Henry can use to dance with his mother and one that I'll be able to use with the person that gives me away at the altar."

Having been quickly shuffling through the records, Michael's hands stilled at her words. He turned to face her, a pained expression set in his eyes. He knew all the family that she had lost, leaving her alone in the world. Weddings were events to share with family, and knowing that Catherine had none to share it with broke his heart.

"Caleb would have been proud to give me away," Catherine said as her eyes brimmed with tears, "and I'm sorry that he's not here to get that opportunity." As Michael placed the records aside and reached for her, she held up her hand to stop him. "Wait. I'm not through." Michael nodded, holding back so Catherine could gain her composure. "And while no one on earth can ever replace Caleb, you've been like a brother to me since the day I met you. You brought me out of the deepest depression I've ever been in and kept believing in me when I didn't believe in myself. You became my family when I had none."

By now, Catherine's tears flowed freely. Michael's eyes also sparkled with tears as he sensed what she was about to ask.

"I want you to pick out a song for us, Michael. Because it would mean the world to me if you'd be the one to give me away."

* * *

"Are you as excited as I am?" Olivia asked as Catherine pedaled up to her. Olivia stood leaning against her car, unable to contain her eagerness to help Catherine find a wedding dress. She had been waiting for this day for a long time, but Olivia didn't want to scare Catherine with her overzealous behavior.

A look of trepidation fell across Catherine's face as she looked at the bridal shop window. The smile she had been wearing on the way over from the club began to fade as she took in the lace and tulle filling the boutique window. Unable to draw her eyes away from the overwhelming window display, she answered, "I'm not setting foot in there with you until we go over the ground rules one more time."

"Catherine! You are *not* going to take the fun out of this."

"And you're not going to dress me up like a doll." She turned to Olivia, gesturing at the window. "Do you see that? A person can get lost in all those ruffles."

"Catherine, need I remind you that I'm pregnant? And need I also remind you that you're planning a wedding *before* I have this baby and get back down to my normal size? You're lucky that I want to help you instead of hurt you. Take advantage of my kindness while you can."

Amused but hiding it, Catherine gave Olivia a defeated look and said, "Okay, maybe we should do this later."

Olivia knew the game Catherine was trying to play. She crossed her arms grudgingly. "Fine. Rule number one: you have the final say, even though I get to choose the dresses for you."

Catherine arched an eyebrow, nodding and waiting for her to continue.

"Rule number two: you're on a budget. So, despite everyone's offer to loan you money to buy an expensive, beautiful wedding gown, you're refusing their help and forcing me to pick from the sales rack." She stuck her tongue out at Catherine when Catherine gave her an encouraging nod.

"That's exactly right. So long as you understand this, then I'm ready to—" She couldn't even finish as Olivia grabbed her hand and forced her into the shop.

If the lace in the window had overwhelmed her, the amount inside the shop stunned her into silence. Olivia, however, felt right at home and immediately started plucking dresses off the racks, not bothering to look at the price tags as they fell into a pile in Catherine's arms. Soon, Catherine lost sight of her and anything else as the pile in her arms towered over her head. A quick glance at the price tag of one of the dresses almost made her drop the entire pile.

"Liv! I thought you understood that I'm on a budget. These are not budget prices!"

"I know that." Olivia didn't even break her momentum to reply as she continued to flick through the dresses. "I'm pulling these for the style and cut. We'll find the perfect style for you and then find the same style on a less expensive dress."

"Why not start with the cheaper ones?" A sales attendant came by at that moment and relieved Catherine of her burden, taking the dresses to set them up in a dressing room.

"Because you're letting me pick out the dresses. So pretend to be enjoying yourself and hush up."

"You're not truly considering *white* are you?" A familiar but unwelcome voice came from behind Catherine's shoulder. She turned to find Susan facing her with a smug look on her face. "I mean, you two were gone for an entire weekend together and came back engaged," she said loudly enough for everyone in the shop to overhear. "Surely you're not in a place to wear white any longer."

Silence filled the shop as customers and employees alike stopped to eavesdrop. Catherine heard Olivia gasp behind her.

With calmness in her voice, Catherine found herself whispering, "Congratulations: that's too difficult a word for you to speak, isn't it?"

Susan arched an eyebrow and leaned in closer before replying, "You only need to tell me what to congratulate you on. Henry's conquest of you?" She looked directly over her shoulder at Olivia. "Is that why he proposed? You know, it only takes one time—"

"You meddling shrew!" Olivia screamed as she tried to lunge past Catherine for Susan's throat. Catherine was too quick for her, though, grabbing her arm and moving her a safe distance from Susan. Olivia struggled against Catherine as she continued to berate Susan. "How dare you come in here and insult Catherine and my family!"

Susan gave Olivia a flippant shrug as she refocused her energy on Catherine. "I'm only trying to figure out why the sudden rush for a wedding, that's all."

"Rush?" Olivia practically spat at Susan. "Do you know how long we've been waiting for this? They both deserve this happiness, and you're not going to spoil it."

"Why, Olivia, I do believe you've been spending too much time with Catherine. Her sharp tongue is starting to rub off on you."

Catherine turned to Olivia, whispering, "I've got this. I'm going to let you go, and I need you to walk away. Let me handle this battle." She released Olivia and turned back to Susan, prepared to handle her with sickening sweetness.

"You did see that article in the newspaper about us, right? Since you seem to believe we're having a quick wedding, you obviously haven't read it. We're planning an autumn wedding—nothing too soon." She snapped her fingers as though the idea had just dawned on her. "I'm sure you can get a copy of that article, or I can even send it to you if you'd like. It really is a great picture of the two of us." Catherine saw Susan's face redden with anger. She opened her mouth to respond, but Catherine wasn't finished.

"You know, Henry is really a gentleman. While he may have proposed to me outside of town, he was and always will be respectful of my wishes. He's not going to do anything to jeopardize my character. But you already know that, don't you? And we didn't spend an entire weekend away. So, whomever you have keeping tabs on me didn't give you the correct information. There will be no reason for me to wear any color other than white at my wedding. And while I'm used to your attacks, I won't tolerate you slinging my fiancé's name through the mud. So, let this be your warning." Then with a gleam in her eye, her smile broadening, she added loudly enough for everyone to hear, "*My fiancé.* I have to admit, that's something I'll never grow tired of saying." She fixed threatening eyes on Susan as she concluded, "The door's over there. You should see yourself out. The staff is too busy helping me to provide you an escort."

For a moment, the two women stood facing each other, complete loathing reflected in their eyes. Finally, Susan found her voice. "Watch your back, Catherine," she retorted. "This isn't over—not by a long shot."

"As far as I'm concerned, Susan, it is." Catherine turned away from her but found that her breathing didn't return to normal until after Susan vacated the shop. She dared look at Olivia and saw the anger still darkening her face.

"Let it go, Liv. I am."

"She has no right," she spluttered, still completely flustered by Susan's accusations.

"It's okay," she said, placing a comforting hand on her shoulder. "I appreciate you standing up for me, though. But come on, you have dresses to find."

Olivia pulled her eyes away from the door. "I don't know. Maybe we should do this later."

"No!" The determination in Catherine's voice took Olivia by surprise. She saw raw resolution in Catherine's eyes as she explained, "Susan only came in here to take a stab at me, to try and ruin what should be a happy time. I am not going to let her get the better of me. She's not taking this away from me. If I have to spend all day here and try on a hundred dresses, I'm not leaving until I find the perfect one."

Olivia couldn't help but admire Catherine's tenacity. No matter how many times someone tried to knock her down, she always got back up again. *She's right; she can't let Susan destroy the happiness she's fought so hard to get. She deserves the perfect dress, and I'm going to make sure she finds it.* Olivia let the corners of her mouth turn up in a conspiring grin and countered, "You may live to regret those words. Don't underestimate my stamina, Cat. You want to leave today with your wedding dress? Consider it done."

That evening, after Henry had left and the house had quieted, Catherine sat on her bed, staring in wonder at the white, lacy dress that hung on the back of her bedroom door, glowing in the moonlight. She still didn't know how Olivia had managed it, but she had succeeded in finding the perfect wedding dress for Catherine. While the latest trend for wedding dresses were tighter, form-fitting styles, Catherine loved that they had discovered an A-line dress that stopped just above her ankles. The full skirt would make dancing easy and keep Catherine from feeling self-conscious about her body's imperfections. While lace accented the waist and bust of the dress, it didn't overwhelm the garment, giving it an affordable price tag. It was the perfect dress for a country girl. It was perfect for Catherine.

Tears brimmed her eyes as she allowed a childlike giddiness to spread from her stomach. This dress signaled that Catherine was about to have her happy ending. Always afraid to dream of something so wonderful and magical happening to her, Catherine had always managed to keep her hopes under a tight seal. For the first time, Catherine allowed a small break in the seal that bottled her deepest dreams.

She was going to marry Henry, a man whom she loved and respected more than anyone. When she told him earlier that evening about finding her dress, she had nearly melted at the happiness that shined in his eyes. He hadn't teased her nor threatened to peek at the dress as she'd thought he would. Instead, he had kissed her soundly on the lips and then silently enfolded her in his arms before whispering in her ear, "All for me. I can't wait."

He had given her so much already, and for now, she was able to forget about her insecurities as she mentally planned their future. She couldn't wait to begin their lifetime together as she tried to give him as much happiness as he had rendered to her.

TWELVE

"How was your dinner last night?" Henry called out to Bobby from across the garage as they both worked on repairs. "Since I left Catherine's before you returned, I know it must have been some nice sit-down place."

Bobby rose up from under the hood of the car he was working on and blew out an exasperated breath. "They were last-minute plans, to be sure. But after I came home and saw Olivia's state of mind, I knew immediately it was an Italian dinner night."

Henry chuckled, asking, "Pregnancy already getting to her, is it?"

Puzzled, Bobby replied, "Not at all. She was furious … wasn't Cat? Surely, she had to be as upset, if not more, than Liv."

It was Henry's turn to give a confused look. "What? What are you talking about? Catherine was great last night. She was excited over finding her wedding dress."

Bobby turned his back to Henry and began methodically cleaning the tools on his workbench. "Did Catherine mention how the dress shopping went?" he asked casually.

Henry hadn't fought in a war beside Bobby without learning the man's mannerisms. Bobby was trying to backpedal. "No, she didn't," he answered. "But something obviously happened."

Bobby remained focused on his task as he spoke, "Well, if it wasn't a big deal to Catherine, then I'm sure it's fine. Maybe you're right; maybe Liv's pregnancy is already creating heightened emotions." He grimaced inwardly as he heard Henry stop his project and take heavy steps toward him.

"If it's not a big deal, why don't you go ahead and enlighten me?"

134

"If Cat didn't say anything, Henry, I don't know that it's my place to—"

"Out with it. Or I'll go to Liv and find out from her."

"No!" Bobby exclaimed. "It took me all evening to get her calmed down. I don't want you to trigger all that again."

Henry didn't speak, but as he crossed his arms, his posture spoke volumes.

Bobby's shoulders sagged in defeat. "I need to learn to keep my mouth shut," he mumbled. When he saw that Henry wasn't budging, he gave a deep sigh and tossed a tool onto the table as nonchalantly as possible. "Liv and Cat bumped into Susan at the bridal shop."

Henry couldn't hide his surprise. "Really? Why would she be …" his voice faded as he answered his own question. As anger flashed in his eyes, he took a step toward Bobby and demanded, "Tell me everything you know."

Had Henry's icy stare been focused on anyone but himself, Bobby would have appreciated the soldier that still lived in Henry. As the target, however, he found the glare unsettling. "Liv said that as soon as Susan came into the store, she hurled insults at Catherine."

"I'm sure Olivia elaborated."

Bobby nodded, his swallow visible in his throat. "Henry," he warned, "promise me you won't go off the deep end. If Cat's over it, we should forget about it too." As he watched Henry's eyes darken, he realized that the more he postponed telling Henry, the worse his reaction would be. "Susan tried to imply that Cat's virtue was compromised by the way you proposed to her. Out on the floor, in front of all the customers, she told Cat not to wear white to her wedding as she might already be pregnant." Bobby couldn't help his own anger from rising with his next words, "Then she threw an insult aimed at Liv before Catherine practically threw her out of the shop."

Anger surged through Henry as he unfolded his arms and scanned the room for a place to release his rage. He grabbed a nearby toolbox and hurled it against the wall away from the automobiles. In that moment, he held the deepest hate he'd ever known for Susan. She had intentionally made those allegations in a public setting hoping they'd fall into the rumor mill and completely tarnish Catherine's reputation. Reflecting on this, he realized that he had created a situation Susan could easily use to her advantage.

I should have never proposed to Catherine that way. I should have never taken her away for a weekend. Even though nothing happened, and we came back before the weekend ended, the appearance alone could ruin her.

Henry tried to shake his head clear of the guilt that had begun to build inside him. He addressed Bobby, who stood a safe distance from him, "You said Liv was furious. Did she say how Catherine responded?"

"With great self-restraint, to be sure. She put Susan in her place and told her to leave." Bobby shook his head and added, "That woman is a rock. She doesn't let anything get to her."

Henry knew that was far from the truth. Susan had already planted deep seeds of insecurity in Catherine, and this latest move was yet another dig to keep her anxieties at the surface. He pulled the towel from the counter to wipe his hands and said, "I need you to stay and watch the shop. I'll be back in a bit."

"Wh-where are you going?" Bobby asked, suddenly worried as the vehemence in Henry's eyes refused to fade.

"I'm ending this," Henry said, now in a hurry to depart the shop. He gave Bobby one last look before leaving. "I'm not going to let Susan spend another day determined to destroy the woman I love. This ends *today*." He stormed out of the building before Bobby could respond.

Although Susan was deeply surprised to find Henry pacing on her front porch, she hid it well as she stepped out of her vehicle and flashed her most disarming smile. As she started to speak, her voice almost faltered at the fury she saw on his face. "Why, Henry, what a pleasant surprise!" she exclaimed. "If I had known you were coming, I'd have made sure that lunch was ready." She gave her hips an intentional swing as she climbed the porch steps up to him. "But if you'd rather, we could go straight to dessert."

This was the wrong thing to say.

Henry looked at her with complete disgust and took a step back to ensure distance remained between them before saying, "I'm not staying, Susan. I just came by to tell you to stop. This ends right now."

"Whatever are you talking about?" she asked with false innocence.

"Leave my fiancée alone, Susan. I heard about the stunt you pulled at the bridal shop."

"Did she cry to you about it?"

"No, she's too classy for that. But I'm not from the same cloth." There was an unspoken threat behind his words. "I'm asking you to keep your distance. Stay away from Catherine. She doesn't deserve your mistreatment."

"My mistreatment?" Now Susan allowed her voice to rise in anger as she said, "I've done nothing to the woman. She's the one who took you from me."

"Are we back to this? I was never yours to begin with. Stay away from her."

"And if I refuse?" she challenged.

Henry countered with the only tool he believed he possessed: money. "My auto repair business has become quite successful. It's brought more revenue into your father's great town. I will do whatever necessary to protect Catherine and give her the life she deserves. If I have to pick up my business and move to a different town to give her that life, I'll do it without a single look back."

Susan caught on to his meaning.

"Are you threatening blackmail?" Susan asked. "Surely you're not stooping to that to protect your little crush."

"She's more than a crush to me, Susan. And I don't want to hear of you ever being near her again. Do you understand?"

Susan's eyes narrowed as she whispered, "You're making a mistake choosing her."

"There was never a choice to make. I want you out of her life."

She sighed. "Henry, this isn't you," she pleaded. "What happened to the man who flirted with any woman in a tight shirt and picked a new dance partner every night?"

"He grew up," he explained. "I've put my wild, foolish ways behind me. I've no intention of revisiting those days."

"Pity," Susan let her eyes slowly roam his body as she spoke. When she met his eyes, she saw determination set in them. "You know, Henry, we can't really change the heart of who we are. We can try to mask our past and pretend that we've always been who we are now, but you and I know it's all a façade. This isn't you, not the real Henry. The sooner you realize that and abandon your fixation on Catherine, the better off you'll be."

"That's not going to happen."

Not yet ... Susan released a sigh of defeat for Henry's benefit. "Listen, Henry, if I never saw her again, it would be too soon. Because I care about making *you* happy, I'll honor your request. I won't have contact with Catherine."

But I didn't say anything about staying away from you.

Henry hesitated at her sudden willingness to comply. Although her mouth spoke one thing, her eyes said something else entirely. Only time would tell if she kept her promise.

That and Catherine's willingness to share any incidents with me.

"Thank you, Susan," he said. He gave her a brief nod before turning and descending the stairs to his truck.

"See you around, Henry," he heard her reply behind him.

The coldness in her voice caused Henry to realize that he may have done more harm than good in confronting her. He had a sinking suspicion that things were only going to get more complicated.

Henry waited until after dinner when they were alone together on the porch before broaching the subject of Susan to Catherine. He wanted Catherine to tell him what had happened at the bridal shop. Even more so, he wanted to know why she hadn't felt the need to tell him about it when it had upset Olivia so much. He held her hand firmly in his and tightened his grip when she started to head to the porch swing.

She looked up to find a serious look on his face. "Henry?" she asked.

Giving her hand a gentle tug, he said, "It's nice tonight. Let's go for a walk."

"Okay," she replied. "Do you want me to grab a flashlight?"

He flashed a smile and held her close, saying, "I think we know our way well enough to get by without it. I'll lead, unless you don't trust me."

"Of course I trust you," she said as she slipped her left hand to latch on to his forearm while he continued to hold her right hand. "Lead on. I'd follow you anywhere."

Henry soaked up the feel of Catherine by his side as they walked along the road leading from her house. As soon as the house lights disappeared from sight, Henry no longer felt the need to show as much restraint. He led her off the road and into the adjoining woods, where Catherine found herself encircled in Henry's arms.

"Sorry, I can't resist," Henry said before seizing her lips with his own.

Catherine momentarily forgot about Henry's seriousness that had concerned her earlier. Yet as his kisses deepened, holding a hint of restlessness, she started to think that one had something to do with the other.

When he finally detached his lips from hers, she didn't have to see him to know how breathless he was. "I thought you wanted to walk," she whispered as she felt his face near hers once again.

"Only if we can visit a few more trees along the way," he replied as he led her back to the road.

They walked together in companionable silence for several minutes before Catherine asked, "Henry? Were you okay earlier? You seemed deep in thought when we first went out on the porch."

"I was just mulling over the day's conversations, that's all." She heard the smile leave his voice as he asked, "Catherine, would you mind humoring me and telling me about how you found your wedding dress again?"

Only the crunching of the gravel beneath their feet sounded. "Sure," she said and began to replay the story once more. As she did the day before, she purposely omitted her confrontation with Susan.

When she finished, Henry let the silence fill the air before commenting, "It sounds like you had a wonderful time."

Catherine chuckled and said, "Once I found the dress, I guess. You know I'm not a fan of the frills and lace."

He released her hand so he could wrap an arm around her shoulders. "I know. It sounds like a day that's more up Olivia's alley." Even in the darkness, he sensed her nod beside him. "But there is one thing I can't understand," he continued. "If Olivia loves this stuff so much, why was she so upset afterward?"

Henry sensed her body tense.

"I'm sorry?"

"Bobby told me Liv was furious about the run-in with Susan," he replied simply. He stopped and faced her so he could read her eyes in the light of the moon. She averted her eyes, but he gently turned her chin so she had to face him. "Why didn't you tell me?"

Water formed in Catherine's eyes, belying her words, "It wasn't a big deal. Olivia throws everything out of proportion. You know that."

"Bobby told me what she said, Catherine. It is a big deal. I didn't believe it would get to this point."

"What point?" she whispered, still trying to turn from him.

"She's harassing you. I won't stand for it. You haven't done anything to her."

"Except steal you … at least, in her eyes." This time, she successfully managed to pull away from him. "But I've got this, Henry. I can take care of Susan." She turned to walk down the road.

She didn't get far.

Quicker than the last time, Henry picked her up and hid them among the woods lining the road. She gasped at the speed he exerted to pin her to a tree once more. "I can see how you were a successful soldier," she said when he didn't kiss her. His face was so close to hers that she felt his breath on her cheeks.

"The thing about soldiers," Henry said quietly but vehemently, "is that they form a bond. They have their comrades' back at all costs. They stick up for one another. They *fight* for one another." His next words came out as a plea. "Let me be that for you, Catherine. We're a team, we're in this together. I want to share everything with you."

"I do too, Henry."

He dropped his forehead to hers and whispered, "Then you have to be willing to trust me. You have to be willing to confide in me. I don't want anything to separate us, especially nothing of our own doing. You know I'd answer any question you'd ask me, right?"

Catherine could only nod.

"Trust me enough with your heart to do the same for me. *Please.*"

Catherine took the initiative to start the next kiss. She leaned up and lightly caressed his lips with her own. "I'm sorry. I should have told you about Susan. I will from now on."

This was all the reassurance Henry needed. He returned her kiss, tracing her jawline with his lips. An involuntary sigh escaped Catherine's lips at his touch.

"Maybe I should have taken you up on your offer to elope," he muttered between heavy breaths.

"Are you *kidding* me?" Catherine asked in exasperation as she playfully pushed away from Henry. "Do you understand how much of Olivia I had to endure to find that dress? Oh no, mister. *You're* getting a wedding ceremony, and *I'm* getting a chance to wear that dress all day long." She made her way hastily up the road with Henry following in cheerful pursuit.

"Your window of elopement is over, Henry Bradley. Don't ever mention it again."

Thirteen

"It's been a while, hasn't it, cousin?" Susan asked of the young woman sitting across her father's desk from her. "Goodness, Natalie, how many years *has* it been?"

"At least ten, I'd venture to guess," the woman replied as she threw quick glances over her shoulder at the closed door of the study. The woman's son paid little attention to his surroundings, preferring the toys generously placed in his lap.

"Too long," Susan said. "No one's going to bother us. You can stop watching the door."

Natalie gave a brief look to her son before focusing her attention on Susan. "I have to admit, I was very surprised to hear that you wanted to speak with me, Susan. The last I remember, you had pretty much written me off when you learned about my *situation*."

Susan waived a dismissive hand. "Who am I to judge?" she asked. "You made a poor choice in your husband. We all make mistakes from time to time."

Natalie looked uneasily at her son before her eyes gave Susan an unspoken warning. "You paid for my expenses to come here, so you have my attention. But why don't we skip the pleasantries and you tell me what exactly I'm doing here?"

Susan responded, "You always were one to cut to the chase." She slid a folded piece of paper across the table. "Please, take it."

"What is it?" Natalie asked cautiously.

"Open it," she replied. She watched as Natalie unfolded the piece of paper and read the number written on it. "That's the total payment I'm prepared to offer you, should you choose to take the job."

Natalie couldn't hide her astonishment. "Why are you offering so much?"

"It's contingent on your silence. I give you the money, you do the job, no questions asked and no opinions voiced."

Natalie gave Susan a skeptical look. "Is this legal?"

Susan nodded to the sum written on the paper as she responded with her own question, "Does it matter? I understand you're hoping to start over somewhere more private. I know how strapped you are financially. This job will help take care of both of those problems."

"How dare you presume to know what I need."

Susan gave her a triumphant look and said, "One word: Edward."

Natalie paled. She cast a worried glance at her son who was playing, oblivious to the adult conversation. "David, honey, can you take your toys and play in the hallway? Mommy needs to talk to Cousin Susan alone for a bit."

David looked up for the first time, casting his eyes first to Susan and then to his mother. Susan gave him a small smile. "Tell the man at the front door, Butler William, that I said you could have cookies."

That was the only encouragement David needed. In one fluid motion, he disposed of his toys and raced to the study's door, calling for William in the process.

Both women waited until he was gone before returning to their conversation. "He doesn't know about Edward. David was still too young when we left him."

"That's perfect for my plans. David doesn't need to know about Edward."

"Susan, he can't find us. I won't do anything to jeopardize him finding us."

Susan tried offering a sympathetic smile through her impatience. "Then I suggest you take me up on my offer. When you're finished, you'll have means to start a brand new life somewhere far from Edward. I'll arrange it so he'll never find you two again," Susan explained.

Natalie nervously folded and refolded the paper in her hands and finally whispered, "Tell me what I have to do."

Susan smiled at Natalie's tacit agreement. "It's simple. You need to introduce your son to his father." She continued before Natalie had the opportunity to refuse, "Not Edward. David's middle name is Henry, right?" She waited for Natalie's affirming nod. "How easy would it be to call him Henry rather than David?"

"I suppose not too difficult."

"Perfect. You need to introduce Henry to his father, Henry Peter Bradley. You need to convince Mr. Bradley as well as his romantic interest that he fathered your child. Once they're convinced, you can leave town without looking back."

"I've no clue who this man is. How on earth am I supposed to convince him we were ever together?"

Susan chuckled as she answered, "Oh, my dear, his wild past offers enough support that it'll take very little convincing."

Natalie thought about the large sum Susan had offered. It would buy her and David an otherwise impossible chance at freedom. She'd been fleeing from her husband, Edward Collins, since shortly after David's birth. She knew her luck at evading him would run out at some point, and the result of him finding her and their son would be anything but pleasant. She knew she'd do whatever it took to keep her son safe.

If that means destroying another man's life, so be it. I have to look out for David. No, not David. Henry.

"I have conditions," she finally said.

"Humor me."

"No photographs. Whatever you have in mind for me, I don't want our photograph taken. I won't risk the opportunity it would create for Edward to find us."

Susan shrugged her shoulders. "Do your job well and that won't be an issue. Anything else?"

"I assume that you don't want this traced back to you. So you'll need to help me acquire a place to stay."

"Consider it done."

Natalie nodded. She shouldn't have been surprised by how easy it was for Susan to pull resources together. Susan had power that she could only ever dream of having. "Do you have a photograph of the man that supposedly fathered my child?"

Susan contemplated showing her the recent newspaper article that announced his engagement to Catherine. She had a sense that seeing their smiling faces might be too much for Natalie and result in her refusal to help. Instead, she turned over a newspaper clipping from when Henry was at war. The article used his military photograph.

Natalie couldn't deny the handsomeness of Henry's face. She fought against the guilt that blossomed inside her at the notion of ruining this man's life. If she had any hope of succeeding, she'd have to leave her heart at home and take up the ruthlessness of her cousin. She took a deep breath, gently placed the clipping back on the desk before rising to her feet, and said, "I suppose I should go collect my son. I need to prepare him for meeting his father."

FOURTEEN

"It's your turn!" Henry called from underneath the truck he was repairing as the bell above the front door chimed, announcing a customer.

Bobby groaned from the vehicle next to him. "You know," he said, waving a tool at Henry, "when I agreed to this venture with you, I thought I'd be in a garage working on cars all day. You didn't mention anything about dealing with the public."

Henry chuckled but didn't break concentration as Bobby continued to grumble on his way to the reception area. When he heard a woman's voice reply to Bobby's greeting, the smile on his face broadened. Since opening the business, he had learned that the female customers were talkative and were often there much longer than necessary.

Soon, Henry saw Bobby's feet reappear next to him. "See?" he called out as he worked. "That didn't take too long. Was it so bad?"

"She's asking for *you*, my friend," Bobby answered smugly. He waited until Henry slid out from underneath the truck before handing him a rag. "I offered to help, but she's asking for you."

Henry frowned as he grabbed the rag and asked, "Who is it?"

Bobby shrugged. "I don't know her. She's got a little boy with her though."

Henry acknowledged with a nod as he left to greet the waiting customer. He gave the stranger a polite smile as he finished wiping his hands. "I'm Henry. How can I help you, ma'am?"

The woman rose from her chair and placed a trembling hand over her lips. With her other hand, she firmly clutched the boy's hand. "You're even more handsome than I remember," she whispered.

146

Taken by surprise, Henry didn't try to mask his confusion. "Excuse me?" The woman giggled softly. "I'm sorry," she apologized. "That was inappropriate of me, wasn't it?" She gave him a shy smile. "It's been so long. Of course I can't expect you to remember me. But I definitely remember you. I remember everything about you."

The implication of her words made the hair on his neck stand. "I apologize, but I don't recall ever meeting you before today." As he spoke, he racked his brain to trigger any memory of her. "Are you from around here?"

The woman shook her head and gave a coy smile.

"What did you say your name was again?"

"I didn't, silly. I'm Natalie. I'm not from around here. I came passing through town a few years ago on my way to visit family further south. I stopped by the local club—Sal's, I believe—for a fun night before continuing my travels. That's where I met *you*." She put a flirtatious index finger against his chest.

Henry struggled to keep up with Natalie's story. "It's entirely possible that I danced with you then. Before the war I spent nearly every evening there. I apologize for not being able to place you."

"We did more than spend an evening dancing, Henry." As she spoke, she lightly raised the boy's hand and encouraged him to take a step forward. "This is my son, David Henry. He's named David after the man in the Bible. His middle name comes from his father."

As Natalie's words sunk in, the color drained from his face. Behind him, the sounds of dropped tools indicated that Bobby had overheard and was just as surprised by the news. Henry remained motionless as he stared at the little boy standing before him.

My son?

As the realization struck Henry, he found his voice. "You'd better come into my office," he said, indicating the small office to his right. He remained still as Natalie nodded and strode into the office, her son in tow.

Bobby stood in the garage doorway, unsure of whether he should proceed. "Henry," he finally said.

"Look after the place," Henry ordered and followed Natalie into his office.

Bobby heard Henry moving around in the darkened office as he closed and locked the door following Natalie's departure. Bobby entered the office to find Henry sitting in a chair facing the wall.

"Hey," Bobby said after gently knocking on the doorframe. "Everything is locked up for the evening." He waited for Henry to acknowledge him, and when he didn't, Bobby continued, "Is everything all right?"

As his world seemed to be crashing in around him, the conversation with Natalie still screamed in his mind. *How could it be possible?* Henry dropped his head in his hands.

Easily enough, you fool. Natalie's just the first to tell me. There could be others.

"Henry?" Bobby said as he placed his hand on Henry's shoulder. "Do you need me to call Cat? Are you all right?"

Henry's stomach plummeted at his fiancée's name. How could he live with himself after breaking her heart? Henry shook his head slowly. "No, Bobby, I'm not all right. But let's get going. I need to see Catherine."

As soon as Henry stepped out of his truck, Catherine knew something was wrong. He lingered at his truck, waiting until Bobby passed him and climbed up the porch stairs.

"Rough day?" she asked, casting a glance at Bobby and seeing concern written across his face.

Bobby glanced over his shoulder to Henry before answering, "I think so." His voice was barely a whisper. "But he's not talking." He gave her arm a light squeeze before entering the house to find his wife and son.

Caleb's squeals of delight at seeing his father carried from inside the house. A look of evident pain crossed Henry's features as his gaze shifted to the front door.

"Henry?" She slowly descended the porch steps.

Hesitation flashed in his eyes before he took a step toward her. Taking her hand, he turned and marched back to his truck. "We need to talk," was the only verbal greeting he offered.

He didn't even try to sound cheerful, and Catherine felt heartache radiate from him. She gave his hand a reassuring squeeze that he didn't

148

acknowledge. When she couldn't catch his eye as he held the truck door open for her, she knew something was seriously wrong.

As much as she wanted to speak, she bit her tongue and waited. It wasn't long before she realized Henry was taking her to his house. Fear laced itself with sentiments of concern.

Henry silently drove across town. He had no idea how he was going to deliver the news to Catherine that he had a son, and he was scared out of his mind at how she'd react. He barely noticed when they had arrived since his mind was racing through every possible emotion Catherine might express.

The one thing he didn't anticipate was for Catherine to scoot next to him in the seat and turn his face to hers after he parked. She lightly held his face in her hands as she studied him. He saw concern in her eyes. She waited patiently for him, but he didn't have the heart to start. Instead, he held onto her and rested his head on her shoulder, burying his face in her neck and hair.

They remained in this embrace for a time until Henry finally found the strength to pull back from her. He held her gaze, and she nodded. Although she didn't know the reason, she understood the need not to say anything until they were inside his house.

As soon as Henry had closed the front door behind them, the security of his home gave him the strength he needed. Gripping her hand, he led Catherine to his bedroom, as if another room could distance him from the day's life-changing events. Still holding her hand, he dragged a chair up to the bed and led Catherine to it.

Sitting across from her, he grabbed her other hand too. Searching for the right words, he studied the hands of the woman he loved. His ring looked beautiful on her finger, and he silently prayed it would always remain there.

"Okay, I'm beyond worried, Henry," Catherine's voice held a hint of trepidation as she spoke. "Just tell me what's wrong."

He forced himself to look up at eyes pooled with tears. *She doesn't deserve this. She doesn't deserve any of this.*

"I love you … more than anything."

She squeezed his hands and replied, "I know that."

He closed his eyes as he spoke the words that he knew would break her heart. "Catherine … I have a son."

FIFTEEN

Catherine sat in stunned silence as her world crashed down around her. Henry had recounted the details of the visitors to the shop. She felt him studying her with pained eyes and knew she needed to say something. *Anything.*

She hated the childish question that left her lips when she asked, "Is it true?"

Henry tightened the hold he had on her hands. "I don't know," he whispered. "Considering the boy's age ... I had some pretty wild days in my time." He took a deep breath. "It's possible."

"But surely you would remember her face, right? I mean, if you don't recognize her, then maybe it's someone's twisted way to try and—"

The hope laced in her words stabbed his heart like a dagger. "Not necessarily, Catherine."

Catherine stilled at his words. Her face suddenly warmed in embarrassment as she understood his meaning. She jerked her hands free from his and saw a flash of hurt cross his eyes. "How many women have you been with, Henry?" Her voice trembled. If he didn't find it suspicious that he couldn't recall this woman's face, she feared the answer.

Henry watched Catherine struggling with her emotions. Not wanting to cause her more pain, he didn't want to answer. Yet if they were going to survive this, they had to be honest with each other. Although it killed him, he held her gaze when he replied, "Too many."

She nodded and bit her trembling lip. A lone tear slid down her face. When he reached out to wipe it away, she quickly rose to her feet. "I need to go," she said before a sob tore at her throat. She ran from the bedroom.

Henry was right behind her.

"Catherine, please!" he called as he hurried past her to put himself between her and the front door. "Let's talk about this."

"You have a child ..." she said, keeping herself out of reach of his outstretched arms. Tears running freely down her cheeks, she didn't hide the pain in her voice as she continued, "I thought I'd be the one to give you that."

"What are you saying, Catherine?" he asked. He reached out before she could step any further away and grabbed her by the shoulders. "You still can. We—"

Although she wanted to bury herself in his arms, she struggled against his grip. "You have things bigger than me in your life now. Is she married?"

Henry dropped his arms in confusion. "What? ... No."

"You found her attractive once before, you might do so again."

He watched as the insecurities he had helped to bury resurfaced. He seized her arm and forced her into an embrace. She struggled against him, but he held her firmly. "Catherine, don't ever doubt this: it's you I want. It will always be you." She leaned back and saw her pain mirrored in his eyes. "I'm not going anywhere. My future is with you so long as you'll have me. Please, don't let the mistakes of my past kill our future."

Despite the heartbreak she felt, she pushed past her own grief to recognize the fear growing in Henry's eyes. This was new for him. Even when she had planned to leave town at one point to give him his freedom, he had never swayed in his confidence to be able to keep her here. Now there was no trace of that self-assurance.

"You're scared," she whispered.

"I'm terrified," he willingly admitted. "This morning I woke up and had the world in my hands." He rested his forehead against hers as he spoke, "And I'm scared that tonight I'll go to bed having lost it all. I'm not going to make excuses for my past. It was wrong, and I know that. I will try to make things right for the child, but I can't do it without you. *Please*, Catherine, I'm asking you to stand by me."

Catherine took in a ragged breath. She grew up knowing that Henry was flirtatious. That was the main reason it took her so long to believe that he truly loved her. She knew about his past. He had never tried to hide it from her. It was foolish to believe there'd never be repercussions for the way he had lived. "You've always been honest with me, Henry. Even when I don't want you to be. I know that had I only asked, you would have willingly shared your past with me. From the moment we stood on the train platform and I realized you loved me, I never looked back." Although it was difficult to speak them, her next words held hope. "And I won't look back now. I'll stand by you, for better or worse."

This was the only reassurance Henry needed. He leaned down and kissed her. He tasted the salt of her fallen tears. It pained him to know he was the cause of them, and he wanted to do everything in his power to make it up to her. He felt her resistance give way as she accepted his kisses. Even though he felt relief that he still had her heart, he couldn't shake the feeling of foreboding that gripped him. As a result, he began to kiss Catherine with a hungry desperation.

She accepted him with just as much need. Even though she knew their lives were forever changed by this news, a part of her wasn't willing to accept it yet, and her response to his kisses was a result of clinging to how things were before this news.

Henry has a son. What troubled her more, though, was the idea that a lover from his past was back in his life. Fighting against Susan was hard enough. *Am I strong enough to fight this one too?* She couldn't stop the doubt from emerging from the hidden place in her soul.

Henry sensed the change in her almost immediately. Her kisses became less confident, and when she pulled away, she averted her eyes. He understood at least part of what she was feeling. He formed a plan in his mind.

"Marry me," he said huskily.

She looked up at him in surprise. "You already asked me, remember?" She held up her hand to display the engagement ring that rested on her trembling finger.

He took her hand and kissed her palm before explaining, "Now. Tonight. Let's elope, Catherine. I should have agreed to it when you first suggested it."

"No," she said as she removed her hand from his, "you can't do that. That's running away."

"How is it running? I want this; I want to be with you in every aspect a husband is with his wife. I want to prove to you that *you* are my world."

"Then don't do anything rash. We have a wedding we're planning. We plan it." She welcomed the calmness that instantly seeped into her pores. "When people find out about this situation, and they're sure to, everyone will be watching you. If we elope, I don't want people to claim it was because you skirted your responsibilities or that I wanted to ensnare you before this child's mother did."

"Or that I put you in the same situation," he realized with horror. Susan's encounter with Catherine at the bridal shop surged to the front of his thoughts.

She nodded. Reaching up, she cupped his cheek in her hand. "We'll get through this together. I promise. I love you, Henry Bradley. I'm not going anywhere, okay?"

Relief filled his eyes as he nodded.

The household was asleep by the time Henry brought Catherine home later that night. After shared tears and reassuring kisses, both felt emotionally drained. As the sound of Henry's retreating truck faded in the distance, Catherine didn't need to look at the clock to know it was in the early morning hours.

She made as little noise as possible as she climbed the stairs and walked to her bedroom. With each step she took, she tried to reassure herself that everything was going to be fine. She was confident in their love for each other. Even as she repeated this thought in her mind, the idea of Henry with another woman weighed her heart with sadness. Susan's cruel words about how quickly he'd tire of her sent off alarms in her mind.

Although she had always known it, the reality that Henry was more experienced with intimacy than she was hit her hard. It wasn't so much her inexperience that bothered her, but rather that now there were two women in Henry's world that knew him on levels she didn't. She was already in a fight against Susan. Would this new woman, armed with Henry's son, join in the battle?

I don't stand a chance.

As the thought entered Catherine's mind, she chastised herself for doubting Henry's love. She opened her bedroom to find the moon casting light through the window and onto her wedding dress, which was lying across a chair.

A shuddered sob escaped her lips as she dropped to her knees. She was engaged to Henry. She wore his ring. Her wedding dress was before her very eyes. Yet the likelihood of marrying him and getting her happy ending seemed farther away than ever before.

Sixteen

The record player was blaring music when Michael arrived at the club the following morning. He took one look at Catherine as she rummaged through a stack of records in an almost panicked frenzy and said, "I think I should have had another cup of coffee." Catherine looked up at him, and when he saw the pained look in her eyes, he added, "Make that two cups."

"Good morning, Michael," Catherine greeted as she turned her attention back to the records.

Michael proceeded with caution. "I didn't think you were scheduled to work today."

"I'm not here to work," she answered as she continued her rapid searching. "Where *is* it?" she fumed under her breath.

Michael causally leaned against a nearby table. He watched as her frustration grew before finally asking, "Something troubling you, love?"

She glared back at him. "What do *you* think?" She turned back to the records to resume her search.

Michael reached out a hand and stilled her. Only when she calmed did he say, "It's too early in the morning for a dance lesson. What's going on?"

A tear escaped her eye.

"I need to find the record you played when you taught me how ... when I needed to feel beautiful. It was seductive ... it was ..."

"Catherine?" he asked patiently.

"Henry has a son," she whispered suddenly.

They stood frozen as Michael regarded Catherine's downturned mouth and tried to process her words.

155

"I thought I could handle this, but now I'm not so sure." A sob escaped her lips and triggered Michael to gather her in his arms.

"Okay, love," he kissed her forehead as he held her. "I need you to start at the beginning. My mind is a mess of confusion at the moment."

He led her to a table and listened as she tried to stay composed long enough to share the previous day's events. Michael made a conscience effort to hold her hand and fidget with her engagement ring. He wanted to remind her of Henry's devotion. When she had finished, he spent time reflecting before responding.

"Well, this definitely explains why you want the dance lesson."

Catherine said in exasperation, "That's all you have for me?"

He held up his hands. "Let me finish, woman!" He waited until he saw the apology in her eyes before continuing, "Catherine, I remember when you first told me about Henry. You admitted to me that he was far from perfect, that he was a playboy, that he was everything you shouldn't want but that you loved him regardless. When he came back from the war, he was different. Even though it took a bit of convincing on your part, you finally saw that. You've been with him ever since. Has he *ever* given you any indication that he's reverting back to his old ways?"

She shook her head.

"And it sounds like he's just as distraught by this news as you are."

She nodded.

"Catherine, listen to me," he said as he leaned closer to her. "Henry has been nothing but faithful to you. This child is the result of a wild, careless past. He doesn't seem like the type to shy away from his responsibilities, so I see him doing right by the child. However, Henry won't sacrifice you for it. This woman is from his past, and I'm sure Henry will make sure she stays there." He held up her hand to show her the engagement ring. "He will be a father to the child, but he won't be a husband to anyone he doesn't love." He gave her a soft smile. "If you want Henry to be the person he is *now* and leave the way he was behind him, then you need to leave it there too. Forgive the mistakes of his past; he's done as much for you."

Catherine let his words linger before answering, "You're right, you're always right. It just hurts."

"Imagine what Henry's feeling right now. He's probably scared out of his mind that he'll lose you. When are you supposed to see him?"

She shrugged as she replied, "I sometimes swing by his shop for breakfast."

"And you didn't today, which means that in his mind, you've already packed up and left town." He gave her a teasing smile and pulled her to her feet. "Listen, go meet him for lunch. Lunch with him will do more for you both than what a dance with me will do. And that's saying a lot ... I know what a *great* dancer I am."

She gave him a nervous smile and agreed. "I shouldn't avoid him. That won't make anyone feel better. I know I'm insulting his love by acting this way. But I'd never imagined this happening. Not now."

"Consider Liv. She went to live with you when she was pregnant with Caleb. Perhaps this woman had to do something similar. Besides, if Henry was so drunk he can't remember her, then maybe she was deep into the cups as well. Maybe only now is she willing to admit how foolish she acted that night."

"You have a good heart, Michael. I've been so obsessed with my own pain that I didn't stop to consider what this might mean for her." She chewed thoughtfully on her lip before continuing, "But is it wrong for me to hope that she isn't too pretty?"

He couldn't keep the laugh from surfacing. "It's good to be reminded that you're human from time to time," he said as he swung her into a twirl. "How about this? I'll let Henry calm those fears, but I'll at least send you to him feeling a little bit better about yourself. You came for a dance, and I know just the music for it."

As he lowered her into a deep dip that would have once mortified her because of its intimacy, she couldn't help but smile. As much as he irritated her at times, Michael was great medicine for her soul.

* * *

Henry tried to ignore the wall clock above the door to the office that showed the afternoon hour. He tried to pretend that Catherine's absence earlier this morning when he stopped by her home didn't bother him. He wasn't successful in either attempt.

Of course, Bobby's nervous pacing wasn't helping.

While Henry tried to focus on the automobile above him, he attuned his ears to the surrounding noises. Bobby's pacing constantly marked the passing time. Suddenly, his feet stopped near Henry's head.

"No word from Cat?"

Frustration filled Henry as he slid out from underneath the car. "You've been here as long as I have. Why don't you tell *me*?"

Henry had arrived at Catherine's house before the sun rose that morning. He had hoped to greet her and give her all the reassurance she might still need. He had tried to hide his disappointment upon discovering she'd already left for the day.

Bobby hadn't missed it, though. He kept Henry there, and Henry used the opportunity to share his life-changing news. Olivia and Bobby were like family to him, and he felt better after sharing his burden.

When Henry explained Catherine's reaction to them, they had said that she probably had left to get a jump on the day. Yet Olivia's furrowed brow and Bobby's now-frequent pacing told him that they didn't believe their own reassurances any more than he did.

Henry rose to his feet with a sigh and apologized. "I shouldn't have snapped like that. I—"

The sound of the bell ringing above the front door announced a new customer. "Hello? Henry? Bobby?"

"It's about time," Henry whispered as he recognized Catherine's voice. He hastily wiped his hands and threw the rag at Bobby to warn him not to follow.

Catherine recognized the determined look in his eyes as Henry emerged from the garage. In one fluid motion, he seized her hand and dragged her into his office, closing the door behind them. Catherine expected him to embrace her. Instead, he backed her up to a wall and took her face in his hands. He forced her to look into his eyes, and the intense fear she saw broke her heart.

Henry remained silent, holding her gaze in hopes of reading her heart. He knew her better than anyone, and he usually had no difficulty discerning her mood, even if he didn't know the cause of it. She had always been so easy for him to read … until today.

Perhaps it was because of his own restless night, filled with worry and regret, that he found it so difficult to read Catherine now. A series of emotions played across her eyes while she stared unblinkingly back at him.

"You left early this morning."

"I did," she whispered.

"Are you okay?" He gently stroked her cheek with his thumb, refusing to relinquish her from her position.

She tried to muster the courage to answer him honestly. The silence was too long for Henry.

"Catherine, I need you to talk to me," he said, leaning his forehead against hers. *"Please."*

His plea pierced her. Slowly, she closed her eyes and forced the tears to remain at bay. "I won't pretend that this doesn't bother me," she started to whisper. "I don't know how long it will take to get past that feeling. But know this, Henry. I love you. This is the result of a mistake from your past. This isn't a mistake from your present ... or from your future."

"I'm so sorry," he whispered as he buried his face in her hair.

"You don't owe me an apology for anything. God's forgiven you, and the least I can do is support you. You're not the person you once were, Henry. It wouldn't do anyone any good to bring up your past actions to crucify you now." Her eyes watered as he took a sharp intake of breath and embraced her. "I'm not going anywhere."

Henry desperately needed to hear that. "When I arrived at your place this morning and discovered you were gone ... and then when you didn't show up at noon ... I have to admit that the nightmare of you leaving me seemed too real."

"I went to visit Michael," she explained. "I needed someone to convince me of what I already knew."

"Which is?"

It was Catherine's turn to regard Henry with determination in her eyes. "I won't let anyone drive a wedge between us. The only one who could separate me from you is *you.*"

Henry gave her a lopsided smile before leaning down to steal a kiss. "Then it's a good thing I don't plan on doing anything that'd push you away," he said as he slid his arms down and tightened his hold on her waist. "On the contrary, all my plans with you will only bring you closer."

Natalie sat in her car a short distance from Henry and Bobby's auto repair shop as she watched Catherine walk across the street and enter the shop. Susan had shown Natalie the recent engagement announcement for Henry and Catherine after Natalie had asked what Catherine looked like.

But seeing her in person is a bit different. It makes all this more real. Destroying a person's life is easier when you're not face to face with them.

Natalie glanced over her shoulder to her son as he slept in the back seat. She couldn't help but smile at the angelic look on his face. He was so young and innocent. She could only hope that he was too young to remember this time in his life. She prayed to God that he'd never learn about the treachery she was about to unleash.

Or about the deal I made with the devil herself.

It had been just the two of them for so long, and the struggles of being a single parent never lessened. That's why Susan's offer had been so tempting. The amount of money she had offered Natalie to ruin Henry and Catherine's engagement and then to simply walk away was impossible to turn down. This money would offer them stability that they've never known. It would give them the chance to start a new life far from everything, including the dangers of her past.

The success of her actions here would ensure that Edward would never have the chance to come back into her life again.

She turned and studied her son more closely, seeing Edward in his soft features. It still amazed her that such a beautiful person could come from such a volatile marriage. She'd been tolerant of Edward's abuse up to the moment he had directed his focus on their son. It had only taken one threat of striking their innocent child for Natalie to pack up her son and never give her life with Edward a second thought.

And we've been running ever since.

She was tired of running, tired of living in fear, and tired of trying to move forward while constantly looking over her shoulder. No matter how badly she felt about potentially ruining an engagement, one final look at her son convinced her that she was doing the right thing. Her son was her priority. He was more important than Henry Bradley or Catherine McKinney.

"Besides," she muttered to herself as she withdrew a small compact and reapplied her lipstick, "if their relationship is so weak that it can be destroyed by one simple lie, it never stood a chance to begin with. I'll actually be doing everyone a favor."

The closing snap that came from her compact caused her son to stir. She watched him with adoring eyes as he began to awake and present her with a sleepy smile. "Hi, Mommy," he said as he rubbed his eye and looked out the window. His eyes instantly sharpened as he held up a chubby finger and pointed out the window. "Look, Mommy! Ice cream!"

Natalie smiled at his enthusiasm. She loved that the ice cream parlor was the first thing he spotted. Situated right across from Henry's auto shop, the location was ideal. She might need this as a place to discreetly keep an eye on Henry and Catherine's meetings. "Would you like some?" she asked, then laughed as he rapidly nodded his head. He slid out of the seat and reached for the door handle.

"Let's go, Mommy!"

"Hold tight there, buster! We have to go across the street first."

"Why?"

"We're going to go see Henry. You remember meeting him, right?"

His eyes followed to where Natalie pointed. His eyes lit up when he saw the garage. "That's the man you said I could call 'Daddy,' right?"

"Yes, darling. That's right. We're going to go say hi to him first. If you're good, we'll go get some ice cream afterwards. But only if you're good—"

"Okay!" he agreed, once again trying to open the car door. "Maybe Daddy will want to come for ice cream too!"

Natalie tried to ignore the pain nipping at her heart as she used her son to assist in Susan's plans. It was wrong, she knew, but she tried to pretend that she didn't care. "You can certainly ask him. Now, how does Mommy look?"

"Pretty, Mommy. You're always pretty."

She blew him a kiss from the front seat. "Well then, let's go see Henry and see if he feels the same way."

* * *

"You could always go where Liv and I went for our honeymoon," Bobby chimed in as he passed the reopened office door. "The one thing I remember about it was that the hotel was *exceptional*."

161

"Stay out of this!" Henry called to him from inside the office. He leaned against the edge of his desk, holding Catherine's hands in his. With smiling eyes, he pointedly looked at Catherine as he spoke loud enough for Bobby to overhear him. "This was *your* idea to have us work together. It's your fault if he knows too much about our personal lives."

Catherine's eyes held a mischievous gleam as she added, "I think that's a great idea, Bobby. I'll probably have to follow up with Liv, though, and explain that you couldn't remember much of your honeymoon ..."

"Okay, I'm butting out now!" Bobby called back to them. The loud slam of the garage door confirmed his declaration.

Henry and Catherine shared a chuckle before he leaned down for a kiss. "I appreciate that you understand why I wouldn't want to go to Europe for our honeymoon. But I refuse to accept your suggestion that we just go to a hotel in a neighboring town or skip it altogether. That's not going to happen," Henry exclaimed. He had hoped that bringing up their wedding and honeymoon plans would be what they both needed, except Catherine's suggestions were doing anything *but* lifting his spirits.

He knew the next protest before she even voiced it, so Henry held a finger to her lips. "Don't you dare mention money either, Catherine. I agreed to let you pay for your dress. But if you remember correctly, you agreed that I could take on the other expenses. At any rate, I have tradition on my side. Groom's side takes care of the honeymoon, right?"

"Yes, but Henry—"

"No, Catherine. I'm not going to let you win this one. In fact, I'm not going to give you another opportunity to even try." In one smooth motion, he pivoted with her in his arms, trapping her against his desk. He leaned in so that all she could see was his face as he said, "I'm going to plan this honeymoon. I'll choose the destination. I'll choose the duration. You won't know a single thing until I take you there. Then I plan to spend the entire time making up for every argument we've ever had and ever will have."

Catherine blushed. There was no mistaking his intentions.

Michael was right; Henry was the best medicine for me. No dance with Michael could substitute what she felt when he looked at her this way.

He wanted *her*.

The bell above the shop's door chimed, but Henry didn't budge.

"You have a customer," she whispered.

"I'm busy." The office was small enough that he easily reached out and closed the door with his foot. "Bobby can take care of it."

"You won't keep customers by acting this way," Catherine countered, knowing it was a lame protest. She knew the right thing to do was to distance herself. Even though they were behind closed doors, they were still in a public place.

"I'm more concerned about keeping my fiancée."

Despite the confidence that Henry usually radiated, his words gave Catherine a glimpse of how badly the news of a son had shaken him. He was as worried about losing her as she was about losing him.

"Daddy!" a small voice called out as a fist pounded on the lower portion of the office door.

That single exclamation stole the very breath from Catherine. She gasped as Henry quickly distanced himself from her. She witnessed a fleeting look of panic cross his face only to fall away to a more stoic expression.

As Catherine's face grew pale, Henry realized that, without warning, the time had come for Catherine to meet his son and Natalie.

No, he inwardly cringed, *not like this. Not until she's ready ... not until we're ready. This is not how I wanted Catherine to—*

Catherine stepped past him and opened the door with a calmness that astounded him. She knelt down to be eye level with the child.

"Hello, young man. What's your name?" she asked him.

"David Henry," he replied as he took a timid step back toward his mother.

Catherine studied the young boy, searching every aspect of his face for traces of Henry. Catherine had known that she would eventually have to come face to face with Henry's son, but she hadn't anticipated it to be today. Summoning her courage, she held out her hand. "Well, David Henry, my name is Catherine. It's very nice to meet you."

David timidly offered a smile and shook Catherine's hand. No sooner did they make contact than Catherine felt Henry close behind her providing a touch of support to her elbow.

"Catherine," Henry began as she rose to stand beside him. He slipped his fingers between hers and gave her hand a loving squeeze. "This is David's mother, Natalie. Natalie, I want to introduce you to my fiancée, Catherine McKinney." He gave Catherine a reassuring wink.

Watching the exchange, Natalie hated Susan for forcing her to destroy a closeness that she had never experienced with her own husband. *Stop it, Natalie, do your part!* Feigning surprise, Natalie's hands flew up to cover her mouth and pretend to stifle a gasp.

Then Natalie reached out and grabbed Catherine's free hand as she said, "I am so sorry to come like this! Oh, you poor darling, I can only imagine how difficult and shocking this must be to find out about Henry's son this way. Had I known you would be here, we most certainly would have given you space. Oh, how embarrassing."

Catherine watched Natalie's flustered state and felt sympathy building inside her. It was obvious that Natalie wasn't ready for this introduction any more than the rest of them. She worked hard to focus on that rather than Natalie's evident beauty. It was easy for Catherine to understand why Henry, or any man, for that matter, would be easily seduced.

I thought Susan was a threat ...

"It's all right," Catherine replied before she let her mind wander too far down an avenue of insecurities. "Henry already told me about the situation."

"I don't keep anything from Catherine," Henry added. He continued to hold Catherine's hand, taking as much strength from the small act as he hoped he was providing. Any other woman would have most likely spat in Natalie's face, but Catherine handled the introduction better than any of them.

Natalie leaned over to pick David up as she frantically thought for something to say in opposition to the couple's solidarity. She brought David, her sole bargaining chip, up to everyone else's level. "Yes, well, while I understand why you might feel the need to discuss our son with Ms. McKinney, I really am protective of him and wished you would have discussed this with me first."

"I only met you yesterday, Natalie."

Natalie nodded her head toward David as she replied, "He suggests otherwise."

Catherine felt her blood pressure rising at Natalie's implication. "Rest assured, I can be trusted to keep sensitive information in confidence," Catherine said.

Natalie saw that her words had affected Catherine and felt a small amount of success at being able to draw that from her. *This is the route to take then* ... "Yes, well, I'm sure that's true, but I came here to have a word with Henry." She focused her attention on him, knowing that her next words would upset Catherine even more, and said, "We need to have a discussion about our son."

Henry felt Catherine tense, and anger sprouted inside him at Natalie's obvious intentions. "Whatever you need to discuss with me, you can say in front of Catherine. If I'm to be part of David's life, she will be too."

As the tension in the room grew, Catherine noticed a small frown growing on David's face. The small child could feel the apprehension too. Catherine could only imagine what the child had already suffered in his life, and she was surprisingly determined not to be someone who added to his distress.

Catherine released Henry's hand and held her arms out to David. "Why don't you come with me while your mommy and Henry talk?" she asked. "We can go to the garage and see some of the cars that Henry's fixing up."

David smiled and reached out for her before anyone could stop him. She set him down and took his hand as he led the way out of the office. When they reached the door, Catherine turned back to face them and said, "Take care of your business. Bobby and I will keep David occupied."

Although Catherine spoke gently, the pain that Henry saw laced in her eyes seared through him. While Natalie began to vocalize her appreciation and need for privacy, Henry gave Catherine a single nod and prayed that the look he gave her conveyed just how much he loved her.

As Catherine closed the office door behind her, she felt as though her heart was shattering into a million pieces. She wanted to be the one to give Henry a family. Yet she had just left him alone with a woman who had already given it to him. A soft sob escaped her lips, and Catherine turned her head to keep David from hearing her.

Bobby, however, heard.

She felt his hand on her shoulder before he said, "Go, Catherine. I have this."

She bit her lip as her shoulders started to shake.

"It's okay," Bobby said reassuringly as he reached down and gave her free hand a squeeze. "I'll cover this." Catherine had never heard Bobby's tone be so serious before, and realizing that he understood her pain made it hurt that much more.

She could only nod as Bobby steered David toward the garage with the lure of automobile tales and promises to let the boy push a few of the car horns.

Catherine stepped outside to a bright, sun-filled afternoon. Henry's engagement ring caught the sun's rays and cast rainbows on the windows and buildings around her, but her tears left her too blind to see them.

Seventeen

"You're late," Susan commented as her butler led Natalie into the private study. She didn't attempt to hide her frustration. "I hate waiting."

"A thousand apologies," Natalie replied, ever so sarcastically. "But it's so easy to get wrapped up in the tours of the mayor's home." Although she said it with a casual shrug, her eyes held a small level of disgust.

Susan didn't miss it. She waited until the butler had closed the door behind him before addressing Natalie, "While I remember distinctly telling you at our first meeting that you aren't being paid to give an opinion, it's evident that you have one. So, you might as well get it off your chest so we can move past it."

"Why do you want them broken up so badly?" Natalie quickly asked. She didn't want Susan to change her mind about giving her a chance to express her thoughts.

Susan, making her way to the study's large desk, stopped short. With narrowing eyes, she replied, "That is most definitely *not* your concern."

Natalie rested her hands on the back of a chair that faced the desk. She leaned forward with a boldness she didn't feel and said, "I disagree. If I'm the one doing the dirty work to destroy this relationship, I have every right to know the reason why."

"The large sum I'm paying you is reason enough." She gave Natalie an innocent smile as she sat at the desk and asked, "Is this an incorrect assumption?" There were teeth behind her next words. "If I'm wrong, then by all means, I'll explain my reasoning to you … but it will cost you every last penny that I offered to pay you."

The two women silently stared each other down. Finally, with a soft curse, Natalie pushed off from the chair she had been gripping.

Susan smiled smugly in triumph. "That's what I thought. Now, be a good cousin and never forget your place in all of this ever again." She held out a hand to motion to the empty chair and said, "Have a seat, Natalie. I want to hear about your progress. They're still engaged, so you haven't had *that* much success."

"That's going to take time," Natalie explained. "Those two ... what they have ... it's strong. *Very* strong. The initial shock of an unknown child would break most people." She shook her head. "That's not the case for these two."

"And what have you done to weaken that bond? Surely you don't give them any opportunity to forget about you."

Guilt over her actions caused Natalie to slowly shake her head. "No, I'm there," she replied. "I take David to the ice cream parlor across from Henry's shop daily. Once I see Catherine arrive to visit Henry, we make our appearance. I've started calling David 'Henry' in front of them both as well."

Susan watched her closely as she listened. "You can do more," she said.

"Excuse me?"

Susan stood up from the chair and walked to the window that faced the street. "You can do more." She kept her back to Natalie as she continued, "If I believed it would be easy enough to destroy their engagement with the meager acts you've done, then I wouldn't have brought you here and offered to pay you such a large sum."

Natalie couldn't believe she felt the need to defend herself, but she did. She had been trying, as much as her conscience would allow. "I've framed a photograph of David for Henry's desk, something I plan to give him soon," she said quietly.

Susan nodded and replied, "That's better. Where do you plan to give it to him, though? At work?"

"Probably."

Susan turned to face her, and the look she gave Natalie sent a chill down her spine. "You won't get any farther unless you give this story of Henry's child some publicity, dear cousin," Susan explained. "It is easy enough for him to hide within the auto shop's walls. If you only visit him there, he and Catherine are able to make sure the story stays there with no one the wiser.

I want that gift presented *publicly*." The laugh that escaped Susan's lips was vindictive. "And I know just the place to give it to him ... a place that spreads news faster than a newspaper office."

The mention of newspapers caused fear to grip Natalie's heart. No matter what, she wouldn't risk exposing her son to the public eye if it resulted in a chance for Edward to find them. She mentally prepared her refusal as she rose from the chair to look Susan in the eye. "What place is that?" she asked.

"You leave Henry and Catherine to me on Saturday, but come Sunday, you'll be joining them in church."

* * *

Catherine lay on the riverbank with her feet floating in the water. This was a place where she had shared many happy memories with Caleb. After the week she'd had, she needed to be surrounded by those happy memories.

It made no difference to her that it was past midnight.

For the past week, Natalie and David—she refused to call him by his middle name—had religiously stopped by Henry's shop for a visit with her fiancé. Although Natalie had claimed coincidence that they arrived whenever Catherine was there, Catherine had found it hard to believe. They always stayed long enough that Catherine had been the first to leave. Although Catherine always tried to leave with a smile on her face, she had never been able to hold it until she left the shop, and Bobby had seen her distress each time.

As predictable as Natalie's visits were becoming, Henry had been just as faithful in spending his evenings at Catherine's home. They had dined with Bobby, Olivia, and their son Caleb, but Henry had insisted they spend the remainder of the evenings away from the others. It had been in the quiet walks around the house or going for drives that Henry had seemed even more determined to reassure Catherine of his commitment to her. She had long ceased being surprised when he would abruptly stop talking, gather her into a long embrace, and release her in silence, forgetting whatever subject they had been discussing.

On Thursday, Catherine had arrived to find Natalie already at the shop with her son. Catherine had pretended that the closed door to Henry's office meant nothing and that David's squeals of laughter, which matched both Natalie's and Henry's chuckles, had been of little consequence. Her insecurities, however, had refused to let her feign nonchalance for long. Once again, she felt like an outsider. The way she had loved Henry from afar before he came back from Europe had reemerged like a lost friend. She had a sinking feeling that she was destined to live like that all over again. This fear had kept her at Sal's that whole evening, having left a message with Olivia that she would miss them all at dinner.

On Friday, she had skipped going by the shop altogether.

Yet she hadn't wanted Michael's advice or Olivia's pity, so she spent the entire day secluded at the river. She had brought her brother's journal that he kept during the war and had pored over the pages as she had done when she had first received it. Although the pages had been painful to read as they explained everything Caleb, Bobby, and Henry had experienced while fighting in Europe against the Axis Powers, it had been a welcome distraction for her.

At the sound of an approaching truck, Catherine knew it was Henry's. She was surprised when the truck didn't continue traveling to her house, but instead stopped by the riverbank. Due to the stillness of the night, she heard Henry exit his truck and close the door behind him.

"It's a little late to go fishing, don't you think?" Henry asked as he descended the riverbank. The moon's glow provided enough light for him to see Catherine lying with her feet in the water.

Just seeing her in person brought him relief. Even though she tried to hide it, he knew Natalie's visits at the shop bothered her. She had kept up a pleasant disposition around Natalie, but Bobby would always tell him later how Catherine had looked when she left each day. And each evening when he would try to lift her spirits, her smiles never reached her eyes.

When she hadn't shown up today, he knew it wasn't because she had been too busy.

He didn't speak as he settled down beside her. After he put his feet in the river, grabbed her hand, and held it close to his chest, he finally said, "I missed you today."

She responded by squeezing his hand.

"When I didn't hear from you, I called Michael to see if you went to the club to work. I thought maybe I would bring you lunch."

"I wasn't scheduled to work today."

"That's what he told me. Liv had mentioned to Bobby that you had been out all day. Are you okay?"

No. Of course not.

"Yes," Catherine replied. "I just needed time with Caleb today." She patted the journal resting beside her.

"I still owe you that trip to Arlington, you know." He turned on his side to face her as he continued, "We could take a few days and go now. We could leave first thing tomorrow."

"It's not time."

Her simple responses worried Henry. "Okay. There's no rush." He was silent for a few minutes before asking, "How are the wedding plans coming? Besides the honeymoon, I mean." He gave her a playful nudge.

"About the same."

Henry reached over and found her face in the darkness. He gave her cheek a gentle caress before saying, "I want you to continue with the plans, Catherine. I've got the honeymoon covered, but I want you to go full steam ahead with everything else. I want this day to be everything you've ever dreamed."

As always, Catherine found it easier to ask difficult questions when night surrounded her. That's how she had first told Henry about her past with Robert, shrouded in darkness. "Will I need to make any changes?" she asked quietly.

Henry propped himself up on his elbow to study her more closely. "Changes?" he asked. "Not unless you want to. Did you have something in mind?"

"Caleb is going to be our ring bearer ..." Catherine couldn't hide the tightness in her voice. "Do you want me to make room for a second? I don't want to remove Caleb, but I can make arrangements for another if you want."

Henry wasn't prepared for Catherine's question. His initial reaction was to scream his refusal. *This wedding is about Catherine and me, our future together. It was planned before David Henry ever came into the picture.* Plus, if David was part of it, then Natalie would certainly be part of it too.

This thought alone made his decision for him. He saw what her presence was already doing to Catherine, and he wouldn't stand for it on the most important day of their lives. "No," he said with determination. "There's no need to make those changes." He sat up and pulled her to a sitting position across from him. "I promised you that while I'll do right by David, I won't jeopardize *us*. I would prefer that they not be at the wedding."

Catherine hated that his words relieved her. While Natalie and David had seemed to invade every other aspect of her world, at least their wedding was still *theirs* alone. "Do you think they'll understand?" she ventured to ask.

"They'll have to."

"Did they come by again today?"

"No." He didn't want to mention that this bothered him. Not because he wanted them there, but rather that he had noticed that their arrivals always coincided with Catherine's. It was as though Natalie wanted to make sure Catherine saw them together each time she was there. He'd spent many sleepless hours trying to remember meeting Natalie. The more he saw her, the more frustrated he became because he had absolutely no memory of her.

With this frustration came the suspicion that perhaps David wasn't his son after all. *But if that's the case, why would Natalie choose me as her victim?*

He couldn't answer that. Until he was able to, he didn't want to share his skepticism with Catherine. He didn't want to give her false hope, nor did he want to give her any reason to be concerned that someone was trying to sabotage them. He wanted time to think this all through and explore his options before sharing any findings with Catherine.

But judging by her disposition, I need to find answers soon. I don't know how much more of this she can take.

This made what he had to tell her all the more difficult. "That being said ..." he began, "Catherine, please don't take this the wrong way ..."

Catherine bit her lip. Any time Henry started a sentence this way, she had reason to worry.

"I think that their visits at the shop are becoming disruptive. Not only to the work Bobby and I do, but to our meetings and any customers that might come by for service."

She heard him hesitating, so she asked, "What solution are you considering to fix that?"

Henry sighed. He could tell by Catherine's guarded voice that she was already trying to set up an emotional barrier to separate herself from his unspoken idea. No matter how he framed his next words, she wasn't going to receive them very well. "I think that it might be better to spend time with David outside of work hours," he whispered. He felt her stiffen beside him.

"But you don't want him in the wedding."

It wasn't a question, so he chose not to respond to it. "This way, I could see him when it was convenient for me ... not every day whenever Natalie feels like it," he explained. "I would be able to have more control over the visits."

As well as set things up for my own investigation, he thought.

Catherine was glad the darkness of night covered her bitter smile. *He sounds like a father with an ex-wife ... and I thought Susan was a threat. Natalie's a threat to Susan and me both. She could steal him away from both of us.*

"Catherine?" Henry tenderly spoke her name as the silence lengthened. "I want to know what you're thinking."

"I'm listening." It was all she could manage to say.

He cradled her in his arms as the water created a calming sound around them. "The idea of me having a son is still really new, and with them coming by every day ... it's been a bit *smothering*." He tucked her head under his chin and continued, "I haven't really thought this part through yet, but I'm not ready to announce this news to the world."

"This is a small town, Henry. I know that more than anyone. If you so much as go to the gas station with them, you're announcing it. Everyone will know about it before you get home."

"And they'll use it against you."

"Only Susan," Catherine said. Despite the painful subject, she found solace in talking about an enemy she was familiar with. "But that's the way Susan operates. You know when she finds out, she's going to capitalize on it."

"She won't say a word to you," Henry said with determination.

"Really?" Catherine asked as she removed herself from his embrace. "Are we talking about the same woman?"

Henry still hadn't confessed to Catherine about the visit he had paid to Susan. He was waiting for the right time, and this definitely wasn't it. "Well, that really only leaves two other places to visit with the boy: my home or yours."

His words caused Catherine to pull completely away from him. She turned and fumbled around on the bank for her shoes. She straightened up to a standing position when she couldn't easily find her shoes. "Forget it," she mumbled. "I'll come back for them tomorrow."

She turned, and with agitation seething from her, started up the bank to the road.

Henry knew he had gone about this the wrong way. "Hold up, Catherine!" he called in exasperation. He reached down for his shoes, felt Caleb's journal next to them, and grabbed it, hurrying after her when she refused to stop. "Will you wait a second? I don't like this any more than you do!"

He continued to mumble under his breath until he finally caught up with her on the road. With a free hand he reached out and managed to catch her arm. "Catherine, stop!"

His tone stopped her from trying to break free from his grip. "I already have one child in this situation. I don't need to deal with a second."

The anger came, and Catherine welcomed it. She had held it in for too long, and his words unleashed a dam in her. "How am I supposed to react? Do you think I'm okay with Natalie being in your home?" She didn't wait for him to respond and continued, "This is a beautiful woman from your past. Even though I trust you, I don't trust *her*. How on earth do you expect me to be comfortable with that? But I don't have a choice, really. The idea of you bringing him here right now ..." She wiped furiously at the tears that had started to fall. "Bringing your son by another woman to my home ... I'm not ready for that."

He dropped his shoes and Caleb's journal and reached out to grab her free arm that she had been waving for emphasis. He hated that she hurt, especially since his actions had caused it. "Catherine, please, calm down. I know this is hard."

"You need to think of a better word than *that*. Because 'hard' doesn't even come close. Yes, I understand your options are limited. I know you're going to have to make some hard decisions, but I can't stand here and pretend that it doesn't affect me ... that it doesn't hurt. I thought I could, but I can't."

A sob escaped her mouth.

"I hate this!" she exclaimed in between her tears, burying her face against Henry's chest. He immediately encircled her with his arms, wanting nothing more than to shield her from any more pain.

Catherine's words mirrored his own emotions. As much as it hurt to hear, he was grateful that she was finally expressing her true feelings. He held her in the middle of the road as she let her anger and frustrations seep through.

Finally, when Catherine's shoulders had stopped shaking and she seemed more collected, Henry shared, "I hate this too. But I don't see how I can turn away from it. Not right now. Things *will* get better. We'll figure this out ... together." He swept his arms under her and lifted her off her feet, taking her to his truck when she didn't protest.

Once they were both inside, they sat in silence, each reflecting on their own thoughts.

"I'm sorry, Henry," Catherine said. "That wasn't fair of me. You're the one who's suffering the most, and I'm too busy wrapped up in my feelings ... I *am* being childish."

Henry let out a deep sigh and said, "Catherine, you've got a passionate opinion about everything. I expect that. It's when you're calm and indifferent ... that's when I get scared." He couldn't look at her as he continued, "I've been pretty scared lately." He reached for her hand and held it tightly as his thumb caressed the engagement ring he had given her. "I don't question your love for me. I haven't since I knew how you felt. But I want you to know that as much as it would kill me, I would understand if you wanted to walk away ..." Henry could barely believe he was saying this out loud. "But I'm begging that you don't."

"Henry," Catherine said softly.

"No, please. I need you to listen. This will get better. Natalie has no permanent residence here. At some point, she'll go back home and take David with her. But he will never go away. In my future, there will be visits ... and as my wife, you'll be his stepmother." Henry stopped speaking when he felt Catherine's gentle finger touch his lips.

"Henry, I know. I understand that. I promised you that I'd stand by you. And I will. My future is with you. It always will be. I'm not angry at David or you. I'm not really even angry at Natalie. I'm just frustrated, scared, and confused. I was having a weak day, and I knew I needed to stay away from them because of it. I can't promise that I won't have any more days like this. I probably will. But I'll try harder, all right?"

Henry's heart swelled. Even though she was innocent in this whole mess, she was still the one promising to do better, to be the rock he needed. He knew that no matter what his next steps were, Catherine would still hurt, so he wanted to make the less painful choice for her.

"Catherine, your home is your sanctuary. You've been robbed of its security once before, and I never want that to happen again. I won't bring David here unless that's something you're ready for. I also want to put your mind at ease in regard to my place. I won't let Natalie set foot in my home— not unless my *wife* ..." He paused for emphasis and squeezed her hand, "... allows it. They won't be in my house without you."

"Henry, then that leaves—"

"I know it's going to be hard, but are you ready for the town to gossip about you once more? When they see me with David at the park, they're going to talk."

Catherine understood how difficult this decision was for him. Yes, the town would talk. Susan would most likely have a field day. Yet Henry was doing what he could to give her peace of mind.

"Yes," Catherine said as she scooted closer to him in the truck. "I'm ready for that. The town hasn't really ever stopped talking."

"I'm sorry, Catherine. You don't deserve this."

She took his face in her hands and found his lips with her own, preventing his next thought from reaching his lips.

And I most certainly don't deserve you ...

Eighteen

Henry and Catherine both groaned internally at the sight of Susan advancing on their table. After everything they'd been through this week, the engaged couple simply wanted to spend the evening dancing in each other's arms. Catherine and Henry both needed a night to laugh with their friends, bask in their love for each other, and forget about the recent consequences of Henry's past.

They did *not* need Susan.

"What is she doing?" Henry hissed under his breath as Susan approached them. Instinctively, his arm snaked around Catherine's waist.

While Catherine appreciated Henry's distaste for Susan, the anger radiating from his clenched jaw surprised her. "This is a public dance club," she replied. "Even though I'd prefer otherwise, Susan can be here if she wants."

"That's not what I meant," Henry replied as he tore his eyes away from Susan to look at Catherine. After Natalie's near-constant presence this week, Susan's appearance was the final straw. "Apparently, it's too much to ask to have an evening dancing with my fiancée without interruptions."

Before Catherine could respond, Susan was at their table. "Hello, Henry," Susan greeted as she slid into an empty seat. She crossed her leg over her knee, allowing the slit in her skirt to climb higher up her thigh.

Henry's voice lacked the courteous patience it normally reserved for Susan as he said, "For Pete's sake, Susan, pull your dress down."

"Thanks for noticing." Susan winked as she responded, making no effort to change the position of her skirt. She threw Catherine a smug smile.

"Bobby and Liv will be here any minute, Susan," Catherine said pointedly. "That seat is for them. You're not welcome at our table."

Susan's eyes narrowed at Catherine as she said, "I just came by to say 'hi,' Cat. There's no need to be nasty. Besides, I came by hoping for an introduction to your new friend."

"Excuse me?" Catherine asked, not bothering to hide her confusion. "Who are you talking about? And why on earth would you think I'd want you to meet any of *my* friends?"

"I'm talking about the beautiful young woman and little boy that people have seen visiting Henry's shop." Susan made certain her face emitted pure innocence as she explained, "I've heard about how you're bringing a gorgeous woman and a small child with you nearly every day you visit. I've heard so much about her beauty, I wanted to see for myself what everyone was talking about." Henry inhaled and Catherine's face paled before Susan added, "Or am I mistaken about this new visitor?"

Catherine felt as though she'd been punched in the stomach, leaving her incapable of breathing. *She knows ... Of course she would know ... she knows everything that happens in this town.* Her thoughts stumbled over one another as she struggled to reply.

Susan basked in the sadness that Catherine couldn't keep from her eyes and felt no guilt in needling, "Perhaps they're new acquaintances for you as well, Catherine." She rose to her feet to make sure Henry's attention focused on her rather than Catherine before asking, "Are they family of yours, Henry?"

"What part of our last encounter do you not understand, Susan?" Henry asked, seizing Susan's arm and dragging her away from Catherine. "I thought I made myself clear."

From the corner of her eye, she saw Catherine watch them with a furrowed brow, which was a beautiful thing to Susan.

He didn't tell her.

Finally, Susan had found a crack in their relationship. She just needed to make sure it remained. "Your visit to my home was very recent, Henry. I don't easily forget treats like that. I was making an effort to be hospitable to Catherine."

Regardless of Susan's interest in Natalie, Henry could see how she carefully chose her words now to imply an intimate relationship between them. "You're making an effort to sabotage!" he hissed, struggling to keep his voice calm but with little success. Fury coursed through him. Between the situation with Natalie and now Susan's meddling, he felt himself beginning to unravel as he lost control of his circumstances.

"I told you to stay away from her!" He practically flung her arm away from him.

Silence followed.

Henry took a step back but immediately felt the coldness in Catherine's stare. Trying to relay an apology with his eyes, he reached for Catherine's hand. Although Catherine allowed him to take it, she wasn't responsive to his touch.

Susan's reaction to this small slight was one of triumph.

"Ah, woman, really?" Michael's voice came from behind him, and Henry was grateful for the interference. "You can't just leave well enough alone, can you? This club is big enough that you could spend the entire night without bumping into Henry and Catherine. But you always come looking for trouble."

"It's much more fun that way," Susan replied to Michael while she winked at Henry.

"Not as much fun as removing you from this club, which I'll be more than happy to do if you don't step away."

Catherine was only vaguely aware of the conversation around her and of Susan's departure from the table. Confused by Henry and Susan's "meeting," Catherine's cheeks flamed from embarrassment. *What confusion? It's easy to discern exactly what happened. Henry told Susan to stay away from me. Henry* ... the light caress of his thumb over her fingers sent her over the edge. She started to wrest her hand from his only to find his grip tightening.

She glared up at him.

Henry knew he had made a mistake in confronting Susan. If he had doubted it before, the cold eyes staring up at him convinced him. He owed her an apology and an explanation. He squeezed her hand as he nodded toward the dance floor as he spoke, "Let's go."

"No."

"Hey, love, blood on the dance floor, not at the tables," Michael chimed in behind them. He covered their joined hands with his own.

"You both have had a trying time of it lately. Take it out on the floor and leave it there."

Michael gave them a small nudge, and Henry seized the opportunity to lead his reluctant fiancée onto the floor and into his arms. As the band's music abruptly changed from a slow to an increasingly fast tempo, Catherine briefly redirected her anger to Michael, who now stood in front of the band.

"Catherine, are you—"

Catherine snapped her head back to face Henry, interrupting, "No! You're not in any position to ask me *anything*. Start talking, Henry. You're only getting one song to explain."

Sensing Catherine had already closed her mind to any explanation he would give, he couldn't help but feel his own frustration building. First Natalie, then Susan, and now to see Catherine so angry with him caused a flint of ire to surface in his own eyes.

He swept Catherine close to him in one strong motion. "Better make this a long one!" Henry called out to Michael as his fierce gaze now mirrored Catherine's.

Catherine and Henry's dance turned into a battle. As Henry tried to explain his actions to Catherine in between moves, their sentiments over both Susan and Natalie meshed into a perfectly orchestrated routine. To anyone looking, their dancing was flawless; but to Catherine and Henry, their anger, frustration, and resentment screamed through the delivery of every move. Lifts were higher. Spins were faster. Every time that Henry's arms encircled Catherine, they turned to iron.

It was impossible to give the couple only a passing glance.

Catherine and Henry also felt the intensity of their dancing, which fueled the argument between them. As the music ended, the two stood separated by the width of the dance floor. Both struggled for breath, and desire now added to their raging emotions.

Catherine hated that despite how angry she was at Henry, seeing him across the dance floor robbed her of her breath more than the intense dance she had just completed. In his eyes, she could see his love for her, and she felt herself weakening and understanding his reasons for speaking with Susan. As much as she wanted to, she couldn't budge as he closed the distance separating them with determined, confident strides.

When he reached her, his arms encased her waist as a slower song began to play. He wasn't going to let her leave the dance floor. Although his eyes still shone with the same hardness, his iron grip softened around her. "That's why I did it," he said. He wasn't sorry for taking action to try to spare Catherine from more suffering. His tone held no apology as he continued, "Is it so wrong to want to do whatever I can to protect the person I love more than anything else in the world?" He saw her flinch at his words, and he took that as a sign of her anger against him waning.

"You had no right to do this," Catherine protested, even as her body betrayed her and drew itself closer to Henry. "This makes me look weak."

"You're anything but weak, Catherine," he replied as he traced her jaw with the hand that held hers.

"*Your* actions beg to differ."

"Maybe my delivery wasn't the best, but I'm not going to apologize for the sentiments that prompted it." His voice softened as he begged, "Please don't be angry with me, Catherine. While it's not my job to protect you, it *is* my desire to." He lifted her chin up to capture her lips in a gentle kiss. "Let me."

Catherine felt herself drowning. Susan tried to control her ability to find a steady job. Henry tried to control her working at the club. Natalie controlled the ability to provide Henry with a future family. Even now, Henry was trying to take on Catherine's battles.

I'm losing power over my life.

The staggering realization caused her to misstep, and she stumbled out of Henry's arms.

"Catherine?" He quickly offered steadying support to her forearms.

Catherine backed away from him. "No, Henry," she said. "While I understand your reasoning, it doesn't justify your actions. That problem wasn't yours to solve." Before her emotions could overwhelm her, she stepped off the dance floor.

It took a minute for Henry to process her words and realize that she had walked away in anger. He recognized that she sought a deeper apology than he was willing to give. While the rest of his world was in upheaval, choosing Catherine, *loving Catherine,* was the one decision he knew wasn't a mistake in his life. Because of that, he didn't want to apologize for his actions defending that love.

As he watched her pass their table and head to the front door, he took steps to follow her. Henry had barely made it off the dance floor when an arm reached out to stop him.

"Hold on there, soldier," Patricia said sternly. "Give her a little time."

Patricia kept a firm grip on his sleeve. Michael stood a small distance behind her. Henry shared a glance with Michael, who offered a helpless shrug.

"I would have gone after her too," Michael explained.

Patricia muttered something under her breath before throwing them both a withering look. "Then you would both be wrong."

"What's wrong with wanting to keep her from pain?" Henry asked as he refocused his vexation on Patricia.

"Not a word!" she hissed to Michael as he started to open his mouth. She turned to Henry and gave him a sympathetic smile. "Nothing's wrong with that, Henry. But what *is* wrong is denying her the freedom to choose if that's what she wants."

"Do you even know what's going on?" he accused.

"You two just had war on the dance floor."

"A beautiful war, I might add," Michael interposed before being silenced by a look from his wife.

Patricia turned back to Henry. "I'm not stupid, blind, nor deaf, Henry. You told Susan to stay away from Catherine, something we've all done in our own way, apparently," she said as she gave Michael a meaningful look, which he returned with a guilty one. "Listen, Henry. I don't think you're wrong in wanting Susan to steer clear of Catherine. I don't trust the woman, and I think she's fanatical about wanting to destroy Catherine. And most likely, Catherine feels the same way we do."

"Then what's the problem?" Henry asked.

"The problem is that you decided what Catherine needed without consulting her, without asking her, without letting her decide for herself what she needs." She made sure to look at both Henry and Michael when she spoke her next words. "I know you two care very deeply for Catherine, and it's this love that drives your actions. But I'm warning you both, if you keep acting on what you *feel* is best for her without asking her, you're going to drive her away from you."

The two men stood by as though reprimanded.

"Times are changing, gentlemen. While the men were off at war, the women back home grew voices."

Michael couldn't help but chuckle as he responded, "And Catherine's is loudest of them all."

Despite his current state of mind, Henry felt pride swell in his heart at Michael's observation. He loved Catherine for being the independent woman that she was.

It was wrong of me to try to stifle that, even if it was unintentional.

"Thank you, Patricia," Henry said. "I see my mistake now."

"Well, don't tell me," she replied, giving him a gentle shove. "Go find her and tell her."

"Just promise me you don't make up too quickly!" Michael called out as Henry walked away from them. "Your dancing was phenomenal!"

Without a word, Henry sat down beside her on the bench. Like her, he stared across the platform into the night's darkness. As difficult as it was to remain silent, that's exactly what Henry did, waiting for Catherine to speak first.

"Am I that predictable?" she finally asked.

"You're anything but predictable."

"How'd you know to find me here at the station?"

Even though Catherine couldn't see him, she felt Henry shrug beside her. "It's closer than home, I guess," he explained. "Besides, if you're trying to get away from it all, what better place than a train station?"

"The last train for the evening went out about thirty minutes ago. I just missed it."

Henry smiled at the dry humor in her voice. "Lucky for me then," he whispered. He waited for Catherine to reply, but when she stayed quiet, he dared to reach out and take her hand. When she didn't pull away, he gained the encouragement he needed. "I'll never forget the moment I first saw you after coming back from the war," he reminisced as he rubbed the back of her hand with his thumb. "I remember feeling very insecure before I stepped off the train. Although I knew without a doubt how I felt about you, I wasn't so sure of your feelings for me. I finally saw you standing across the platform. You were breathtaking."

Catherine recalled the dirty, unkempt state she had been in that day. After a full day's work at the factory, little sleep, and an empty stomach, she had looked anything but breathtaking. "The train smoke must have really affected your eyes."

"No, Catherine. For the first time, I saw things clearly. It was as though my future, every fiber of my being, surrounded you. I couldn't get to you fast enough."

Catherine couldn't help but be affected by Henry's declaration. "I remember."

"The euphoria I felt when I saw you coming to me, running to *me* ..." his voice caught in his throat, and he moved to embrace her. "It gave me my first real hope of a future with you. I had dreamed of your face for so long in Europe. To finally see you in the flesh made me forget about everything but you. I wanted nothing more than to sweep you up in my arms and kiss you exactly as I had imagined doing almost every night in Europe."

Although he paused, Catherine sensed that he wasn't finished. She felt his grip around her shoulders instinctively tighten. Before she had decided to protest, Henry touched her chin and turned her face to him.

"I should have never let her keep me from kissing you that day," he said huskily. Catherine couldn't help but give a slight tremor at the intensity she saw in his eyes. She watched as a look of pain passed over them before he continued, "If I would have stopped her when I had the chance, things would have played out differently. I would have gotten my kiss. More than likely, Robert never would have been a threat to you like he was because we would have been together even then. We would be married by now, Natalie would never have been able to create the insecurity that I see in you, and Susan would no longer be a menace to either of us. By trying to fix a mistake I made back then, I tried to take matters into my own hands and made the mistake of assuming I knew what was best for you. I'm really sorry about that, Catherine."

The guilt emanating from Henry floored Catherine. Without realizing it, her free hand found his cheek, as though her touch might erase the remorse he shouldered. "Susan will always be a menace, Henry," she said, sighing when he lowered his head to rest his forehead against hers. "I'm sorry. I know you meant well. I think I've been excessively defensive lately."

"You have every reason to be. It's like you're being attacked on all sides just for loving me."

She gave a simple smile as she leaned back to look at him. "Loving you has always been my war, Henry. But it's one I've been willing to fight."

Her words touched him in a way that caused both joy and sadness. Her devotion meant everything to him, and he was glad to hear her verbal reconfirmation. However, the fact that she felt she had to fight at all tore at him.

"It won't always be this way, Catherine."

"There will always be obstacles, Henry. We can't let them destroy us. Yes, if you had kissed me that day, things would have played out differently, and we would have had an entirely different set of problems. Don't regret what happened. Everything, both good and bad, led us to this moment together. Focus on that."

Because it'll destroy us otherwise.

He studied her a long time before whispering, "I love you."

She gave him a small smile as she squeezed his hand. "In the end, that's all that matters."

"Does this mean I'm forgiven?" he asked as he nuzzled her neck before taking a gentle nibble at her earlobe.

As much as Henry's playfulness encouraged her to reply with physical affection, a serious plea left her lips: "Promise not to let me go, Henry. No matter how difficult it gets."

He sensed the desperation in her voice. He positioned himself so that he could cradle her face in his hands and look directly in her eyes before answering, "I swear that I won't let go. I'm hanging on for dear life."

He silenced any further dialog with a kiss not unlike the one that he had dreamed of giving her when he first came home from war.

NINETEEN

The week's frustrations, fears, doubts, and even the noise of Olivia calling for Bobby to corner their son Caleb faded the moment Catherine opened the door the following Sunday morning to find Henry standing at the doorstep with a bouquet of wildflowers in his hands. A loud crash followed by Bobby yelling his son's name caused the corners of Henry's lips to turn up.

"I see my timing is perfect," he said as he held the flowers out to Catherine.

Her smile reached her eyes as she eagerly took the bouquet and shut the door behind her. "Absolutely," she agreed. "It's amazing how much demon we see in Caleb on Sundays."

He took in her image as he tucked her hand into the crook of his arm. Although her hair was still short from the night Patricia had cut it for Catherine's dancing debut, it had started to grow out. Fortunately, it was still too short to pull back in the ponytail that she favored and that he loathed. Her yellow dress was simple and added to her natural beauty. She looked charmingly sweet, and he found himself unable to resist the urge to lean down and plant a chaste kiss on her cheek as he escorted her to the truck.

"You're beautiful."

Catherine offered a shy smile while giving him a sideways glance. "You clean up pretty well, yourself," she complimented. She loved seeing him in his Sunday best. His khaki slacks, white dress shirt, and tie vastly differed from his usual greasy work clothes. He appeared clean and fresh, as though he had scrubbed away all the problems from the week.

"Save us a seat, you two!" Olivia's voice suddenly called out to them from the front porch. Another crash sounded that prompted her to add, "Preferably in the back pew!" The couple acknowledged Olivia with an overhead wave.

"He certainly keeps them on their toes," Henry commented after they were on the road on their way to church.

She nodded in agreement and said, "As it should be. That house should always be filled with the vibrancy of a child. It reminds me of how loud it used to be when my brother and I were little. That house had been getting too quiet."

"Little? I remember it being pretty loud with you and Caleb as adults, too. You had some pretty heated discussions."

"To which you should take credit for being the cause of most of them." She chuckled as she remembered the fights she had with her late brother. "We fought a lot, didn't we?"

"'We' as in you and Caleb or 'we' as in you and me?" He gave her a wink, adding, "Because you and I definitely had our share too."

"We *still* do."

Henry reached over and gave her hand a squeeze. "What can I say? You're cute when you're angry."

She stuck her tongue out at him in protest.

"See? You're absolutely adorable right now."

By this point, they had arrived at the church. Both were surprised to see so many vehicles in the parking lot. As Henry searched for a vacant spot, he asked, "Is there some special luncheon today or something?"

Catherine shook her head, just as confused as he was. "Not that I recall."

"Maybe this week was rough for everybody else too." He pulled his truck to a stop at the far end of the parking lot. Shutting off the engine, he turned to find Catherine looking at him earnestly.

"Thank you," she said, watching a wave of confusion pass across his face. "I know you were never a frequent churchgoer before the war. I want you to know that I appreciate you making the sacrifice to come with me now."

"It's not a sacrifice, Catherine. War causes people to self-reflect. Plus, almost losing you ... I'm not going to pretend that I'm perfect, and I'm sure I still do a lot of things that make some of the church members cringe. For example, I want to kiss you right here in the middle of the church parking lot." He waited for her shy smile before continuing, "But I'm trying. I'm not above dropping my knees to the floor."

Especially now ... learning I have a son. I'll need all the forgiveness I can get.

Henry must have said something right because Catherine scooted closer to him in the truck, reached up, and turned his face to hers for a kiss. Henry's arms circled around her, but Catherine pulled away from him. Seeing the reluctant look in her eyes was his only consolation.

"It's time to go," she said as she laced her fingers through his.

He nodded, opening the driver's door and waiting for her to slide across the seat before helping her step down. Her impromptu kiss had distracted Henry, preventing him from noticing who else was entering the church. Had he been paying attention, he would have never gotten out of the truck in the first place.

"It must be sinner's Sunday," Bobby mumbled as drove into the full parking lot several minutes after Henry and Catherine. He chuckled softly as Olivia reached out and slapped his shoulder. He winked at her before asking, "Do you want me to drop you and Caleb off at the front while I park the car? It'll save you a walk."

"Nice try," Olivia replied as she returned her hand to her slightly swollen stomach. "I'm pregnant, and there is *no* way I'm handling Caleb in my present condition on my own. If you do a drop-off, it'll be for me only. I can't handle him single-handedly."

"I could make a tasteless joke right now," he said as he held up his partially amputated arm, "but I won't."

Olivia gasped and covered her mouth. "Oh, Bobby, I didn't even think!"

He gave her a mischievous smile as he braced himself for another smack. "You know it doesn't bother me. I'm only trying to get a rise out of you." He parked their car at the curb and hurried to open the door for his wife. "Go on inside, Liv. I'll park and take care of getting Caleb. With the extra crowd today, I can't have the entire town thinking I'm not considerate of my pregnant wife." He planted a kiss on her nose as he helped her out of the vehicle.

"Thank you. I wouldn't want you being run out of town because of your lack of consideration," she returned the banter. Nodding to the parked cars behind them, she continued, "Especially since it looks like we have the mayor's company today."

"The mayor?" Bobby couldn't hide his surprise as his gaze fell on the car Olivia had singled out, which had spent quite a bit of time in his and Henry's repair shop. "There must truly be something worth seeing today if he's gracing us with his presence. He hasn't passed through these doors since the war ended."

"Maybe it's Susan here instead." As she spoke the words, Olivia felt uneasy. She noticed that Bobby shared the same worried brow.

"Surely not after last night," he whispered, as though he half-expected Susan to appear at the mention of her name.

"Park the car quickly, Bobby. I'm going to find Cat and Henry."

Bobby needed no further direction.

Susan feigned interest in her hymnal as she discreetly kept tabs on everything around her. She had situated herself in the middle pews of the sanctuary. From her vantage point, she could easily see Natalie up at the front corner with her son. Natalie looked extremely uncomfortable as the nearby congregants offered her polite greetings.

Susan didn't care about her cousin's discomfort. If anything, Natalie's unease would only aid in executing her plan. Even from across the church, she sensed Natalie making a deliberate effort to avoid any eye contact with Susan. This didn't bother Susan in the least, and in fact, she thought it was better this way.

Susan turned to engage in conversation with the woman next to her. By turning slightly, she could also see the back of the church. She smiled inwardly when she saw Henry and Catherine enter and take a seat in the far back of the sanctuary. Their seat selection was perfect. Their eyes would fall on Susan long before they noticed Natalie, and this was exactly what Susan wanted. It was her goal to keep Natalie a surprise until the end of the service.

"Excuse me, Susan?"

Susan turned from her neighbor to find the minister kneeling over the pew in front of her in order to have a word with her. "God's house is full

189

today. I thought I might have forgotten it was Easter or Christmas, but after a few inquiries, I learned that you were responsible for inviting most of them." A smile spread across his face as he continued, "I can't tell you how inspiring this is."

Susan pasted on her most charming smile as she answered, "Yes, Reverend. I'm doing what I can to witness to the community."

The reverend observed the full congregation and couldn't help but reply enthusiastically, "I applaud your successful efforts. God bless you."

"Thank you." She made certain to sound humble as she allowed him to squeeze her hand.

She waited until he had left before looking around again. It was true that much of the congregation were individuals she had reached out to over the weekend, calling in any favors that were outstanding to anyone not so close to her family that they might recognize Natalie. She doubted that they would, since her father insisted on keeping better company once he was elected mayor, but she didn't want to chance it.

Knowing that it wouldn't be until after the sermon that her plan would come to fruition, she settled herself more comfortably in her seat.

"Scoot over," Olivia whispered as she slid in the pew next to Catherine. "Are you okay?"

Confused, Catherine replied, "I'm fine. Are *you* okay? You seem to have lost your family along the way."

"Bobby has Caleb and is parking the car. I thought it best to get in here as soon as I could to make sure you both were okay."

Henry leaned in to join the conversation. "What on earth are you talking about, Liv?" he asked. "This is church. It's a sanctuary. Why would you think that there was a problem?"

Due to Olivia's odd behavior, Catherine had already started scanning the large congregation. "Because Susan's here," she whispered, as her eyes zeroed in on the center pews.

Henry followed Catherine's gaze to find Susan engaged in what seemed like a friendly conversation with the reverend. Instantly wary, he started to rise to his feet. Catherine pulled him back into the pew.

"No, Henry. She has a right to come here. Lord knows she *needs* to be here." She made sure to meet Henry's eyes before adding, "If we're truly going to get her out of our lives, we have to let things go. Leave her be, Henry."

Henry closely studied his fiancée's face. He saw the silent plea in her eyes. He knew all she wanted was some semblance of peace. Although he couldn't provide much of that in regard to Natalie, he could at least try to grant that with Susan. He nodded in compliance and draped his arm over her shoulder. Appreciation filled her eyes, and he was reminded of his promise to her last night.

As the sermon commenced, he stole a glance at the blonde-haired nemesis who worked so hard at destroying Catherine.

War games with men were easy for Henry to understand, but he had no clue how to fight these games against Susan.

Bobby and Caleb arrived, forcing everyone in the pew to make room. As Henry shifted down, his view of the congregation changed slightly. His stomach plummeted when he recognized Natalie seated near the front. Prayers instantly flew through his head as he hoped to be spared an embarrassing scene, especially for Catherine's sake.

Paying little attention to the sermon, Henry's mind raced for a way to handle the situation. He realized that leaving the church now was out of the question. All eyes would follow them, and attention was the last thing he wanted. The only other option would be to try to slip out with Catherine immediately following the end of the service.

It wasn't that he thought he could keep Natalie's situation a secret forever; he just wanted to do it on his time line.

Why, of all Sundays, did there have to be a crowd today? He glanced over to find Susan listening to the sermon with rapt attention. *Maybe it's not so coincidental after all.*

Natalie felt sick. Sitting in the front of the church with her son, despite Susan's insistence, was a mistake. The reverend's sermon as well as the feeling of an entire congregation's eyes focused on her served as a weight, making her guilt feel heavier. The lie she currently lived strangled her, but she knew there was no way to escape from it. She needed Susan's money. She felt it was the only way to create a haven for her son. As her eyes fell on the package jutting out from her purse, she recoiled internally and turned to focus on the crucifix hanging on the wall behind the reverend.

God, forgive me for what I'm doing. You know my situation better than anyone.

She numbly rose to her feet for the final hymn as her own beating heart drowned out the organ. As the service concluded, she contemplated saying another quick prayer for strength but deduced it was useless.

Surely God does not favor me in this.

Catherine lost her balance as Henry seized her hand and started to head to the church's exterior doors as soon as service ended. He didn't relinquish her hand, and she practically had to climb over Olivia, Bobby, and Caleb to keep up with Henry. She muttered apologies as they went, embarrassed and confused over why Henry was hurrying.

He didn't stop until they were outside of the church. He turned in time to catch Catherine as she stumbled into him. She looked up at him. "Henry, what's the matter?"

He steadied her as quickly as he could, saying, "We need to leave. *Now.*"

"Why the rush? Because of Susan?"

He leaned down to tuck a loose strand of hair behind her ear in order to whisper, "No. Partially. *Natalie is here.*"

The color drained from Catherine's face. She took an involuntary step back, but Henry kept a grip on her and drew her close to his side. She saw pain deep in his eyes. Even though she understood his wanting to leave, she knew there was no way to escape the inevitable. Whether Henry was ready or not, today the town would learn of his son with Natalie.

And with Susan here, things are going to go from uncomfortable to painful in no time.

"Of all the churches in town, why ..." Her question fell off as the answer dawned on her. "You, of course."

"Please, let's just go."

Catherine wanted nothing more. She wanted to get in Henry's truck and drive to the ends of the earth with him. But that couldn't happen, and she inwardly cringed as the next words tumbled out. "Leaving isn't going to help, Henry. It'll only make things look worse."

"Do you realize what Susan will do with this once she finds out?"

Catherine was nearly sick with the thought. Susan would take whatever she could to create a wedge between her and Henry. Catherine refused to let that happen. With courage that she barely felt, she gave Henry's hand a gentle tug back to her. "She'll find out sooner or later. Better to do it now, and let the whole community see us united than to give Susan the opportunity to learn of this and spread rumors," she explained.

By this point, the rest of the congregation had started to leave the church. "Catherine, I—"

"I have never seen you back down from anything, Henry Bradley," Catherine said with steel in her voice as Bobby, Olivia, and their son came up behind them. "Don't you dare start now."

Olivia and Bobby realized immediately that they had walked into a private conversation. They stood in uncomfortable silence as Catherine's command hung in the air. Right as they prepared to interrupt the discussion, if only to say a quick good-bye, the sound of Henry's name came from the church doorway.

"Henry!" It was impossible for anyone within earshot to miss the eagerness and excitement in Natalie's voice. Holding David's hand and waving her free arm above her head, she plowed through the crowd as politely as she could.

While most of the people gave way, some frowned at Natalie's hastiness. However, when David called out to Henry, the townspeople parted like the Red Sea.

"Daddy! Daddy! Daddy!" David yelled. He squirmed out of Natalie's grip and ran with all his might toward Henry. Henry had little choice but to accept the hug the child offered.

Catherine realized that no matter what, Henry's simple act of accepting David spoke greater volumes than anything else said or explained would. Catherine felt everyone's eyes on her small party as people started to take longer to descend the church stairs.

Henry's face was expressionless as he knelt to hug David while refusing to relinquish his hold on Catherine's hand. He waited until Natalie reached them before acknowledging her, "Hello, Natalie."

If Natalie sensed his coolness toward her, she hid it well. With a sunny smile, she greeted him, "Hello! I daresay, Henry, you look quite handsome today."

"My fiancée said nearly the same thing to me earlier," Henry replied with an indication of his head to Catherine as he rose back to his feet. "Though I must say, I pale in comparison to her beauty."

Natalie turned to Catherine, and Catherine saw Natalie's smile slip slightly before she recovered herself. "Of course. Good morning, Catherine. How lovely to see you again." Her gaze passed over Catherine as she moved on to the other members of the party, hoping to prevent Catherine from speaking. "Oh, Bobby, hello again as well! This must be your family."

Bobby looked from Henry to Catherine to Olivia, unsure of how to proceed. It was Catherine who finally gave him a slight nod of her head. "Yes, Natalie. This is my wife, Olivia, and my son, Caleb. Olivia, this is ..." he hesitated.

"Hello, Natalie. My goodness, it's sunny. And I'm pregnant. Can we all move out to those shade trees at the end of the parking lot if we're going to continue this conversation?"

Olivia kept Bobby from announcing to any bystanders the relationship Natalie had with Henry, and Catherine was eternally grateful. She gave Olivia a look of appreciation and bit her lip to hide her smile.

"My goodness, that's wonderful news! Isn't it, Henry?" Natalie exclaimed as she moved to stand beside Henry while David clung to his leg. "I hope you're not too ill from it. I was so sick when I was pregnant with David."

Catherine's heart felt a pang of jealousy. By placing herself so close to David and Henry, Natalie could demonstrate to anyone watching what a perfect family they would make.

Ever since David had hurried into Henry's arms, Henry had focused his attention on Catherine. He faintly heard the conversation going on—a conversation that would result in everyone knowing about his newly discovered son. When he sensed, rather than saw, Natalie move closer to him, he understood from Catherine's look the image it created. He watched as Catherine challenged him once more with her eyes.

I have never seen you back down from anything, Henry. Don't you dare start now.

As her words echoed in his mind, he gave her a nod before taking a step closer to her and distancing himself from Natalie. "It was nice seeing you both," he said as he gently guided David back to his mother. "We shouldn't be keeping you from your plans."

Natalie, however, was not to be discouraged so easily. "Oh, I've no plans today. What about you, Henry? Maybe David and I can talk you into having lunch with us."

"I have plans with my fiancée."

Again, Natalie's gaze only briefly landed on Catherine before darting back to Henry. "Yes, of course. Well, perhaps next time. I'm so new to the area that—"

"Excuse me, but did I overhear you say you're new here?"

Henry clenched his teeth at Susan's arrival to the group. He removed his hand from Catherine's in order to slip it around her shoulders and draw her closer to him, ensuring there was no confusion as to which woman he loved.

Natalie turned and gave Susan a timid smile before answering, "Oh, I'm sorry. I forget how easily my voice carries." She held out a hand. "Hello, my name is Natalie. Yes, I'm new in town."

Susan returned Natalie's smile with a warm one of her own and said, "There's no need to apologize, dear. I'm the mayor's daughter, and I couldn't help but overhear your conversation. I believe it's my civic duty to make sure you're acquainted with our quaint little town."

"That's a most generous offer, Susan. Thank you, truly."

"Of course!" Susan regarded the others as if noticing them for the first time. "I see you've met some people already. Should I finish making introductions?"

Natalie giggled as she replied, "There's no need. I already know most of this party. Olivia and her son are the only ones new to me."

Susan studied each of them, certain that the dawning look in her eyes was convincing. "Oh, you must be the woman and young man I understand have been visiting the repair shop!"

Natalie gave a shy nod of her head. "Guilty as charged."

"Well, dear Natalie, good luck with those visits. Any time I try to stop by for a friendly 'hello,' I'm always told to leave. Surely they're more welcoming to you than that?"

"That's quite enough, Susan," Catherine said, putting an end to the conversation. She turned toward Natalie, forcing the young woman to pay her more attention than just a passing glance. "Natalie, it was nice to see you again. But please excuse us; we really need to be going. If you want to see more of the town, Susan will make an excellent tour guide. Good-bye." In sync with Catherine, Henry was already turning to escort her down the stairs.

"Good-bye, David. Good-bye, ladies," Henry said as he cast a quick glance backward and started down the stairs with Bobby, Olivia, and Caleb close behind him.

"Oh, Henry, I nearly forgot!" Natalie called out to stop him. He was halfway down the stairs by the time she reached him. "I've been carrying this around to give to you."

"It can wait," Henry said, not wanting to accept anything from her, especially since he already felt so many sets of eyes on him.

"But you're here now," Natalie insisted. "Please, it's just a small token in appreciation for how you've handled everything thus far." She pulled the package out of her purse and opened the wrapping for Henry as he refused to take the package. "I thought you might like it for your office," she explained as she held up a framed photograph of David.

A sharp gasp escaped Susan's lips.

Bobby muttered a curse, and Olivia reprimanded him, if only to find something useful to do in the increasingly awkward situation.

Catherine took one glance at the frame and quickly looked down at the hand gripping her own. Her vision blurred as she felt a tremor tear through Henry.

A painful silence followed. Henry cast a weary eye at the frame as his grip on Catherine's hand tightened. "Why are you doing this?" he whispered, though their little group heard his question.

Natalie wasn't immune to the obvious pain her single act produced. Everyone's reaction caused her to hesitate. *I'm sorry, Henry.* "I thought you might want it. I see now that this probably wasn't the best timing."

When she met the hardness of Henry's eyes, a shiver passed through her.

"You don't like it?" David's small voice timidly asked.

Something snapped inside Catherine. She saw the sorrowful look in David's eyes, and her heart broke as he reminded her that a young child was also an innocent victim in this nightmare.

But he may see Henry as a dream come true rather than a nightmare.

Before she could change her mind, she released Henry's hand, took the frame from Natalie, and knelt down to David's level and commented, "This is a very handsome photograph of you, David."

"He doesn't think so," David said as he pointed up at Henry.

"Nonsense. He's just so amazed at your gift, that's all. It's left him speechless." Catherine turned to Henry, silently pleading for him to agree.

He could only nod.

"See?" Catherine asked, praying that she provided a convincing tone of excitement.

David studied Henry for a long while before nodding in agreement.

Convinced she'd lost all soundness of mind, Catherine made a show to David of grasping the frame to her chest and kissing him on the forehead. "Thank you. I'll help Henry find a special place for this."

Natalie hated herself, Susan, and any other person who had forced her hand in bringing such conflict to Catherine's and Henry's lives. In this single act, Natalie saw how brave and considerate Catherine truly was. Despite every reason to be nasty, Catherine was anything but, and she handled David in a remarkable way.

Natalie started to feel sick at being on the wrong side of the war Susan had waged.

When Catherine rose to her feet again, Henry seized her hand and brought it to his lips, hoping that this small act conveyed to her all the love he felt for her. She gave him a timid smile before turning back to face Natalie and Susan once more.

As Henry prepared himself to give a second, curt good-bye, Natalie did the job for him and said, "Well, we've taken up enough of your time today. Come, David, we should be going. Say good-bye."

It wasn't until Natalie and David had left, with Susan hurrying behind them, that the rest of the party dared to move. They were all silent as they made their way to the parking lot.

Henry kept his eyes glued on Catherine as they walked, oblivious to the good-bye Bobby offered. Based on his own turmoil of emotions, he could only guess at what Catherine was feeling. Embarrassment? Anger? Fear? Sadness?

"I have to admit," Bobby said softly, "this will be one of the most memorable services I've attended."

The sound of Olivia smacking Bobby's side as they walked behind Catherine and Henry caused a giggle to escape from Catherine's lips. She glimpsed over to see a hint of humor in Henry's eyes as well.

"Go take care of your loved ones," Henry called to Bobby as they passed Bobby's vehicle and left the small family behind.

I intend to do the same.

TWENTY

"All things considered," Susan began after taking a sip of water and setting the glass back down on the diner's table, "I think that was a success. Wouldn't you say so?"

From across the booth, Natalie gave her son the rest of her French fries before acknowledging Susan's remarks. "I suppose so."

"You could show a little more enthusiasm, Natalie."

Despite the warning in her head, Natalie cast a glare at Susan. When she was about to speak, the busboy came offering to clear the plates. His arrival caused Natalie to hesitate.

Susan waved impatiently for Natalie to speak. "Todd works for me," she explained. "You can speak freely in front of him."

The nervous look on Todd's face and his eagerness for a quick departure from Susan confirmed to Natalie that he most likely did work for Susan in some capacity; however, Natalie wasn't quite willing to trust him. She refused to say anything until he was some distance from the table. Only then did she practically hiss across the table, "*Success?* Are you serious, Susan? It's a wonder that God didn't strike me down for doing that in a church."

"It was outside His doors, so I'm sure He overlooked it," Susan replied nonchalantly. "We had two goals today," she explained as she counted them off on her fingers. "First, we needed the town to know about David's daddy." She gave a wink to the little boy who played with his food, oblivious to their conversation. "I made certain that there were enough people at the service today to have this news spread like a wildfire. Now we have only to sit back and wait for the fireworks to begin."

"And second?"

"By being publicly introduced to you, it's going to be so much easier to get together and make plans. While my home is still the best place to meet, it's no longer the only option for our planning." Susan couldn't help but laugh triumphantly. "The town will be witness to our budding friendship."

Natalie refused to join in the laughter.

Miffed, Susan leaned across the table and warned, "Don't start getting a conscience on me now, Natalie. You're lucky that Henry is buying this story."

"*You're* lucky he's buying it."

Susan's smile completely dropped from her face. Today's events had rattled Natalie more than Susan had expected. *She's going to break. I'm going to need to get as much use out of her before she does.* "You do recall how much I'm paying you, right?" She waited with a glare until Natalie nodded, then added, "Good. And I hope you realize that if you should decide to quit, none of that payment will come your way."

Natalie took a visible deep breath and nodded once more.

"Good. So I suggest you be more enthusiastic in playing your part." She waited until Natalie nodded once more before continuing, "Excellent. Now, as I was saying, you're lucky. I noticed at the church that you slipped in calling me Susan without me first introducing myself."

Natalie paled.

"I don't think anyone caught it, but don't misstep again," Susan warned, reaching into her purse to pull out money to cover the lunch. "With the town soon watching your every move, it's imperative that you make every move count and that you follow any instructions I give you with precision. Don't worry, my dear, if everything goes according to plan, you'll be on your way soon enough." She slid out from the booth. "I insist on treating you to lunch," she said in a voice that carried throughout the diner. "It's been such a pleasure to meet you, Natalie. And David, you're such a treat! I insist on meeting up with you later this week to show you more of our town. What do you say?"

Susan's voice was inviting, but her eyes dared Natalie to refuse her.

"That sounds wonderful, Susan! Doesn't it, David?" Natalie's voice carried as far as Susan's and with just as much enthusiasm. Playing the part once more, she hurried to her feet to give Susan a warm embrace.

Susan maintained a smile on her face until she was alone in her car. Once there, her smile vanished completely.

I'm running out of time. Natalie had a weaker constitution than Susan remembered from their childhood. *She's going to need a push. I've got to come up with something fast ... before it's too late.*

*   *   *

Henry parked his truck in front of his house, amazed that he had no recollection of the actual drive there. He had been reflecting repeatedly on the events at the church, and he had finally realized something: Susan had never formally introduced herself.

Natalie already knew her name.

He tried to rationalize that perhaps they had met earlier but quickly dismissed this. Susan had acted as though the meeting he witnessed at church was their first meeting.

He had a nagging suspicion that this wasn't a coincidence.

With that in mind, a strong part of him wanted to share this with Catherine. He wanted her insight and opinion. Although it was only a suspicion, it was enough of one to drive hope into his heart, which he desperately wanted to share with Catherine.

But it will kill me if I had to take it away because I was wrong.

That alone sobered him and kept him from voicing his thoughts.

"Is it all right if we stay here for the day? I've got enough food for lunch and dinner, and I can drop you off at your place later tonight." He turned and gave Catherine a small smile as he explained, "I figure it might be best to stay in today."

"Good call," Catherine said. "I'm sure the town is buzzing with rumors already. Susan will make sure of that."

Henry didn't respond until he opened her passenger door. "Even so, I don't mind a day of having you to myself."

Catherine felt a blush creep up her neck as he pulled her from the truck. Rather than allow Catherine to gather her things or smooth out her dress, Henry instead seized her in a dizzying kiss.

"Henry!" she gently scolded when she was finally able to catch her breath. "There's probably already enough talk about us in town. What will your neighbors think?"

He flashed a roguish smile and replied, "That you're one lucky lady."

His response elicited the desired reaction from her. She fought to suppress a grin, rolled her eyes, and playfully pushed at him. "You're so full of yourself."

"Having you with me, how can I not be?"

"You didn't always think that," Catherine teased as Henry closed the front door behind them. She liked seeing this side of him. *It's a side I haven't seen much of lately.* She wanted to keep his carefree temperament as long as she could, knowing it was a balm for both of their spirits.

"You convinced me otherwise."

"It took you long enough."

Henry's grin widened as he took Catherine's purse that held David's picture and placed it with his keys in the small hall closet. *I don't want any distractions today.* "Well, I'd counterargue that you took your sweet time convincing me."

Catherine smiled as she allowed Henry to draw her into his arms and plant a series of kisses along her neck and jawline before finding her lips. She gripped the sides of his shirt.

"Thank you for today, Catherine," Henry whispered. "I know that had to be hard; it was for me. The way you handled it, though, was amazing. I love you."

She gave him a sympathetic smile. "Handling it any other way would have only made things worse."

"Especially with Susan there as a witness."

Susan, Natalie, and David were the last things Catherine wished to discuss as she shared this private moment with Henry. The idea that he had been more intimate with both Susan and Natalie than he had ever been with her was unsettling to her. It drove a sobering blade of fear straight to her heart.

Susan's claims that Henry would one day compare his intimacy with Catherine to his time with Susan suddenly echoed through her mind, with Natalie's voice now joining Susan's. Catherine couldn't help but tremble slightly.

Henry felt it and searched her eyes deeply. "Are you all right?"

"Yes," she nodded. Disentangling herself from his arms, she took a step back.

Henry was having none of it. "Where are you going?" he asked, reengaging his arm around her waist and pulling her back to him. His voice grew husky as he said, "I was enjoying your company right here."

The insecurities started to well up inside her once more. *You have to tell him, Cat. If you want any fighting chance, you need to let him know what you're feeling. While Susan may eventually leave us alone, Natalie never will.*

Catherine took a deep breath to gather her courage. When she spoke, her voice was soft, and she found it impossible to meet his eyes. "It's hard to hear you talk about Susan and now Natalie when you're kissing *me*." She felt Henry's grip loosen. She knew he was angry, and that was the last thing she had wanted. "I know it's stupid," she rambled. "I'm the one you're marrying ... but I can't help but wonder if you *compare*, even if you don't mean to."

There. She had said it.

Henry's arms dropped from her waist. Silence ensued as Catherine focused on a spot on the ground. She couldn't look at Henry. He had so much of his life in turmoil; he didn't need her insecurities added to it.

But if I don't say anything, this is only going to fester.

Henry took no additional steps to distance himself from her nor did he say anything to contradict her. Catherine felt like a lifetime passed before she finally found the strength to look directly at Henry.

He stared at her with intensity. She couldn't tell if he was hurt, angry, or something else entirely. She opened her mouth to speak, though she had no idea what more she could say.

However, Henry held up his hand to stop her. "I apologize. That clearly wasn't the right time to say anything. However, Susan has found a chink in your armor, Catherine. Why do you let her attack you there? And Natalie ... *I can't even remember being with her!*"

Catherine bit her lip as Henry continued.

"And you know something else? I don't remember any of them anymore! When I was in Europe, you consumed my thoughts. And that was before admitting to myself that I was in love with you. Now, every moment with you has successfully erased every memory of my past. You're in my thoughts when I'm awake, and you visit my dreams each night." He ran a hand through his hair in frustration. "There is nothing to compare, because for me, there's only you."

Tears welled in Catherine's eyes as she choked out, "I—"

"Follow me," Henry interrupted. "I want to show you something." He took her hand and led her into his bedroom. Once inside, he released her hand and ordered, "Open the closet, Catherine. And the drawers."

"Henry, I don't need to invade your space."

"Open them." His tone told her that he wasn't going to be dissuaded.

Hesitantly, Catherine went to Henry's closet and opened the door. She gasped in surprise. Dresses filled part of his closet, some of which Catherine recognized as the ones she thought Olivia had packed away when redecorating Catherine's bedroom after Robert had invaded her home. Here they hung, next to Henry's clothing. She reached out to touch them, but Henry stopped her.

"Now open the drawers."

She turned to the opposite side of the bedroom. Although she had to travel only a few feet, the distance seemed longer. When she reached them, she faltered.

"Top one on the left," Henry instructed, not moving from his position in the doorway.

Catherine's hand visibly shook as she opened the indicated drawer. Inside were blouses and nightgowns she didn't recognize.

"You said you didn't need to invade my space," Henry explained, now so close behind her that his breath tickled the hairs on Catherine's neck. "But, see, Catherine? You already have."

"I recognize the dresses," her voice whispered.

"These are yours too. I bought them for you." He reached around her and gently picked up a pink, discreetly laced nightgown and handed it to her for inspection.

Catherine knew she was supposed to protest. Words associated with modesty jumbled themselves in her mind, but she couldn't form them into a sentence.

It was as though Henry could read her thoughts. "They're for later, Catherine," he explained, "when you're mine exclusively. When going home means coming here. Or wherever we decide to live the rest of our lives

together. When you have my last name. These are yours, and yours alone."
He took the nightgown back as he looked at her with smoldering eyes.

Catherine's throat felt dry as she asked, "When did you do this?"

Henry said unflinchingly, "When I bought you the dress for the proposal, the feeling was amazing. Then when I saw you wearing what I had picked out ... that was the start."

Warmth spread through her body, and she didn't know if it was the clothes or the look Henry continued to give her. She stumbled over her words, "H-how ... why didn't you tell me?"

Henry began to trace light circles on her arms with his fingers as he spoke. "I'm not going to lie and say that a part of me doesn't already want you here wearing them. But to have you wear them and then have to drop you off somewhere else ... another place that isn't here with me ..." He lifted her chin to look directly into her eyes, forbidding her to break eye contact, as he said, "Just know, Catherine, you're already here. You've already infiltrated so deeply, there isn't room for anyone else. Not here," he said as he touched his temple to imply his memories. "And certainly not *here*." He covered her hands with his and placed them over his rapidly beating heart.

She nodded. A tear escaped her eye when she blinked. Henry was quick to catch it. Henry could see in her eyes how much this act meant to her.

"Thank you," she whispered, giving him a shy smile.

"Do you want me to show you the rest?" Henry asked, indicating the drawers with his head. He arched an eyebrow suggestively, hoping it would render the reaction he needed to lighten the mood.

It did.

"*No,*" Catherine said as color reddened her face. She glanced around her as though realizing for the first time exactly where they were. "Henry, we should probably see to lunch."

"I'm not hungry," he said. Henry silently scolded himself. He struggled to resist Catherine; he had wanted to be the one to stop this before it went too far, and yet when she had given him the opportunity, he had refused to take it.

His stomach growled.

"Liar," Catherine said with a smile. The chuckle that followed was contagious.

"I tell you what," he said as he kissed her lightly on the nose, "why don't you look at it all yourself while I make us some lunch?" He recognized the look on her face as one of refusal and continued before she had the opportunity to rebuff him, "I won't bother you. I'll call you when lunch is ready, and nothing more will be said about this. Okay?"

Catherine didn't want to admit how much she wanted to look through the things Henry had purchased for her. Yet she didn't dare do it in his presence, and the solution he had offered suggested that he was just as eager to have her see the items. "Okay," she agreed. "I promise I won't take long."

Henry kissed her once more before leaving the bedroom. "Take all the time you need," he called over his shoulder.

Catherine appeared indifferent until Henry closed the bedroom door behind him. Then she was back at the drawers, going through each piece with meticulous care. While nothing was scandalous, the fact that Henry had put thought into each one kept her cheeks rosy. The drawers held beautiful blouses, practical work clothes, and several nightgowns. While her fingers skimmed each item, she knew her favorite was by far the pink nightgown. The full-length, chiffon material was thin, but Catherine hardly noticed. Small rosebuds adorned the scooped neckline and sleeves. It was so delicate but unlike anything Catherine ever wore. For Henry to believe she was feminine enough to wear it meant a lot to her.

The fact that he had pushed forward with plans for their future, even as she had allowed insecurities to stall her, meant even more. She smiled as she gently tucked the nightgown back into the drawer. Then she turned and eagerly made her way to the kitchen, prepared to spend the rest of the day playing catch-up with Henry.

And if he wants to get married as soon as tomorrow, I won't stop him.

TWENTY-ONE

Catherine sat at the table watching the surprised expression of her two friends. They remained silent for so long, Catherine started to worry they hadn't followed her through the entire story. *"What?"* she finally asked.

"We're waiting for you to finish your story," Michael said with a wink as he leaned in conspiratorially against the table. Patricia followed suit.

"What do you mean? I just finished it."

"Tell us about you hitting her," Patricia said a bit too enthusiastically. "Surely you hit Susan for her actions. Or Natalie?"

"Or both?"

Catherine gave Michael and Patricia a bewildered look. "You both are crazy, you know that?" She rose to her feet, grabbing the dish towel off the table as she went, and asked, "Did you miss the part of the story where I said we were on the stairs of the church?"

"I've got to hand it to her," Michael said as he rose to his feet. "Susan sure knows how to take full advantage of any situation and bend it to her favor." He reached over to steal the towel from Catherine, implying they weren't quite finished with the conversation. "So, what are you going to do?"

"What do you mean? I'm going to take back my towel and do what I'm paid to do: clean this place."

"And then?"

Catherine couldn't hide her frustration as she glared at him and demanded, "What do you want me to say?"

"Michael," Patricia warned.

He ignored her and said, "I want to know what your plan is, Catherine."

Although he smiled, his eyes were dead serious. "Susan has some powerful information. Although it's true that she would have found out eventually, I know you and Henry weren't planning on sharing this news so soon. She's going to take this, and she's going to use it to her advantage. When she does, I need to know what you plan on doing about it."

"*Michael!*" Patricia hissed.

"I'm not going anywhere, if that's what you're worried about. If Henry wants me to stay, I'm staying. My future is with *him*, not with Susan or Natalie. So, his opinion on the matter is the only one I care about."

"Well said, dear," Patricia said, also now rising to her feet.

"Commit that to memory, love," Michael advised. "If you thought Susan already had the town turned against you by refusing to hire you, just wait. She's going to capitalize on this information and do everything she can to use it."

"You think I don't realize that?"

"I know you do. I think it's good to remind yourself, *aloud*, that Susan isn't part of your future with Henry."

"Nor Natalie, for that matter," Patricia chimed in.

She looked at her friends and basked in the warmth of their friendship. "Well, it's good to know that if things get messy, you're in my corner," she said.

Michael flashed a charming smile and declared, "You're stuck with us, love. And it's best you commit that one to memory too."

* * *

"No," Natalie said with anger. "That's crossing the line. That's going too far."

Having expected such a reaction, Susan watched Natalie pace in the small living room of Natalie's newly rented home. It was a month-to-month rental. The woman couldn't plan any further into the future, not when she might have to drop everything and leave with her son.

"I agreed to help you create a division between the two, but what you're asking ..." Natalie's voice came out in a harsh whisper, hoping her sleeping son in the next room wouldn't awaken.

"And you don't think this will do the trick?"

"You're asking me to destroy them!"

"I'm not paying you to have a conscience, cousin."

"No, you're paying me to whore myself!"

Susan patiently shook her head and countered, "I'm not asking you to sleep with Henry. I actually forbid you to do that."

"It'll all be the same in Catherine's eyes."

"*Precisely.*"

Natalie regretted getting involved with Susan with each passing day. "Why do you hate her so much?" she asked.

"Again, I'm not paying you to ask questions."

"You're not paying me enough," Natalie said, surprised at her unwavering tone.

Susan's eyes narrowed. "*Excuse* me?"

Natalie prayed Susan couldn't hear her heart pounding in her chest as she demanded, "The amount you originally offered me, that's only half the payment." She waited for Susan to protest, but when she didn't, Natalie continued, "If you want me to go through with this new plan of yours, it's going to cost you twice as much."

Susan had to give Natalie credit; the woman had more nerve than she had first believed. Her slow smile caused Natalie to swallow with unease.

"Well done, cousin. How reassuring it is to know that even *your* conscience can be bought at a price."

Susan tried to ignore the memory she had of the one person she hadn't been able to buy—Catherine.

Twenty-Two

The great thing about small towns was that patterns soon became common knowledge among its residents. It wasn't a secret that the local diner was a favorite of Henry's. Therefore, when Catherine periodically stopped by to pick up food, there was no question that the meal was for Henry.

Susan sat at a booth and waited for Catherine's arrival. Meeting Catherine here was pivotal to her plans, and she had enlisted the assistance of the diner's busboy, Todd, to make certain she would be here when Catherine stopped by to pick up the food order. The timing had to be perfect, and as she glanced at the wall clock, she became slightly concerned.

When Todd passed her table, she reached out and grabbed his attention with a wave of her hand. "You missed a spot," she scolded as she indicated an imaginary stain on the table. Todd muttered an apology and leaned over to scrub at the spot.

"You told me she placed an order to pick up at five this evening because she was getting off from work early. It's already a quarter past."

Todd swallowed nervously and gave a slight bob of his head as he responded, "She did. I imagine this rain is slowing her down. Especially if she's coming by bicycle like she normally does."

As if giving the cue himself, thunder rolled.

Susan watched as the child across the table jumped. He looked up at her with wide, frightened eyes. "It's okay, David," she soothed. "It's just a bit of rain. We're safe in here, and once the storm ends, we'll meet up with your mommy, okay?" She held her smile as customers nearby gave her warm looks for the comfort she offered David. She nodded to Todd. "You're probably right. I hadn't really considered the storm."

Todd took that as a dismissal and hurried from the table.

A few minutes later, Catherine entered the diner. One look at her soaked appearance fully supported Todd's suggestion.

With water still dripping from her hair, Catherine strolled to the counter and offered the waitress an apologetic smile as she accepted a bag of food. "Sorry I'm late."

"You poor thing!" the employee behind the counter replied. "Why don't you sit here a minute and wait for the rain to pass? I'll get you a cup of coffee."

Catherine shook her head even as she sat down on a barstool. "I can't stay long enough for coffee. I'm already late, and it looks like the rain is here to stay for the evening. If you would double-bag the food, that should keep it until I get to Henry's."

"I'll triple-bag it," the waitress replied, taking the bag of food and heading back to the diner's kitchen.

While Catherine waited, Susan seized the opportunity. "David, how about you wait here like a good little boy, and I'll go to the counter and order you some ice cream?" she asked. "How does that sound?"

His eyes shone as he eagerly nodded his head. It was too easy.

I have to give Natalie credit; she's doing a good job raising her son.

Susan could tell when Catherine noticed her approach. Catherine's smile was still present, but its warmth had vanished. But she was too close to her goal to let Catherine's coldness bother her. "Hello, Catherine," she greeted.

Catherine merely nodded.

"I thought your shift at the club ended at seven."

If Catherine was surprised that Susan knew this, she didn't show it. "I'm surprised to see you here, Susan. The diner doesn't really seem like your type of eating establishment," she countered.

Susan gave a small laugh as she pointed behind Catherine's shoulder to her booth. "It isn't. But it suits *him*," she explained, taking pleasure as Catherine's smile slipped when she noticed David.

Perfect.

"Natalie asked me to babysit him tonight, and I don't know the first thing about babysitting. But she's such a darling, you know? I felt that I couldn't refuse her. I mean, who could refuse her anything?"

Catherine caught Susan's implication, and she turned back to face the mayor's daughter. "Say whatever it is you're dying to say," Catherine ordered. "I don't have time to sit here and play your games."

Oh, yes, Catherine, you do.

"No games," Susan said, making sure her face gave away no hint of pleasure at her plan now unfolding. "I just wanted to say that, despite our differences, I have to admire how well you're handling the news of David and Natalie."

"It doesn't change anything."

"*Of course* it doesn't. I, more than anyone, know how strong your love for Henry is. And to show so much trust to allow him to meet Natalie tonight to discuss David's future—"

"What are you talking about?" Catherine asked too calmly.

"Well, that's the whole reason that I'm watching David this evening. When I met Natalie, I gave her my phone number and told her that should she need anything, I'd be happy to help. She called me this afternoon and asked me to watch David while she went to Henry's to *talk*."

Even as Catherine kept a stoic face, she felt her world being yanked out from underneath her. *She's at Henry's home. He promised he'd never have her there. And she's there without her son.*

Just then, the waitress came back with Catherine's food. Catherine took it and barely whispered a thank you. She turned back to Susan, fighting against all the words she wanted to hurl at her nemesis. The two stood while their eyes waged a silent battle. Finally, Catherine broke eye contact, saying firmly, "The rain let up. Excuse me." She shouldered past Susan and headed back into the rainstorm, which had done anything *but* lessen.

Susan couldn't contain a triumphant smile as she watched Catherine clumsily get on her bicycle and pedal as fast as the pouring rain permitted in the direction of Henry's house.

Okay, Natalie, I've done my part. Now it's your turn.

* * *

Henry leaned back against his couch and closed his eyes as the rain beat against the living room windows. Catherine wasn't scheduled to get off work for a couple hours still, and the weather was perfect to catch a quick catnap. No sooner had the idea of sleep entered his head than he felt his body already succumbing to the idea. He knew he wouldn't sleep for very long, as the military had trained him on how to practically sleep on his feet. Henry also wanted to make sure that he had plenty of time to pick Catherine up from the club when her shift ended if it was still raining.

I don't care how independent she is; I won't let her ride her bicycle over here in a downpour.

He always wanted to pick her up regardless of the weather conditions but was smart enough to know what battles to fight, and this wasn't one of them. So instead, he sat on his couch and let the recent stress roll off his shoulders. Now that everyone in town seemed to know about David, Henry's days certainly hadn't gotten any easier.

But they will ... When Catherine and I are finally married, it will be easier.

He had only dozed for a few minutes when the sound of someone knocking on his front door jerked him awake. He rose to his feet as he gained his bearings. He glanced at his watch. It was too early for Catherine, yet that was the only company he was expecting for the evening.

"If she got off work early and rode over here in the rain, I'm going to *seriously ...*" he spoke under his breath as he reached the door. Any additional words remained unspoken as he opened the door and saw his visitor.

Natalie stood on his doorstep, soaking wet, shaking from coldness, and sobbing nearly uncontrollably.

He barely had enough time to speak her name before she threw herself into his arms, almost at the point of hysterics.

He instinctively pulled her into the house as fear gripped him. "Natalie," he said, giving her a shake, "what's wrong? Where's David?"

"He's fine," Natalie managed to splutter before returning to her sobs.

While bewildered at Natalie's state, Henry felt relief course through him at learning David was all right. "You're freezing," he commented, releasing her and heading to his bedroom. "Stay there. I'll be right back with a blanket."

He was back quickly, having grabbed the quilt that covered his bed to wrap around her shoulders. By this point, her sobs had turned into deep sniffles. He waited as patiently as he could, but when it seemed Natalie was reluctant to speak, he finally questioned her, "What are you doing here, Natalie? I thought I made it clear my home was off limits."

"I'm so sorry, but I didn't know where else to go!" Natalie exclaimed as her sniffles turned back into larger sobs.

"You didn't—" Henry said as he ran a hand through his hair in frustration.

"Please, give me a moment, okay? Let me use your restroom and pull myself together, then I'll explain everything."

Henry wanted Natalie to explain her presence out on the front porch, in public view. He absolutely didn't want her using his bathroom. She'd have to go through his bedroom to get to it.

Although his instincts told him to refuse her, he reasoned against them. *The sooner I find out what's going on, the sooner I can get her out of here.*

He sighed and said, "There are towels in the bathroom. It's small, so you won't have any trouble finding them." He didn't want to be in his bedroom with her, even if it was merely to escort her there. "It's at the end of my bedroom, on the right."

Natalie gave him a grateful look. "Thank you," she whispered before heading to his room.

The moment that Henry heard the bathroom door close, he began pacing the living room. It didn't matter that Catherine wouldn't be there for another couple of hours. He had assured her that Natalie would never be in his home.

Now, she was.

As soon as Natalie had stepped into Henry's room, her tears vanished. She went straight to the bathroom and closed the door. She knew Henry wasn't comfortable with her in his home. Therefore, he wouldn't come near her while she was in the proximity of his bedroom. As long as he heard the bathroom door close, he would rely on that sound alone to believe she was in his bathroom.

That left her a little time.

She heard him pacing back and forth in the living room, and although she felt guilty over his obvious discomfort, she steeled herself into action. She darted to the drawers along the back wall of his bedroom and prayed they were silent as she opened them. The first few drawers revealed nothing that would help her. When she opened the top left drawer, both relief and dread filled her.

Seeing the pink chiffon nightgown, she found *exactly* what she needed.

Blinded by a mixture of tears and rain, Catherine pedaled to Henry's as if her life depended on it.

It does *depend on it.*

She tried to force calm breaths through her nose and rationalize the situation. If David hadn't been at the diner, Catherine would have accused Susan of scheming. His presence had confirmed Susan's words, and Catherine realized that for once in Susan's life, Susan was innocent. While Susan had clearly taken pleasure in seeing Catherine upset, Susan had only been relaying information.

There has to be more to the story. I just need to get to Henry. He'll explain this. He'll explain everything.

She cried out in relief when Henry's house came into view. Only his truck was present. Natalie's automobile was nowhere in sight. *She's not here.*

Without hesitation, Catherine practically jumped off her bicycle when she reached Henry's lawn, grabbed the food, and ran across the lawn. Mud from puddles on the ride over caked her legs, but she didn't care. She stumbled once, her hands keeping her from completely falling. She ignored the small scrapes bestowed on them as well as the bag of food she had dropped. Her goal was to get to Henry and away from Susan, Natalie, and the insecurities the two women created in her.

When she reached the front door, she didn't bother knocking.

Henry spun around as his front door burst open and Catherine filled his sight. Relief surged through him even as he took in her disheveled appearance. Though she was covered in mud, he had never seen her look more beautiful. "Catherine!" he said in surprise as he hurried to her. "Look at you! You're not supposed to be off work for a couple hours still, and if it was still raining, then I was going to pick you up."

"Don't reprimand me now," Catherine said as she rushed over to Henry and buried herself in his arms. "Just shut up and hold me, all right?"

Momentarily forgetting about Natalie, he readily agreed. As she trembled in his embrace, he kissed the top of her head. "You're freezing. You should have called me."

"I'm not cold."

"You could have fooled me. You're shaking from head to toe."

"I was scared," Catherine found herself whispering.

"A flashback?" Henry asked as his arms tightened around her.

"No. I ran into Susan at the diner, and she had David with her. She said Natalie was—"

"Henry?" a voice from the doorway to Henry's bedroom interrupted Catherine. "Do you have company?"

Catherine jerked her head from Henry's chest at the sound of Natalie's voice. *Oh, God, no ...*

Both she and Henry turned to face Natalie at the same time.

Henry took a sharp intake of breath.

Catherine's world crumbled.

"Oh my goodness, I'm sorry!" Natalie said as she placed her hands modestly over the part of her chest Catherine's nightgown didn't cover.

Catherine felt her knees give as she recognized what Natalie wore. *Oh, God.*

"*Catherine!*" Henry said, reaching out and catching her as she started to fall.

His touch burned her. *Don't touch me!* In a frenzy, she pushed away from him. He reached back for her, his movements just as desperate.

"Catherine, let me explain. This isn't what it seems." Henry didn't try to hide the pain from his voice nor his desperation. His worst nightmare was playing out before his eyes.

No, apparently, we're not at all as it seemed. Catherine couldn't find her voice to say these words. Her mind was tangled, and the only thing she could recognize was the hurt that now pulsed where her heart used to.

"Sweetheart, listen," Henry begged as he watched Catherine take a step away from him. She looked like a wild animal cornered and unsure of where to go, but it was clear on her face that her goal was to flee.

"Catherine," Natalie called out, drawing the attention back to herself.

Seeing Natalie shamelessly wearing the nightgown Henry had bought for her was all it took for Catherine. She turned to go, but Henry caught her arm as she reached the still-open doorway. If he was still speaking, she no longer heard him. Pain muffled her hearing. She felt his fingers slide down her arm and encircle her wrist. He aimed to keep her here, but she knew she couldn't last another minute in this scene of infidelity. Before she realized what she was doing, she turned on him and slapped him with all her strength across his cheek.

The sound echoed through the house.

Henry was too stunned to move.

Natalie couldn't suppress a small gasp.

Catherine fled, stumbling down the stairs and to her bicycle, where she grabbed the handlebars and hastily pushed it to the street. She didn't dare stop as she got on the bike and blindly pedaled away from Henry's house.

Once Catherine had stepped outside, Henry knew he was on borrowed time. He turned to face Natalie, still standing in his bedroom doorway. She stared worriedly at the empty doorway.

"What are you *doing*?!" he bellowed, not trusting himself to get any closer.

I'll murder her.

Natalie looked at him, stricken. "I'm sorry, Henry. My clothes were soaking wet. I didn't think—"

"Clearly! *Why* would I allow you to wear Catherine's clothes? And *why* would I give you something like this to wear? *I wouldn't.*"

"Henry, I—"

He closed the distance between them, grabbing her arm and holding her close so she wouldn't miss the fury in his eyes. "I'm going to get my *fiancée*. When I return, you'd better not be here." He turned and ran out of his home, yelling Catherine's name and not bothering to give Natalie a second glance.

Natalie waited until she could no longer hear Henry calling after Catherine before she went and closed the front door with trembling hands. She didn't know who she hated more in that moment: Susan for creating this scheme or herself for executing it.

I'm a monster, like Susan.

Natalie had sold her soul. She hoped the price was worth it.

Twenty-Three

Faster ... faster ... keep pedaling. The command was a repetitive cycle in her mind, each one more frantic than the one before. If the rain wasn't already blinding her vision, her tears would sufficiently do the job.

He lied ... he lied. The hurt from what Catherine had witnessed was destroying her. *Henry wasn't expecting me for a couple more hours ... enough time to have Natalie ...*

A sob tore through her and was as audible as the rain that pelted her. She heard a car honk its horn, followed by the sound of screeching tires, but Catherine didn't care. She pedaled recklessly, daring anyone to hit her. At least that wouldn't be nearly as difficult to endure as the pain she currently felt.

In an instant, Catherine's past, present, and, more importantly, future had changed. As her mind replayed Natalie coming out of Henry's bedroom, Catherine chastised herself for being such a fool. Henry hadn't changed.

No, that's not true. Even as she struggled to analyze everything, she knew the man she had loved from so many years ago *had* changed when he came back from Europe at the end of the war. Even though it had taken quite a bit of convincing, Catherine finally had believed Henry's declarations of love. Tonight, the pain she had seen on his face before she fled told her that he loved her still.

But it's not enough. Whether he was sorry that he got caught or was sorry for the entire incident didn't matter to Catherine. Both were unforgiveable.

Henry punched a nearby tree in frustration. He had been certain that because of the weather, Catherine wouldn't be pedaling her bicycle so fast that he couldn't keep up with her on foot. Not only had the time he had taken to order Natalie from his home cost him valuable seconds, but he had also underestimated Catherine's determination to be as far from him as possible. His cheek still stung from the blow she had delivered as shock turned to pain and then rage in her eyes.

He knew how Catherine had interpreted the situation, and he couldn't blame her. And, by his own admission, this scenario wouldn't have been too surprising for someone to find him in had it been before the war. *But things are different now. I'm not that person anymore.*

He hadn't been that person for a very, very long time.

Yet, how could she not assume the worst when the evidence was so tangible and Catherine's world had already rocked by Natalie's allegation that she'd been with Henry before?

I have to find her. I have to make her listen. The sound of a blaring horn and screeching tires a few streets away alerted him as to which direction Catherine had taken. As much as he hated to, he turned and ran back to his house. The distance was already too great to reach Catherine on foot. He'd have to use his truck to make up for lost time.

When he reached his truck, he refused to look at his house. He assumed that not enough time had passed for Natalie to leave, and seeing her face from a window would send him over the edge. Instead, he took his anger over the situation out on the road, squealing his tires on the wet pavement as he tore out of the driveway. He sped off, knowing his future was in serious danger.

Catherine silently cursed living in a small town. She didn't dare go home. Olivia and Bobby would be there and would insist on an explanation on why she was so distraught. She couldn't go to the club. Henry had tried to keep her at his house, so she knew he would try to find her. The club would be the first place he would check. Every place she thought to go to was either so public that someone would be bound to contact Henry, or it was so secluded and personal that Henry knew about them.

I don't want to be anywhere near Henry. She didn't want to hear his lies or whatever excuse he would offer to explain away the image burned in her mind. She didn't want him close enough to touch her and try to erase all the anger and hurt she was feeling. She roughly wiped a hand across her lips, as though the action would erase every kiss he had ever given her.

How many kisses did he give Natalie before I arrived? The pain tore at her heart anew as the rain lessened to a drizzle. The absence of the heavy rain made approaching automobiles more audible. Catherine was grateful for this one stroke of luck. She'd be able to hear the distinctive sounds of Henry's truck coming, giving her enough time to evade him.

It was still too early in the evening for all the shops to be closed for the night, and although they each offered a warm haven as she pedaled past them, she refused to enter any of them. She was cold and wet, but her anger and hurt blanketed her physical discomforts.

She approached the park in the center of town where, what seemed a lifetime ago, a young soldier had requested the support of the townspeople, resulting in her brother, Bobby, and Henry enlisting and being sent to Europe. Here, she could be alone. The weather would keep people away, and there were enough bushes to conceal her from anyone searching. She could stay there for a while to try to see past her heartache and to plan her future.

No sooner had she dropped her bicycle and crumbled to the muddied ground behind a tangle of bushes than she heard Henry's truck pass. She tightly closed her eyes and tried to shut out the desperation she heard in his voice as he slowed down and called her name. Only when she was certain that he had continued past the park did she allow herself to breathe.

With her breath came a brand-new torrent of tears.

Henry could now add a new sentiment to what he was feeling: *fear.*

"Liv, please, if you're trying to cover for her, I respect that. But I need to know she's okay."

Olivia stood in the kitchen as Bobby slipped in next to her at the counter. She shook her head, her face rapidly changing to a level of concern that matched Henry's. "Henry, I swear to you, I haven't seen her," she said.

"A phone call?"

"Why would we have expected her or a call?" Bobby asked. "We thought she'd be with you."

Henry started pacing as he felt himself becoming frantic.

"What's happened?" Bobby asked calmly.

Henry didn't break stride as he answered, "She left my home over five hours ago. I haven't seen her since."

"Did you check with Michael?"

Henry shook his head and said, "The place was closed every time I drove past it, and I didn't want to lose the time it would take to stop and call him. I've been looking—"

"Let's call him," Bobby interrupted.

"What happened?" Olivia demanded a response as they followed Henry into the living room.

"Hold on a minute, okay, Liv? If I reach Michael, he'll be demanding the same information." Henry's voice came out as a mournful whisper as he said, "And I don't think I can stomach telling this story twice."

Olivia wanted to ask more, but Bobby silenced her with a warning glance.

"Michael?" Henry said suddenly into the telephone. He hardly waited for a response before asking, "Is she there? Is Catherine there with you?"

Bobby and Olivia didn't need to hear Michael's response; Henry's face said enough.

"And you haven't heard from her?" Henry gave a solemn look to Bobby before speaking to both Michael and Bobby, "I need your help finding her. There was a great misunderstanding. Natalie came by my house and tried … I don't know what she was trying. Catherine thought she'd walked in on Natalie and me."

Olivia's eyes teared up as Henry continued to explain in anguish, "She thinks I'm cheating on her with Natalie. She fled my house upset and angry, and I've been looking for her for over five hours."

Henry paused as Michael spoke on the other end of the line, to which he replied swiftly, "She's on a bicycle, Michael! How far could she go?"

Bobby laid a hand on Henry's shoulder to calm him, but it was with little success.

"You can yell at me later, Michael. You all can. For now, I just want to find Catherine. *Please.*"

A few seconds of silence passed in the McKinney house before Henry finally spoke again, "Thank you. *Hurry.*"

Henry hung up the telephone and turned to his two friends. Bobby looked at him like the soldier he was, awaiting his orders. In contrast, Olivia shot him a murderous look.

"*What did you do?*" she hissed.

Henry held up a hand. "Not now. I need you to stay here in case Catherine returns. Patricia is staying at their house with the same instructions. Bobby, I need you to get in your car and help us continue the search. We don't stop looking until we find her." He headed for the door, not bothering to see if Bobby followed.

Catherine lost all sense of time as she sat hidden in the park. She had no clue if minutes or hours had passed, and she didn't care. She had thought sitting down and thinking through everything would help. However, all it did was cause her to be even more distraught.

Just when she thought she had shed her last tear, the undeniable image of Henry's infidelity would start them flowing again.

Oh, Caleb, we were wrong. We were so wrong about him.

Catherine hated how fragile she had become. She hated that this single act yielded more emotion from her than the deaths of her mother, father, and brother.

Enough! You're the one who acknowledged there could still be something between the two of them. You're the one who considered giving them their space but then decided against it.

Determination filled her core as she came to a decision. She had thought about distancing herself from the situation before, and now she would do just that. She rose to her feet and resolutely pedaled toward the train station.

If he wants distance, I'll make sure he gets it.

Before she could talk herself out of it, she allowed her grief to take full control of her actions.

Henry felt a small bit of comfort in passing Bobby's and Michael's vehicles at different points throughout town. He was no longer alone in his search. He knew it was only a matter of time before they found her.

He slowed his truck to a stop at the railroad crossing near the edge of town as the warning gates lowered. Soon enough, he found Michael and Bobby stopping their vehicles behind him. As late as it was, most of the town had already closed for the night, so he didn't think twice about loitering as he shifted the gears and jumped down from the truck.

Michael and Bobby were already thinking the same thing.

"Not even a hint of her?" Henry yelled to be heard over the passing train.

Bobby shook his head as Michael eyed him underneath the streetlight. Bobby turned to the club owner and asked, "Do you have any guesses?"

Although now wasn't the time to bring it up, Michael couldn't help himself. "What exactly did you do to her?"

Henry shook his head. *Nothing. That's the problem. I didn't insist on marrying Catherine sooner. I didn't do enough to make sure there was no question about where my loyalty lies. I didn't stop Natalie from entering my home. I didn't do enough.*

Henry shook his head as he turned away in frustration from his two friends.

He kicked at the ground and then stood with his hands on his hips as he watched the train continue to pass.

The train reminded him of the history he had with Catherine. It had been at the train station when he was leaving for Europe that he had first seriously considered his best friend's twin sister. It had been on that same platform when he had arrived home after the war that he had realized his future was with her. It had been at that station when she had sought to leave him, and he had somehow successfully begged her to stay.

When she sought to leave me, to free me ...

"No," Henry whispered. As his panic threatened to paralyze him, he mentally pushed it aside. "No!" He turned to Bobby and Michael as the last of the train crossed the road.

"What is it?"

Henry looked at Michael, his face visibly pale under the streetlight. "The station," Henry choked out. He didn't wait to see if they followed as he jumped back in his truck and weaved around the gates that were just starting to lift.

As Henry raced to the train station, he didn't blink as he passed through every stop sign and traffic light. He focused only on getting to Catherine. He swerved his truck into the station's parking lot and heard two more vehicles repeating his entrance as he hurried from the truck.

"Catherine!" Henry yelled frantically as he ran to the platform. Bobby and Michael were close behind, also calling her name. As they approached the far end, Michael grabbed Henry's arm.

"Henry, look." Michael nodded to the bench in the shadow of the station's wall.

Catherine's bicycle rested against the back of the bench.

Even though it was evident that she wasn't there, Henry hurried to the bicycle while Bobby and Michael went to the ticket counter.

"How long has that bicycle been there?" Bobby demanded as he pointed to where Henry stood, clasping its handles tightly.

"Did its owner purchase a train ticket?" Michael added.

The station employee peeked over Michael's shoulder then helplessly held up his hands. "I'm sorry, I don't know. I just started my shift."

By this point, Henry had left the bicycle to join the small group. He was close enough to hear the man's response, and it wasn't good enough for him. "The train that just went through town, where is it heading?"

"It's been over five hours, Henry," Michael warned. "She could be on any—"

"Henry, did you say?" the station employee interrupted. He turned to Henry and asked, "Is your name Henry?"

Henry nodded.

The man bent behind the counter and came up with a folded piece of paper in his hand. "This must be for you."

Dread filled Henry as he reached out and took the paper with his name on it. He recognized Catherine's handwriting instantly. As soon as the paper was in his hands, his heart crumbled. Without opening it, he already knew what it contained. As though delaying the process would keep it from becoming a reality, Henry took his time opening the letter.

He caught Catherine's engagement ring before it fell to the floor from the page that displayed two words he vowed to disobey:

Don't follow.

PART II

Twenty-Four

"I'm sorry, Sarah," the man said as he stepped out from behind the ticket booth to greet the approaching young woman. "I didn't want to call the police. She didn't seem dangerous enough for that."

Sarah Geoffrey gave the man her friendliest smile as she looked in the direction he pointed and said, "It's okay, Tom. How long has she been here?"

They both watched the woman as she sat stoically on a bench near the station platform. "A couple of hours, maybe? Long enough that it's clear she plans to spend the night there," Tom whispered with concern.

Sarah didn't turn her focus from the woman as she asked, "You didn't speak to her?"

Tom responded, "I tried. But she either can't hear me, or she's ignoring me." He ran a nervous hand through his hair and added, "Your brother will be furious when he realizes you're out this late."

"It's a good thing that he's still out of town on a business trip, then," she countered, feeling Tom place a hand on her shoulder.

"Maybe I should have called the police. It's too late in the evening for you to be here."

Sarah turned and gave him a sharp look, her brown eyes visibly flashing in spite of the darkness. "Nonsense," she argued. "This woman clearly needs help. If she was a dangerous criminal, she wouldn't have stayed here for so long."

The telephone rang in the ticket booth office, interrupting their discussion. "Sarah, I need to answer that. Promise you won't approach her until I get back," Tom requested.

Sarah waved a dismissive hand at him. Once she heard Tom answer the phone, she approached the woman on the bench. The woman made no indication of being aware of her. When Sarah reached the bench, she slowly sat down.

"I have no problem hearing."

Sarah looked up, startled to hear the woman speak to her without prompting. She used this time to take in the woman's appearance. She was covered in dried mud, as though she'd waded through a swamp instead of ridden a train to get here. Her hair was a tangled mess, and she carried no luggage. "Pardon me?" Sarah asked. When the woman turned to her, Sarah saw a hollow look in her eyes.

"I have no problem hearing," the woman repeated as she gave a slight nod of her head in the direction of the ticket office.

"Oh."

"However, my forward planning could use some work." Staring at the train tracks, she whispered, more to herself, "I obviously didn't think this one through."

The woman's words surprised Sarah. She expected this stranger to be simpleminded. She hadn't expected sarcasm from her. "Are you meeting someone here?" Sarah asked with concern.

The woman shook her head and replied, "No, but do you mind telling me where 'here' is? I missed hearing the name of this town before I got off the train."

"You have no place to stay, then?"

The woman shook her head. "I should probably find a hotel," she concluded. "Do you know where I can find an inexpensive room?" She turned and looked back at Sarah.

Sarah saw the pain in her eyes. Wherever this woman had come from, it was clear the trip to this point had been rough. Sarah watched as the woman clenched and unclenched her small purse, the only personal item she seemed to possess. When the woman's stomach made audible sounds of hunger, Sarah had already made up her mind.

"You can stay the night with me," she volunteered.

The woman seemed bewildered. "Really?"

Sarah gave her a warm smile and repeated, "Yes, you can stay the night with me."

The woman's eyes brimmed with tears as she returned Sarah's gaze. "You trust me?" she asked.

"I don't have to," Sarah said. She took the woman's hands in her own, and when the woman didn't protest, Sarah gave them a squeeze. "I just have to trust *Him*. The question is, do *you* trust *me*?"

A small smile rebelliously curved the woman's lips. She gave Sarah's hands a squeeze of her own and answered, "I guess I don't have to, do I?"

Catherine sat next to the young, vibrant stranger who had opened her home to her. From the time the two had entered the cab, the woman had talked nonstop. Fortunately, the woman had asked no questions of Catherine. Instead, she had spoken with the sole purpose of putting Catherine at ease, and it had worked. Distraught, Catherine had left her hometown. She remembered very little about the train ride, only that she had been so lost in her thoughts that she had missed her paid exit. When the conductor had viewed her ticket and realized she should have departed the train three stops prior, he had escorted her from the train at the next stop.

Catherine had no idea where she was.

"Thank you again, Sarah," Catherine spoke softly when the woman paused to take a breath.

Surprised, Sarah said, "You know my name."

Catherine nodded, explaining, "Like I said earlier, I have no problem hearing. I heard the greeting when you arrived at the station."

Sarah looked like she wanted to ask a question but bit her lip to keep from speaking. Soon enough, the cab came to a stop in front of a two-story white house. The lights on the first floor glowed from the front windows.

"Come on!" Sarah said with childlike enthusiasm as she grabbed Catherine's hand and practically pulled her out of the cab.

As they climbed the steps of the front porch, an older woman met them at the door. "Sarah, you've had me pacing the floor with worry!" the woman exclaimed.

"This is my mother, Irma," Sarah explained to Catherine as they were both ushered into the house. Sarah directed her next words at her mother. "And I already told you where I was going. You didn't need to worry."

"I wasn't worried about *that*," she said as she took the coat from her daughter. Turning to Catherine, she assessed her from head to toe before saying, "Hello, dear. I daresay you look like you had a long day. May I get you something to eat or drink?"

Catherine couldn't hide her surprise at their generosity. They were welcoming a complete stranger into their home, and they hadn't so much as asked her name. Her broken heart couldn't help but warm to their kindness. "A piece of bread will suffice, if it's not too much trouble," she replied.

"And warm milk, I think," Irma added as she continued to study Catherine. "Sarah, why don't you see to that while I take our guest upstairs to a room?"

Irma ushered Catherine upstairs to a guest bedroom. Tears sprang to her eyes at the comforting room. "I … I can pay for this room for the night," she offered.

"Nonsense! Why would I charge you to sleep in a bedroom we have no use for?" Irma dismissed the suggestion with a wave of her hand. "Now, I'm going to make sure you have a warm bath ready shortly. I don't mean to hurry you along, but I want to get you tucked in bed as quickly as possible. Although by the looks of you, I don't think that will be an issue."

"Why the hurry?" Sarah asked as she brought the milk and bread into the room. "Tomorrow's Saturday. We can sleep in if we'd like."

"That very well may be, but I'd rather not have to explain everything that's happened with your brother until then."

Sarah asked in confusion, "What are you talking about?"

"He called while you were out. Apparently, he'll be back in town before morning. He didn't want to startle us when he returns in the middle of the night, so he called to let me know. *That's* what I was worried about. I want everyone in bed before he gets here."

Sarah rolled her eyes and gave Catherine a reassuring smile, explaining, "Edwin's bark is bigger than his bite. Don't worry about him."

"I don't want to be bothersome. I could go somewhere else." *I have no idea where, exactly …*

"No!" Irma and Sarah said in unison.

"I'm going to go get your bath ready. Sarah, take Catherine with you and see if you have a spare nightgown for her to wear," Irma ordered. With that, she turned on her heel and left before Catherine had the opportunity to protest.

In no time at all, Catherine stood in the doorway of what would be her bedroom for the night. She was bathed, in clean clothes, and at a complete loss over how the day had transpired. *Just this morning, I was home ... I was looking at my wedding dress and thinking about Henry. Now that dream is gone.*

An involuntary sob tore from her. No sooner had she emitted the sound than Irma approached from behind her with a pile of extra blankets. Without a word, Irma placed the blankets on the bed. Facing Catherine, she held open her arms and said, "My dear, I don't know the details of what brought you to us, but I don't need to know. I've been around long enough to recognize a broken heart when I see one. So why don't you come here and let me be the comfort you look like you desperately need?"

That was the only encouragement Catherine needed.

TWENTY-FIVE

The sun's warmth peeked through the curtained window and kissed Catherine's face when she woke the next morning. The moment she opened her eyes, the heart-wrenching details of the previous day came hurtling back to her. *I'm not in my own bed. I'm not in my home. I'm not anywhere near it. Henry ...*

She gazed at her left hand, her ring finger naked. She made a fist and tightly closed her eyes. She had wallowed in her sorrows instead of thinking things through. An evening of hurt had delivered her to an unfamiliar town, family, and house. She had acted impulsively. She had no clothing, little money, and no plan. While she was fairly certain she was safe with Sarah and Irma, she couldn't allow her emotions to prompt anymore rash decisions.

As she assessed her surroundings, she soon detected voices from the rooms on the first floor. While she couldn't make out the words, she could sense their intensity and knew it would be better for her to be dressed and ready to leave at a minute's notice. The one thing she didn't want was for Sarah and Irma to receive a reprimand for the charity they had offered her. She climbed out of bed and searched the room for her dress. She found her shoes, now spotless, next to a chair with a folded skirt and blouse on it.

Catherine couldn't help but smile at the kind gesture. As quickly as possible, she dressed, combed her hair with a brush resting underneath the borrowed clothes, and took a tentative step into the hallway.

The voices, clearly angry, rose to her more easily in the hall. By the time she reached the top of the staircase, she could make out every word spoken as well as surmise that the argument was coming from the kitchen.

"Seriously, Mother! You let Sarah bring in every riffraff she meets on the street. Your heart's too big." Catherine was unsure to whom the last statement was directed, but she didn't have to wait long to find out.

"It makes up for yours being too small, Edwin!" Sarah practically screeched at him.

Thinking of the two women's hospitality as the heated exchange continued, Catherine felt herself grow defensive as she descended the stairs.

Catherine stopped at the kitchen door, hesitating to open it.

"You don't know anything about her, sis!"

"Oh, for goodness' sake," Irma responded. "Edwin, be serious."

"She could be up there right now, robbing us blind."

The anger inside Catherine was too easy to conjure up, and she used it to give her the courage to push open the door. "Or murdering you all in your sleep, right? I'm assuming that'll be your next argument." Although her insides raged at the insults he had thrown, she did her best to remain calm. Her words silenced them, and Catherine tried to ignore the awkwardness as she stood in the doorway and causally crossed her arms.

Whatever argument rested on his lips disappeared when Edwin turned and took in the stranger his sister had allowed in their home. He was dumbfounded that someone who had taken advantage of his mother's and sister's generosity dared to speak so boldly to him. *She* was the stranger, after all. As he mentally fumbled to come up with a response, he used the opportunity to fully assess her. His delay in responding created a prolonged silence, but he didn't care. Edwin recognized the clothes she wore as belonging to Sarah. They fit well enough, and the stranger appeared average in her physical appearance.

When he gazed into her eyes, however, he realized average wasn't a word that should be used to describe this woman. Her eyes held a depth he had seldom witnessed before, and it was easy to detect every emotion she currently felt. She was hurting, and the darkness under her eyes attested to that. The iciness in her eyes made it obvious that she was also angry.

Something akin to attraction stirred in him, irritating him and causing him to wish for her departure more than ever. He tore his eyes away from her, but not before narrowing them into a glare that mirrored hers.

"I'm sorry to insult you," he finally said.

Catherine kept her arms crossed and countered, "You're just sorry I overheard."

"Perhaps."

Catherine heard a gasp from Irma or Sarah but paid it no attention. "Besides, you didn't insult me," she explained. "You insulted your sister." She watched as Edwin's glare deepened, and she bit her tongue to keep from saying anything more to him. She turned to Sarah and Irma and said, "Thank you both for your kindness, but I think I've trespassed too long. If you can provide me with the clothes I arrived in, I will change, give you money to compensate you, and then be on my way."

"Edwin! See what you did!" Sarah said, scowling at her brother.

Meanwhile, Irma gave Catherine a quick wink and motioned to the table. "Have a seat, dear," she ordered. "I'll get you a cup of coffee. Your clothes won't be clean until the end of the day, so I'm afraid you'll have to *trespass* a bit longer."

"Please, I insist—" Catherine started to protest.

"I won't have your malnourishment on our hands too," Edwin's masculine voice interrupted right behind her. "If my mother is offering you breakfast, it's best you accept the offer."

Although his words told her she could stay, his tone reflected otherwise. She looked up and found him uncomfortably close. Without breaking eye contact, he leaned across from her and pulled out a chair.

"Please, sit. What did you say your name was?"

"I didn't," Catherine replied as she quickly accepted the seat.

Sarah gave a small snort as she joined Catherine at the table. Edwin cast a warning glare to which his sister responded by sticking out her tongue at him.

He sat directly across from Catherine. "Well, then, what is it?" he challenged.

"I'd rather not say," she responded, giving Irma an appreciative smile as she placed coffee before her on the table.

"Did you kill someone?" he asked without missing a beat.

"Do you automatically assume the worst in everyone?" she easily countered.

Edwin paid no attention to the breakfast plate now sitting in front of him. "Do you always give everyone so much trouble?" he asked.

Edwin watched as something flashed in Catherine's eyes. He had seen that look often enough from living with two women—heartbreak. However, he was grudgingly impressed at how quickly she recovered from it.

"It's Grace," Catherine said, regretting the lie as soon as she spoke it. However, she remembered the last stranger, Robert, who had nearly destroyed her life, and she knew the alias was necessary.

The man sitting across from me could be another Robert, for all I know, and Henry's not here this time. Tears surfaced in her eyes at the thought of Henry. *Forget Robert; Henry's taught me an even harder lesson of not trusting anyone.*

Edwin watched as a mix of emotions played across her face, and his reply was softer after seeing her fight against tears. "That wasn't so hard, was it?" The pain in her eyes was apparent to Sarah as well, who swiftly delivered a hard kick to his shin.

"Apparently it is for you, son," Irma said as she joined the table. "You have yet to introduce yourself."

Edwin watched a small smile creep up on the woman seated across from him. When she looked up to find him watching her, she tucked the smile away.

He hated to see it go.

"I'm Edwin."

Catherine nodded but then focused on the food before her. When she had first entered the kitchen, the smells of breakfast had enticed her. But thoughts of Henry had snatched away her appetite. She was grateful that she was able to delay taking a bite as Edwin led them in a morning prayer.

As the family descended on their meal, Edwin wasted no time in interrogating the new addition to their table. Even though he felt remorse over upsetting her, his mother and sister were his priority. It was for their well-being that he continued his inquiries.

"So, tell me, Grace, what are your plans? Where do you plan to go now?"

Catherine abandoned the fork she had been pushing around her plate. Although Edwin had asked the question, she saw that both Irma and Sarah were also interested in her answer.

I have no idea. My world was ripped out from under me yesterday. I'm amazed that I had the strength to get out of bed.

"I can't answer that until I know where I am." She looked at Irma's motherly face, puckered with concern, and asked, "What city am I in?"

At her question, the family shared a look that Catherine didn't quite understand.

Edwin cleared his throat, suddenly looking uncomfortable. "Grace, you don't know what city you're in?" When she shook her head in response, he could feel Sarah and Irma turn to him. "I apologize in advance for being so blunt, but is there a chance that you suffered an injury that would cause you to be confused or lose your memory?"

On the contrary, I remember everything all too well. The memory of Natalie in Catherine's nightgown rushed forward, and she gave a sharp shake of her head when she answered, "No. I fell asleep on the train and missed my original destination. When they discovered my mistake, they promptly asked me to exit the train at the next station. That's why I have no idea where I am."

"You're in Mattisville, and you'll be staying with us for a spell," Irma said without hesitation. She gave Catherine a wink. "You need to take time to find your bearings, my dear. Here you're safe to figure things out. We'll help in any capacity you need."

"Of course!" Sarah squealed with delight. "Please stay."

It felt good to be wanted. While Irma and Sarah's enthusiasm was comforting, she refused to allow herself to get caught up in their generosity. She kept her eyes on Edwin, trying to read the emotions he masked. He remained silent, but Catherine was sure he wanted to protest.

"I'll stay on two conditions," Catherine said. With a slight lift of his eyebrows, Edwin regarded her with interest. She made sure to hold his gaze as she continued, "First, I insist on earning my keep. Let me take on some of the chores."

The women started to protest, but Edwin held up a hand to stop them. "Let Grace finish," he said. "And two?"

"I won't stay unless you agree to it. I refuse to be the cause of tension in this family."

Catherine watched as something like admiration crossed over Edwin's icy blue eyes. He studied her for a moment, and though his eyes thawed slightly, there was still an undeniable coldness to him when he finally nodded his head.

Relief filled Catherine, and only then did she realize she'd been holding her breath.

"Thank you."

Edwin rose to his feet, leaving most of his breakfast uneaten. "Don't thank me yet, Grace," he warned. "This in no way means that I trust you."

An hour later, Catherine was alone with Irma and Sarah. She didn't want to acknowledge the sense of relief that had consumed her once Edwin left the house, but it was hard to deny when she saw it clearly written on Sarah's and Irma's faces as well.

"Don't mind my son, Grace," Irma said as she patted the empty space next to her on the sofa, indicating that Catherine should join her. "He appears gruff, but it's all for show. He'll warm up to the idea."

"He's also not used to people standing up to him," Sarah said as she sat against the front windowsill.

"You seem to be able to hold your own against him," Catherine complimented from where she stood at the base of the stairs.

"I'm about the only one who does."

"Don't make your brother sound like a tyrant, Sarah," Irma gently scolded. She turned to Catherine. "While he appeared overbearing and argumentative this morning, he's only being protective of us. People don't normally stand up to him because there's never a need to. He's well respected in the community."

"I understand wanting to make sure you're safe," Catherine commented, "but I'm definitely not a threat."

"Of course not. I knew that from the beginning," Sarah said with satisfaction in her voice. "So, Grace, what would you like to do today? I can show you around town, or we could take in a movie."

"Or maybe you want to take time to yourself," Irma added. "You seem to have a lot to think through."

Catherine's mind jumped to Henry and the very real heartbreak of leaving him. *Of losing him.* The one thing she didn't want was to dwell on her ruined dreams.

Catherine forced a polite smile and shook her head. "As tempting as both sound, I'd rather get to work on earning my keep," she said. "I saw a few things that I could work on and repair for you."

Sarah made a raspberry sound and rolled her eyes. "You can't be serious? You know we're not going to make you work here. No matter what Edwin says, you're our guest."

"Your brother didn't say anything to me about working. That was my suggestion, and I insist on doing it. I'll have plenty of time tonight to work on figuring out where I go from here."

Sarah looked to Irma for help, saying, "Mother, will you please tell her—"

"I have a feeling that Grace isn't going to back down from this," Irma interrupted as she gave Catherine a look of admiration. "We need to respect her wishes. For now."

"At least let us help, then," Sarah protested, pushing off from the windowsill. "What do you have in mind?"

Catherine smiled at the young woman barely out of her teenage years. Catherine appreciated Sarah's resiliency and her refusal to let anything get her down for too long. "What I have in mind is for you two to go about your regular business. Don't change your plans on my account. I aim to keep myself busy today."

If I have to clean this house from top to bottom to keep the thoughts of Henry at bay, I'll do it. Then I'll do it all over again tomorrow.

Irma studied her a moment before turning to Sarah. "There's that quilting circle at the church I had planned to attend today."

A mischievous smile spread on Sarah's lips. "And it would really get under Edwin's skin if he came home later to find that we trusted Grace enough to leave her to her own devices, if only for a few hours." She was already making her way to the closet to retrieve her and Irma's purses. She smiled and said, "I'll accompany you, Mother."

Irma rose to her feet, rolled her eyes as she smiled at Catherine, and took the purse that Sarah offered her. "The church is right down the street," she explained as she pointed to the street on the right side of the house. "If you need anything, we'll be at St. Michael's."

The mention of her friend's name sent a wave of longing over Catherine. *Michael ... I should have gone to him. He would have given me better advice on how to handle everything. He's probably worried sick and furious with me.*

Catherine barely registered Sarah's and Irma's words as they left her suddenly alone in the house. As she headed to the kitchen to wash the dishes and see to any other chores she might be able to do, she realized that no amount of work would keep her mind off yesterday.

She was fighting a losing battle.

Edwin expected silence to greet him when he returned home later in the afternoon. His mother had mentioned an activity at church earlier in the week, so he knew she would most likely be there with Sarah and now Grace in tow. What he didn't expect to find was Grace alone in his house and underneath the kitchen sink.

He stood in the doorway to the kitchen, not fully believing his eyes. This stranger who hadn't even been in their home a full twenty-four hours was dressed in more of his sister's clothes, this time run-down dungarees, and positioned so far under the sink he could only see her legs.

"What on earth are you doing?"

Grace started in surprise at the sound of Edwin's voice, nearly dropping the tools she held. She pulled herself out from under the sink and rested against the lower cabinet doors as she said, "You startled me."

"Let me ask again. What are you doing?"

Catherine dropped the tools in the toolbox that rested by her feet and replied, "Earning my keep and saving you quite a bit of money." She wiped at her brow, unaware that it spread a large smudge of grime across her face.

"When you offered to earn your keep, I didn't have sink repairs in mind." He came forward and offered his hand to help her to her feet.

Catherine couldn't help but give a small chuckle. "I imagine not," she said as she accepted Edwin's hand and came to her feet. Once righted, she tried to pull her hand from his grip.

Instead, his hand tightened around hers. He placed her hand in both of his and turned it palm side up. "Just as I thought," he began as he traced her palm with his fingers, "callouses." He continued to stroke her hand as he looked up at her. "You're not a city girl, are you?"

Catherine wanted to reply that his hands were just as calloused, but the words wouldn't come. The intensity she saw, but didn't understand, in his eyes and felt in his continued touch caused a tremor to race through her.

They remained this way longer than Catherine wanted.

She finally found her voice, though still unable to remove her hand from his secure grip. "I'll be gone in a few days," she whispered. "It'll be like I never existed for you." She pleaded, "Please, don't pry. Don't dig too deeply."

This only served to convince Edwin that she had a secret.

Even as his mind screamed at him to do the opposite of what she asked, the look in her eyes caused him to soften. "You're trembling," he said, his voice barely above a whisper. "Do I frighten you?"

She tried to pull her hand from his grasp once more, but he refused to relinquish it. *Yes ... no.*

Her struggle to respond and attempts to remove her hand from his intrigued him. "Why are you afraid of me?" he couldn't help but ask.

"I-I didn't say that."

"You didn't have to." Keeping a firm grip on her hand, he took a step closer. He didn't want to frighten her, but his primary responsibility was protecting his family. So, he needed answers. *If this is what it takes to get her to talk, then so be it.* "I'm not leaving until you answer me. Do I frighten you?" he asked again.

"We're home!" Sarah called from the front door.

Edwin dropped Catherine's hand as though burned. Together, they took an extra few steps back to separate from each other. "We're not finished," he managed to whisper before Sarah and Irma entered the kitchen.

Every aspect of Edwin's nearness left Catherine unsettled. She had been fine until he touched her. While Edwin had questioned her, his touch hadn't been harsh. Realizing that left her more shaken than she cared to admit.

"Grace, you're filthy!" Sarah's exclamation brought Catherine back to the present.

Catherine needed the excuse Sarah's words offered. "Yes, you're right. If you'll excuse me," she replied, leaning over to retrieve the box of tools. She felt Edwin's gaze on her as she spoke, "I'll go clean up."

"I'll take that, Grace," Edwin said, reclaiming the tools from her as she tried to brush past him. His voice so close to her ear, and her relief from the tools caused Catherine to give a small stumble.

As she hurried from the kitchen, her mind was finally able to form a definitive response to Edwin's question.

Yes, Edwin, you frighten me. Everything about you frightens me ... especially when she realized it wasn't in the same sense that Robert had frightened her.

TWENTY-SIX

Henry sat on his bed, staring at the wall across from him. Darkness filled his bedroom, and he finally had peace from the telephone's rings from the other room. With the first few phone calls, he had practically broken his neck trying to answer it in hopes that Catherine was on the other end of the line. Each call was a disappointment to him, and as days had passed with no word from Catherine, despair began to smother him. Yesterday, he had thrown the telephone against the kitchen wall with enough force to shatter it. If he couldn't talk to Catherine, he didn't want to speak with anyone.

As the memory of their last encounter surfaced, he felt another wave of sickness at the pain in her eyes. He had said and done things that had hurt Catherine in the past, but it had never been at this magnitude. He gripped his fist around the engagement ring she had left behind at the station. He was clueless on how he was going to fix things.

I've got to try. Catherine, if I could only find you, I could explain. It wasn't what it seemed.

Henry had spent the last several days thinking of every way possible to locate his fiancée. He refused to think of her any differently, and he knew that if he could get to her, he could make things right. Unfortunately, her note indicated a willingness to leave, so he wasn't having any success with reporting her as missing to the police. The only lead he had been able to secure was the train's schedule from that night.

I've got a list of possible cities that she could have gone to, but no lead beyond that. But it's enough ...

The ticket clerk who had covered the ticket booth during the hours in which

Catherine had left town had tried to be helpful when Henry, Michael, and Bobby had confronted him at the station the day after her departure. Although he had clearly remembered Catherine, since she had personally given him the note for Henry, the station employee had been of little help beyond that. He hadn't been able to tell them the destination of Catherine's ticket, having been adamant that he hadn't sold a ticket to Catherine. But she had gotten on the train, so Henry and the others had been left to conclude that another passenger had purchased the ticket for Catherine—creating the largest stumbling block for him.

He knew he'd eventually have to ask Bobby to hold down the shop while Henry took a leave of absence. Henry planned on stopping at every station in the cities on his list to ask if anyone had seen Catherine. He'd take as long as necessary to find her.

The sudden pounding at his front door pulled Henry away from his planning. He could tell by the force of the knocks that a man stood on the other side. It wasn't Catherine, so he didn't care to answer it.

"Go away!" he bellowed from his bed. Although he knew the visitor couldn't hear him, it had felt good to yell and unleash a bit of his frustration.

The knocks morphed into outright banging, forcing Henry to answer the door, if only to demand the visitor's immediate departure. Henry jumped out of bed and took agitated steps to the front door. "I said to go away," he practically screamed as he opened the door.

Michael and Bobby stood on the other side.

"It's about time," Bobby said, an annoyed expression on his face. "We've been trying to reach you for a while. Thanks for answering the door. *Finally.*"

"Call next time," Henry grumbled, refusing to give them access to his home.

"We tried," Bobby said as Michael pushed past Henry into the house.

"You're not welcome," Henry said.

Michael turned on the light in the kitchen, its brightness filling the room. "Obviously," he replied as he touched the remains of the telephone.

"You wouldn't stop calling me," Henry answered as he begrudgingly allowed Bobby to also enter.

"That was Liv," Bobby explained, "not us. But when you stopped answering the calls, she grew more concerned."

"I'm fine," Henry said as he scratched at the beard that now framed his face.

"What if Cat was trying to call?" Bobby asked.

Henry gave him a painful look. "She's not calling. I hurt her, Bobby. She's not coming back to me. I have to be the one to find her."

"How long has it been since you shaved?" Michael asked. "You look terrible."

Henry ignored Michael's observation. "Has Liv heard from her?" As gruff as he wanted to sound, he couldn't hide the hope emitted by his question.

Bobby found he couldn't look at Henry as he answered, "I'm sorry. She hasn't."

Henry turned to Michael, asking him the same question with his eyes.

"Sorry, friend," Michael said. "I haven't heard from her either."

Henry nodded as he fell back against the wall and let his body sink to the floor. "She's hurting," he said, his voice a hoarse whisper. "I have to find her."

Michael and Bobby exchanged a look before refocusing their attention on Henry. It was obvious Henry hadn't bothered taking care of his personal hygiene over the past several days. His clothes were wrinkled and in desperate need of laundering, and the beard hadn't grown overnight. It was clear Henry was hurting as badly as Catherine.

"Sorry for my bluntness," Henry continued, "but if you're not here to bring word of my fiancée, would you mind leaving? I need to finalize plans. I'm going after her."

"Tell him, Bobby."

Bobby gave an uncomfortable nod as he felt all eyes on him. "While we haven't heard from Cat, Henry, we *have* heard from Natalie."

Hate filled Henry as he rose to his feet. "She is the root of all of this! I don't want her name mentioned in my presence ever again."

Bobby stole a glance to Michael before continuing, "I understand that. Really, I do. But Henry, you need to hear this."

"I'm not giving her the time of day."

"Henry, you need to go back to the shop tomorrow. You need to make an appearance through town."

Henry whirled to face Michael and demanded, "What does that have to do with anything?"

Michael gave a shrug. "This is a small town, Henry. Word has spread that Cat's gone. Natalie is new, but she does have a few friends."

"Susan, in particular," Bobby added. "Your current state is giving credit to her story."

Henry looked at them in bewilderment and asked, "*Her* story? What *story?*"

"Let's just say that Natalie's version of what happened the night Cat left is a bit different from yours, Henry, and it's one that can fully support Catherine's decision to leave."

Dread seized Henry and sent a wave of shivers down his spine. He ran a hand through his unwashed hair and rubbed his neck before answering, "I'll put on some coffee. I have a feeling whatever you have to say is only going to make things worse."

Twenty-Seven

Catherine remained in a panicked state of mind through the next few days. Edwin's presence unnerved her, and she did her utmost to keep her distance from him. The hole in her heart from losing Henry refused to fade with the passing days, and Edwin's nearness made the pain more real. As a result, staying away from him was an act of self-preservation.

On the other hand, Edwin became increasingly convinced that Catherine—Grace, as he knew her—held a secret worth knowing. The closer he tried to get to unearthing it, the more effort she put in widening the gulf between them, and he couldn't help but become increasingly intrigued by their game of cat and mouse.

He almost found it comical, especially when his mother and sister thwarted her obvious desire for distance. No matter how much Grace tried to discourage bonding, it was becoming apparent to everyone that Irma and Sarah loved this stranger more with each passing day. While they appreciated the help she offered, they loved the natural kindness that Grace emitted, even as she tried to hide it. Each day Irma's and Sarah's love for Grace grew, and each night they begged Edwin to permit their new guest to stay indefinitely.

Edwin tried to convince himself that it was their begging, along with his own desire to learn Grace's secret, that led him to agree to their pleas rather than the long-abandoned emotions that Grace's presence resurrected in him.

He pretended his need for her to stay was purely based on his desire to protect his family.

I only want her here in order to keep an eye on her. My family's affections for her grew too quickly, and I need to make sure it's not going to come back and hurt them. But even as he thought the words, he knew they were a lie. *At least partially ...*

"It seems my mother and sister are quite taken with you, Grace," Edwin began one morning at breakfast. Out of the corner of his eye, he watched her stiffen in the chair situated farthest from him. "They've asked me to extend an invitation for you to remain as our guest ... indefinitely."

Catherine stared at her bowl of oatmeal as she frantically processed his words. Without looking to her left, she felt Irma's warm, motherly eyes on her. The nudge Sarah gave her under the table was meant to encourage her to accept the invitation Edwin had yet to formally offer. Her heart nearly burst at the love she felt from these two ladies who had grown from strangers to cherished loved ones in a short period of time. Their love was what she needed in trying to adjust to a life without Henry.

But it was Edwin's role and his unknown motive in this that left her unsettled. She looked up at the sound of him politely clearing his throat. It was easy to look past Sarah's and Irma's stares. Edwin's was impossible to ignore.

His bright blue eyes protruded her defenses. His face was an unreadable mask.

And he's not going to give me anything else to help gauge the situation, is he?

"What do you think about that, Grace?" he asked as if reading her mind. "How does it make you feel to know that you've so quickly won my mother's and sister's hearts?"

Tread softly, Cat.

"Irma and Sarah have shown me nothing but kindness since I've been here trying to figure out the next steps in my life. I'll be forever grateful for their endless hospitality. I'm both flattered and humbled by their wish for me to extend my stay."

"To forever," Sarah whispered.

Catherine couldn't help but smile at Sarah's quiet comment before continuing, "They are as dear to me as I apparently am to them."

Edwin hated how he immediately noticed the blush tinting Grace's cheeks at Sarah's whispered desire.

"Does that mean you'll stay?" Sarah asked, unable to mask her excitement. "You'll be like the sister I never had."

Catherine focused her attention to Edwin and asked, "How do you feel about it? *My* opinion is irrelevant at the moment."

Edwin tore his eyes from her and focused on buttering his toast as he answered, "I'll admit, I'm not completely comfortable with the secrecy you're maintaining about the cause of your arrival in the first place ... especially if you're to become the sister Sarah apparently has always dreamed of having. However, everything you've done since coming here has been nothing less than considerate to my family. You've respected all of us and offered your help in any way. That being said, I'm willing to consider a trial period—"

Sarah's squeal of delight cut off Edwin, but he didn't protest. He watched as his younger sister jumped up from the table, hugging first him and then practically launching herself into the arms of their guest. His mother was watching him with pride in her eyes. She gave him a quick nod of approval before turning to Sarah.

"She hasn't agreed to the arrangement yet, Sarah," Irma said. "Give the poor woman a chance to answer."

"And give your brother the chance to finish." While Sarah disengaged herself from Catherine's embrace, Catherine looked at Edwin and added, "I think he still has something to say about the matter."

"Thank you," Edwin continued. "As I was saying, I'm comfortable with a trial period. You said yourself that you need to figure out the next steps of your life. You've proven that you don't have idle hands. While I appreciate that, staying here and 'earning your keep', as you dubbed it, will not help you in the long run. A paying job would. It would help you to save money for wherever you go next. If you choose to stay in this town, a job will provide the way for you to get established. Despite Sarah's wishes for you to remain here forever, you're too independent to want to rely on someone else for too long. I can try to help you find work ..."

Catherine watched Edwin as he spoke. A new wave of respect for him coursed through her. She hated to compare him to Henry, but the gift he offered her made it difficult not to. Edwin offered her a job, or at least help in finding one. The arguments she had shared with Henry over her work replayed in her thoughts.

Stop it, Cat ... Henry was supportive of you working. He just didn't want you working like a dog at the club. He wanted better for you. Catherine mentally shook her head, trying to stop the way she automatically jumped to his defense. Henry had cheated on her with Natalie, and still she tried to defend him?

"A job would be wonderful, thank you," Catherine said. "If I can find work, then I'd be happy to stay on here for a while, but only if you're okay with it."

Edwin was pleased as he watched her embrace the idea of a job. "I am," he said simply and flashed a hint of a smile before he realized it.

Catherine couldn't help but return the smile with one of her own.

It practically disarmed him.

Scrambling to regain his composure, Edwin rose to his feet. "Good. Why don't we go to my study to brainstorm what kind of work you can do?"

"Can't we help?" Sarah protested.

Irma watched her two children and their guest closely. Edwin's plan was evident. He was going to ask questions about her past, and if Grace was already reluctant to share it with them, a full assault from all of them would cause her to withdraw completely. She smiled at her son's foresight.

"Sarah, I need help with some errands," Irma said as she rose to her feet. "Let's leave this with them. If they need our help, they'll ask for it."

Sarah nodded begrudgingly and began to clear the table. Edwin motioned for Catherine to follow him but didn't wait to see if she did.

"Before you ask," Catherine said as she closed the study door behind her, "I have a high school education. I did factory work and housekeeping. I grew up on a small farm."

"I conclude, then, you're no stranger to hard work?"

"I am not."

Edwin nodded. "I didn't think so." He motioned at the empty chairs sitting in front of his desk and said, "Please, have a seat."

She sat and was surprised when he took the seat next to her rather than behind the desk.

"I'm a hard worker," she rambled on, trying not to let his closeness bother her.

"I know that, Grace. You mentioned a high school education. Can you type?"

"Excuse me?"

"Type?" He mimicked the action with his fingers. "It's obvious you have parts of your past you want to keep hidden, and I'll respect that for now."

"Thank you."

"But if that's what you want, then I'm wondering if it's a good idea to find work in a field that will remind you of where you've been."

"I can manage," Catherine offered.

Edwin studied her for a moment, contemplating whether to make the suggestion. While it would ensure that he'd be able to keep a close eye on her, he wasn't sure if he was ready to share a workplace with her.

You're not sure if you're ready to share her with the world ... admit it, Edwin.

"I can't promise anything," he blurted out before he lost his nerve, "but there's a clerical position open at the office where I work. I can inquire about it if you'd like."

"How about I join you on your way to work tomorrow and inquire about it myself?"

Edwin let a chuckle escape him and said, "Bring that spirit with you, and you're as good as hired."

TWENTY-EIGHT

"She sure is a quiet mouse," Edwin's coworker said as they watched Grace deliver mail to each desk in the large room. "She comes in, she works, she eats lunch by herself, she works, and she leaves. She's too shy to speak with anyone." He asked Edwin, "How did you say you found her again?"

"I didn't. My sister found her."

"Well, despite her quietness, or maybe because of it, I'm dying to get to know her. But she's not making it easy."

"Did it ever occur to you, Paul, that maybe she's like that because she doesn't want to know you?" Edwin couldn't help but tease him as Grace disappeared from their view.

Paul took the teasing in stride and said, "Of course not! But she only ever acknowledges you."

"That's only because we walk to and from work together. She doesn't say a word to me during the shift."

"That's more attention than she gives any other guy here. She's just shy, right? Or are you two—"

"We're not an item," Edwin interrupted. He didn't want to admit that Grace was almost as distant with him as she was with the others.

Grace had been employed for two weeks now and had quickly elevated to an essential asset to the company. She was a quick study and worked harder than most people. His own boss had thanked him several times for suggesting the job to Grace.

He was proud of the reputation she'd created.

It was obvious that Grace was pleased with the situation too. Just this week, Grace had relaxed enough to tease Edwin on their walks to and from the office. Even though Edwin continued to try and unearth pieces from Grace's past, she evaded answering by offering conversation subjects impossible to ignore. As a result, Edwin was no closer to knowing who Grace was. But he was closer to understanding Grace now, in the present.

The thought brought a smile to his lips.

"Well, will you at least put in a good word for me, then?" Paul asked, interrupting his thoughts. "If you're not claiming her, I'd like to throw my name into the hat."

"But I could be a murderer for all you know," a voice said behind them, startling both Edwin and Paul.

Paul nearly came out of his skin, causing him to spill his cup of cooled coffee down his shirt and onto his desk. With a reddened face, he hurriedly tried to save the papers on his desk while Grace placed a stack of envelopes on the desk's corner.

"Besides, you have enough fan mail. You don't need anything from me."

She left them without another word.

"Shy she may be," Edwin say, hardly believing his ears, "but there's no denying that she's got a wry sense of humor."

Edwin still had a smile on his lips when he left work that evening and found Grace waiting for him outside the building. As always, he was the last to leave the office, and when he met Grace, he didn't think through his actions.

"That was amazing!" he said, as he grabbed her arm and slid it through the bend at his elbow and began to escort her home. "Did you see the look on Paul's face when he realized you had overheard him? And then when you scared him half to death!" He threw his head back and let a hearty laugh escape him.

While Catherine was surprised at the familiarity Edwin displayed in taking her hand and slipping it through his arm, his laugh left her speechless. Up to this point, she had only witnessed small smiles and light chuckles in which to measure Edwin's pleasure. This laugh opened up a new side of him that Catherine hadn't thought existed.

She waited until the laugh had completely faded before responding, "I hope I didn't embarrass him too badly. I didn't mean to create any problems. It came out before I could stop myself."

Edwin shrugged beside her. "He'll get over it."

They walked in companionable silence for a while before Edwin realized he held her hand in the crook of his arm. "I apologize," he said as he removed her hand from his arm. "I didn't mean to take such liberties."

"It's okay," Catherine said. She hated to admit that it was nice to be held once again in a protective manner, even if it was a simple escort. Yet she hated the feel of its absence even more. "You were obviously caught up in the moment." She gave him her most convincing smile and added, "I'll try not to hold it against you."

Edwin caught the gleam in her eye and felt relief that he hadn't offended her. "You tease, Grace. Who knew that was in you?"

Henry knows ...

"Yes, well, it's gotten me into a bit of trouble in the past, so I try to keep it contained as much as possible."

"I see."

A lengthy silence followed until Edwin broke it. "So, today was your first payday. How does it feel to have a bit more change in your pocket?"

"Good," Catherine replied. "Although I want your family to have most of this paycheck."

"What? Grace, no," Edwin argued as they neared his family's home. "You earned every penny and deserve to keep it for yourself—"

"You all fed me, gave me a room, and gave me my space for no charge. I insist on doing this. You think I have a mischievous streak? Just wait until you see my stubborn side."

Edwin sighed heavily as they reached his home. "I'll leave this up to you and my mother," he said. "And if for some crazy reason she accepts your money, it's a one-time occurrence. I *will* put my foot down on that."

Catherine didn't try to hide the triumphant smile on her face as she bounded up the front porch stairs. "Fair enough," she agreed.

"But Grace," Irma argued as she noted the amount of wages placed in her hand, "this doesn't leave you with very much at all." She faced Edwin. "And you agreed to this?"

Edwin held up his hands in surrender, explaining, "I told her that if you decided to accept the money, this would be the only time. I guess she's making the most of it."

"It's fine," Sarah chimed in. "If she gives you most of her wages, that means she'll have need of us longer. I'm fine with that."

"Please." Catherine held up a hand to stop them all. "The remainder is more than enough money to get me through to the next pay period." She held out the few bills in her hand, adding, "To be honest, this is all I really need right now."

"That will barely get you a long-distance phone call," Edwin observed.

Catherine suddenly swiveled to him. She could tell he had guessed correctly how she was planning to use the money.

Edwin studied her carefully before saying, "Use our phone, Grace. We'll cover any costs."

Catherine shook her head and adamantly argued, "No, I'm going to take a walk and use the phone that we pass on our way to work. I won't be long."

"I'll escort you," Edwin said, stepping toward the door.

"No!" Sarah objected. "You had her all day. I want to spend time with her. I'll go. And I won't be nosy about any phone call she makes," she added with a wink to Catherine.

"I'll accompany you both," Edwin countered.

"Ugh," Sarah said as she grabbed Catherine's hand and pulled her to the door. "We're *fine*, Edwin." She pushed past her brother, closing the front door in his face.

Edwin stared in disbelief at the inside of the door.

"Leave them be, Edwin," his mother said behind him.

"I mean only to walk with them."

"And then try to figure out who Grace is calling," Irma finished for him. "Give the poor girl a break. You have her under a microscope every second of the day."

"It's to protect you and Sarah, Mother. I want to make sure—"

"Edwin, she's a girl with a broken heart. She's not a criminal. It's high time you stop treating her like one and treat her like the treasure she is." She rolled her eyes in exasperation and added, "It's any wonder how she handles working with you every day."

"She has nothing to do with me at work," Edwin explained. The day's earlier events came back to him, and he couldn't help but chuckle. "She refuses to fraternize with anyone at the office. But today she made an exception." This time a full laugh escaped his throat.

"What's so funny?"

"The way she put Paul in his place ... make yourself comfortable, Mother. I have a story that you're sure to enjoy."

"I'm not a particular fan of Paul's."

Edwin nodded and said, "That will make this even more enjoyable for you."

Twenty-Nine

From where Catherine stood in the telephone booth, she saw Sarah give her a friendly wave before turning her attention to a nearby store's window display. She returned the wave with a confident one of her own, but Catherine couldn't hide the tremble in her voice as she provided the information the operator needed to connect her to Michael.

It had been weeks since she had last seen him, and she could only imagine the fury and concern he must be feeling over her. She had considered telephoning Olivia but knew her best friend would likely fall apart at the sound of Catherine's voice. *And that's not what I need right now.*

She needed stern, truthful Michael. When his voice finally broke through the phone, sternness was exactly what she got.

"Hello?"

His voice was home. She felt tears well up in her eyes before she found her voice and whispered, "Michael, it's me."

"Cat?"

It took a minute for her to feel strong enough to speak and say, "Yes, Michael."

"Thank God!" his voice held relief that quickly turned to anger. "Where on earth are you? Do you realize how worried I've been? How worried *Henry's* been? I swear, I—"

"Don't yell at me, Michael."

"Well, someone needs to! Cat—"

"I'll hang up, Michael. I'm warning you."

"No. Listen to me, Catherine. You need to—"

"I'll call again later, when you're actually in the mood to listen."

Catherine ended the call without saying goodbye. At first, she distanced herself from the telephone as much as the booth would allow. While she had wanted Michael's sternness, she didn't want his lecturing.

And mentioning Henry ...

She felt alone. Michael had always been *her* friend first, and hearing him mention the man who had broken her heart felt like a betrayal.

As emotional as Liv is, at least she'll understand.

Finally, Catherine reached for the telephone once more.

Olivia picked up right away. "McKinney residence."

Catherine's voice sounded shattered as she responded, "Hey, Liv."

Catherine could hear Olivia take a deep breath, but she didn't give Olivia the chance to speak.

"Liv, before you start giving me a hard time too, will you listen?"

Silence was her reply.

"I'm all right, Liv. I needed to get away ... and quickly. I'm sorry I didn't let you know what was going on." As she tried to explain, to apologize, tears surfaced once more.

Eventually, after Catherine had exhausted her tears, Olivia asked, "Where are you, Cat? Henry told us what happened."

"Did he?" Bitterness lined her words.

"He's lost without you. Cat, please come back home. There must have been some misunderstanding."

"Misunderstanding? He ripped my heart into a million pieces, and you call that a *misunderstanding*?"

THIRTY

Olivia cringed at the pain she heard in Catherine's voice. *Of course it wouldn't seem like a misunderstanding to you, Cat. You're the one whose heart is broken.*

"I'm sorry, Catherine. You're right. I'm here for you, no matter what. I'm worried about you." Olivia turned to face the front door as she heard Henry's and Bobby's vehicles pulling up to the house.

Stall, Olivia. Stall ...

"You left with only the clothes on your back. Do you have enough money?"

"I will soon. I have a safe place to stay, Liv. I also have a job."

"A job?" Catherine's words surprised her, and she frantically waved at Bobby and Henry for silence as they entered the house. "Catherine, how long are you planning to stay away?"

As soon as Henry heard Catherine's name, he was at Olivia's side. Relief surged through him that Catherine had finally called. He began to reach for the phone, but Olivia shook her head. Instead, she held the phone out so that they could both listen to Catherine speak.

"Liv, I need you to look after the place for a while. Do you think you and Bobby can do that?"

Henry's eyes watered at the sound of her voice. He had spent so many sleepless nights worrying over her. It took every ounce of self-restraint not to take over the conversation.

Olivia glanced at Henry, and when he nodded for her to reply, she said, "Cat, we can watch this place for as long as you need. But why don't you come home? Bobby and I can come get you. Tell us where you are."

Henry could hear the pain in Catherine's silence.

"Liv, I think it's best that I have some distance for a bit. Nothing has gone as I planned, so I don't want to rush into anything. I need space, and I need time."

"Cat, but Henry—"

"Liv, please, this is hard enough as it is."

"He deserves better than this, Cat. You should at least talk to him. He's been frantic over your disappearance. What am I supposed to say when he finds out you called?"

There was a deep sigh through the phone before Catherine whispered, "He doesn't have to know. No one has to know that I called you."

"Catherine, are you listening to yourself? This is Henry we're talking about." Although Olivia knew it was risky, she asked, "Have you forgotten him so quickly?"

Both Henry's and Olivia's hearts broke at the sound of Catherine's bitter, sad laugh. "Liv, tell me, do you think my love for him is so simple?"

"I only meant—"

"Forgetting him is like forgetting how to breathe … only death can bring that."

Henry heard what he needed to. Despite Catherine leaving and telling him not to follow, despite her lack of contact with anyone before now, despite the pain that was in every word she spoke, she still loved him.

There's hope.

He seized the telephone from Olivia's hand and spoke, "Catherine, are you all right?"

His question was met with her quiet breathing.

"Catherine, please," he pleaded, "let me explain."

The silence that followed his plea was more definite; she was no longer on the line.

"Let me guess," Olivia said from behind where he stood gripping the telephone. "She hung up?"

He could only nod.

"So, I guess she's still upset?" Bobby asked from across the room. Both Olivia and Henry turned and glared at him.

Henry collapsed on the sofa, dropping his head in his hands. "Before we got here, before I went and messed everything up—"

"That's right you messed it up!" Olivia scolded him as the sound of another automobile approaching reached their ears.

"It's Michael," Bobby said after looking out the window.

Olivia gave a slight nod as she kept her focus on Henry. She wasn't through yelling at him. Catherine was her best friend, and she had been deeply worried about her. She had known the moment Henry had taken the phone from her that Catherine would refuse to talk with him. "It's obvious she isn't ready to talk to you. So, if you want to find out anything more about Cat, I suggest you *not* take the telephone from me when she calls again … *if* she calls again."

"You heard from her too, then?" Michael asked from the doorway.

Henry glanced back at Michael, his words like a lifeline. "You heard from Catherine?"

Michael nodded and answered, "Sort of. She called, at any rate. When I started to lecture her, she hung up on me."

"She hung up on us too," Olivia said with a glare at Henry.

"I'm sorry, Liv." Henry explained, "Liv was on the phone with her, and I couldn't help it. What I heard her say gave me reason to hope … I was so desperate. But when she heard my voice, she ended the call."

Although Michael wanted to offer words of comfort to Henry, he knew now wasn't the time. He focused his attention on Olivia and asked, "What did you find out? Did she say where she's staying?"

Olivia shook her head. "No. She wouldn't tell me where she was staying. She *did* tell me that she's somewhere safe and that she's found work."

Michael frowned slightly but said nothing.

Henry, on the other hand, was more vocal.

"A *job?*" he exclaimed. "How long is she going to stay wherever she is?" He didn't wait for an answer. "You know what? That's not important. I'm not waiting around to find out." He rose to his feet as though planning to go and find her that instant.

"You are if you want to actually find her," Michael said as Henry started to push past him at the front door. "You have no idea where she is. But wherever she is, she's situated. If you go on a wild-goose chase now—"

"Finding my fiancée is *not* a wild-goose chase."

"It is if you have no idea where to begin," Michael countered. "She's reached out to us. We know she's safe. Now we have to wait for her to reach out again."

"So we can upset her again?" Henry couldn't keep the frustration out of his voice.

"We know her state of mind now. We'll do better next time," Olivia added. Michael nodded in agreement.

"Plus," Bobby added, "if you go now, with no idea where you're going, and Cat calls back, you won't be around to learn anything more."

Henry stood facing the door, his back to them. "I hate this," he whispered. "I feel helpless."

Michael had been mulling over an idea for a few days and now was as good a time as any to voice it. "You don't have to feel that way, you know," he said slowly.

"If you're going to start with one of your motivational speeches, save it for someone else," Henry snapped.

"No, I meant that there's something you *can* do while we wait to hear back from Catherine."

Henry turned his head to give Michael a sideways glance. "What?"

"I need you to promise to hear me out first."

Henry threw his hands in the air and said bitterly, "Seeing as I have nothing else to do …" Despite his sarcasm, Henry gave Michael a curt nod.

"You can use this time to figure out Natalie's angle."

"Excuse me?" Olivia asked. "You want him to go to the person who caused this whole fiasco? "

"I have to agree with Liv," Bobby said. "That doesn't make sense."

"Let me explain." Michael held up his hands to stop their protests and continued, "Patricia said something that got me to thinking. Natalie set Henry up. Although she may swear it differently, we all know that has to be the case. After all, David wasn't even with her at the time. This leads Patricia, and now me, to believe there's more to Natalie's story than we know."

"What do you mean?" Henry asked.

"You don't remember being with Natalie, do you?" Michael asked point-blank.

Henry shook his head. "No, but—"

"Up until Natalie, you remembered all of them, right?"

Henry didn't want to talk about his past mistakes, but Michael's suggestion sparked an interest, and he wanted to hear him out. "I thought I did. But Natalie's shaken my confidence in my memory. There were times that I was pretty drunk ..."

"It's eating at you that you can't recall her, isn't it? Do you think there's a possibility that Natalie was never with you? That David isn't yours?"

Henry turned to fully face him and asked seriously, "But why would she do that?"

Michael looked at each of them before responding, "Well, now that's the question, isn't it? And that's what I'm suggesting you try to uncover while we wait to hear back from Catherine."

"We'll help," Bobby offered.

"Natalie went after Cat with that move," Michael said. "We need to watch her ... give her time to make a mistake."

"At the risk of losing Catherine?" Henry asked.

Michael shook his head. "Henry, Catherine obviously needs time to cool. If any of us so much as mentions your name, she clams up. She needs time, and the truth needs time to reveal itself. As much as you hate this, Henry, you need to give everything more time."

As much as Henry wanted to argue, he couldn't. From the moment Michael suggested David might not be his son, it validated the nagging feeling Henry had been feeling and revealed the need to uncover the complete truth about Natalie. Guilt over his past had kept him from believing this was a possibility, but now that someone not directly involved had mentioned it, it seemed entirely plausible.

If I discover that David isn't mine, that all of this is a hoax ...

"Patricia has more of a detective's mind than I do, and she's already come up with some ideas that might work if you want her help."

Henry nodded. He wanted to put this entire nightmare behind him. But more than anything, he wanted Catherine back in his life.

"I'll go along with all of this," Henry began, "for *now*. But the moment I discover where Catherine is, I'm going after her." He focused on Michael as he asked, "Do I make myself clear?"

Michael saw the promise in Henry's eyes and understood the determination in his voice. Michael could only hope they had enough time before Henry acted out in desperation and did permanent damage. "Yes, soldier, you do." He gave Olivia and Bobby a final nod before leaving.

It was only after Michael departed and Olivia was putting their son to bed that Bobby brought up Michael's departing words.

"You know I'm not one to give advice, right?" Bobby said as he and Henry stood on the front porch.

Henry kept his eyes focused on the darkness as he replied, "Don't let that stop you now."

Bobby glanced over at his friend's profile before replying, "Michael … he called you a soldier for a reason before he left."

"To tell me that I'm fighting to win back Catherine? Tell me something I don't know, Bobby."

"A soldier, a good soldier, doesn't make rash decisions. You know this. It's what kept you alive in Europe. He's telling you to *think* before doing anything. I know this whole situation seems desperate, Henry, but we faced a lot of desperate situations in Europe too. You need to treat this the same way."

Despite everything Henry was feeling, he couldn't help but chuckle and comment, "It never leaves us, does it? Once a soldier, always a soldier."

Although Henry couldn't see him, Bobby nodded in agreement before adding, "And I'd say it's a good thing. Because with everything you're up against, you're going to need to be that soldier in order to survive."

THIRTY-ONE

Edwin walked into the kitchen to find his sister and mother at the table, deep in conversation. They both looked up at the sound of his entrance, their eyes hopeful. As they registered Edwin, their disappointment was impossible to ignore.

"Expecting someone else?" he asked as he leaned between them to take an apple from the bowl of fruit set in the center of the table.

"No," Sarah muttered. "We were only *hoping* it was someone else."

"You just went with her to the phone booth less than an hour ago. Did you lose her already?" he teased, winking at his mother. "See? I knew I should have gone with them."

"Oh, be quiet, Edwin!" Sarah growled at him. "I didn't lose her! She's in her room. I was hoping she'd come back downstairs. She was pretty upset when she ended her call."

Edwin's teasing smile faded from his lips. "What happened?" he asked, sliding into a seat next to Sarah.

Sarah shrugged her shoulders. "I don't know. I didn't eavesdrop on her conversation. I noticed when she finished that her frame of mind had changed."

"Was she angry? Scared?"

Sarah struggled to find the right words to describe the silent mood that had engulfed them on the way back home. "She was *shaken*," she explained. "I didn't want to pry, so I tried to bring up any subject that might boost her spirits. But she didn't say a word the whole way back. She didn't cry or anything, but it was obvious the phone conversation left her reeling."

"As soon as the girls got home, Grace went straight to her room and hasn't left," Irma contributed. She gave Sarah a meaningful look as she continued, "So even though we may want to check on her, we're respecting her desire to be left alone."

"And sitting on our hands until she does come back down," Sarah grumbled.

Edwin saw once more the deep impact their new guest was having on his family, yet he wasn't surprised. His short time working with her and sharing the walk to and from work had been affecting him as well. The idea that the bright disposition Grace had earlier in the day had faded as the result of a telephone call didn't sit well with him.

And I learned a long time ago, from my own experiences, that the longer a person is allowed to wallow, the harder it is to get up again.

He drummed his thumbs on the table while he struggled with conflicted feelings. "Let's go," he said as he rose to his feet.

"Edwin, we can't go up there!" Sarah hissed as she rose to follow her brother.

Edwin turned to look at his sister and said, "We're not going to. At least, not like you're thinking. We're going to sit on our hands as Mother suggested, but we're at least going to make it memorable."

"What are you talking about, dear?" Irma asked as she followed them from the kitchen.

He shrugged and explained, "You both always said that ice cream was the balm for a woman's hurting soul ... so we'll go get some. And in the process, we'll show Grace another part of our charming little town."

Irma and Sarah stopped and stared at Edwin as though he had two heads. "What?"

"Who are you, and what have you done with my brother?" Before Edwin had a chance to answer, Sarah's hand flew up in mid-air to stop him. "Wait!" she exclaimed. "Don't answer that. Then you might change your mind." She turned and hurried up the stairs, calling Grace's name as she went.

Irma smiled as she watched her daughter hurry up the stairs then turned to face Edwin. She gave him a knowing look.

"What?" he asked.

"Nothing."

He gave a deep sigh and said, "I don't believe that for a minute. Say what you're thinking. You've got something on your mind, so you might as well get it off your chest."

She gave him a motherly pat on his cheek before saying, "It's good to see, that's all."

"What is?" Edwin whispered as he heard Sarah's and Grace's footsteps through the ceiling, although he already knew what his mother was implying.

Irma whispered in reply so that the two women at the top of the stairs couldn't hear. "It's good to see that she's affecting you too."

"You presume too much, Mother."

"I'm just telling it like I see it."

"So am I … two sulking women is hard enough to live with. I don't want to make it three."

He frowned as his mother simply smiled and led the way out of the house. *You're wrong, Mother. Nothing's changed. Some things are too hard to come back from. There's no fear of me losing my heart, or my head, again.*

THIRTY-TWO

Bobby arrived at the auto repair shop early. He had hoped to beat Henry in and get a head start on things. Although he couldn't do anything to help with Henry's problems over Catherine and Natalie, he could at least help with the shop.

But Henry had beaten him there.

"You know," Bobby said as he entered the garage, "it'd be a whole lot easier to help you if you'd give me the chance to." He didn't hide his frustration. "I may not be able to help you in other aspects of your life, but this ..." he paused to indicate the cars around him, "this is something I can handle."

Henry didn't pause in his frantic movements as he worked at the side table. He only spared Bobby a single glance before refocusing on his work.

Bobby studied Henry. To say that Henry looked rough was an understatement. A short beard now splayed across his face. There was an emptiness in his eyes that Bobby knew only Catherine could fix. Henry's clothes were dirtier than usual, especially considering how early in the day it was. The darkness under his bloodshot eyes told Bobby that Henry hadn't been sleeping well.

"What time did you get up this morning to be here so early?"

"That," Henry said as he prepared to do repairs underneath one of the automobiles, "would mean a person actually had to go home—"

"You *spent* the night here?" Bobby interrupted.

"In the office, actually."

Bobby shook his head and said, "You need to seriously get yourself

267

together. Sleeping at the shop, allowing yourself to look like a lumberjack ... none of this is helping."

"I know that," Henry whispered.

"You look awful and smell even worse."

"I know that too."

Bobby shook his head. "Is the coffee on?" he asked as he moved toward the office.

Henry didn't respond but rather stood in the garage to wait for Bobby's reaction. He closed his eyes, expecting Bobby's cries of disgust and disappointment to soon reach his ears. When the sounds didn't come, he opened his eyes to find Bobby standing in the doorway, holding a shattered coffee mug.

"How bad?" Bobby asked seriously.

Despite the turmoil in Henry's life, relief coursed through him. Bobby understood. "You saw the state of the office," he replied.

"How often are they?"

Henry shrugged and answered honestly, "They were practically nonexistent before Catherine left. They were under control. Now, I have them every few days or so."

Bobby hesitated and said apologetically, "I don't know what to say."

Henry shook his head. "There's nothing *to* say. My demons came back, and I have to find a way to deal with them. End of story."

Bobby processed Henry's words. He knew all too well the demons of war. He supposed every soldier did. "Henry, is there anything—"

"The nightmares in my head will stop when the nightmare I'm currently living ends."

"Speaking of which," Bobby threw the broken coffee mug in the trash as he came back into the garage, "you know, eventually, Natalie is going to come back around, if she hasn't already."

"I haven't seen her since that night. She left knowing full well that she wasn't welcome back in my home ever again."

"Well, you'll see her again. She'll either come back to apologize or to pursue you further, especially when she finds out about Cat."

"You're not helping."

"I'm trying, Henry. Don't forget, when she does come back around, we've got an objective, okay? If you want Cat back, we need Natalie here."

It took every ounce of self-restraint not to throw a punch at his friend's face. *He has no idea what it's like. He's not running the risk of losing the person he loves.*

The sound of the front door opening broke into his train of thought. "Hello?" a woman said.

Henry turned to Bobby as they recognized Natalie's voice. "Did you set this up?" Henry accused in a harsh whisper.

"No, I swear it! I'm as creeped out by the timing of her arrival as you are." Bobby turned to the garage entrance and called out, "Be right there!" Then, turning back to Henry, he asked, "Do you want me to tell her you're not here?"

"No," Henry said with an edge in his voice. "You said it yourself—she needs to be here if I want to find out the truth and get Catherine back home." He wiped his hands on a rag and gave Bobby a quieting glance. "I'll take care of this."

Natalie wasn't sure what to expect when she finally found the courage to enter Henry's repair shop. She assumed he'd still be angry at her, but she never imagined the hollowed-out shell of a man who appeared before her now. A short beard covered his jaw, and the empty look in his eyes sent a shiver down her spine.

Not quite empty, though ... no, there's no mistaking the hate glaring back at me.

Guilt seized her, and it was a struggle to bring a smile to her lips. "Hello, Henry," she greeted him.

Henry offered no reply.

Natalie swallowed, understanding fully that she was to blame for what happened at his home. However, she didn't want to dwell on that. "David's been asking to come see you," she said.

"Where is he?" Henry asked, making sure not to come any closer to Natalie. He was barely keeping his anger in check.

"I didn't want to bring him by until I got the opportunity to apologize and see how things were with you."

"Was that your apology?" he asked brusquely.

"No." Her voice was barely above a whisper as she continued, "I feel terrible, and I want to apologize for any misunderstanding my carelessness might have created."

Henry raised his eyebrows in disbelief. "*Misunderstanding*? Is *that* what you'd call it?"

On the verge of breaking, Natalie could only nod. His sharp and undeniably bitter laugh cut into her. He was hurting, and it pained her to know she was the cause.

Susan, I hate you for what you're making me do.

"I want to apologize to Catherine too," she continued. "Although I completely understand if she doesn't want anything to do with me."

"With *you*?" There was no mistaking the anger in his eyes now as he anguished, "She doesn't want anything to do with *me*."

I know ... I feel terrible. "Really? Well, maybe if she gave me the opportunity to explain—"

"You don't get it, do you? She's not here. I haven't seen her since that night. My foolish decision to let you into my house resulted in Catherine leaving town."

Heartache crossed his face before he regained his composure.

"But where is she? When will she be back?" she asked meekly.

"Look at me, Natalie. Do I look like I know?" Henry pointed to his disheveled state.

There, Susan! She's gone. Are you happy now? Will this be enough for you? It had better be, because Natalie didn't know if she could bear to see Henry like this again.

When her bottom lip started to quiver, Natalie wasn't acting. "I-I'm so sorry, Henry. I never meant for any of this to happen."

Henry looked doubtful but refrained from speaking his mind. Bobby's and Michael's warnings about needing her around to make a mistake entered his thoughts.

Easier said than done. I want nothing more than to yell at her to leave my life, permanently. But if David truly is my son ... I can't allow that to happen, can I? Frustrated that so much remained beyond his control, he felt his body sag in defeat.

"Wait," he said as she turned to leave.

"Yes?"

He took a deep breath. "Look, no matter what's happened between us adults, David shouldn't be penalized for it. If David's asking to see me, he can."

Natalie's smile was genuine even as she thought, *He's such a good man. That's what makes this all the more difficult to do.* "Really?" she tentatively asked.

Henry gave a small smile as he nodded. "Really. But not here. There's nothing fun for him to do here. There's a park where I could meet you both."

The park is a great place to watch the fireworks in July ... Catherine showed me that once.

He only hoped that he'd get the opportunity to watch them with her once again.

* * *

"So, he confirmed she's gone?" Susan asked after Natalie had reported her recent encounter with Henry.

"Yes," Natalie said, sickened by the smile she saw on Susan's face.

"This is great news. You've done a great job so far."

"So far?" Natalie said in horror. "Wait, no. This ends now. I came and did what you asked. I accomplished what you wanted: Catherine's gone. He doesn't know where she is. This is *exactly* what you wanted." She pounded her fist on the desk in front of her for emphasis.

"You're right, dear cousin," Susan practically purred. "In any other circumstance, you'd be right. But this is Catherine McKinney. She's a fighter. She doesn't give up easily, and she's not the type to walk away."

"Well, that proves you don't know her like you thought. She's *gone*, Susan."

Susan tapped her chin and thought out loud, "But for how long? Once she reaches out and communicates with Henry, which she's eventually bound to do, will she forgive and forget this one occurrence?"

Natalie watched with dread as Susan's face became more animated. *No. No. No.*

"You've laid a good foundation, Natalie. But I want to make sure it's solid. If you leave now, she'll know it was a hoax. Then all of your hard work would have been for naught."

271

"How much longer do you want this to go on, Susan? I've destroyed a relationship, and now I'm destroying what's left of a man."

Susan laughed as she replied, "Oh, Natalie, you are quite dramatic when you want to be. And while I appreciate it sometimes, now isn't one of them." Her voice suddenly grew stern as she demanded, "You're going to finish this."

Natalie, weary of the continued scheme, glared at Susan and threatened, "I could tell him everything, you know."

"And I could locate Edward."

Natalie felt stung by Susan's threat. "You wouldn't," she whispered in fear.

"Try me."

"Double what you're paying me, and you'll buy my silence." She put on the bravest face she could muster and added, "I can fight too."

Susan's eyes narrowed. "You're costing me."

"Nothing more than what this is costing the people involved."

"I'll pay you more, but only if you stop growing a conscience. It makes you weak."

You agreed to my demands, Susan ... but somehow, I don't feel this is a victory.

THIRTY-THREE

Olivia stood at the kitchen sink, lost in thought as she stared out the window. She gently rubbed her growing stomach as she gazed out at the open field behind the house. She and Bobby had been married there, and Olivia found herself welcoming the memories of happier times at the McKinney home. She loved this house and the memories tied to it. It had been more than generous of Catherine to allow Olivia's family to continue to stay here.

We owe her so much. She's given us all more love and patience than we deserve. She's always been there for us, and now, when she's hurting the most, we can't get to her. Olivia shut her eyes to keep her tears at bay. No one had heard from Catherine since the disastrous night she had abruptly ended the calls to both her and Michael.

"Daddy!" her son cried out from the living room at the sound of Bobby's car. She glanced down at the vegetables in the sink and realized she wasn't nearly as far along with dinner preparations as she should be. Even so, her heart wasn't in it enough to prompt her into action. When Bobby entered the kitchen with Caleb in his arm, he found her studying the food.

Bobby saw that Olivia was out of sorts. He set his son at the table and placed a few of his discarded toys in front of Caleb so he could entertain himself. Bobby came up behind his wife, wrapping his arm around her while planting a gentle kiss on her neck.

"Can I help with dinner?" he asked.

Olivia shook her head and replied, "No, I'm on it. It'll be a bit later than usual though." She moved out of his embrace and picked up a green bell pepper.

Bobby seized it and gently set it back in the sink. "How was your day? Are you feeling all right?"

Even as Olivia nodded that she was well, tears filled her eyes. "Never better," she managed to whisper.

"You and I both know that's a lie," Bobby said as he caught a tear as it escaped down her cheek.

"How's Henry?"

Bobby knew Olivia wasn't trying to change the subject. What bothered his wife was the same thing that bothered his best friend: Catherine. He glanced over his shoulder to see that Caleb had already vacated his chair and had gone to play in the living room before responding, "Not so good. He's working, but it's nearly nonstop. I made sure he left the shop today because he was in desperate need of a shower. He's trying to be patient and follow Michael's suggestion to bide his time and wait for Natalie to do something that might reveal anything sinister. But he's unraveling."

"It'd be so much easier to cope with if we would hear from her again," Olivia responded. She didn't try to stifle the tears now. "It kills me that she's in so much pain over a misunderstanding."

Bobby nodded in agreement, adding, "If she could see him now, she'd have no doubt he loves her."

"You should invite him over for dinner."

"I'm lucky if he takes a lunch break at work."

"Ask anyway."

"I will." Bobby grabbed Olivia's hand and pulled it to his lips. "Now, do you want to tell me what else is bothering you?"

Olivia gave a small shrug of her shoulders and said, "I'm just being selfish."

"Humor me."

Olivia allowed Bobby to guide her to the kitchen table. She waited until her husband sat across the table from her before explaining, "When you all were in Europe fighting, things were tough here. It wasn't life-and-death or anything, but I was pregnant and unwed."

Bobby reached across the table and took her hand. The pain he felt over her experience was evident in his voice as he said, "I'm so sorry about that, Liv. I wish—"

"It's okay," she interrupted. "What I'm trying to say is that Cat was here for me. She was here for every step of Caleb's pregnancy. It's what brought us together. I'm scared that this child will be born and Cat won't be here for it." She rubbed her stomach for emphasis.

Bobby hated seeing the sadness in his wife's eyes. "This whole thing is a mess," he commented. "Henry's in a terrible situation—he's being forced to face skeletons from his past, and he needs Catherine to help him face them. You need your best friend. And Catherine ... I can only imagine the pain she must be feeling to think that Henry, the love of her life, was unfaithful to her."

Olivia nodded in agreement. "The child was never the issue, you know." Olivia spoke confidently, "As hard as it was for her, she was willing to accept that and move forward with Henry. She wasn't going to leave him because of his past."

"It's what she thought was happening in the present," Bobby agreed. He paused in contemplation before giving Olivia a determined look. "I have to believe this will all work out somehow, Liv. I don't know when Cat will come home, but I promise to do everything in my power to help make that happen."

Olivia gave him a small smile. "I know you will. And we can't forget about Michael. I've seen firsthand how he can pull Catherine from places beyond where any of us can reach."

"Well, then, with all of us fighting to bring her home, there's no way we can lose."

*　*　*

"That's the last of them," Michael said as he tossed a small notebook to his wife, who was seated at one of the club's tables. They had a few hours before the club opened for the evening, and Patricia had just dismissed the two new employees hired to clean the club. Although he was close enough to whisper to Patricia, he waited until the two employees had completely vacated the building before continuing, "I've telephoned every name in my uncle's address book that is affiliated with a club or dance hall in the cities that the northeast-bound train travels to."

"No luck?" Patricia asked as she motioned for Michael to join her at the table.

"She hasn't shown up at any of them yet."

Patricia thumbed through the pages of the notebook as she asked, "You're so convinced she will? She's hurting. I know that if I were in her shoes, I'd probably want to avoid all things that reminded me of Henry. Dancing, unfortunately, is one of those things."

Although Michael understood his wife's perspective, he shook his head in disagreement. "Maybe you would, but it wouldn't be for long. Dancing is in your blood, love. You wouldn't be able to stay away from it indefinitely. You'd simply find a way to channel any hurt and anger you'd be feeling to the dance floor." He gave a teasing wink as he added, "Believe me, my dear, I've seen it time and time again with you."

Patricia couldn't argue. "You're right about *me*. I hope your belief that Catherine is the same isn't misguided."

"It might take her longer to get there than it would you or me, but she'll get there eventually. She's passionate, in every temperament. She's learned how to channel that through dancing. It's only a matter of time before she's doing that again."

"And then what?" Patricia countered. "I understand the need to do something, for Henry's sake, but even you have to admit that calling dance clubs and providing a physical description of Catherine seems unlikely to be successful."

"You're right. That would be a complete waste of time."

She arched an eyebrow, silently demanding further explanation.

"I described her *dancing*. You and I both know her style leaves an impression. If anyone sees her dance, they would remember her."

"But they haven't?"

"No, but now I have several people eagerly anticipating when she finally does surface." He watched his wife rub her expanding stomach and momentarily forgot about his search for Catherine. "Come here. Prop up your feet on my knee and let me feel instant gratification at being successful at *something* today."

Patricia laughed and happily obeyed. She waited until he started massaging her feet before saying, "You're a good man, Michael. I'm sure Henry really appreciates what you're doing."

"I haven't told him what I'm doing. He's so desperate to have her back;

he'd be at my doorstep every day asking for updates if he knew the extent of my searching. The real struggle will be when we *do* find her."

"He loves her. Don't complain about that. You'd be doing the same thing."

"I'd be worse," he said as he lowered his head and kissed the top of her feet. He smiled when she let out a soft giggle and wiggled her toes. "But in all honesty, Henry, his son, and the events that *prompted* Catherine's departure aren't my main concern. How much tragedy and heartbreak can one person take before it destroys them? Catherine is like a sister to me, and my goal is to find her to make sure *she's* okay."

"You'll find her. I know you will. And if you do manage to bring her back to us, we need to double her wages. We've had to hire two people to replace her, and still, they aren't able to complete all the duties Cat was able to."

"You're not picking up their slack, are you?" Michael asked, his concern for his wife edging past his worries for Catherine.

"I'm not overdoing it."

"You're avoiding giving me a direct answer." He held up her feet, examined them closer, and said, "These aren't swollen from dancing, and I think this is from more than your pregnancy."

"I know my body better than you, Michael. I know how much I can handle."

Michael wasn't the type of person to beg, so when he spoke his next words, the plea disarmed Patricia from arguing.

"Patricia, you know how small the probability was for this pregnancy. As much as I want to forbid you to do work around here, I'm not that type of person. However, I'm begging you to think twice before doing anything that might jeopardize you or the baby. I don't want anything to go wrong. I can't—"

"Michael," Patricia interrupted as she pulled her feet from his lap and leaned forward to place her hands in his.

"Promise me you'll be careful," he countered quickly.

Patricia's heart felt ready to burst at seeing this rare vulnerability and fear in Michael. She rose to her feet, pulling him with her. Planting a kiss on his lips, she replied, "I promise."

"Thank you."

"Now I want something from you."

"Name it, love."

"I want another foot massage. What do you say we give my feet a *real* reason to swell up by taking me out on the dance floor for a couple spins before we open the doors tonight? It's been a while."

Michael smiled as he led her onto the dance floor by tugging her into a spin. "You just proved my point."

"What's that?"

"Dancing is in your blood. It's in Catherine's too. We have to be patient, but she'll find a dance floor. It's only a matter of time."

*　　*　　*

Bobby has to learn to lock that front door! Henry thought as he heard the chiming from the bell above the door. It was well past closing time, which would deter normal customers. It was too late for Natalie to be out with David, and Michael was working at the club—a place Henry hadn't visited since Catherine had left.

"We're closed for the evening," Henry called as he made his way to the front door. He hated the sound of hope in his voice. Even though he knew it wasn't Catherine, he couldn't stop wishing for her with each chime.

"Then you should lock your door," the voice replied with a hint of teasing.

Henry stopped the instant he recognized the woman's voice. Although he knew he had no reason to blame his current misfortune on her, a large part of him wanted to do exactly that. He forced himself to take the necessary steps to stand just outside the garage so that he could face his visitor.

"I guess I was wrong to assume customers could read the 'closed' sign in the window." Henry tilted his head to indicate the sign hung hurriedly by Bobby.

"Good thing I'm not a customer then." She smiled as she reached behind her and locked the door, adding, "But let me help you out."

Her actions sprung Henry into motion. "Oh, no you don't, Susan," Henry said as he hurried past her and unlocked the door once more. "I'm not having that."

Susan shrugged and gave him a smile. "Fair enough."

Henry turned to face her with crossed arms. "What do you want, Susan? Are you here to gloat?"

"Come now, Henry, give me *some* credit. Believe it or not, I heard about Catherine leaving some time ago. While I won't pretend to understand what you ever saw in her, it's clear that you saw something. I see how much you're hurting even now. So, I've purposely given you some space."

"And now you're here to try and dig your claws back into me again, is that it? Now that Catherine's out of the way, you're planning your next move."

That was exactly the plan, but Susan would never admit it to Henry. Instead, she gave him a pleading look and said, "Henry, please. I'm your friend. Just let me be your friend. No strings attached." Before Henry had a chance to avoid it, Susan placed a hand gently on his forearm. "You're hurting, and I want to help."

"And if I don't want you to?"

"Seriously, Henry, look at yourself. If Catherine were to come through these doors, would you want her to see you this way?"

As much as he hated to admit it, she was right about that.

"She fell in love with the strong, confident, handsome Henry whom everyone in this town knows and loves." She motioned to him as she continued, "She wouldn't want what you've become."

"And you do?" he asked with bitter sarcasm.

"Of course, I do, but that's irrelevant."

"When has your own personal desires not been pertinent to your motives?"

Susan gave him the warmest smile she could muster. "I'm here to help you heal, Henry," she explained. "That's all. Take my advice and go home … get cleaned up."

Henry knew her advice was reasonable, having already heard it from Bobby, but he didn't want to hear it coming from her. He wanted nothing to do with Susan, and he felt that by taking her advice now, he'd be opening himself up to Susan's plan.

There's no doubt she has one.

However, Henry was determined to quash her plans before they had a chance to take root. He was tired of her schemes and lies, and there was no way he was going to let her do anything to destroy his chance of getting Catherine back.

"How did you learn about Catherine, Susan?"

The question took Susan by surprise. "Why, I've become friends with Natalie. She was heartbroken over the misunderstanding at your home that night. She—"

"Let me get one thing straight," Henry pounced, "I love *Catherine.* No matter how long it takes, when she comes back—and she *will* come back—my heart will still belong to her. *I* will still be hers. If you're trying to come up with a scheme to use Natalie, David, or anyone else to try and worm your way back into my life, give it up now. You won't win."

A cold look passed across Susan's eyes before she forced a smile to her lips. "Henry, I'm appalled that you would think so poorly of me," she said with a small pout.

"You're not used to losing. Remember this, Susan, I know you better than most people do. I know how little good there is in you. You don't do anything unless you can profit by it."

Anger boiled inside Susan as Henry saw right through her. She had been a fool to believe that with Catherine now gone, the challenge of winning him would disappear as well.

Well, he's right about one thing: I refuse to lose.

She would have to alter her plans and play nice a bit longer than anticipated. However, Susan was up to the challenge. She hadn't worked this hard to lose Henry to the memory and hope of Catherine's return.

"Well then, Henry, dear, I look forward to proving you wrong. I don't know what Cat's said about me to make you think I'm a monster. You didn't always feel that way."

"Catherine didn't say a word, but your actions spoke volumes."

Susan knew angering Henry wouldn't help her. She gave Henry a remorseful look and said, "Henry, we all make mistakes and do things we wish we could change. I'm asking you not to hold my past against me and let me be the friend to you that I truly wish to be."

Her words were like a slap across the face. *Susan's asking what I asked of Catherine ...*

Susan watched the emotions play across Henry's face. She inwardly smiled in triumph, congratulating herself on choosing the right words. Already she was thinking of ways to use his relationship with Catherine to her advantage.

And if she ever does come back and learns that I've won Henry by using the structure of her relationship to him, the victory will be even sweeter. I can hardly wait ...

Thirty-Four

Tonight, there is silence. No gunshots, no fires, nothing but calming silence as Henry huddles in the bunker. For the first night in a very long time, the men seem to have a reprieve from the fighting. Henry isn't the only one to notice the change. Sitting next to him, Bobby can't help but give a soft whistle as he pens a letter to Olivia.

"Tell your wife I said 'hello'," Henry says. "And to your son too."

Bobby acknowledges him with a nod and replies, "Of course. It won't be long before the next little one comes. I'm hoping for a daughter this time."

Someone laughs, and Henry looks behind him to see Caleb standing there with a small smile on his face. Henry finds his lips moving to match Caleb's smile. He has no clue what Caleb is thinking, but he knows it will be humorous.

"You want to add to Olivia and Catherine's ranks? Are you crazy?" Caleb asks.

Henry laughs. This feels familiar to him. This feels right.

Bobby laughs too and says, "Maybe you're right. Those women are hard to handle at times."

Caleb crosses to Bobby and gives his shoulder a squeeze. "You're doing fine with her. Finish your writing. We'll leave you in peace."

Bobby loses himself in his writing as Caleb joins Henry. They back up against the trenches and look up to the sky, quietly studying the stars.

Finally, Caleb whispers, "You're doing a good job too, Henry."

Henry gives him a sideways glance before asking, "I am? What do you mean?"

"*My sister.*" *He chuckles and adds, "I don't know how you did it, but you managed to win her, didn't you?*"

"*I love her,*" *Henry replies.*

Caleb nods. "I know you do. Have you decided on a date for the wedding?"

Henry shakes his head and answers, "Not yet ..." Remorse fills him as he struggles to explain to Caleb what's happened.

"*I'm sorry I won't be able to be there,*" *Caleb says with evident sadness in his eyes.*

His words interrupt Henry's thoughts. "What do you mean you won't be there?" *he asks.*

Caleb solemnly nods to the length of the trenches and replies, "I'll still be fighting. I'll always be fighting." He gives Henry a sad smile. "You know I won't be going home."

Henry feels his chest tighten. "No!" he argues with Caleb. "Don't talk like that. Of course, you'll—"

"*How is she?*" *Caleb interrupts. "How is my sister doing? Is she as argumentative as ever?*"

Pain sears Henry as the sound of gunshots fill the distant air. He's running out of time. He reaches for Caleb's arm, but he's unable to grasp it.

"*How is she, Henry? How is my sister?*" *Caleb persists, as Henry unsuccessfully tries to touch him.*

"*Caleb, I don't—*"

"*How is she?*" *Caleb's voice sounds impatient. "You promised to protect her, so you should know.*"

Henry's eyes burn with frustrated tears as the sounds of battle grow louder. "I don't know, Caleb. She's gone."

"*Gone? Where'd she go?*"

He shakes his head, defeat in his answer. "I don't know. I lost her, and I can't find her anywhere."

Wild anger fills Caleb's eyes as he asks in disbelief, "You lost my sister? How did you lose her?"

Henry feels frantic as he tries to explain before the fighting gets any closer. "I ... there was a misunderstanding, Caleb. I have a son, and his mother tried to seduce me ... Catherine thinks we're together." His words sound confusing and desperate to his own ears, but he continues, "But we're not. I would never be unfaithful to your sister."

The anger doesn't leave Caleb's eyes, but hurt is now also present. "You promised, Henry," he whispers.

"I know! Believe me! I'm lost without her!"

A grenade lands near them, but Henry and Caleb remain standing in place. When the smoke clears, Henry is unharmed, but Caleb's body now burns, and blood covers him.

"Caleb!" Henry cries, once again frantically trying to reach Caleb and offer help. Henry can't touch him, and he watches in horror as Caleb painfully perishes. "No!" he cries above Caleb's own screaming.

He's losing Caleb all over again.

Henry's heartbreaking cry is so great, it momentarily silences Caleb. Even though Henry is unable to touch Caleb, Caleb has no issues reaching out and grabbing Henry by the shirt. Despite the pain he is obviously experiencing, Caleb garners enough strength to pull Henry close so that they face one another, their noses nearly touching.

"Find my sister, Henry," Caleb says, gritting his teeth as he tries to keep the pain at bay.

"I'm trying, Caleb." His heartache at losing Caleb deepens as it focuses on the loss of Catherine. He bursts into tears as Caleb places his forehead against his own.

"We're seeing too much of each other, Henry. You need to stop coming here. You need to find her. Don't stop trying ..."

Caleb begins to fade, and his grip on Henry loosens. He's going to lose Caleb once again.

"Promise, Henry."

He lost Catherine, and he knows he'll die trying to find her. Henry doesn't need Caleb's prompting, but he nods his head and promises, "I swear, Caleb, I'll find her. When I do, I won't lose her again."

If Caleb responds, Henry doesn't hear him. Explosions appear all around and heat covers his body. He looks down to find his hands slick with blood. Despite the probability of injury, he knows the blood isn't his. He looks up, hoping to catch one last glimpse of his brother-in-arms, certain the blood is Caleb's.

He finds Catherine there instead.

"Catherine!" he yells as he frantically tries to reach her.

Henry woke as his body made contact with his bedroom floor. His bedclothes tangled about him, he sat up, searching about in a mad frenzy. Only when he scanned his hands by the light of the small lamp on his nightstand did he realize that Catherine's blood wasn't covering him.

She's not injured. Caleb's not here. There's no war.

As he tried to calm his rapid breathing, he closed his eyes and focused on the backs of his eyelids. He was covered in a sheen of sweat, brought on more from fear than heat.

The dream had taken him back to the trenches in Europe. But it was neither the reminders of what he had faced while fighting there nor Caleb's repeated death that disturbed him. Seeing Catherine in his nightmare, injured and bleeding, brought on a whole new level of terror inside him. Had Catherine still been in town, he would have immediately gone to her house to see for himself that she was safe, despite the late hour.

But she's not there, and I have no way of knowing if she's safe.

Therefore, even though he was now wide awake, the fear from his nightmare refused to subside. He leaned his head back to rest it against the wall after pulling her photograph down from his nightstand. He held the small photograph originally intended for Caleb in his hands and gently brushed his thumb across her image.

"Where are you, Catherine?" he whispered, his voice growing rough with emotion. "If I can't come to you, please come home to me. I'm helpless without you."

Helpless, but not hopeless.

Ashamed he hadn't thought of it sooner, he closed his eyes and prayed.

Thirty-Five

Edwin stood at the window of his study, watching his sister and Grace help one of the neighborhood boys rake up the season's last fallen leaves from their backyard. He had already paid the lad for his services. When Sarah had argued that the payment was too little for the job, Grace had simply gone outside, located a second rake, and helped. Sarah, seeing this as an act of protest, had valiantly joined them. Grace had found a way to turn the chore into a game, and the three individuals' laughter drifted through the air.

"You could go join them," his mother commented from behind him.

"Not today," he replied with a small shake of his head.

"I take it your leg is bothering you?"

Edwin didn't acknowledge his mother but continued to watch the scene play out in his backyard.

"With the change in the weather, it's completely understandable," Irma tried again as she entered the study. When her words still didn't elicit a response, she let out a sigh. "You know, Edwin, you mask your pain so well, no one would be able to tell you'd suffered an injury."

"Then I see no need to bring it up," he quipped.

Irma bit her lip to keep from speaking further. They then watched as Grace led the small entourage to the next-door neighbor's house to commence raking up their yard as well.

"What is she doing?" Edwin whispered more to himself than to his mother.

"The same thing you'd be doing if you were able to be out there," Irma said with a smile. "The widow Mrs. Betts is too old to do the yardwork herself. Grace—"

"I know what she's doing. Perhaps I should have asked *why* she's doing it." Although he spoke to his mother, his eyes never left the yard. "It seems that Grace is here because she was trying to escape *something*. Even though she's been here long enough to gain employment, I can only assume the stay is still temporary. She hasn't ventured much beyond work, church, our home … basically, our company. Surely, she realizes something like that," he paused and inclined his head toward the neighbor's yard, "will undoubtedly create a connection beyond us."

"Just because she keeps her distance with you doesn't mean she's doing that with everyone else." Irma gave Edwin a sidelong glance before continuing, "Or maybe that's what has you so miffed. She's letting down part of her guard to people other than you."

"You speak nonsense, Mother."

"Maybe," she said as stretched up to give her son a soft kiss on his cheek. "But at any rate, they'll be in soon, so I'd best get some hot tea ready for them when they finish." She headed for the door but added before she exited the study, "Getting Grace to tear down some of her walls might be easier for you if you tear down your own too. She won't care that you were injured—"

This time, Edwin did nothing to soften the harshness in his tone as he said, "If you'll remember correctly, Mother, I stopped caring what others thought about me some time ago."

Edwin did not follow his mother to the kitchen to greet the raking party. Nor did he choose to join them later at dinner. While he would never admit it to anyone, especially his mother, his injured leg bothered him with the day's hint at the oncoming winter. His injury had given him no grief worth mentioning since Grace's arrival, but the change in the weather had more than made up for his temporary reprieve from pain.

It shouldn't be any of her concern. I shouldn't care whether she knows … But it irked him that he did.

Now, with his family and Grace finally retired to their rooms for the evening, he went downstairs to the kitchen. He wasn't expecting to find

Grace on the other side of the kitchen door, coming in from the back porch.

It was evident that she was as surprised to see Edwin as he was to see her. She stood inside the kitchen with an arm full of firewood. Even in the kitchen's low light, Edwin could see her reddened cheeks. "Grace! What are you doing?" he demanded, forgetting about his injured leg and hurrying to relieve her of the firewood.

"Your mother said you weren't feeling well," Catherine explained, unwilling to release the wood to him. "It's getting cold outside, and I figured that your mother, and you too, might benefit from a warmer house tonight."

"And you thought it best to do this late in the evening, *after dark*?"

"No," Catherine argued. "Although you all tolerate some of my assistance, I thought this task might be met with opposition. So, I waited until I thought no one would be awake to protest and try to stop me."

"That didn't work out for you, did it?" Edwin refused to let her see how touched he was by her thoughtfulness.

"Just let me finish the job, Edwin."

He shook his head. "Nonsense. I'm here with empty arms. Let me at least carry a portion of them, all right? My mother would never forgive me if she saw you doing a man's job while I looked on."

Catherine gave him a skeptical look.

"I'm not budging. I can jerk them from your arms, or you can give them to me willingly."

Although it was a short walk to the fireplace in the living room, Catherine was too cold to argue any further. She gave a brief nod and shifted the majority of wood to Edwin's arms, her body relieved for the help.

Holding the door open for her, he said, "After you, Grace."

Catherine made her way to the fireplace as quickly as her cold legs permitted. Once there, she knelt and hastily dumped the logs into the fireplace in order to relieve Edwin of his load. Although she wasn't quick enough to take the firewood from him, she was quick enough to notice that the few steps he took to close the distance between them came with a noticeable limp. "Edwin, you're limping!" she exclaimed with concern.

"It's nothing," he said dismissively. He deliberately turned his back to her as he placed his portion of the firewood into the rack beside the fireplace. As he knelt down, pain shot through his leg, but he gritted his teeth to keep from grimacing. When he straightened back up, he turned to find Grace scowling at him.

"You're injured." She stood with her arms crossed and a disapproving look on her face. "You shouldn't have carried—"

"It's nothing."

"You were fine yesterday. When did you injure yourself?"

"It's not important," he replied, not bothering to hide his irritation.

"Of course not, but it apparently *did* keep you behind closed doors for the day."

"Well, while we're on the subject of injuries, how about yours?"

"Excuse me?" Panic seized Catherine as her hand involuntarily went to her waist to cover the scars Robert had given her.

Did he see them when I unloaded the firewood? When else could they have shown?

Before Catherine had time to think, Edwin's hand shot out and grabbed her wrist. She instinctively tried to pull away, but Edwin's strength was too much for her. He twisted her arm and tugged at her already pulled-up sleeve to reveal her forearm. Red welts and scrapes covered it.

He studied them carefully before raising his eyes to hers and asking, "From the firewood?"

She could only nod. He still held her arm, and the warmth from his hands seeped through her. She closed her eyes, willing the rest of her body to warm up too.

Edwin then seized her other hand. If he saw the welts on that arm, he ignored them. "Your hands are as cold as ice, Grace. Why didn't you wear a coat?"

"I don't have one," she responded. She politely tried to tug her hands free from his grip.

He held them tighter as he looked at her and replied, "No, you wouldn't have. You arrived with only the clothes on your back. I'd forgotten."

"I'll warm up soon enough," Catherine replied as a shiver went through her. "If you'll let me start the fire—"

"Of course, where are my manners?" He released one of her hands long enough to grab the afghan blanket resting on the nearby chair. In a single motion, he had the blanket draped over her shoulders and tucked under her chin. "Not used to this cold weather?" he couldn't help but ask.

Catherine sensed the deeper inquiry behind his question. She chose to answer his question with silence.

Tight-lipped, Catherine cast him a wary look. The sound of her teeth chattering ceased his interrogation. "Never mind, it doesn't matter," he muttered as he instinctively began to rub her upper arms. When she pulled her hands free from the blanket to blow on them, he grabbed them and guided her toward the chair the afghan had previously occupied.

"Stay here," he instructed as he turned to the fireplace. The angle at which Catherine sat allowed her to see Edwin's grimace as he knelt to start the fire.

"I can do it," she said softly.

Edwin ignored her. Only after the fire burned strong enough for its warmth to permeate the room did Edwin turn to face her. Catherine saw his lingering pain in the tightness of his lips as he stood up. When he took a step toward her, he stumbled.

The pain blinded him and chased away any other thoughts. When it subsided, Edwin found Grace at his side, her arms already reaching out to support him. At first her look of concern angered him, but the gentleness in her touch as she placed her cool arms around his waist to steady him disarmed him.

Edwin stared down at her with a storm of emotions in his eyes. Catherine could easily read the pain and anger present in them, but there also seemed to be something deeper. It left her unsettled. She didn't know how long they stood like that, but when she suddenly felt his arm fall to her waist and tighten around her, something shifted in his eyes.

"What can I do?" she whispered, not daring to move and cause him further pain.

Don't let go. The thought broke through without warning, sobering Edwin instantly.

Despite the pain in his leg and the risk of falling flat on his face, Edwin pulled free from her embrace. Despite her cold state, the warmth that had radiated through him at her touch wasn't something he wanted. "Next time you decide to do anything like this again," he said as he pointed to the firewood, "wear a coat. If nothing else, I have one hanging behind the back kitchen door. Use that. It'll keep you warm and protect your arms." He turned away from her and began a concentrated walk to the stairs. It took all his effort not to limp.

When he reached the base of the stairs, he glanced over his shoulder to find Grace where he had left her. It was clear she saw through his attempt to hide his injury. Behind her, the fire had started to blaze.

"Bringing in the firewood ... it was a thoughtful gesture. Thank you, Grace."

She nodded.

It was enough for him. "Good night."

Catherine watched him slowly climb the stairs. The earlier look in his eyes left her unsure how to reply. Only after she heard his footsteps fade and his bedroom door close did she find her voice and reply, "Good night, Edwin."

* * *

From behind her coffee mug, Catherine sat at the table and watched Edwin move about the kitchen. Slightly warmer temperatures and a full night's sleep had made a world of difference for Edwin. There was no limp in his gait. He even offered smiles for his family, who sat on either side of Catherine, discussing their plans for the day. He gave Catherine a brief greeting as he sat down across from her.

"You seem ..." Catherine began, searching for the right word as Edwin's eyes narrowed in warning, "*improved*."

Sarah and Irma paused their conversation to gauge Edwin's response. They both understood that Edwin's injury was an off-limits subject. In the past, when either Irma or Sarah had tried to discuss what had happened to him, Edwin would normally leave the room. Would he do the same today?

Edwin forced a smile to his lips as he replied, "With today's warmer weather, I could say the same for you, Grace. You're really not used to these colder temperatures, are you?" *Oh, yes, Grace, two can play at this game.*

Catherine and Edwin held each other's gaze, neither wanting to respond.

"And that, my friends, is what we call a stalemate," Sarah said, chuckling as she stood up from the table. "Well, I'm off to work. Are you sure you don't want me to walk you to the church, Mother?"

Irma's eyes gleamed as she watched the two still engaged in a stare-down, and she gave a dramatic sigh. "Just when it was getting interesting. I'll come with you, Sarah. Let me grab my coat from my bedroom."

"I'll get it for you," Edwin muttered. He quickly abandoned the table and followed Sarah into the living room, leaving Catherine alone with Irma.

Catherine waited until he was out of earshot before saying, "Last night, after you and Sarah went to bed, I was still awake when Edwin came out of his room. He had a noticeable limp, but he wouldn't let me help him. He wouldn't tell me what had happened. And now, he acts as though he never had an injury. I *know* what I saw."

Irma's lips thinned as she glanced at the door, expecting her son to re-enter the kitchen any minute.

"Irma, I wouldn't be concerned if it was a simple scratch or bruise. But he was in obvious pain last night."

Irma reached over to give Catherine's arm a comforting squeeze. "I appreciate your concern, Grace. You have such a caring heart. But this … let it go, dear. If Edwin wants you to know, he'll tell you. It's his story to share, not mine."

Catherine had no argument to offer. As private a person as she was, going so far as withholding her true name from them, she couldn't hold it against Edwin for keeping his own secrets. *Besides, finding out his story would most likely cost me mine.*

* * *

Two weeks passed, bringing colder temperatures than Catherine had ever experienced. Having already borrowed so much of Sarah's clothing, Catherine had refused to borrow a heavy coat from her as well. While she had received paychecks from her new employer, Catherine had saved all but the bare minimum to send home to Olivia and Bobby. They were taking care of her house while she was away, and she wanted to make sure they didn't have to use their own money for any repairs. She had only recently sent them the first payment, and Catherine planned to call them soon to ensure they had received it.

The idea of calling Olivia sent waves of anxiety through Catherine. She missed home. She missed Olivia, Bobby, and little Caleb crowding around her kitchen table for meals. She missed Michael and his bluntness. She missed their dance lessons. She missed how he knew how she felt about things before she did. She smiled at the idea of telephoning them. Yet if she telephoned any of them, she'd be forced to deal with Henry.

She missed *him* most of all.

Henry. Even now, as she sat curled up in a chair in front of a blazing fireplace in a house miles from Henry, he still consumed her thoughts. Although it was never easy, Catherine was able to keep memories of him at bay while she was in Irma's, Sarah's, and Edwin's company. It was only at night, and in the rare moments like this when she was left alone, that she couldn't keep the memories from overpowering her.

Although the memory of discovering Natalie at Henry's home, in the nightgown he had purchased for *her*, was what normally strengthened her resolve to stay away, it wasn't painful enough to prevent the happier memories from seeping through. The way his arms had felt around her, the way his eyes had shined when he smiled at her, the way he had incessantly teased her, and the way his kisses had claimed her as his own lacerated her heart in ways their last encounter never could.

"Oh, Henry," she whispered as she stared into the warming fireplace. The sound of his name on her lips released pent-up anguish, and a sob escaped her lips. She dropped her face into her hands, allowing the grief to consume her. She hated him. Her mind told her she needed to, at least. She *should* hate him …

But her heart told a completely different story. *Admit it, Catherine, after everything that's happened … after all he did to you … you still love him. You're pathetic.*

Frustrated at herself, Catherine flung the cover she'd been curled under across the floor. It landed at Edwin's feet as he entered the living room from the kitchen. Catherine gasped as she realized he could have witnessed her distress. "I didn't realize anyone was home," Catherine explained as she jumped to her feet to retrieve the blanket.

"I just got back," Edwin said, obviously surprised by Catherine's actions. "It's like you were waiting for me before pouncing."

"I thought you were shopping with your sister and mother."

"I was. But they tend to make it an all-day event. Once I have what I need, I don't linger."

She hurried over to him and picked up the tossed blanket with haste. "I'm sorry, I shouldn't—"

Edwin grabbed her upper arm, forcing her explanation to fade from her lips. He turned her to face him. "You've been crying," he commented, his face folding into a frown as he studied her face.

"It's nothing," she replied, wiping at her face with her sleeve.

"I don't believe you." Without thinking, he used his free hand to help to wipe away her tears. New ones formed from this act of kindness. "What is it?"

It had been too long since a masculine hand had brushed away her tears. With Edwin's unexpected touch, Catherine felt the loss of Henry even more. As Edwin caught the next wave of tears, she felt his hand tighten on her arm.

If he offered to hold me while I mourn, would I let him?

She tore her eyes away from Edwin, more embarrassed by her wish to be held rather than by being found crying.

Edwin felt her stiffen in his hold and watched as embarrassment replaced vulnerability in her eyes. "I'm glad to see your leg is much improved," she whispered to him.

Edwin regarded her as he held her for a bit longer. *Fair enough, Grace. You win this round of secrets.* With a slight nod, he released his grip on her.

The break in contact allowed Catherine to collect her scattering thoughts and frantically push back the painful memories that had been forefront in her mind. Grasping at any bit of normalcy, she cleared her throat before asking, "Your shopping trip was successful?"

Edwin smiled at her choice of words. "Please don't call it that. You make it sound like a fun adventure. Although it's not something I do on a regular basis, it definitely doesn't fall into the fun category. I went out for the purpose of a single purchase." He held up his finger. "Wait here. I'll show it to you."

He left and returned from the kitchen holding a large box. He placed it on the sofa near the fireplace before taking a step back. "Open it," he said.

Curious, Catherine stepped forward and removed the lid. The box contained a cherry red, woman's winter coat.

Edwin smiled with satisfaction in seeing her reaction.

"Edwin, this is gorgeous. Sarah will love it."

"It's not for Sarah."

Catherine felt his eyes on her. "Your mother, then?" she asked.

"It's for you, Grace."

Grace slowly turned her face up to him. The warmth in his eyes took her by surprise and rendered her speechless. *Has he been standing this close the entire time?* Catherine swallowed, a sudden shortness of breath dizzying her.

"It's going to get colder before it gets any warmer, Grace," Edwin explained. "You need this."

"This is too nice, Edwin. I can't accept this."

He leaned past her to pull the coat out of the box. Holding it out to her, he said, "It's an early Christmas gift, Grace. One that you need."

"Edwin—"

"It's obvious you're from somewhere south of here ... I could pry more, Grace."

"Th-thank you," Catherine stuttered a reply, reaching out to take the folded coat from Edwin.

"That's better," he replied. However, rather than surrendering the coat to her, he flipped it open and held it out for her to step into. "Allow me."

Reluctantly, Catherine nodded and slowly shrugged into the coat. As she slid her arms into the sleeves, Edwin's hands lingered on her shoulders. A sensation leaving her confused and nervous filled her the moment he gently pulled her hair free from inside the coat's collar.

"It's lovely," Catherine whispered as she kept her back to him.

Even though she couldn't see him, he nodded in agreement. Unable to ignore the way her hair tickled his hands as they rested lightly on her shoulders, he offered, "I hope you like the color. There were other choices ... we can exchange it easily enough—"

"Why *did* you choose red?" Catherine asked, unable to face Edwin nor step away from his touch.

His response was so close to her ear, she felt his breath on her cheek as he answered, "It was the only color I could imagine you wearing. It seemed to scream your name when no others would." He turned her to face him. He appreciated how the coat flattered her before looking back into her eyes. "Red suits you."

Catherine remembered when she had worn a dress that nearly matched this coat's color. Michael had selected it for her dancing debut with the purpose of winning Henry's heart. Although the dress had been destroyed, the memories of Henry telling her how beautiful she had looked that night hadn't.

"Where are you, Grace?" Edwin asked, lifting her chin so he could focus on her face.

The sound of the front door opening saved Catherine from answering. Edwin quickly placed a safe distance between them as Sarah and Irma came into the house. Sarah took one look at Catherine and yelled at Edwin, "You gave it to her already? You're supposed to wait for Christmas!"

"Christmas is weeks away." Edwin's gruffness resurfaced, distancing himself from everyone in the room. "If she chooses to stay, she'll freeze to death if I wait until Christmas to give it to her."

"It's stunning," Irma said, observing Edwin and Catherine closely before commenting, "You did well, Edwin. The coat is perfect for her."

"Yes, thank you again, Edwin."

As she started to remove the coat, Sarah stopped her. "No! Let's go test it out!" She hurried over and grabbed Catherine's hand. "Let's go get some coffee. I'll tell you all about Christmastime in our little town and convince you to stick around long enough to see it. You can tell me about your own Christmas traditions too …"

Catherine failed to hear her as Sarah rattled on. At the mention of Christmas traditions, a new wave of homesickness swelled in her heart. *Christmas … have I really been away from home so long? I've stayed too long.* Time was supposed to have healed her heart by now. But if the state Edwin had found her in was any indication, her heart was a long way from being healed. The heartache of losing Henry was still too raw.

THIRTY-SIX

Catherine stared at the merchandise lining the shelves, trying hard to focus on the Christmas shopping she was forcing herself to do. Christmas would soon arrive. If the toys displayed in the storefront window and carolers singing at the street corner weren't proof enough, Sarah had attacked the decorating with gusto, making sure every available spot in the house had been adorned in red and green. Had it been any other year, Catherine would have been ecstatic to have a kindred spirit to celebrate the holidays with.

But not this year ... This year, it's too hard to celebrate.

This holiday season of hope reminded Catherine of everything she had lost. Gone was her bright future, gone were her hopes and dreams of a family, and gone was Henry's love. Although she had yet to call home, she'd been gone long enough for Henry to have moved on with Natalie. The break had nearly destroyed her. Even though Catherine was still with Henry in her dreams, in reality, having seen Natalie with Henry, Catherine had convinced herself that the woman who had Henry's child was the one who had Henry's future.

And that's not me.

Yes, she was still hurt and angry about their last encounter, but Catherine wasn't so blinded by hate that she couldn't recognize it'd been for the best. Although she would never intentionally try to sabotage Henry's relationship with his son, she knew her marriage to him would have done just that.

And that poor boy has been without a father for so long.

Catherine shook her head to clear her thoughts. She may have fled her home in a fit of anger, but the rash decision had been the right one. She was giving Henry, Natalie, and David a chance that they never would have had with her being in the mix.

Even though it was the right decision, it hadn't made the task at hand any easier. Catherine didn't want any part of Christmas. She wanted to hide herself in a room where self-pity was her only companion. While Edwin might allow that, Catherine knew Sarah and Irma never would. Even Catherine's employer, by granting a week of paid vacation between Christmas and New Year's Day, fed into the problem.

Perhaps it's time I leave. I could get a hotel room, figure out my next steps from there ... and completely crush Sarah's heart. Leaving now, after everything Sarah, Irma, and Edwin had done for her, would be insulting. Catherine decided she should stay. She owed it to her new friends to spend the holiday with them at least. With the decision made, she looked around her with new determination.

"This isn't hard," she muttered to herself. "Just think like Liv."

By the time her shopping was finished, she was pleased with herself. While she tried to remain in Olivia's mindset for the gifts, Catherine had purchased items that she would have liked herself. For Irma, Catherine had purchased a bottle of lilac-smelling perfume. Its scent was soft enough that had Catherine owned any perfume, it would be this. The purchase for Sarah was a pair of small pearl earrings. They weren't flashy, but rather classic enough to go with any of Sarah's outfits.

Edwin's gift, however, was more difficult. Although ultimately pleased with her purchase, deciding on gloves for Edwin had been a slightly selfish choice. The memory of the day he had given her the coat, wiping at her tears with his hand, had left her unsettled. Before that day, Catherine could easily describe Edwin as a mostly private but sometimes grumpy person. He was fiercely protective of his family, and he'd destroy anyone or anything that threatened them. However, after Edwin had given Catherine the red coat, she couldn't help but feel that he was starting to include her in the protective circle he held for his family. The comfort she had felt in his touch startled her, and rather than try to figure out why, she had decided that distancing herself from it would be better. As a result, she had thought of gloves—something that would keep his skin from touching hers.

It's stupid, but it makes me feel better. She hoped they were impersonal enough. Her heart was already a tattered mess. She didn't need any further complications. As she left the store, the season's winds cut through Catherine, causing her to burrow into the warmth of her new coat.

She glanced down at the red material enveloping her body. She hadn't wanted to complicate things, but she had a feeling she already had.

*   *   *

Henry watched the traffic from the window in his living room. Although car headlights blurred by, the Christmas candles in the windows of his neighbors across the street held his attention. Christmas was one of Catherine's favorite times of the year.

This would have been our first Christmas together, as a couple. Instead, his fiancée was in a town lost to him. He had no clue where she was. No one had heard from her since her first phone calls to Michael and Olivia. He prayed without ceasing that she was safe. While a part of him understood Michael's reasoning for Henry staying put and figuring out what prompted Natalie to come now with a son he had no previous knowledge of, his patience for sitting on his hands grew thin. When he closed his shop for two weeks to celebrate the holidays, Henry planned to take a train ride north—and not return until he had found his fiancée. He was tired of waiting for other people. If he wanted Catherine back, *he* was going to have to be the one to fight for her. In Europe, no one had fought his battles for him, and he wasn't going to let that start happening now.

His bag was already packed and shoved in the back of his closet. Catherine's ring rested in its original case, adorned now with Christmas wrapping paper. If his constant prayer was answered and Catherine came home before Christmas, he planned to propose to her all over again. If she didn't, his plan was still the same but merely delayed. Regardless of when he saw her, a battle to regain her trust awaited him. He prayed that once he had the opportunity to explain the terrible day that tore her from him, her heart would see that his love for her had never faded.

They had faced so many trials to find each other. Their love was too deep for a misunderstanding to destroy it. Yes, Catherine was hurting. He could easily see why she would be. Hadn't his own jealousy surfaced when he had believed Michael was more a love interest than friend to Catherine?

The sight of another woman in a fiancé's bedroom would shatter anyone.

But that doesn't mean she's stopped loving me. When, not if, I win her back, I'm going to marry her so quickly she won't have another chance to escape me ... and I won't have another chance to lose her.

*   *   *

Catherine felt Edwin watching her as the two walked home. They had just finished the last day of work before the Christmas break. She couldn't help but feel saddened at the thought that she most likely wouldn't be returning in the new year. Although the work had been different from anything she had done before, she had enjoyed it. But once the holidays ended, she planned to be gone. She had been relying too heavily on this family to help her heal. She used to take pride in her independence. She needed to learn how to rely on herself alone for survival.

Edwin, on the other hand, was in better spirits now that their employer had suspended work for the holidays. Catherine could see his breath in her peripheral vision as he softly whistled a Christmas melody into the cold, early evening air. His step was lighter insomuch that Catherine found she had to quicken hers in order to keep up with him despite the slight limp that continually plagued him in the cold weather.

"You weren't this jovial at the office party earlier," Catherine commented as she pulled her new coat more tightly around her neck.

He turned and faced her as he began to walk backwards. "We were at work. Even if it was a party, it's *still* work," he explained.

He winked at her, and Catherine couldn't help but giggle. "Fair enough," she agreed.

"Besides, Grace," Edwin continued, "I think most anyone would be this happy when facing the beginning of a small vacation."

"You're right. I've never had an employer this generous with leave."

Edwin turned and stepped back to walk alongside Catherine once more before asking, "What kind of employer did you have before?"

"Ah, the fisherman is back!" Catherine teased.

"You're the one who brought it up!" he countered, giving her shoulder a small nudge with his own. He looked down at her, his body forgetting the coldness around him as her smile filled him with warmth.

Catherine was the first to shift her eyes away from his. Once she did, she expected Edwin to step a respectable distance away from her. He didn't, and as they continued to walk, their shoulders brushed several times.

Also aware of their nearness, Edwin needed to devise a plan to maintain it. He spotted a Christmas tree lot across the street that also sold wreaths and poinsettias. An idea struck him, and he pounced on it before giving it lengthy consideration.

"Let's stop and purchase a wreath for my mother. Do you mind staying out in the cold a bit longer?"

"Not at all. Irma would love the gift."

Without thinking, he reached for her hand, interlacing his fingers with hers as he escorted her across the street. As soon as they were safely across, Catherine freed her hand from his. Rather than draw attention to the action with awkward silence, she immediately began to study the wreaths on display.

It took her no time at all to find the perfect wreath for Irma. She placed herself directly in front of it before bringing Edwin's attention to it by declaring, "*This* one. There's no need to go any further in our search."

Edwin watched Catherine's face light up as she pointed to the wreath, and he couldn't help but feel pleasure. He had noticed her somewhat melancholy mood at the office party earlier in the day, and he had assumed it was due to homesickness. Knowing so little about what brought her here in the first place, he wasn't sure how easy it would be to lift her spirits—he only knew that he wanted to.

Edwin considered the other wreaths before answering, "That's the largest one."

"That makes it the best."

"*Of course*," Edwin said as he made an exaggeration of picking up the wreath, eliciting laughter from Catherine. Her laughter grew as he pretended to fumble under its weight and bulkiness.

"Edwin?"

The sound of the voice behind him caused him to stagger. He turned sharply, never in a million years anticipating seeing the woman now standing before him.

"It *is* you!" she exclaimed as she held out her hand for him, but he refused to take it.

Catherine tried to make sense of the exchange. Even though she had no idea who this woman was, it was evident that Edwin wasn't happy to see her. Catherine could sense hostility radiating from him.

"Vivian," Edwin could barely reply as anger and pain threatened to resurface.

"You look well," Vivian said as a man came up next to her and snaked his arm around her waist.

"Time heals."

Vivian was clearly uncomfortable with his response and took a moment before saying, "This is Carlyle—"

"I remember," Edwin quipped.

"Yes, of course," Vivian replied.

Catherine couldn't help but feel a small degree of sympathy for Vivian. Then Vivian turned her attention to Catherine, who was standing off to the side.

"Oh, excuse me, I didn't realize you weren't alone, Edwin," Vivian commented, her eyes focusing on Catherine.

"I'm not alone," Edwin replied.

When it was evident nothing more would be said, Catherine stepped forward and slid her arm through Edwin's in the hope of offering some form of support.

The ice that had filled Edwin melted a small degree as he felt Catherine give his arm a reassuring squeeze. She didn't know the history between him and Vivian, but it didn't matter. She was there for him. He pulled her closer to him and offered a warm smile before turning back to Vivian.

"This is Grace."

Vivian smiled and said, "It's a pleasure to meet you, Grace."

No, it obviously isn't. Catherine gave a quick nod before turning to Edwin. "Dear, should we make our purchase and head home? We wouldn't want to keep your mother waiting, and it is getting colder."

Catherine gave an internal smile as her words provided the desired effect. Edwin's brief glimpse of confusion soon turned to relief.

"Of course," Edwin said, taking her tucked hand and bringing it to his lips. "Forgive me." He turned to Vivian and Carlyle and said, "Merry Christmas." With the wreath in one hand and Catherine's hand in the other,

Edwin led her away from the couple without waiting for a response.

They purchased the wreath and were on their way home before either of them spoke.

"I suspect you want an explanation, or at least to hear the story about my acquaintance with Vivian."

With her arm still secured in Edwin's, she smiled and said reassuringly, "Not at all. We all have parts of our past that we want to remain buried."

"Ah, I should have known you would use this against me."

Catherine laughed and gave his arm a supportive squeeze before trying to remove herself from his nearness. "I'm only teasing. But seriously, I recognized in your eyes something I know all too well."

"What is that?" he asked as he tightened his hold on Catherine, unwilling to let her go. Edwin stopped in the middle of the sidewalk and turned to face her fully.

"Heartache. And everything that comes with it."

She understood, whether or not she meant to, she had just offered the root of her reason for being in this town. He slid her arm off his elbow and clasped her hand. "How badly did he hurt you, Grace?" he asked. Still holding her hand, Edwin lifted his hand up to her chin and forced her to look at him.

Catherine flinched at his words, and she immediately stepped back from him, removing her hand from his.

As pain flashed across her eyes, Edwin knew he had hit on the truth. "Grace, I—"

She held up her hand to silence him. "We all have scars on our hearts, Edwin. The thing is, heartache doesn't normally consist of stories that warm the heart and are eagerly shared. I'm not prying for your story. Don't pry for mine."

Edwin watched her walk away, more surprised by his own reaction than he was by her words. When this woman had entered his life weeks earlier, he would have relished having this small nugget of information. But he didn't care about that anymore. His desire to unearth her motives and determine if she was a threat to his family was gone. He hadn't asked her that question to pry. He had asked because the pain in her eyes, even in that brief glimpse, was still very raw.

And I want to help her heal.

The private admittance caused him to stumble as he hurried to catch up with her. The slight misstep caused his injured leg to twist, and pain unexpectedly shot through him. "Grace!" he called out. He extended his hand and grabbed a streetlight pole to prevent a fall.

Catherine was irritated at Edwin's constant investigation. She thought her earlier support in the presence of a woman from Edwin's past would have won her a bit of a reprieve from his interrogating questions. As she distanced herself from him, she felt her anger subside. Embarrassment at her quick and childish departure took hold so that when she heard him call for her, she was secretly relieved he had given her a reason to stop and wait for him to reach her. She took a deep breath before turning around.

"Edwin!" Catherine cried out as she took in the scene. The newly purchased wreath lay on the sidewalk, and Edwin stood braced against the pole, making her forget all about her frustrations.

While Edwin hated to publicly show pain, he appreciated the concerned look in the eyes of the woman who hurried back toward him. While he had once recoiled from her sympathy, his self-revelation now caused him to welcome it.

Catherine reached Edwin in no time and tentatively held out her arms to him. "Edwin, what happened? Are you hurting? What can I do?"

"I'm fine. Give me a moment ... can you hand me the wreath?"

Catherine scooped down and picked up the wreath. Rather than giving it to him, she slid her arm through its center. "I've got this."

Edwin slowly released his grip on the pole and stood with most of his weight on his good leg.

"Are you all right?" she asked.

Edwin didn't want her to hear the pain in his voice, so he merely nodded. Finally, he said, "I just need a minute, Grace."

Placing herself next to the side of his injured leg, she took his hand and slipped his arm around her shoulders, whispering, "Lean into me. I'll help you get home."

"I don't need—"

"Edwin?" Vivian called out as she and Carlyle approached them from behind. "Are you okay?"

Edwin bit his tongue to keep the forming curse at bay. *Of all people, I don't need Vivian here witnessing this.*

Catherine heard him take in a deep breath, and she thought of a quick response. "Yes, he's fine," she answered as she laced her fingers through his and snuggled into his side, lending support at the same time. She peered up at him and offered her sweetest smile as she explained, "I wasn't expecting … he's such a spontaneous romantic at times … when he tried to steal a quick kiss, I'm afraid I was a bit clumsy." She hoped the blush crawling up her cheeks was convincing. Turning to Edwin, she leaned in and lightly kissed his cheek. "Your toes aren't too bruised, are they?" she asked.

Edwin was speechless. Once again, Grace had come to his aid and saved him from embarrassing himself in front of Vivian and Carlyle. The warmth that had only begun to course through him at the tree lot now burst into a full flame in his blood.

This woman is incredible.

Briefly forgetting about the pain in his leg, he leaned his body against the pole and joined his free arm to the one already wrapped around her shoulders. He pulled her close to him. "No permanent damage," he managed to whisper huskily, his eyes solely on the woman in his arms.

"Of course," Vivian said, clearly uncomfortable. "Well, then, we'll be on our way. It really was good to see you again, Edwin."

Edwin kept his eyes locked on Grace. He nodded, not offering Vivian a verbal response.

A rush of emotions consumed Catherine. As she stood trapped in Edwin's intense gaze, she told herself that her actions were simply to help Edwin. She had wanted to protect him. Recalling how unwilling he had been to discuss his injuries with her, she had assumed he'd be even less willing to share them with someone who had obviously hurt his heart. She was surprised how easily Edwin had played along with the ruse. Yet now that Vivian and Carlyle were gone and Edwin still held her, she wasn't so sure they were both acting any longer.

"They're gone," Catherine whispered, unable to look away.

"Thank you," he said, maintaining his hold on her. The wind blew a strand of hair across her face, and Edwin reached up and gently tucked it behind her ear.

Pain lanced through her at the intimacy. Edwin's action felt so strange, yet so heartbreakingly familiar. Henry had performed the same act so many times, a part of her still felt that it was his task, and his alone, to perform.

Henry, even now, you still have my heart.

This realization forced Catherine to remove herself from Edwin's embrace as she replied, "You're welcome. Seeing as private as you are about your injury, I figured you wouldn't want Vivian to know about it."

As reluctant as he was to release her from his arms, Edwin's facial features hardened at her words. Memories of Vivian came hurtling back to him. "You're absolutely right," he agreed, offering his arm to escort her back home. "Let's get home. We have a wreath to deliver."

Catherine lightly slid her arm through his. When they took a step together, Edwin's heavy limp caused Catherine to forget about keeping her distance. She took his arm and slid it once more over her shoulders. "Lean on me."

"Grace, I'm—"

"The limp is less noticeable this way." Her tone was matter of fact and full of determination.

Edwin nodded. As he walked with his arm around her, he realized she was right. But he couldn't tell if it was because she was truly assisting him in walking or if it was her nearness that distracted him and made the old, cumbersome injury easier to bear.

THIRTY-SEVEN

"Before you tell me to leave, this was your mother's idea," Catherine said at the door to Edwin's study. "I suggested leaving you alone, but Irma wasn't having it. It was either me or having her come and most likely spoon-feed you." Without waiting for Edwin's reply, Catherine entered the study and placed the tray of food at the edge of the large desk he sat behind. "Don't worry, I won't try to spoon-feed you."

"Thank you," Edwin responded with a small smile. The near fall as he had left the tree lot had bothered him more than he liked to admit. As a result, he had retired to his study to elevate his leg in hopes of alleviating his injury from further aggravation.

"At the risk of sounding like your mother, can I get anything more for you or help with ..." She inclined her head in the direction of his leg.

"No, thank you."

An awkward silence followed as Catherine stood, her eyes focusing anywhere but Edwin. He watched her, silently appreciating her attentions, even though a day full of painful memories preceded it.

"Okay, well, I'm going to retire for the night. Once I'm asleep, know that I can't stop Irma from coming up to check on you." When Edwin smiled slightly, she added, "Good night, then."

Edwin waited until Catherine was at the doorway before stopping her. "Grace, wait. I'd ... I'd like to speak with you."

Catherine turned slowly and faced Edwin. She knew what he wanted to discuss. "You don't have to explain," she said.

Edwin motioned for her to take the seat across the desk from him. "No, you're right about that. If there's one thing I've learned since you came here, it's that people don't have to reveal anything they don't wish to."

The look in her eyes indicated she had understood his small jab.

He waited until she seated herself before he spoke again. "Vivian was once my fiancée. Carlyle was the final stake that drove us apart."

"I'm sorry."

An almost bitter laugh escaped his lips. "I'm not. While I was devastated at the time, I see now how fortunate I was to learn the type of person she truly is."

"I've heard that hindsight is 20/20."

"So they say … We didn't always live in town, Grace. Before the war, my family lived several miles outside of town. We owned farmland—"

"You're a farmer?" she asked in disbelief.

"*Was* a farmer. More, my father was a farmer with expectations that I'd share the passion and take over at some point."

"But you didn't."

"*Au contraire*, Grace. I did. My father's passing was completely unexpected. I was away at college when I received the call that he was gone. It had been a massive heart attack."

"I'm sorry. I know loss like that as well. I lost both of my parents in a car accident when I was still in high school."

Edwin nodded, choosing not to comment for fear it would make her realize she had disclosed a piece of her past. "I came home as soon as I could. Mother loved the farm. Devastated by my father's passing, my mother and sister needed my help. I had initially planned to take only a semester away from school to deal with everything. My plans were to sell the farm and move my family to the city. I had been so confident I'd be able to find a job after college that would earn enough to support them." He paused, taking a cup of coffee from the tray and swirling its contents before continuing, "But when I returned home, my father's presence was *everywhere*. I couldn't sell the place. Before I knew what I was doing, my education was suspended indefinitely as I poured my heart into making the farm a success." He looked over at Catherine and smiled, asking, "Would you give me your hand, please, Grace?"

Catherine didn't want to interrupt the progression of his story, so she readily offered her hand to him. He held his up next to hers, their palms facing up.

"See the calluses? Our past follows us, Grace. This is how I knew you weren't a city girl."

"Because you're not from the city yourself."

"Correct. So, I had come back home. But academics weren't the only thing I put on hold. I had met Vivian at school. We had been dating for nearly two years. Upon graduation, it had been our plan to find jobs in the city, marry, and live out our lives in luxury. I couldn't wait until graduation to ask for her hand though, and the summer before my father passed, Vivian and I became engaged. We were happy. She was extremely sympathetic at the loss of her future father-in-law. She even came with me initially to offer support to my mother and sister. But as my plan was to be away from school for a semester, she went back to school when the semester started, fully believing that I'd soon be following."

"But you didn't."

"No, I didn't. Like I said, the farm got to me; it got into my blood where it never had before. It took my father's passing for me to find that my passion was in the land. I'm sorry that he never saw that."

His pain at losing a parent was so apparent that Catherine couldn't help but reach out to him. She leaned over and grasped his hand with her own. He returned her squeeze but didn't relinquish her hand.

"When it became certain that I was going to stay at the farm for longer than originally planned, Vivian was livid. My actions affected her dreams, too, you see. She didn't want to be a farmer's wife. She wasn't cut out for that kind of life. I didn't blame her for feeling this way. The thing is, though, I was still so in love with her. The idea of her not in my life ... it was something I couldn't fully accept. She was my future, and I had wanted so badly to be able to do whatever was necessary to keep her. When the war broke out and the United States entered it, I saw my opportunity. Due to the immense success of our farm, I had a job essential to both the military and nation. Left and right, Vivian's and my college friends received draft notices. She cried nearly every day as she received news about another friend going off to war. My essential job kept my name from being selected."

"By having a farm, you could help your country and still be here, out of harm's way."

Edwin unconsciously began to rub the back of her hand with his thumb.

"Exactly. Because of my job, I'd be able to keep her from worrying. I thought for sure she'd embrace the idea of being a farmer's wife when she realized this. Unfortunately, I was mistaken."

Edwin carefully lifted his leg down and rose to his feet. He still held Catherine's hand and gave it a small tug so that she stood up next to him. She allowed him to lead her to the study's window and a nearby chair. After seating her, he turned and looked out the window. "I think Vivian had hoped that the war would do the opposite: pull me away from the farm. When I explained that I wouldn't have to fight in the war, she ... *changed*. She claimed that I was being a coward and using the farm to hide behind my responsibilities."

"Edwin, but you had more responsibilities than most people on your shoulders already. What would have happened to your mother and sister—"

"I'm afraid that in a moment of desperate weakness, I didn't think of them. I thought only of Vivian. I'll spare you the many horrible details, but know that in an effort to save my future with Vivian, I gave up everything else. I sold the farm, moved my family to this house, and enlisted in the United States Army."

Catherine felt her stomach plummet. Already Edwin's story held so much heartbreak and disaster, a part of her wanted him to stop telling it.

"Had I actually fought in the war, maybe my story would have ended differently. But as it happened, before I was able to report for boot camp, I was in an automobile accident. My leg was severely injured, and I nearly lost it. Needless to say, my military career ended before it began. I was hospitalized for a long time. Vivian visited me only once, in the beginning. I thought that, perhaps, it was the idea of hospitals that kept her from seeing me. Some people have those phobias, you know. When I finally was released—she had no way of knowing since she hadn't visited—I wanted to surprise her and show her how much I had healed. Apparently, she had done some healing on her own—or at least, *moving on* ... she had found her soldier."

"Carlyle."

His lips formed a grim line as he nodded.

"Edwin," Catherine rose from the chair as she spoke, "I'm very sorry."

"I'm just one life, Grace. I would have made no difference whatsoever in the war."

"Edwin, don't ever think that way." Thoughts of her own brother sacrificing his life to save a small child and Bobby prevented her from continuing.

"No," he agreed with bitterness in his voice, "you're right. Because my actions, the actions of *one man*, have damaged my family more than I could have ever imagined. So, one life may not be instrumental in helping, but it's certainly effective in *ruining*."

"Edwin—"

Edwin held up a hand to stop her. "Think carefully before you speak, Grace. I can tell you're itching to correct my point of view. But before you do, reflect on what brought you here, to an unknown town. Although you share so little about yourself and your history, I can't help but draw my own conclusions that I'm right with my theory. I'm guessing it wasn't an entire town that brought you to your knees."

Henry, Natalie, and their innocent son entered her thoughts as she unconsciously took a step away from Edwin. *He's right ... one person, one misguided deed, destroys everything.*

"I've taken up enough of your time," Catherine said as she turned to leave.

Edwin reached out to grab her arm and stop her. He waited until she turned back around and faced him before speaking. "I've struck a nerve." She pursed her lips, unwilling to acknowledge this.

I struck deeper than I thought. Edwin found himself softening at the evident emotions written on her face.

With contrition, he continued gripping her arm as he took a step to close up the space between them and apologize. "Please, Grace, pay me no mind. My bitterness will be gone by morning."

Catherine looked away from his intense gaze before giving a slight nod.

With an internal sigh, Edwin released his hold on her arm. "Thank you again, Grace, for what you did earlier today."

"It was nothing," she replied, her voice little more than a whisper.

"I think after hearing my story, you and I both know that's not the case at all." He gently tucked an errant strand of hair behind her ear.

The act triggered the memory of Henry performing this gesture and nearly brought her to her knees.

Edwin saw pain in her eyes and almost regretted touching her. "What you did, Grace, it was *everything*," he said.

Catherine refused to hold the gaze that bore into her. Instead, she gave a simple nod, not caring how he interpreted the act. When she reached the door to his study, she dared to look back at him and found his eyes bearing into her soul.

"Good night, Grace."

She couldn't help but smile as she offered him her own departing words, "You said it yourself, Edwin: the actions of a single person *can* help heal. Thank you for winning the argument for me."

THIRTY-EIGHT

Sarah sat at the kitchen table on Christmas Eve morning, sorting through various-sized pine cones she wanted to add to the Christmas wreath Edwin and Grace had brought home the day before. Her mother had loved it, but Sarah wouldn't let her hang it before she added the pine cones as a finishing touch. She had been up before the sun this morning, hoping to finish the project before everyone else came to breakfast. She had opened the kitchen door to find her brother already awake and gathering items to make breakfast.

He had been relieved to see her.

"What are you doing up so early?" Sarah had asked, unable to hide her surprise.

Edwin answered, "I thought I'd try to make everyone breakfast today."

"You'll poison us."

"Nonsense! I *can* cook."

"We can cook better, big brother. Besides, making coffee doesn't count."

"I'm not planning on only making coffee! I thought pancakes should be easy enough for me."

"Pancakes??" A third voice had entered the conversation.

"Grace … uh, yes … I was planning on surprising everyone with pancakes for breakfast."

The brief argument that had followed had been fun for Sarah to watch. Edwin had looked extremely embarrassed to be caught trying to cook for the family. Grace had practically begged for the honor instead. The result now had Grace preparing pancakes with assistance from Edwin.

Sarah pretended great concentration on the pine cones in her hands, but her focus was really riveted on the action before her. She observed her brother as he continuously stole glances at the woman beside him. He no longer regarded her with mistrust. Edwin's glances held an affection Sarah hadn't seen in him since Vivian.

Oh, goodness! Sarah dropped a pine cone to the floor at the realization. *Is my brother opening his heart again?*

Sarah's eyes focused next on Grace, who worked quickly, with an almost nervous energy.

She knows! Yes, Edwin's fallen for Grace, and Grace knows!

"Now for the cinnamon," Catherine explained. She saw the jar of cinnamon sticks on the other side of Edwin, whose hands were buried in the bowl of pancake mix. "I'll just reach—"

"Here, allow me," Edwin said at the same time. As they both reached for the cinnamon, their hands briefly collided.

Catherine pulled back as though burned, muttering an apology.

Edwin took her hand, placing the sticks in it.

The look they exchanged caused Sarah to clap her hands in delight.

Having forgotten Sarah was in the kitchen with them, they both turned in astonishment.

It was Sarah's turn to blush as she tried to cover her excitement by saying, "Um … cinnamon. You mentioned adding cinnamon. I've never had cinnamon pancakes, but they sound heavenly."

Catherine, who had been trying all morning to keep her emotions from the previous night at a distance from Edwin, was grateful for the distraction Sarah provided. "Yes," she explained, "that's the only way I ever made them at Christmastime. They were my brother's favorite. He used to beg for cinnamon other times of the year when I made them, but I refused. That's part of what makes them so special, right? Having them only at Christmas?"

Silence followed at this admission.

"You have a brother?" Sarah asked.

Catherine then realized her mistake. She had spoken too freely, having focused too much on trying to avoid Edwin. She found him staring at her, his eyes unreadable.

Oh, no. How am I going to backtrack this one?

"You can trust us, Grace," Edwin whispered.

Catherine saw only concern in the two siblings' eyes. Her heart seemed to break at the similarities between them. Missing her own brother more than words could describe, she turned back to the counter and managed to reply, "Had. I *had* a brother."

The silence that followed made Catherine want to scream. She hadn't meant to say anything. She didn't want to be the cause of any sadness in this household.

Sarah watched as Edwin extended his hand to comfort Grace, only to reverse course at the last minute. It was evident that his heart hurt for Grace as much as hers did. *Was this why you left? Because of your brother's death?* She wanted to ask, but the look Edwin threw her way discouraged the idea. In fact, it insisted she leave.

"If you have enough help from Edwin, I'm going to hang this wreath," Sarah said. Before she exited, wanting to offer some amount of comfort, she added, "I'm so sorry, Grace. I can only imagine how difficult it would be to lose a brother."

Catherine nodded, not trusting herself not to cry. She continued to work on the pancake batter until Edwin's hand covered her own.

"She's gone."

"Do you like cinnamon? I didn't think to ask. I could make some without if you want," Catherine rambled as she tried to pull her hands away from him. His hands tightened around her own.

"Grace."

Don't ask me about Caleb. Please. Caleb leads to Michael, who leads to Henry, and I cannot think about them right now.

When Edwin spoke again, his voice was at her ear, his breath warming her cheek. "Did you lose your brother at the same time you lost your parents?"

"No." She blinked rapidly to keep the tears from spilling down her face. "He ... he was in Europe. The Army."

Edwin closed his eyes, inwardly berating himself for sharing his story with her last night. *She lost her brother in the same war I practically bragged about being able to avoid. What an insensitive—*

"I'm sorry, Grace. I had no idea."

"No," she said as she forced her best smile. "My brother was always a hero to me. When he died, he became a hero to many more people. By sacrificing himself, he directly saved the life of a young French girl as well as one of his best friends."

"And who says one person's life can't help others?"

Catherine gave Edwin a genuine smile and whispered, "Exactly."

"I'm truly sorry, Grace. Had I known … I never would have told you about how—"

"Edwin," Catherine interrupted. It was her turn to comfort him. He still held her hands, so she gave them a strong quick squeeze before releasing them and refocusing on breakfast. "Stop. Let's start the day with the knowledge that, whether we planned it or not, we know a little more about each other. I won't bring up Vivian if you promise not to bring up Caleb."

He studied her a moment before agreeing with a nod. "You can trust me, Grace."

She dared not fall victim to his gaze as she replied, "I know, Edwin. But it's what I've left behind that I can't trust myself to revisit."

* * *

Please, please, please *still be open!* Sarah prayed as she hurried into town. She had been struggling for days over what to get Grace for Christmas. After seeing Grace's interaction with Edwin earlier that morning, Sarah knew exactly what she wanted to get her new friend.

Of course, it would have helped if they hadn't waited until the last minute …

She smiled when the dress shop came into view. The display window still held the party dress Sarah planned to buy for Grace. She stopped in front of the window to admire the emerald green dress that would look amazing on Grace.

And with my brother wearing a dark suit with a matching green kerchief in his pocket … what a pair they will make at the company New Year's Eve dance!

Sarah let out a squeal of delight and clapped her hands together triumphantly. His broken engagement had kept Edwin's heart locked up for too long, and Sarah couldn't contain her excitement at seeing it finally resurface.

This is going to be perfect!

"Oh, pardon me," the storeowner said as he opened the door to let the last customers exit the shop. "I'm closing up for the holiday now."

"No!" Sarah said to the owner at the entrance. "You can't close yet!"

"It's Christmas Eve. I can't believe I stayed open as late as I did."

"But I have a purchase to make." She frantically pointed to the dress in the window. "That dress. I want to purchase that dress."

The storeowner glanced at her and shook his head, saying, "I'm sorry. It doesn't appear to be your size, and our seamstress has already left for the day."

"Sir, *please*, I need to buy that dress. It's not for me … it'll fit my friend, I just know it. If it doesn't, I'll bring her by after Christmas for alterations. Please, sir, I'm asking only to make the purchase today. Alterations can wait." Sarah tried to wait patiently as he looked from the store window to her to the store window again.

He scratched his chin and said thoughtfully, "Well, seeing as tomorrow's Christmas, I won't have any customers since we'll be closed. Plus, everyone will be at home with their families, so if the window is bare for a day, it won't hurt me." He gave a heavy sigh but smiled when Sarah leaned over and hugged him. "Come on inside, dear. You can tell me all about your friend while I ring up the purchase."

Sarah was happy to oblige. As she pointed to a matching kerchief in the display case, she told the owner all about her hopes to keep Grace in the family.

When she left the shop with her wrapped packages and the owner's best wishes, she fought the urge to run home as fast as she could. Instead, she forced herself to take a leisurely pace, passing by the same tree lot where Edwin had purchased the wreath for their mother. She had one more purchase to make that would take no time at all.

When she left the lot, Sarah already had an idea of where she would hang the mistletoe.

"Cutting it a little close this year, aren't you?" Edwin asked as he stood near the front window, watching the snow and adjusting his tie at the same time.

Sarah smiled as she placed the wrapped boxes underneath the tree and said, "Better late than never, big brother. But no snooping; this big one's for

Grace anyway." She gave it a gentle tap before rising back to her feet. She went to Edwin and took over adjusting his tie. "You look quite dapper this evening."

Edwin regarded her closely. "It's Christmas Eve, Sarah. We're all supposed to look 'dapper' for the midnight service." He glanced at his wristwatch before adding, "We'd better be leaving soon."

Sarah grabbed her coat from the hall tree. Before slipping into it, she tossed Grace's coat to Edwin and suggested, "If you're in such a hurry, why don't you meet Grace at the bottom of the stairs with her coat?"

Edwin caught the coat and, as Sarah rearranged the gifts under the tree, humming Christmas carols to herself, asked suspiciously, "What are you up to?"

She gave him an innocent look that Edwin didn't believe for a moment. "Nothing," she replied. "Since it's Christmas Eve, and you bought Grace that coat for Christmas ..." She gave a deliberate head nod to the coat in his hand before continuing, "you should be the one to help her with it tonight."

He shook his head as he walked to the bottom of the stairs and stood in the hall's doorframe. "I'd help her whether or not the coat was my gift to her. I'd help you, too, for that matter."

"Who wants their brother to help them with their coat?"

"Well, I'll take any assistance he offers," Irma said as she came through from the kitchen. She started toward her son, but her daughter stopped her.

"No! Let me help you, Mother! Edwin can help Grace when she comes down."

Edwin watched in silence as Sarah steered their mother toward the front door before helping her with her coat. He was about to ask how much eggnog Sarah had already consumed when he heard an upstairs' bedroom door close and soft footsteps follow. His mother and sister forgotten, he waited with nervous anticipation for Grace to come down the stairs.

What is wrong with you, Edwin? You are not a schoolboy nor is she anything more than a friend. Just because she helped spare you from embarrassment with Vivian does not mean that you should pursue this ...

"I'm so sorry; you all should have told me to hurry up!" Catherine said as she reached the bottom stair to find three pairs of eyes focused on her. Irma and Sarah were by the door with large smiles on their faces, and Edwin stood near her, his face unreadable. "The dress Sarah loaned me for tonight has more buttons than I'm used to." She gave Sarah a sweet smile and added, "It was a bit difficult to figure out."

With his hands tightly gripping her coat, Edwin stepped up to her, holding it out. He waited until she had slipped her arms in the sleeves before saying, "It was well worth the trouble, Grace. You look lovely." He smiled as a faint blush crept into her cheeks.

"Thank you," Catherine replied, taking a step away from him only to have Sarah intervene.

"Wait! Stop!"

Edwin and Catherine froze, startled expressions on their faces.

A mischievous gleam filled her eyes as she motioned above their heads. "Look! You're standing under mistletoe!" she explained.

Edwin's eyes narrowed as he glared at his scheming sister. *You did this on purpose.*

As though reading his thoughts, Sarah gave a slight, triumphant nod.

An awkward silence followed. Irma and Sarah secretly held their breaths, waiting for the kiss under the mistletoe. Edwin saw apprehension and a silent plea written in Catherine's eyes.

I can't do this. She doesn't want—

"It's okay," Catherine whispered to Edwin.

But it obviously wasn't.

Edwin towered over Catherine, making it easy to place a chaste kiss on her forehead. "I'd like to apologize for my family," he said the moment his lips were free.

The gentle caress of Edwin's kiss involuntarily brought tears to Catherine's eyes. He was sparing her from as much embarrassment and awkwardness as possible, and she was grateful for his thoughtfulness. She gently shook her head and whispered, "It's nothing. Thanks for keeping it from being any more uncomfortable."

Edwin nodded and held his arm out for her. "Let's get going," he said loud enough for everyone to hear. "It's not a far walk to the church, but this weather and the lateness of the evening will make it seem longer."

The small group filed out of the house and briskly made their way to the church. While Edwin was grateful the mistletoe scheme hadn't turned into anything bigger, he couldn't help but feel a little trepidation for what else his sister had planned.

It appears I've been unsuccessful in concealing my feelings for Grace.

It had been a long time since Catherine sat through a service that left her squirming in her seat, but this Christmas Eve sermon was making up for it. Although she usually enjoyed being in church on the holiday, the minister's words made her regret coming. Sandwiched between Irma and Sarah, with Edwin on the other side of his mother, they all listened with rapt attention to the message of forgiveness.

It appears that I'm the only one having issues with that.

Catherine started to reposition herself in the pew but stopped when she caught Edwin giving her a sideway glance.

"Your refusal to forgive your neighbor, friend, or loved one defines your heart. Your actions tell the world that you thrive on despair and that you are choosing to remain miserable." The minister's gaze glided over everyone, but Catherine felt as though he was targeting her when he added, "So don't complain about your self-inflicted misery."

His words caused Catherine to skim the church pews. His perspective mirrored Michael's so closely, she was convinced her former dance instructor was here, feeding the minister words. He had berated her so many times for intentionally sabotaging her relationship with people out of fear of losing them.

Homesickness, sudden and heart-wrenching, racked her body. She missed Michael's sharp and always truthful tongue. *And Patricia ... how is she doing as her pregnancy progresses? And Liv, too, for that matter? And is little Caleb even little anymore?*

The realization of all she was missing smothered her, and she dropped her head in her hands from the weight of the loss. *My unwillingness to forgive, to listen, has cost me more than Henry.*

Without a word, nudge, or any other indication of curiosity, Catherine felt an arm gently wrap itself around her shoulders. It was Irma comforting Catherine while her eyes focused on her hymnal, ready to sing the service's final song.

This simple motherly act, one that Catherine had been without for a long time, brought tears to her eyes. A sob nearly escaped her lips as Sarah gently took Catherine's hand in a sisterly manner. The love from this family filled her.

Even though I've lost so much, I've also gained. Catherine lifted her eyes to the church's cross and gave a silent prayer of thanks for the three people sitting in the pew with her. She looked past Irma to find Edwin focused on her with an intensity she didn't understand.

Catherine had little time to dwell on it, however, as the service concluded. Christmas greetings circulated among the members of the congregation, and with each greeting that passed from Catherine's lips, the pain of homesickness heightened. It was close to midnight, but the desire to speak to someone from home was so strong, she gave no thought to the hour.

Edwin walked silently beside Catherine during the short walk home. Although it was close to midnight and darkness surrounded them, only to be interrupted occasionally by streetlights, Catherine could feel him watching her.

"If you all don't mind, I'm going to make a phone call. I'll meet you at home."

Irma was the first to protest, saying, "It's the middle of the night, Grace! And it's cold."

"You don't have to use a pay phone, Grace. Just use ours," Sarah chimed in as she came up and linked arms with Catherine.

Catherine smiled but remained rooted to the sidewalk as she said, "That's kind of you to offer, but I'd rather take the call out here. I only need a few minutes alone. I'll be home shortly."

While it was clear that Irma and Sarah wanted to argue, Edwin stopped their protests by saying, "I'll stay with her and see her home safely."

Catherine turned to Edwin and replied, "There's no need for that."

"I wouldn't leave my mother out here alone, nor my sister. The same goes for anyone living under my family's roof. While Christmas encourages peace on earth, this is not often the case. I'll give you your privacy, but I'm staying."

Catherine was too homesick to refuse him.

THIRTY-NINE

Michael settled himself next to his wife in their bed before giving her a good-night kiss and whispering, "Merry Christmas, love."

He leaned over to turn off the bedside lamp while Patricia rubbed her swollen stomach and replied, "Merry Christmas to you too, dear. It's hard to believe we'll be sharing next Christmas with a new baby."

Michael smiled in the darkness as his hand found hers resting on her stomach. "That's a nice thought," he agreed.

"Do you think we'll have *all* our family home by then?"

Michael hesitated in responding. When he finally did, his words were anything but cheerful. "I hope so. I have to admit, I'm surprised I haven't heard any more from her," he said, unable to hide the concern in his voice.

"Catherine hung up on you the last time she called, dear. I'd be surprised if she did call again. But what about Olivia? I would say if anyone would hear from Catherine, it would be Liv."

"While that may be true under normal circumstances, this definitely isn't normal circumstances. If there's even the smallest chance Henry will be with Liv and Bobby, Catherine won't call."

"While I love your little protégée dearly, and I understand why she's been so stubborn about Henry, after seeing his heartache firsthand, I wish she'd at least listen to his explanation."

"If you'll recall, it took a lot for her to finally open her heart to him. If she showed up on his doorstep right now, he could explain that night, but there would still be things he couldn't explain."

"And despite everything, Natalie is still here, and Henry is trying to

322

build a relationship with a small child he doesn't have definitive proof of being his."

"It's an absolute mess. Catherine's hurting, Henry's—" The sound of the telephone ringing spliced his thought. "What in the world? It's too late for calls." Michael stumbled out of bed to hurry and answer the telephone in the kitchen. Patricia, despite her pregnancy, was close on his heels.

"Hello?" Michael asked as he held the telephone to his ear.

"Michael … it's me," a timid and somewhat shaky voice replied.

"Catherine." Relief filled his whispered word. Behind him, Patricia excitedly squeezed his arm. "My God, Cat, it's good to finally hear your voice. We've been worried sick about you."

"I probably should have called sooner." There was an evident tightness in her voice as she choked with emotion. "But I was pretty angry at you for a long time after my last call."

Michael hoped his chuckle sounded light as he responded, "I shouldn't be surprised by that. And I'm sorry I handled the last call so badly."

"It's what makes you *you*," Catherine said. Although she tried to sound carefree, she was anything but. "I wanted to call to wish you and Patricia a Merry Christmas."

"Love, don't take this the wrong way, but it's almost eleven. Why did you wait to call so late?"

He was met with silence before Catherine said, "I miss you all."

Michael heard the quiet sob that followed her words. He patiently waited for her to collect herself before he told her, "Catherine, come home."

The sounds of church bells drowned out her reply.

"I'm sorry, Cat, you'll have to repeat that. There are church bells in the background."

"Oh, sorry. Those are St. Michael's church bells," she explained as they started to fade. She waited until they were over before saying, "Merry Christmas."

"Cat, you sound miserable. Please, come home."

He heard her take a hitched breath before responding, "Michael, I can't do that."

"Why?"

"You know why."

Michael ran a hand through his hair in frustration and said, "Love, let the bloke explain. Then if you still decide to stay away, it can be a decision that will bring closure."

"I need to go," Catherine replied, her words barely audible through her tears.

"Okay, love, now you're just being stubborn." He winced as he felt Patricia pinch his arm.

"I love you and will call again soon, okay?"

"Cat—" The call ended before he could say another word.

Patricia slapped his arm as soon as he hung up the phone. He gave her a bewildered look. "What was that for?"

"You did it again! One minute you're gentle with her because she's obviously upset. The next minute, you're telling her she's stubborn! It's no wonder she hung up on you." She gave him one last glare before asking, "How is she?"

"*Homesick*."

Patricia sighed and laid her head against Michael's shoulder. He wrapped his arms around her, grateful that he hadn't lost his love to a misunderstanding like Henry had.

"She still loves him, doesn't she?"

"If the pain in her voice and refusal to speak with him is anything to go by, then yes." He kissed the top of her head before adding, "However, she did give me a clue to where she's at."

"She did?" Patricia asked.

"Yes. Church bells were ringing while we talked. She briefly mentioned St. Michael's."

"So, you have the name of a church …"

"And a time zone. We have another hour until midnight, love, so the church bells shouldn't be ringing yet, unless she's an hour ahead of us. Tomorrow, I'll start to narrow down Cat's whereabouts." He smiled at the small victory. "She doesn't know it, but she gave us all a valuable Christmas gift."

* * *

Olivia gave a small squeal of delight at the scene before her. Bobby and Olivia had just finished placing the last of their son's Christmas gifts under the tree and had taken a moment to enjoy how beautiful it all looked in Catherine's living room. Christmas was one of Catherine's favorite times of year, and Olivia loved the multitude of decorations Catherine had collected over the years.

"The only thing missing is Catherine," Olivia commented as Bobby came and draped his arm over her shoulders.

"I had thought she'd be back by now."

Olivia wiped a tear from her cheek and nodded. "Me too. But when she sent that money to us . . ." She dropped her head on her husband's shoulder. "She'll have to come back at some point, right?"

Rather than give an answer he wasn't sure was true, he said, "Henry's about to lose his mind. If she doesn't come back soon, Liv, I think he's going to look for her on his own, without our help."

"And where will he start? Cat's left no trail. The only contact we've had from her since her phone call was the money. And she even made that untraceable—cash in an envelope, with no return address."

The telephone ringing startled them both. Bobby hurried to answer it, but Olivia pulled at his shirt. "No! We agreed that I answer all phone calls. If it's Cat, she might hang up at the sound of your voice."

When Olivia answered the phone and heard "Merry Christmas, Liv," her eyes instantly teared up.

"Cat!" Olivia broke down in sobs. Both women cried for the next several seconds.

Finally, Olivia was able to speak. "Merry Christmas, Cat." She took in an audible gulp of air and added, "We received the money."

"Good."

"You didn't have to do that, Cat."

"How's the baby? And little Caleb?"

Olivia chuckled, "The baby isn't here yet, but I've only a little ways to go. And Caleb, well, he misses his aunt terribly."

"I miss him too."

"Maybe you can talk to him the next time you call."

"I'd like that," Catherine replied, her voice shaking with emotion.

Olivia prayed for courage as she spoke, "Cat, he's lost without you. It's like he's a shell of a human being now."

"Caleb?" Catherine asked, trying to keep her voice light.

"No, Cat. Now, are you going to ask about him or not?"

The silence that followed was so long, Olivia feared her friend had hung up.

"How are Henry … and Natalie?"

"I wouldn't know about Natalie, Cat. I rarely see her. And as often as Henry is over here or working himself to death at the shop, I doubt he sees her much either. He's here a lot, hoping that one of us has heard from you."

"I'm so sorry, Liv. I never meant to cause you to worry this much. I—"

Olivia's tears matched Catherine's. "You were hurting," she interrupted. "It was your instinct to protect your heart. I just wish you two would talk. You've always had a level head on things."

"But with Henry, I don't."

"No, sweetheart, you don't. Maybe it's because you love him so much. You've always been so passionate, whether loving or hating him, when it comes to Henry. Have you thought about calling him?"

"Too much for someone whose heart he broke."

Olivia was so grateful to be talking to Catherine for longer than the few minutes their previous conversation had lasted. *Maybe it's because she's homesick, or because it's Christmas, but at least she's listening.*

"Do you remember the day he came home from Europe? When he stepped down from that train, his focus was you. And I've never seen that focus waver since."

"But Natalie was wearing …" Catherine couldn't continue as she choked on the memory.

"And Susan was the first person to kiss Henry when he returned home, but that didn't mean he belonged to her. He had already given his heart to you."

"You think I should go back to him."

"I think you should talk to him. Listen to what he has to say. Catherine, yes, I want to believe that there's a very good explanation for all of this. I hear it in your voice that you still love him. And I know, without a doubt, that he still loves you. It's Christmas."

"Maybe I could."

Olivia's heart broke at the uncertainty in Catherine's voice. The distance was hurting Catherine as much as it was hurting Henry. "I'd like to talk with you longer. I've a million questions to ask you, but I think you need to make another phone call more than you need to answer my demanding questions."

Catherine chuckled, warming Olivia's heart, before she replied, "That's saying a lot that you'd willingly give up the opportunity to ask questions."

"Call him, Cat."

"Okay ... wish me luck."

Olivia felt a smile spread across her face. "You're not going to need it."

* * *

Henry lay on his bed, the letters Catherine had written to him during the war spread out around him. The hand resting above his head held her boxed engagement ring. The hand resting on his chest held the tattered and worn photograph of her that she'd first given to her brother. Even though it was approaching midnight on Christmas Eve, every light in his house was on.

He had spent the earlier part of the evening with Bobby's family. He had regretted it the moment he had arrived at their doorstep. *Catherine's doorstep. That's* her *home. We, Catherine and I, should have been celebrating Christmas together there, or maybe even at a new place of our own by now. It was not supposed to be like this.*

The sound of someone knocking on his door pierced through his thoughts. Although it was too late for any visitor worth talking to, a small part of him held out hope that Catherine was on the other side of his door. However unlikely, the thought was strong enough to propel him to open the door.

Natalie stood alone at his front door, holding a small present in her hands. "Merry Christmas, Henry!" she greeted.

He couldn't hide his disappointment. "What do you want, Natalie?" he asked coolly.

"To be asked in, for a start. It's freezing."

Henry turned and walked away, leaving the front door open. "Why are you here?"

Taking a small step inside, Natalie held up the gift in her hands and replied, "To present a peace offering."

Henry turned and glared at her. "It's the middle of the night, and you don't have David with you. I don't want your 'peace offering'."

Natalie set the present on the table near the kitchen. "Look, Henry, I know I've brought a lot of change to your life. But I'm asking that you give me a chance. I can't replace Cat—"

"No," Henry interrupted. "You can't. Don't even try."

Natalie continued as though she hadn't heard him, saying, "I can keep you from being alone."

Henry lost his patience as he hissed, "I'm not alone! My heart is with Catherine, and it's not going to leave her anytime soon."

The telephone ringing prevented Natalie from replying. Without thinking, Natalie picked up the telephone. "Hello, Bradley residence ... Hello? Hello, is anyone there?"

Suddenly, Henry jerked the telephone from her hand. "Hello?" he asked in the phone. His voice was weary but hopeful. "Hello? Catherine?" Although no one spoke, he heard deep breathing on the other end of the line. "If that's you, Catherine, please don't hang up."

His voice was pleading, but it held the caller. "I'm sorry I disturbed you."

He could hear the tears in her voice, and his own eyes quickly filled as well. "Catherine ..." he whispered, not knowing where to begin. He had so many things he wanted to say. The fact that she had called him spoke volumes.

She still loves me.

"I miss you so much," he said softly.

The pain shown through Catherine's words as she replied, "She's there, Henry ..."

Already feeling her distancing her heart, Henry cursed the unfortunate timing as he realized she once again assumed he was in a relationship with Natalie. He knew no matter what he said, his next words would sound pathetic. "Please hear me out, Catherine. This isn't what you think."

Her laugh was bitter, harsh, and full of despair. *"Isn't* it?"

"Natalie and I aren't together."

"She's in your home on Christmas Eve ..." Her voice broke, but she continued, "... in the middle of the night. How else would I view this?"

He glared at Natalie, ignoring the guilty, pained look on her face.

"Catherine, she's nothing to me. My heart, my very being, belongs only to you." He closed his eyes in pain as he heard her break down on the phone. "Please, Catherine. Let me come to you. Let me bring you home," he begged.

"I will always, *always* love you, Henry," Catherine said. Even over the phone, he could hear the determination in her voice to stay strong. "But I can't keep doing this to myself."

FORTY

"Merry Christmas." Blinded by the tears in her eyes, Catherine couldn't see the telephone as she placed it back on the receiver. Every instinct in her wanted to collapse right there and succumb to the pain. Any portion of her heart that had started to heal over the last several weeks ripped open once more.

Curse you, Catherine! What dream world do you live in to make you think a phone call would help? He's moved on. You need to, too. Walk away, and keep walking ...

Catherine knew she could not easily erase the grief from her face. *I don't have the strength left to try and hide it.* So with that thought, she exited the phone booth to join Edwin, who had waited a respectable distance away. She silently berated herself for showing any weakness.

She couldn't see the concern in Edwin's eyes as she approached his still form. His brow creased, it took extreme effort to keep from reaching out for her. Judging from her unsteady gait, he suspected that whomever she had spoken to had made her regret the conversation. Anger rolled through him. He didn't know who she had telephoned, but he hated them for the state they had left her in.

Catherine stopped shy of his arm's reach. She dared to glance at him, and when Edwin saw the despair in her eyes, he found the courage to pull her into his comforting arms.

Although Edwin didn't speak, the strength Catherine felt as he folded her in his embrace chipped away at her. She needed comfort more than anything, and as much as it hurt not to be receiving it from Henry, Edwin's

330

arms offered a solace that shattered any remaining barrier for her tears. Before she could stop herself, she lost herself in such grief that Edwin's arms were the only things keeping her on her feet.

The sorrowful sobs emitting from the woman in his arms reminded Edwin of his own heartbreak. "He's a fool, Grace," he whispered into her hair as he held her head tucked under his chin. "He doesn't deserve you."

The deepness of Edwin's voice vibrated through her. She barely comprehended his words as she felt his arms tighten around her and his hand cradle her head against him. Although she knew she should remove herself from his embrace, she stayed cocooned in the protection his arms offered.

"He was a fool to let you go."

Catherine heard a roughness in his voice that slipped past her own grief. It was a warning that, despite her longing to stay, she needed to pull away from him.

She started to lift her head, but Edwin continued his confession as his embrace grew more intimate. "If you were mine, I'd be hanging on for dear life," he said as his lips met the top of her head. Edwin felt a large weight drop from his shoulders as he cupped her face and turned it up to him.

"I wouldn't let go."

Despite the pain that still seared through her from hearing Natalie's voice, Catherine managed a moment of soberness. "Edwin, you don't—"

A calloused finger, cold from the evening's air, silenced her lips. He shook his head and continued, "At first, I thought I was watching out for my family. But even when I realized that you refused to give more than your first name and your past was a mystery I couldn't unlock ..." He cupped her face and caressed her bottom lip with his thumb. "Your unknowns no longer matter to me."

Catherine felt her entire world shift, leaving her dizzy and unsure of everything. She didn't know what to say because she didn't know what she was supposed to feel. She loved Henry, but he was with Natalie now. Even though Henry had denied it, the fact that Natalie was in his home convinced her otherwise. *And here's someone who understands what it's like to lose love but has found a way to dare to open his heart again—for me. But he has feelings for Grace, not Catherine.*

As these solemn thoughts swirled through her head, she struggled to lend sound to her voice, so instead she shook her head.

Edwin stilled her movement. He made sure her gaze didn't waver before speaking again. A degree of sadness marked his words. "Don't worry, Grace. While your heart still belongs to him, there is nothing I can do. I will not take anything you do not freely give."

Catherine tried to convince herself that relief was the only emotion she felt, but his words had made more of an impression than that. Coldness surrounded her as Edwin stepped back, grabbed her arm, and tucked it through the crook of his own. They walked home in silence, and Catherine appreciated that he didn't continue to express these sentiments. Edwin had drawn a distinct line regarding how he felt about her, but she felt assured that he would not cross it unless she asked him to. Still, she felt she owed him at least some response to his heartfelt confession. When they reached the porch, she stopped Edwin from turning the doorknob. If he was surprised by her desire to linger on the porch, he didn't show it.

"It's Catherine," Catherine said, her own chest less constrictive with the admission. "My name is Catherine Grace."

Edwin gifted her a slow smile. Before she had the opportunity to let new tears flow, Edwin said, "Okay, Grace. Let's go inside." Warmth flooded him as she had finally decided to share something more with him. He said her name repeatedly in his mind as he ushered her inside the house and helped her out of her coat.

For a moment they stood there, facing each other, unsure what to say. Finally, Catherine dipped her head and whispered, "Good night, Edwin," before turning to head to her bedroom.

She took only one step before Edwin seized her hand and wordlessly pulled her to the hallway entrance. He pointed above his head.

Mistletoe.

"I may never have this opportunity again." He took both of her hands in his and whispered, "So I'm going to seize it and use it to kiss you."

A flicker of panic came over her, and Catherine began to pull her hands out of Edwin's.

His grip tightened. "It's mistletoe. No strings attached. But I *am* going to kiss you, Catherine."

The sound of her true name on his lips did something to them both and silenced Catherine's protests. Her breathing stilled as Edwin gently cupped her face in his hands. Her eyes instinctively closed as he kissed her forehead, eyes, and cheeks.

Edwin watched for a discouraging reaction after each kiss he planted on her face. He tasted the salt from her tears but could also sense that a part of her welcomed his affections. He murmured her name, her *true* name, once more before covering her lips with his own. What began as a slow, gentle kiss quickly progressed to something more ardent. His hands left her face to hold her waist and back of her head. A soft moan escaped his lips as he felt her soften in his arms.

The sound brought them both back to reality. Edwin took a step away from Catherine. Guilt washed over him for taking advantage of the situation as well as having enjoyed it more than he should have. So, when he saw a new set of tears make paths down her cheeks and her fingertips cover the lips he had just enjoyed too much, he kept his distance.

"I'm sorry … that was too forward of me."

Catherine tried her best to smile, but her lips faltered. "Mistletoe, right? It's nothing." Another tear streaked her cheek. "No one's held accountable past this moment, okay?" She excused herself without waiting for an answer. She was homesick, heartsick, and too confused to remain.

As Catherine hurried up the stairs, Edwin waited until he heard the sound of her bedroom door close before retreating to his study. Once there, he sat at his desk and let his head drop into his hands. He wasn't sure what his next move should be, or if he should try to do anything at all. Still, the shared intimate moment with Catherine had confirmed one important fact: he very much wanted to be held accountable for kissing her.

FORTY-ONE

"Wake up, Grace! It's Christmas!!" Sarah called up the stairs from the living room. "Wake up, wake up, wake up!"

Catherine buried her head deeper in the pillow as Sarah continued to insist that everyone within a mile needed to get out of bed. Catherine had slept little; her late-night tears and the memories of her phone conversations and mistletoe kiss had faded enough to finally allow her to succumb to sleep. It seemed she had only closed her eyes when Sarah had begun crowing like a rooster.

Whoever this Grace person is deserves to be ... oh, wait, that's me.

Catherine had felt such relief at sharing her real name with Edwin that she wanted to completely abandon the alias.

Edwin.

Catherine's pillow absorbed her smothered groan. She didn't know how to handle what had transpired between them. While discovering Natalie at Henry's home on Christmas Eve had told her everything she needed to know about the death of her relationship, she had hoped the conversation would have gone differently. *Olivia had been so encouraging.* She sat up suddenly and threw her pillow across the room in anger. *It doesn't matter anymore. He's moved on, Catherine. You need to, too.* A new wave of tears cascaded from her eyes.

A soft knock at her door made her hastily wipe them away. She hurried out of bed, nervous about who stood on the other side.

"Grace?" Irma's gentle voice revealed the visitor.

"Please, come in." Catherine quickly opened the door for the older woman. "I'm sorry; I'm running a little behind this morning."

"No, you're fine, dear. It's Sarah that's been itching to wake everyone before dawn." She regarded Catherine before adding, "But you could probably do with a bit more sleep. It looks like you had trouble sleeping."

"I'm sorry, Irma. Give me a few minutes, and I'll be—"

"No apologies necessary, dear. You're away from home, and it's Christmas. I'd be more concerned if that combination *didn't* bother you." She gave Catherine a comforting smile and held out a house robe. "Now, there's no need to get dressed. Put this on over your pajamas and come on down. You'll find yourself blending right in."

"*Everyone* is still in their—"

Irma winked at her. "Everyone, dear. Now hurry. I'm not sure how much longer I can keep Sarah from ripping into those packages or Edwin away from the bacon." She held out her hand. "Come, I've been ordered not to come back down without you."

Catherine couldn't help but smile as she slipped into the robe and took Irma's hand. Memories briefly assaulted her—memories of sharing Christmas with her own family, in particular, her mother. However, her heart was too heavy to allow the memories to be an additional burden. Instead, she chose to bask in the motherly comfort from Irma.

The two descended the stairs with their hands still joined to find Sarah bouncing giddily at the bottom. Edwin was coming in from the kitchen with one piece of bacon in his hand, one piece in his mouth.

"You took too long," he said, winking at Catherine as Irma broke free from her grip to scold her son and attempt to snatch the bacon from his hand.

Catherine sobered, not knowing if Edwin's wink implied a deeper message. However, when Edwin looked more closely at her face, his own smiled faded, and she knew that the wink had been in jest. He allowed his mother to snatch the bacon from his hand and return it to the kitchen, giving him time to greet Catherine.

"Merry Christmas, Grace." Edwin took a step closer and said so only she could hear, "I'm sorry if you had problems sleeping last night due to … I'm sorry if I was a contributing factor."

Catherine appreciated that Edwin didn't draw any nearer to her. Despite their shared kiss, which Catherine had finally admitted to herself that she had participated in, he wasn't claiming possession of her. It seemed he was going to stand by his promise that while her heart still hurt for another, Edwin wouldn't pursue her.

"Will you two stop already and get over here?" Sarah called out, preventing Catherine from replying.

Edwin winked again, telling Sarah, "We were only strategizing, little sister."

"Strategizing?" Irma asked as she reentered the living room.

"On how to avoid Sarah's cursed mistletoe." He pointed an accusing finger at his sister and teased, "We're on to you. And rest assured, we've outsmarted you."

Or strategizing on finding a way to keep kissing after the mistletoe is gone, Sarah fought the temptation to add. She flashed them both a wide smile. "Well, strategize later. There are gifts here with your names on them!"

Despite the sadness in her heart, Catherine felt joy at the surprise each of them expressed when they discovered she had gifts for them. Edwin seemed more surprised than the others, and he gingerly held the gloves in his hands.

"Grace," *Catherine.* "these are ... I'm surprised. Thank you. I know my attitude toward you has been trying at times." He wanted to say something more but didn't dare around the others.

Catherine sought to ease his struggle by saying, "Oh, don't worry. I was only thinking how useful they'd be in handling the lumps of coal you'd be getting from your family."

Her words caused the desired effect, and soon mother, sister, and brother were laughing and bantering with one another.

Suddenly, the only thing Catherine could think about was the letter Catherine had written to Henry at Christmas during the war. She had teased him, drawing a picture of coal for his gift.

Stop it! Stop it! Stop it!

Sarah stood in front of her, holding a box and coaxing Catherine from the memory. "Enough about Edwin, this gift is for you."

"Me?" Catherine asked. "The coat was too much as it was."

"And that was from Edwin." Sarah's grin widened as she noted, "This is from me."

Catherine felt all eyes on her as she held the box in her lap. Based on the box's size and lightness, she guessed its contents were clothing. What she didn't expect, however, was to find a green dancing dress underneath the lid.

"I hope you're planning on going with us to the New Year's Eve dance," Sarah immediately jumped into an explanation. "You do dance, don't you, Grace?"

Catherine couldn't look away from the dress as she replied, "Yes." Her reply was nothing more than a whisper. "But it's been a while."

"We'll have to practice beforehand." Sarah continued to talk, but Catherine didn't hear her.

Oh my ... Although the dress was made for winter and more modest than her previous dancing dress, it wasn't the green fabric she saw as she slowly reached out to touch the dress. Red clouded her vision—a red fabric that she had seen torn and stained with blood.

Robert has found her again. She doesn't know how, she doesn't know why, but he has. She's evaded him for so long; she's dared to believe she'd finally ridden herself of him. But he's found her. He is here now, in this house. She looks down and sees her bloodied hands, and she knows the bathrobe is the only thing keeping the blood on her stomach and legs from appearing.

There is so much blood. She hopes it is only hers and not Henry's.

The sound of Robert's gun explodes again in her ears. She needs to keep him from Henry. She has—

"Grace! Grace!" Edwin knelt beside Catherine as her eyes maintained a distant look. When she hadn't acknowledged Sarah's gift, but rather had stared blankly at it after Sarah's chatter had faded, he knew something was wrong.

Irma had, too, and had immediately asked for Sarah's help in the kitchen to prepare breakfast, allowing Edwin to focus on Catherine.

But no matter how many times he had called her name and gently shook her, she seemed lost to him. *But her name's not Grace ...*

"Catherine!" Edwin hissed in her ear so that no one else could hear him. "Where are you?" Casting a glance to the kitchen to watch for his family, he wanted to make sure he stopped calling her by her real name before they reappeared. When she still didn't respond, he cupped her face in his hands and turned her to face him. "Catherine. Look at me, dear. Focus on me." He drew her face to within inches of his own. "Come back from whatever world you're visiting." His thumb lightly caressed her lower lip. "*Catherine*," he pleaded with her. "Come back." Edwin exhaled a worried sigh, his breath caressing her face.

Catherine suddenly jerked, her eyes refocusing on her surroundings. He dropped his hands from her face but kept a hand on her shoulder. She blinked quickly, her breathing labored as she looked around franticly.

"Where is it?" she whispered, panicking. "I need the jacket. His jacket, I need to find it." The man next to her seemed vaguely familiar. *But that's not important. I need Henry's jacket. Robert was here, and Henry said his jacket would always bring me back.*

Edwin saw her panic rising. He had no idea what she was talking about, but he had to do something to calm her. He took her face in his hands once more and turned her to face him. "Look at me, Catherine," he whispered, his tone gentle yet firm.

Still feeling the need to find Henry's coat, she focused on the man in front of her.

"Catherine, you're okay. You don't need to find someone's coat. You're here. You're *safe*."

"Safe?"

Edwin nodded. "You're safe with us. With Irma, Sarah, and me." He bore his gaze into her, hoping that something he said would help the situation.

"Edwin?"

He released a sigh of relief and nodded. "Yes," he said, giving her a small smile.

Edwin ... Edwin! "Oh, no," Catherine whispered as she realized she had just come out of a flashback. The green dress was clutched in her hands. This was a gift from Sarah. It had nothing to do with Robert. Tears of embarrassment struck her cheeks before Edwin could wipe them away. "I'm so sorry."

"Are you okay?" he asked, only allowing a slight distance between them.

"I ... yes." She looked down at the dress. "Sarah? She doesn't—"

"She's with Mother in the kitchen."

"I offended her." She hastily rose to her feet. Edwin quickly followed her.

"I think we're all more concerned about you rather than about the gift."

"I love the dress," Catherine said, trying to change the subject.

"Of course. You can tell Sarah that at breakfast."

She didn't want to face them. She didn't want to have to explain how Robert, though dead, still haunted her. "I'm just tired. Please, can I get some rest? I ... I can't give them an explanation right now."

Edwin knew they'd want one. He wanted to ask about what he had just witnessed.

"Perhaps food—"

"I need sleep," she countered.

Edwin watched her momentarily before nodding. "I'll let them know they can expect you later, after you've had a good rest."

"Thank you, Edwin."

He nodded again, the look in his eyes unreadable. "Do you need assistance?" he asked softly.

She shook her head. "No, thank you. I'll only need a few hours."

"We'll talk later, then," he commented, his words confirming Catherine would have to offer an explanation at some point.

Clutching the dress to her, Catherine turned to head back up to her bedroom. However, Edwin gently reached out to stop her as she passed him. He waited until she looked up at him before saying, "I meant what I said last night. Whatever just happened, wherever you were, it doesn't change anything."

She forced a trembling smile to her lips. "The past is always there, Edwin. It's always there ready to trip us up and cause us to stumble." *And deny us our happy endings.*

It was well past midnight, but Edwin was no more tired than when he had prepared for bed hours earlier. Once Catherine had retired to her room after opening Sarah's gift, she hadn't resurfaced. The entire day had passed with concern for Catherine forefront in everyone's mind. Whether Catherine had feigned sleep, every meal brought to her room had remained untouched and on the floor outside her door.

When he had first seen her that morning, it had been difficult to act as though the previous night's kiss hadn't happened. *Pretending not to care is nigh impossible now.*

A blood-curdling scream filled the air.

Edwin shot to his feet. Another cry met his ears before he could get to the door.

It was easy to determine the owner of the screams as his mother and sister both hurried out of their rooms and met him in the hall.

Catherine.

Sarah's eyes were full of fear as she searched Edwin's. "Stay here," he told both women. If there was an intruder, he didn't want to put them at risk.

Irma grabbed his arm before he hurried to Catherine's room. "No, son. I've got this."

Edwin looked incredulously at his mother. "Nonsense," he refuted.

But Irma wouldn't budge. "Listen," she said as she held up a hand to silence him. The screams had now turned to soft, muffled cries. Irma gave her son an unyielding look. "I've got this. I've woken up enough times with you and Sarah when you were growing up to be able to discern a nightmare."

Edwin cast a long look at Catherine's closed door and nodded. "Okay, but leave the door open in case you're wrong."

Catherine felt as though her heart was ready to explode. Her screams had awoken her from her nightmare, but only just. It had taken frantically kicking the covers off of herself before she was convinced Robert wasn't in the room with her.

It's the blanket smothering me ... not Robert.

A whimper escaped her at the realization of having both a flashback and nightmare in the same day. She had gone for such a long time without either. *Why am I regressing?*

A gentle knock on the door informed her that her outburst hadn't gone unnoticed. Irma entered before Catherine had the chance to speak. The older woman stood at the door with concern in her eyes.

"I'm sorry, I didn't mean to wake you," Catherine whispered. "Are the others—"

"Don't worry about them. They won't bother you. May I?" She motioned to the bed, and Catherine moved to allow Irma to join her. Once settled next to Catherine, Irma took her hand and asked, "Bad dream?"

This small act of motherhood, something Catherine hadn't felt since she was a teenager, brought on a new wave of tears. She nodded, placing her free hand to her mouth in an effort to quell the tears.

Irma gave an understanding nod before gathering Catherine into her arms and laying back into the bed.

Edwin listened as his mother sang the song to Catherine that she had sang to him and his sister every time they had nightmares growing up. Edwin stood against the wall opposite Catherine's room. Sarah stood next to him. Sarah took his hand, and they both slid to the floor. Although they knew it was wrong to eavesdrop, their concern for Catherine as well as their mother's song prompting cherished childhood memories kept them both with their ears straining to hear their mother's conversation with Catherine.

Their words were hushed and muffled, but neither Edwin nor Sarah dared move to improve their ability to hear. Instead, they continued to sit in the hallway in silence with their hands held in sibling affection. When the bedroom's bedside lamp came on, Edwin was glad he and his sister were too far down the hall for anyone in the room to see them.

However, his mother's gasp made him regret his inability to see into the room. Edwin and Sarah exchanged a glance as they both leaned forward.

"Goodness, child!" they heard Irma explain in a sharp whisper. "Who … what … I don't even know what to say."

"There's nothing to say," Catherine answered. "I wanted you to know that some nightmares are harder to run away from. They leave their impression on you."

"It's a wonder you're not in the nightmare around the clock."

The siblings heard a soft chuckle. "Yes, well, no one goes through life without earning a few scars."

Irma tried not to grimace at the scars she saw splayed across the young woman's stomach. She could only imagine the story behind them. Pushing her curiosity aside, she reached out her arms. "If there's anything we can do, Grace, to help, please let us do it."

Catherine lowered her shirt to cover the scars Robert had given her across her waist and said reassuringly, "You've done plenty. I hope I haven't awakened Sarah and Edwin."

Irma patted her cheek. "Nonsense. Don't worry about them. Focus on *you*. Okay? I'll see you in the morning."

Catherine nodded, both embarrassed and grateful for Irma's attentions. "Thank you, Irma. For everything. It was nice having a mother again."

Irma winked as she made her way to the door. "I'll be your mother any time you need me," she said over her shoulder. "And don't forget it."

At the first sounds of their mother preparing to quit Catherine's room, Sarah raced to her room to avoid being caught eavesdropping. Edwin knew his mother wouldn't be surprised to find him in the hall, and he remained until his mother closed Catherine's door and stood facing him.

"Is everything okay?" he mouthed.

Irma took her son's hand and led him to his bedroom. Once inside, Irma clasped a hand over her own stomach before turning to face Edwin. "Be gentle with her, Edwin," she warned. "That poor girl has been through something horrific."

"What did she say?"

Irma shook her head and replied, "That's her story to tell. I'm just warning you because no one should ..." Her voice trailed off as both hands now protected her stomach. She gave a small shudder.

Edwin noticed the subconscious action.

Her stomach ... He noticed the pained look on his mother's face. *Dear God, what had Catherine endured?*

FORTY-TWO

Olivia stood in the doorway as Henry came up the porch stairs, his eyes searching even as his shoulders sagged in defeat. When he reached the door, he hesitated as he fought to contain the grief that had nearly destroyed him from the moment Catherine had ended their phone call. "Did you hear from her too?" he finally managed to whisper.

Despite Henry's obvious low spirits, Olivia couldn't help but feel hopeful. She placed a hand over her heart as she replied, "She listened to me? She called you? I didn't know if she would."

"Merry Christmas!" Bobby called out from behind Olivia, unable to see Henry's face.

Olivia ignored her husband's joyous tone and placed a reassuring hand on Henry's shoulder. "Caleb just went down for a nap. Come on in, and I'll make some coffee."

Whatever happy greeting Bobby had prepared to say next, it died on his lips as Olivia ushered Henry inside. "You'd better make sure the coffee is strong, Liv," he said, following them into the kitchen.

Olivia nodded and motioned for them to sit at the table. "So, Catherine called you?" she asked tentatively, her back to Henry as she worked. "I'm glad for it. That's great news."

Henry's laugh was bitter, and anger laced his words as he spoke, "Oh, yes. It *is* great news."

"Then why do I—"

"It was an answer to a prayer," Henry interrupted Bobby, his voice edgy. Olivia turned slowly to face the men. It was clear that Henry's

343

conversation with Catherine hadn't gone well, but the only way to figure out why was to ask. "I spoke with her, encouraged her to call you and at least hear you out."

"We never got to that point. She ended the call after a few short minutes."

"What happened?" Bobby asked, casting a worried glance at Olivia.

"Natalie answered—that's what happened."

Olivia gasped and Bobby stared in disbelief. "Natalie?"

Henry could only nod.

"But it was so late when she called us. I don't—"

"Let me explain, Liv. I think unseen forces are working against me. Natalie stopped by, uninvited, right before Catherine called. She waltzed in, *alone*, with the nerve to offer herself to comfort me." He clenched his jaw as anger radiated from him.

Olivia, having just poured him a cup of coffee, held off handing it to him for fear it would end up shattered on the wall.

"I was in the process of getting rid of her when Catherine called. Natalie had the nerve to answer it."

"Oh no," Olivia whispered as she slipped down next to Bobby. "She didn't."

Bobby groaned at Henry's confirmation.

"She was already so emotionally fragile when I spoke with her," Olivia reflected. "Hearing Natalie's voice …"

"Destroyed her," Henry finished for her. "It was worse than a nightmare. It didn't matter what I said."

"Of course not," Olivia agreed. The sound of a vehicle approaching kept her from saying anything more.

"I'll get it," Bobby said as he rose to get the door. Soon thereafter, he returned with Michael following him.

"Michael, Merry Christmas!" Olivia greeted as she rose and placed a kiss on his cheek. "Where's Patricia? You shouldn't have left her alone on Christmas."

"It wasn't my plan to, but she insisted I come to see if anyone else heard from Catherine last night."

"We all have," Olivia said, motioning for Michael to join them at the table.

Paining him more the second time around, Henry told Michael about his phone call with Catherine.

Michael simply nodded before asking Bobby and Olivia, "What about you?"

"It was good. We spoke long enough to know she's homesick."

Bobby nodded in agreement. "And she wanted to be sure we received the money," he added.

"Money?" Henry and Michael asked almost simultaneously.

"What money?" Henry asked with a new edge in his voice.

"Catherine had money sent to us to help cover any expenses that might have incurred with the upkeep of the house," Olivia said matter-of-factly, unable to meet anyone's eye.

Henry looked at her in bewilderment. "How is it that I'm just *now* hearing about this?"

"Because she didn't leave a way for us to trace it," Bobby said, defending his wife's actions. "What good would it have done?"

Henry seethed in frustration. "While I don't want to see her destitute, … she's a step closer to staying *there*, wherever there is, rather than coming home." He rose to his feet and began to pace the room. "She was blacklisted here. You all know how she struggled with finding work outside Michael's club." He ran a hand through his hair, trying not to scream. "We had so many arguments over this. This is a *very* big deal."

Michael watched Henry's impatience grow. Henry was close to losing all self-control, and the information he had yet to share might send Henry over the edge. As if reading Michael's mind, Henry focused his attention on him.

"And you, Michael? What have you heard?"

Michael hoped what he had to say would be encouraging. "She called, but we didn't speak for too long. However, it was long enough to learn she's an hour ahead of us."

"You know where she's at?" Hope filled Olivia's question.

"I have a pretty good idea of where to start looking. I have to wrap up a few things, and then I'll head out in a couple of days to look for her."

The room grew uncomfortably silent as Henry gave Michael a long, hard look. Hope was ready to burst from his chest at Michael's words: perhaps the nightmare of living without Catherine would soon be over. He couldn't get to her soon enough.

"We head out tonight," Henry said. "I've waited long enough. My things are already packed."

He made to leave, but Michael stopped him, placing a hand on his arm. "Not so fast, Henry. I think it best if you stay here."

Bobby saw Henry's death stare aimed at Michael's hand.

"Excuse me?"

"I know this is hard, but I think it's best if you let me go alone."

Henry snapped. He was tired of listening to everyone else tell him how to handle the situation. "No, Michael! I'm going. I've been sitting here listening to all of you long enough. I should have gone for her a long time ago." He jerked his arm free from Michael's grip.

Michael knew he was putting himself at risk, but he stood firm in front of Henry and said, "You're staying." He felt Henry's fist in his face before he saw the punch coming. He heard Olivia's surprised scream as his head jerked back.

Bobby had anticipated the punch, and he was quick to reach Henry and restrain him before Michael fell victim to a second one.

"Easy, Henry!" Bobby said, using all his weight to restrain him.

Henry saw red as he struggled to reach Michael once more. "She's *everything* to me!" he yelled. "How can you expect me to stand by? Would you do the same if this was Patricia?"

"She's convinced you're with Natalie, Henry. *Convinced.* And with Natalie being in your home again last night … you know your past." He licked at the blood coming from his busted lip, hoping that his harsh words were enough.

"But I didn't—" Henry started to protest, still struggling against Bobby.

Michael held up a hand in understanding. "I know that. Everyone in this room knows that. But only showing the truth behind Natalie's motives will clear you." He dared get close to Henry, grabbing his shirt to put extra emphasis on his next words. "Natalie doesn't seem to have any family here, right? None that she's claiming, anyway. What I want to know, and what you all should be asking, is why she wasn't with her son on Christmas Eve? And if she wasn't with him, where on earth was he? Who, but a close friend or relative, would watch a young child on a holiday so his mother can go and try to seduce the alleged father?" He gave a small shove to show he was getting as angry as Henry. "Who would do that?" he demanded.

Henry hadn't thought of these questions, and he begrudgingly gave Michael a conceding glare. Michael nodded to Bobby, who slowly released Henry.

Olivia stood in the corner with her hands over her mouth as the three men, breathing deeply, tried to regain their composure.

Henry finally broke the tension. "Bring her back to me, Michael," he coolly demanded.

Michael nodded. "Catherine is a very stubborn woman, Henry. I can't make her come back against her will. But when she nearly died, I had promised myself that I'd do everything in my power to bring you two together. I know you love her. Trust me, Henry, I'll do all that I can. *You* need to focus on finding out everything you can about Natalie. There's more to her story."

At least, Michael mused, *I hope so.*

*   *   *

"I'm done, Susan," Natalie said, entering Susan's office without bothering to knock.

"Merry Christmas to you too, cousin," Susan replied with a sweet smile. "I have to admit that I'm surprised to see you out of bed so early today. Didn't you have a late night last night?" She gave Natalie a knowing look. "You'll find that I've been a great babysitter for your son."

Natalie crossed her arms and shook her head. "Stop it. I'm not playing these games any longer. I did what you asked. I helped you destroy a beautiful relationship. Catherine is gone—"

Susan's smile widened as she replied, "She is, isn't she?"

"Yes! So, why are you still making me do this?"

Susan walked over to face Natalie before saying, "Tell me what happened last night."

"You didn't answer my question."

"But I am. Tell me what happened, and then I'll explain to your simple mind why I still require your assistance."

Natalie knew that Susan would get the information one way or the other, and if she could find a way to at least gain something in return, it was worth it to answer her. She sighed and then said, "I went over there like you asked me. Henry was not happy."

"And?"

"And I made the offer like you asked me."

"*And?*"

"Well, he obviously refused me, thankfully. But you knew he would. And when Catherine called—"

"Stop right there." Her eyes narrowed before she continued, "That's why you're still here. Because *she* is."

Natalie shook her head as Susan pace the room. "Nooo ... she's not physically here."

"Maybe not, but despite everything you've done to them, she still reached out to him. And he's still refusing you. So, you see? You haven't completely severed the tie between them."

"You're sick."

"Just thorough."

"It's not going to work, Susan. Henry *loves* Catherine. He'll spend the rest of his life trying to win her back. There's nothing I can do that will change that."

"Sounds like you need my assistance," Susan said with calculating coolness.

That was the one thing Natalie certainly *didn't* want. Since she didn't trust Susan, Natalie could count on any aid Susan planned to lend as being destructive to all parties involved, herself included. She saw the veiled threat for exactly what it was.

If I want any chance of coming out of this unscathed, I need to keep Susan at bay.

Susan smiled as Natalie's shoulders slumped in defeat. She grabbed Natalie's hands and squeezed them. "That's better. Now, go spend the day with your son. Soon enough, we'll need to make our plans for New Year's Eve." A gleam filled her eyes as she crowed, "I'm certain that holiday will be a success for us."

Us? Natalie wanted to scream. Instead, she glared at her cousin. "I'll play along a bit longer, Susan. But here's an idea you might want to consider: What will you do if he stops refusing me? Will you play this same game to destroy me if Henry's affections turn toward me?"

"That's ridic—"

"Let me finish. I have one more thing to say. God help you if either of them ever find out about this. You'll have a war on your hands."

"Well, Natalie, it's a good thing you're in the thick of it too. It evens the playing field."

FORTY-THREE

Judging by the brightness of the bedroom, Catherine had slept well into the late morning. She hurried out of bed, knowing she had a full day of apologies and making it up to Irma, Edwin, and especially Sarah for her behavior the previous day. After quickly dressing, she went downstairs only to find the house empty.

Empty but not forgotten. Catherine smiled as she entered the kitchen and found a plate of breakfast pastries waiting for her. She sat at the table and picked at a muffin, her mind slipping back to last night's nightmare and the *real* nightmare that had caused it. She hated that Irma, and most likely Sarah and Edwin, had heard her screams in the middle of the night. While Irma had told her not to worry about Sarah and Edwin, she couldn't help but wonder what they all thought of her. She was certain they would have questions that she wouldn't be able to answer.

A light touch to her shoulder caused Catherine to jump from her chair and race across the kitchen. Safely on the other side, she turned and discovered Edwin standing behind her vacated chair.

"I'm sorry I scared you."

"I thought the house was empty," Catherine said at the same time.

"It was," Edwin said. "Mother insisted we leave you to rest this morning. But as head of this house, I couldn't easily do that, so I backtracked." He noticed an expression of hurt cross her face before she quickly masked it.

Tension filled the room as Catherine tried not to read too much into his statement. Yesterday's actions must have left him thinking poorly of her, which bothered her. She took a few steps toward the table, hoping to dismiss the look of fear that lingered on her face. He regarded her, waiting for a reply. Already embarrassed, she didn't want to explain anything more than necessary, so she simply said, "I'm sorry ..."

Before Catherine knew it, Edwin was right next to her. The storm in his eyes caused her to take a step away from him. But Edwin closed the distance, slowly backing her to the counter next to the sink. As Catherine looked up, her pulse quickened. Edwin couldn't hide the desire in his eyes, and as he focused on her lips, almost within kissing distance, the memory of their kiss was foremost in Catherine's mind. He clearly wanted to kiss her again.

Edwin struggled with the desire flaming within him. He had intended to hold a conversation about what had happened to Catherine the previous night, but being this close to her and seeing the vulnerability in her posture, he wanted to abandon conversation and caress her lips with his own. He shook his head to clear these thoughts.

What's happening to me? I've gone from keeping women at a distance to not being able to get enough of this one.

"I ..."

Catherine's timid voice brought him back to task, and he tore his eyes away from the temptation of her lips. *No, I have to know what happened.*

Edwin's mental struggle resulted in a harsh edge settling into his eyes. Catherine was reminded of the first time she'd met Edwin. He had been an imposing figure, fiercely protective of his family.

"Do you trust me, Catherine?" he asked, his soft voice demanding an honest answer. His face closed in on hers as he waited for a reply.

Catherine had lost the ability to speak. She swallowed and gave a single, small nod. She then lost the ability to breathe as Edwin came closer, his body nearly pressed against hers.

"Then I'd like to be able to return the favor."

Once again, her heartbeat quickened when he placed his hand on her stomach, at the exact spot she had shown Irma the previous evening. *He knows.* He must have overheard her conversation with Irma and now wanted to know the full story.

"I know what you're asking," Catherine responded, surprised at the strength in her voice. "Your priority is to protect your family, and you need to know if I bring any threat to them."

Edwin felt torn at seeing the resignation in Catherine's eyes, and he felt bad for the implications his words had created. *I trust you.* He wanted to reassure her, but he owed it to his family to learn if Catherine's stay created a threat. As much as his feelings had grown for Catherine, his affection for his family was stronger.

And I'm not going to fail them a second time.

He reluctantly removed his hand from her stomach and nodded. "You understand, then."

"Of course I do," Catherine replied. "I ... please, not here."

He fought the urge to place a reassuring hand on her shoulder. "No one will bother us here."

Exactly. "I don't want to risk them coming back before I finish."

He studied her closely before giving a nod to grant her request. "Come," he said, taking her hand and entwining his fingers with hers. "I know just the place."

She reluctantly allowed him to lead her to the living room to retrieve their coats, dreading the painful memories she was about to revisit. Besides the nightmare of Robert, she feared facing the memory of Henry's devotion to her during that time as well as the heartache of knowing that devotion no longer existed.

Edwin kept his eyes focused on the sidewalk as he walked next to Catherine. They had just left an isolated park bench where she had told him about her nightmare, and Edwin now regretted forcing her to relive it. He silently berated himself, abhorring that he had ever questioned her. Catherine was the type of person who would never knowingly put others in danger. Knocking her attacker down the stairs in an effort to spare her friends had been a testament to that. He could only imagine the scars she carried both physically and mentally.

"I apologize, Catherine," Edwin said in a low voice as he tucked her arm more securely at his elbow. "It was wrong of me to demand to know the cause of your nightmares. When I think of all you've suffered ..." He shook his head as he continued, "I'm so sorry that my actions added to your suffering." He stopped their progress as they entered a snow-covered park near St. Michael's church. "I was wrong to doubt you."

When Catherine returned his gaze, the sadness in her eyes tore at his heart. "You were right to ask. I admire you for protecting your family, at any cost. I only hope that you're not too ashamed to call me your friend." The burst of intensity that filled Edwin's eyes told Catherine she had been mistaken.

Almost instantaneously, he raised his hands to cup her face between them. He studied her a long time, as if his gaze were strong enough to heal her wounds and squelch her fears. Emotion laced his words when he finally said, "On the contrary, Catherine." His thumb caressed her bottom lip.

"Edwin," she pleaded.

"I know, Catherine," Edwin whispered as he struggled to keep his emotions in check. "I know where your heart is at present."

She stared into his eyes, and tears swelled in her own at the compassion she saw. "Thank you."

He nodded, gently kissing her forehead and pulling her into a comforting embrace. Catherine was reluctant, but when Edwin offered no other advancements that would suggest anything more than friendship, she allowed herself to draw comfort from the hug.

At present, Catherine, but should you ever decide to give your heart away again, I pray that I'm here to receive it.

FORTY-FOUR

Olivia nervously twisted her purse's handle as she waited at Michael and Patricia's doorstep. Having never been to their personal residence, Olivia wasn't sure how well they would receive her uninvited arrival. While she loved them both, Patricia intimidated her. Patricia was independent, strong-willed, and extremely self-confident. At this moment, Olivia felt lacking in all of these traits.

She's never going to agree to this ... never. When Patricia opened the front, Olivia dismissed her internal panic.

Patricia was surprised to find Olivia on her doorstep. "Olivia?"

Olivia gave a nervous smile as she asked, "Michael, has he—?"

"He left early this morning." She stood in the doorframe, waiting for Olivia to explain her reason for coming. When no response seemed forthcoming, Patricia regarded Olivia's swollen belly before glancing down at her own, commenting, "We make a fine pair, don't we?"

Olivia chuckled.

"What brings you by, Liv?"

Olivia smiled, saying, "I can see why Cat loves you so much. You're right to the point."

"I'll take that as a compliment," Patricia replied as she motioned for Olivia to follow her inside. "Where's Caleb?"

"I dropped him off with Bobby's parents," she replied, following Patricia. "I wasn't sure how long I'd be and didn't want to test his attention span."

"This must really be good, then."

Olivia sat in the chair Patricia indicated as she asked, "What do you mean?"

Patricia gave her a conspiratorial wink and explained, "You never come by, you dropped your son off before coming, you're alone ... you have something to say that you don't want others to hear." She lowered herself onto the couch across from Olivia. "So, spill it."

Trying to take a lesson from Patricia, Olivia blurted, "I want to know where Michael went."

Patricia considered the request carefully before responding, "Michael doesn't want any help right now, Liv. He doesn't want Bobby, or especially Henry—"

"I won't tell them. I plan to follow Michael without either of them."

Patricia couldn't hide her surprise. "Liv, look at you! Look at us! There's a reason Michael left me behind. And it's the same reason you should dismiss this crazy idea. You're not in any condition to travel."

"I still have some time before—"

"You can't be serious," Patricia interrupted. "You'd end up getting out there and having the baby before you can get back home."

Olivia gave a triumphant smile and replied, "Exactly."

"You *want* to have your child away from home?"

"I want Catherine home, Patricia. If I have this baby away from here, Bobby will be too distraught and concerned to stay behind."

"You've got that right," Patricia quipped.

Olivia continued, "He'll want to be with me, but he'll obviously be in no condition to drive himself. He'll need Henry to drive him."

Patricia sat in silence as she reflected over Olivia's plan.

"I believe Henry needs to be there," Olivia whispered. "It kills me how much they're both hurting, and we're holding him back. I understand Michael's reasoning, but I'm not entirely sure we should rob Henry of the chance to go after Catherine. Actions speak louder than words for Catherine, and Henry staying behind, no matter whose idea it is, cannot be productive."

Patricia leaned back in her chair and sighed heavily before responding, "For the record, I love my husband dearly—with all my heart. But he thinks he can solve all the problems of the world. And he knows so little about women. I have to agree with you that no matter the reasoning, Henry's presence *here* won't endear himself to Catherine. Your plan, though, might just work."

Abandoning her nervousness, Olivia squealed in delight. "You'll tell me where she's at, then?"

"No, Liv, not yet. I haven't heard from Michael since he left, so I have no clue where he is."

"But once you hear from him?"

"On one condition: you bring Bobby into this. He has to know the full scope of what's going on, *and* he has to agree with it before I'll tell you anything. If he doesn't want you to go, especially because of your pregnancy, I won't go against him."

Olivia clapped her hands. "He'll agree with it, I know he will."

"Don't be so sure, Liv. If he's anything like Michael, you won't be going anywhere. And while I would normally be in full support of a fellow woman and her scheme, I don't believe in keeping such a huge secret from a spouse." When she saw that her warning did nothing to dampen Olivia's spirit, she couldn't help but smile. "I see why Catherine loves you, Liv. You're so optimistic. How about you both come here tonight for dinner?"

"So you can help convince him?"

Patricia laughed. "So I can be certain you're not leaving out details in order to persuade him."

"I have to admit that tonight's dinner invitation caught me by surprise," Bobby said as he sat next to Olivia and across from Patricia. He gave Olivia a questioningly look, adding, "Especially since you demanded that I not mention it to Henry, so I assume this dinner is to discuss him, right?"

Patricia bit her tongue to keep her chuckle at bay. *Oh yes, Liv, you're going to have a great time convincing him to go along with your plan.*

Olivia laughed softly and looked to Patricia, silently pleading for help.

"This was your idea, dearie," Patricia said. "I'm here to make sure you tell him your whole plan."

"What plan?" Bobby asked with trepidation. His wife gifted him with her most charming smile. "Liv?"

"Well, I was hoping to have dinner first," Olivia countered. "I don't know about anyone else, but I'm starving."

"It can wait," Bobby said. "What scheme are you trying to delay telling me about?"

Olivia looked squarely at Bobby before replying, "Bobby, I need you to hear me out before you say anything."

Bobby groaned and cast a glance at Patricia. "This isn't going to be good, is it?"

"I figured out a way we can help Henry and Catherine."

"Liv, Michael's already working on it."

"But I think I can help."

"How?" Bobby narrowed his eyes and asked.

Bobby remained silent as Olivia laid out her plan to follow Michael in the hopes of actually delivering their child in whatever town Catherine was residing. He could scarcely believe his ears. While he agreed with her logic that Henry needed to be there, he found one glaring flaw in her plan: her absence from him.

"Absolutely not," Bobby said as soon as Olivia had finished. "You are too far along in your pregnancy. In fact, I wouldn't let you do this if you were only a week into your pregnancy."

Olivia's jaw dropped in surprise. "Bobby!" she exclaimed. "How can you say that?"

"Easily, dear. You're my wife who's carrying our unborn child. You and our child's safety take priority. I won't sacrifice either for this plan." He paused as he saw his wife's eyes pool with tears. "Liv, I understand you want to help. I admire that and love you for it. But you have to think about yourself now."

"Cat never did," she countered. "When I was pregnant with Caleb, she sacrificed everything to make sure I was taken care of. Now I want to do something for her."

"That's my point! I wasn't here for that pregnancy, and the worry over it nearly drove me mad. I can't do that again. It nearly killed me."

"And don't forget," Olivia continued as though Bobby hadn't spoken, "Henry looked out for you in Europe. You've told me countless times how his presence helped you, and he's gone into business with you."

"Olivia," Bobby pleaded.

Bobby was starting to waver, and Olivia recalibrated her argument to focus on Henry, not Catherine. "It's because of him that we have what we have. We owe it to him."

Bobby nervously ran his fingers through his hair and said reluctantly, "If Henry finds out about this—"

"Not if, but when," Patricia interjected.

Bobby nodded. "You're right. *When* Henry finds out about this, he's going to be furious."

"Not for long. Especially if it brings Cat home," Olivia argued.

"And what about Caleb? Do you plan to take him with you?"

"Your parents or mine can watch him."

Bobby studied her before finally asking, "You've got your heart set on this, haven't you?" When Olivia nodded with fervor, Bobby released a deep breath. "I want to think about this some more. If I agree to it, and I have the right to completely change my mind, you won't be leaving until after New Year's."

"But why? That's nearly a week—"

"I'm not backing down from this," Bobby interrupted. "I want you with me on New Year's."

"And the request that Henry not know about this?" Patricia prompted, a bit shocked that he was even willing to consider Olivia's idea.

Bobby let his shoulders drop. "I won't tell him. Not yet. But if this happens, God save us when he *does* find out. Although he'd eventually be happy we'd be bringing him to her, the fact that nearly everyone else would see her first would get him riled up. Let's hope Michael finds her and brings her home before then."

*   *   *

Henry smiled as Caleb finally fell asleep in his arms. Although Henry had been surprised that Bobby had asked him to babysit Caleb at the last minute so he could take Olivia out for dinner, Henry hadn't minded. His other alternative for the evening would have been to pace the floors at home, waiting to hear from either Michael or Catherine herself. He hadn't even cared about where Bobby and Olivia were going for dinner or how long they'd be gone. Henry needed a distraction from everything, and Caleb provided that.

As gently as he could, Henry carried the sleeping child up the stairs and to the room that Bobby and Olivia shared. Although no McKinney resided here, both Catherine's and Caleb's rooms remained untouched as though waiting for their return. While one would never be coming back, Henry prayed fervently that the other would. After Henry had placed Caleb in the crib and closed the bedroom door behind him, he made his way to the first of the two empty bedrooms.

Henry had only been in Caleb's bedroom a few times since his return from the war. Each visit had been tough on him. Tonight's visit, however, was the hardest yet. Caleb McKinney's death still tore at Henry, and even though he no longer felt guilt over his inability to save his friend, Henry still missed him.

"Oh, my dear friend," Henry whispered to the silent room, "I could use your advice right about now. If you could see the mess I've made with Catherine ..." He shook his head and continued to speak to the empty room. "I swear to you, Caleb, I have been nothing but faithful to your sister. Natalie ... she's from a past I can't remember and want nothing more than to forget." He leaned against the door and slid down to the floor. "I can't figure her out. She claims the boy is mine, but instead of trying to work with me and figure out what's best for him, she's tried some crazy antics to ... seduce me? When Catherine found Natalie in my home, I was as surprised as your sister. But it wasn't for the reason she thinks. I can only imagine how seeing Natalie there ... how it must have devastated your sister. It *did* devastate her." Henry felt his throat tightening with emotion. "She's hurting so badly over a misunderstanding. And I can't make it right. I haven't seen her since that night. She won't come home, and I have no clue where to find her. Michael does, but he's not telling."

He dropped his head in his hands as he fought the tears blurring his vision. "Her absence has shattered me," he whispered. "And *I don't know how to fix it.*"

The sound of the telephone ringing reached him, and Henry hurried to answer it, hoping it wouldn't wake Caleb.

"You're not answering the phone as quickly as you used to. Is it getting more difficult to waddle?" the caller asked before Henry could offer a greeting.

Henry held his breath at the sound of Catherine's voice. Her teasing tone warmed his heart, and he found himself reluctant to reveal that he wasn't Olivia.

"Liv?"

Henry swallowed before replying, "She has begun to waddle, but she's still pretty fast moving around." Before he had finished his sentence, he heard her sharp gasp.

"Henry," Catherine said after a very long pause.

"Hello, Catherine," he replied. As hard as it was not to launch into an array of apologies and requests for her to come home, Henry held back.

"I'm sorry, I meant to dial—"

"You didn't misdial," Henry interrupted. "Liv and Bobby are on a date, and they asked me to watch Caleb. So I'm here."

"Oh," Catherine said hesitantly. "I see."

Henry sat on the sofa, clenching his fist to keep from pleading. "How are you?" he asked as calmly as he could.

"I ... I should let you go."

Her stumble chipped at his self-control. "Please, Catherine. Let me listen to your voice a bit longer, okay?"

"Henry ..."

The one word held pain, but Henry found no trace of anger. It gave him hope. For Catherine, anger came spontaneously, but hurt brought caution. He could work his way through caution and guardedness. Since anger had caused her to leave in the first place, that would be a harder battle to fight.

Either way, he planned to fight for her.

"I miss you."

He heard her voice catch as she replied, "Henry, I can't—"

"Come home, Catherine. Where are you? I can come get you. I need you here ... *with me.*"

"Henry," Catherine said with a pronounced tremor, "you need ... you have a son now. And Natalie—"

"*No,*" Henry interrupted with determination. "There is no Natalie. I know what you *think* you saw, Catherine. This has been a complete misunderstanding."

"What I saw, Henry, was another woman who wants you in her life. And she has the means to make it happen. You have a son together. I can't be in the way of that, no matter how much I want to."

Henry latched on to her words before she could backtrack. "Do you still want to? Be with me, I mean."

He heard a tired sigh from the other end of the line. "In the end, Henry, what difference does it make?"

Despite everything, Henry couldn't help but smile. He felt a renewed energy beat from his heart to the rest of his body. He was ready to do battle, confident that he could win. "It makes all the difference in the world," he replied with hope.

"It's late, and I'm starting to get cold standing in this phone booth."

"Catherine, are you in any danger?" Concern over her physical state overpowered his desires. "Are you staying someplace safe?" Her experience with Robert swept through his thoughts, and it scared Henry that he had no way to protect her.

"Catherine, I'm worried about you. Promise me that you're—"

"I'm safe, Henry. I'm with a family who takes good care of me. I don't want to trouble them by using their phone to make calls."

Henry had no choice but to trust her judgment. "Okay," he conceded. "I … I *love* you, Catherine."

"Henry … I'm … I can't respond to that. I'm trying to hate you right now."

Trying.

"It's okay," Henry replied, feeling now that he still had part, if not all, of her heart. *It's a start.* "I'm not asking you to. I want you to know what I feel—what I'm *always* feeling." He hesitated before adding, "You promised me once … promised that you'd always believe in me and let me find you no matter what."

He waited, believing she must remember when he had extracted that promise from her.

"That promise was made because of my flashbacks," Catherine argued.

"I wasn't talking solely about flashbacks then, Catherine," Henry said solemnly. "And I'm still not." Then, as difficult as it was, he robbed Catherine of the chance to end the call first. "Good night, Catherine. Have sweet dreams. I'm counting the days until you're home."

The only sound in Henry's house was the opening and closing of the case that contained Catherine's engagement ring. He gripped it tightly in his hand, wishing that his will alone would be enough to bring her to his doorstep. But his far-fetched wish was met with silence.

Wish ... no ... this stopped being a wish but rather became a fervent prayer almost as soon as she left. And I've been in constant prayer since.

Henry smiled bitterly in the darkness of the early morning hours. While his wild past had finally caught up with him and was now costing him dearly, he recognized the irony of the situation. His time fighting in Europe and coming back to find himself in the most amazing relationship with Catherine had changed him. Prayer was something he found himself engaged in more often. Although he still struggled with who he had once been and who he wanted to be, he was trying to be better for Catherine and for himself.

A lot of good that's done me. My past is costing me everything. In the end, it doesn't matter how much I've changed.

Frustration filled him, and he suddenly sat up in bed to turn on the lamp on his nightstand. As light filled the room, he left his bed and went to the drawers holding the new clothes he had purchased for Catherine. Paying them little attention, he pawed through the items until he found the stack of letters he kept there. He dropped down to the floor and, with his back against the drawers, held the stack of letters to his forehead. Heartache consumed him as he slowly lowered them to his lips. His letters from Catherine while he fought in the war would always be dear to him. Now, they were the only link he had to the woman he loved and to the woman he prayed still loved him.

Henry gave a small smile as he began reading through the threats Catherine had made to destroy his truck. The threat was repeated in nearly all her early letters to him. While in Europe, he had cherished every word from her, biting words and all, and her letters had served as his lifeline. They had encouraged him in a way that nothing else did. He took his time reading the memorized words, and when he finally got to the last letter she had written to him during the war that he hadn't received until that horrific night he had almost lost her to Robert, his vision blurred.

Catherine had bared her soul in this letter, thinking Henry would never receive it. Anyone who read this letter would know the depth of Catherine's love for Henry. It described a love that matched his own for her, a love that he believed still existed. This letter was a testament to the magnitude of

Catherine's feelings for him. He read her confessions of how she had loved him for such a long time, from a distance she had never expected to bridge.

Catherine had never been one to express verbally her innermost feelings and, based on their last phone conversation, that hadn't changed. Yet, hearing everything she *hadn't* said along with her trembling voice convinced him that there was still a chance.

They weren't beyond reconciliation.

FORTY-FIVE

"Well, it certainly took you long enough to call," Patricia scolded her husband. His hardy chuckle made her smile.

"I've missed you too, darling. Tell me, how are things back home?"

She reflected on the scheme Olivia had presented to her earlier in the day before saying, "They're all waiting to hear from you—impatiently, I might add."

"Is Henry harassing you?"

Now it was Patricia's turn to laugh. "Goodness, no. Olivia and Bobby had dinner here tonight, so they charged Henry with babysitting Caleb."

"Really? They've never been over before," Michael commented, more to himself than to Patricia.

"Like I said, they are quite eager to hear from you. I know it's too soon to ask, but—"

"I haven't found her," he interrupted. "But I have found something that looks promising."

"Oh?" Patricia asked as she lowered herself to the kitchen chair.

"When Catherine left, it wasn't anything she'd planned. So I seriously doubt she had much money with her, meaning there is only so far north she could have taken the train. Only time will tell if I'm right, but this town looks promising. Not only does this town have a St. Michael's church, but I searched the area looking for a phone booth within walking distance of it. I've done this in a couple other towns along the way, but this one seems ... I've got a good feeling about this one."

"Michael, you're crazy. You have a *feeling*? Seriously? So, what are you going to do now? Set up surveillance and wait for Catherine to appear?"

"Something like that. I'm hoping Catherine will call again soon. When she does, I need you to somehow convince her to call again on Sunday afternoon, right after the church service."

"And people say I've lost my mind due to the pregnancy."

"She's religious. No matter where she's at, she'll find a church. I need to figure out if this is the one."

"Okay, handsome detective. I have to be the voice of reason—what if she doesn't call?"

"She's homesick, love. Don't worry, my dear, she'll call before Sunday." Not waiting for a response, he asked with concern, "Patricia, are you holding up okay?"

"Yes, Michael. It's busy here, though. I could really use you *and* Catherine right now."

Michael gave a heavy sigh. "I hate leaving you with the New Year's Eve dance right around the corner."

"Think nothing of it," she replied dismissively. "You had to go now. Because once this baby is born, I'm not letting you go anywhere."

"Fair enough. Are you sure you can handle all the planning? Don't be afraid to ask for help—especially from Catherine's friends. It'd keep Henry busy."

Patricia laughed before responding, "I have to visit the mayor to finalize his part in the celebration tomorrow. I'm sure Henry would *love* to accompany me there."

"Okay, never mind," he agreed.

Patricia was silent for a moment before asking, "Sweetheart, have you considered that this may not work? Even if you find Catherine, you may not be able to bring her back."

Michael's voice grew somber as he replied, "The thought never leaves my mind."

* * *

Catherine stared at the phone in her hand as the late evening's winds cut through the air. While Edwin waited for her at a respectable distance, her unexpected conversation with Henry replayed in her mind. She tried to wrap her mind around how she felt. *I hate him ... he hurt me so badly.*

Although Henry had frantically pleaded with her in their previous conversation, this one had been different. His wish to continue speaking with her had been evident, but so had something else. Henry hadn't begged for forgiveness for what had happened. Instead, he had displayed extreme confidence in trying to explain to Catherine that what she had witnessed had been a mistake. His confidence had shaken her, so much that she had unknowingly let her guard down. She hadn't realized it had happened until he had taken her words and turned them on her, asking if she still wanted to be with him. Her instinct had been to end the call, to do anything possible to avoid answering that question, but Henry had chosen to end the conversation before she had the chance.

She gently placed the phone back on its receiver, feeling alone and uncertain of what she was doing. Michael had always told her she was afraid of taking chances, that she was always quick to run and hide. *And now I'm far from home, running again. Maybe Michael is right.*

He would probably scold her, but she didn't care. The need to talk to the man who was practically a brother to her outweighed the risk of reproach. She picked up the phone once more and dialed. Knowing the late hours her friend kept, she didn't feel bad for calling so late.

"Hello?"

"Patricia!" Catherine replied, surprised Michael's wife was the one answering.

"Catherine? Goodness, how are you?"

"I'm doing all right," Catherine said, fighting hard to sound upbeat and positive.

Patricia chuckled. "You can't fool me, dear."

"I never could. Is Michael there?"

"Oh, Cat, I'm sorry, but you missed him. He's out running an errand for me."

"Really?" Catherine asked in surprise. "I figured you would still be awake, but isn't it late—"

"I'm pregnant," Patricia interrupted. "I have cravings at all hours of the day and night."

Catherine laughed and said, "Fair enough. Goodness, I've missed your sharp tongue."

"It's been out of use since you've been gone." Catherine could hear her chuckling through the line, then yawning.

"Oh, Patricia, I'm sorry. You should get to bed. I'll call back later. Can you tell Michael I called?"

"Of course, dear. Hey, I have an idea. Why don't you call around noon on Sunday? I'll make sure he's available to talk to you then."

"Um, okay." Catherine glanced at the church over her shoulder. "It might be a little after that, since I'll be at church. But I'll call after the service, okay?"

"Perfect. And Catherine? It's good to hear your voice. We all miss you, love."

Catherine found it hard to swallow as tears filled her eyes. It took her a couple of tries before she could say, "Thanks, Patricia. I miss you all too."

"We'll talk to you soon, okay?"

"Of course," Catherine whispered after the call had ended. She hung up the telephone, a small tremor in her hand. It had been a rough couple of days. Nightmares of Robert, reliving the story to Edwin, aching over Henry, and now missing advice from Michael emotionally drained her. With her steps as heavy as her heart, Catherine made her way to where Edwin stood waiting.

She was so lost in her thoughts that she didn't notice him appear suddenly at her side, having taken long strides to meet her. "Catherine?" he offered, holding his arm out to escort her.

She looked up at him, but before she could take his arm, Edwin pulled her into a hug. She accepted the embrace, burying her face into his coat. Catherine felt his arms tighten around her. With her face upturned, she stuttered, "Edwin ... I ..."

Edwin shook his head. "Don't. There's no need to explain. Shadows from our past creep up to haunt us. But remember," he said as he tucked a flyaway strand of hair behind her ear, "it's our choice to turn from them and focus on the future. Don't keep them here with you. Let them go."

Please, Catherine, let your past go.

Forty-Six

Patricia grumbled under her breath as she pulled into the mayor's driveway. She had no idea why she had agreed to come to his house to plan the New Year's Eve dance. *I'm pregnant. The dance isn't being held here—it'll be at Sal's. Why should I be the one to come out here?*

Pulling the key out of the ignition, Patricia glared at the mansion and said, "Oh yeah, I figured I'd be able to charge you twice as much for coming out here. If the outside of this home is anything to go by, you can afford it."

She studied her surroundings as she stepped out of the vehicle, noticing that hers wasn't the only "poor man's" car parked in the driveway. *Must be the villagers' day at the castle.* At the front door, she had barely knocked before the butler opened it and ushered her inside.

With only a curt, impersonal greeting, the butler led her to the mayor's office and indicated for her to sit. "He'll be along shortly."

"Other peasants, I assume," she whispered after he had left her alone. Patricia was tempted to poke around the office. However, she knew her swollen stomach wouldn't afford her the speed she'd need. With a small sigh, she slumped back and waited for the mayor's arrival.

She didn't have to wait long, as the mayor came rushing into the office a few minutes later. He replaced the frown on his face with a large, campaign-like smile, but not fast enough for Patricia not to notice. "Good morning! Had I known I would be meeting with you rather than your husband, I would most certainly have insisted on meeting you at the club." His eyes fell on her stomach as he said, "I had no idea your condition was so—"

"Well, it's a good thing, then," Patricia interrupted him, "that we aren't here to discuss my 'condition,' as you put it." She sat up straighter in her chair and put on her best game face. "I apologize if this is a bad time for you. We can reschedule."

The mayor dismissively waved his hand. "Nonsense. You're my only business this morning."

"Oh, I saw another car in the driveway and assumed—"

The frown from earlier returned to his face as he replied, "It's nothing. I have a niece in town with her son. I haven't seen her in ages, and I can only assume she's shown up wanting some handouts. But never mind her; Susan is handling it."

Patricia's mind narrowed on the words "a niece and her son" asking for handouts. *Could it be?* She tabled the thought while she focused on discussing plans for the New Year's Eve dance. The plans were simple enough: a band more renowned than the usual local groups would provide the music, a meal more substantial than the regular food and drink would be available, and the club would naturally be open past midnight.

"We'll need to sell tickets or something," Patricia commented as she checked her notes.

"Pardon? Tickets? We don't have time to sell tickets!"

Patricia stared pointedly at the mayor. "With all due respect, sir, you were the one who asked for this to be turned into a more extravagant event on such short notice. Our club often has standing room only, which isn't a big deal since most people are dancing. You want a sit-down meal. If we don't sell tickets or at least increase the cover charge to compensate, we're going to have too many patrons and not enough space for them to sit, let alone eat."

"I see your point," he acquiesced. "But while increasing the price of entry would discourage some participants, would it also make me look bad? Greedy for charging more?"

"Not if you announce you'll donate the money."

The mayor regarded her with a deepening frown on his face and asked, "Meaning that I'm footing the entire bill?"

Patricia nodded. "When you explain that all proceeds will go to the Disabled American Veterans organization, you'll be guaranteed a successful evening with media coverage. Plus, it'll be a surefire way to get votes come next election." She remained serious, careful not to give away any emotions while he brooded over her suggestion.

Finally, he gave her a slight smirk, saying, "You should be a politician, or their assistant, at the very least. You know how to push an agenda, I'll give you that." He gave a consenting nod as he rose to his feet, crossed over to her, and offered his hand to help her up from her seat. "Make it happen. Pull together the contract and bill, and I'll see to it that you're paid promptly."

"Thank you, sir."

"Of course," he replied as he reached the door and ushered her into the hall. "My butler will see you out."

Patricia turned to find the butler that had brought her in earlier engaged in self-preservation as a young boy continuously took aim at his shins. Patricia studied the young boy, memorizing his face quickly before saying, "It's okay. He obviously has his hands full. I can see myself out, thank you."

Patricia wasted no time leaving, heading straight to Henry's and praying he was home. When she stopped her car in front of his house, she saw him heading to his truck. "Don't leave yet!" she yelled before getting out of her vehicle.

Henry turned, surprised to find Patricia waddling toward him. "Patricia! I didn't see you. I was just heading back to the shop." He hurriedly met her halfway across his lawn. "Are you all right?"

"Can you spare five minutes?" Patricia asked as she took his arm and allowed him to escort her to his porch.

"Of course. Can I get you anything?"

"Let's go inside," she directed. "I promise this will only take a minute."

Henry helped her inside and waited while she sat on the living room sofa. Finally, his patience ran out. "I'm sorry, but I have to know, is this about Catherine? Have you heard from Michael?"

Patricia understood his focus but answered, "Maybe, but this is about something else. Catherine had mentioned that Natalie had given you a picture of your—her son—as a gift. Do you still have it?"

Confusion crossed his facial features, but he nodded slowly. "I do. I think she wanted me to have it on my desk at work, but I can't. Especially now that Catherine—"

"May I see it?" Patricia interrupted.

"Hold on." Henry left and quickly returned from his bedroom with a frame in his hand. He held it out to her.

An image of the young boy she saw at the mayor's house stared back at her, and Patricia couldn't help but offer Henry a triumphant smile.

"What is it?" he asked cautiously.

"I think I may have found the master puppeteer." She handed the photo frame back to Henry.

"What do you mean?"

"Does Cat have any enemies?"

"Catherine? I don't see how any of Catherine's enemies have anything to do with my son—"

"I was at the mayor's office today," Patricia explained, "and so was this child. The mayor was complaining to me about a niece and her son trying to freeload off him ... but that Susan was taking care of it." She waited for comprehension to dawn on his face before adding, "Susan ... she claims she's a new, close friend to Natalie, doesn't she?"

Henry collapsed on the sofa next to Patricia and groaned painfully. "Of course. Susan! How did I not *see* this before?"

When he looked back at Patricia, fury filled his face. "She's taken this to an entirely new level," he whispered.

Patricia felt a sense of satisfaction. Although she hated being the bearer of such news, she was pleased to provide Henry with something to take action on. Having stumbled on this discovery, she hoped it would give him the means to get Catherine back.

As a spark of an idea flashed in his eyes, Patricia asked, "What are you thinking, Henry?"

"If Susan's hand is in this ..." Henry stopped himself from completing the vocalized threat. Instead, he focused on Patricia. "Will you be able to meet with me later this evening? I'd like to have Bobby's and Olivia's thoughts on it all too."

"A brainstorming session? Of course."

Henry nodded. "I'll come by and get you so you don't have to drive," he said as he helped Patricia to her feet. He grabbed her hand and kissed it. "Thank you. You just gave me back a piece of my life."

Henry hadn't felt this hopeful since before Catherine had left town. Although they didn't have any incriminating proof yet, puzzle pieces had started to fall into place.

Susan has been trying to come between Catherine and me for so long ... had she finally found a way with Natalie?

Henry looked up to find everyone at the table looking at him, waiting for a reply to a question he hadn't heard. "I'm sorry, what was that?"

Olivia gave him a sympathetic smile from across the table. Bobby, Olivia, Patricia, and Henry were at the kitchen table at the McKinney residence.

"I asked," Bobby repeated, "if you thought Natalie might confess to Susan's part in all of this if you asked her directly?"

"And that question was after I asked if you're absolutely sure you've never been with Natalie ... in a way that would result in a child," Patricia clarified.

Focus, Henry.

Henry rubbed a hand across his face. "I'm not proud of my past—especially when it comes to my past with other women. And I'll admit, there have been times when I've woken up not completely sure how I ended up there. However, I always thought I was able to remember at least a portion of each evening of flirting, and I have no memories whatsoever of Natalie. I don't recall *ever* meeting her before she showed up at my shop. But she was so convincing, and based on who I had been ... I thought it possible."

"And if Susan is involved in some sort of scheme," Olivia added, "I think it best to find tangible proof of her involvement."

Patricia nodded, saying, "I think, based on what Michael has told me about Cat and Susan's past, whatever plan we make should attempt to remove Susan from our lives."

Bobby said to Henry, "I want you happy, Henry. And I want Susan out of Catherine's life. I think if we can find something tangible, then great. But if we can't, I think a confession from Susan will hold more weight in the end."

"I should have stopped this long before I left for Europe," Henry said with regret. "If I had handled things differently *then*, Susan wouldn't be at war with Catherine *now*."

"We'll each do our part, Henry," Olivia said with conviction. "We'll get to the bottom of this and counterattack from every side if we have to."

"You've been hanging around your military husband," Henry said with a grateful smile.

"Nonsense," Olivia replied dismissively. "It wasn't my husband or you, for that matter, who taught me this type of warfare."

"Cat?" Patricia asked.

Olivia shook her head. "I come from the same roots as Susan," she explained. "I can think like her if I need to."

Henry smiled. "Thank you all," he said. "And if we hear from Michael that he's found Catherine, I can only pray she'll be home soon."

"Do you think Natalie would come clean if Susan is manipulating her?" Patricia asked, carefully avoiding Henry's comment.

"No," Olivia answered promptly. "Susan's the type that always gets her way. She's controlling. Cat's about the only person I've ever seen really stand up to her, and look at all the repercussions she's suffered for it."

They were silent, each lost in their own thoughts, until Patricia mentioned cautiously, "Henry, seeing that little boy at Susan's could be innocent enough. After all, didn't Susan befriend Natalie after they met at church? While I hope there's something here, I could be wrong."

Henry nodded. "I know. But the more I think about it, the more it makes since that Susan has her hand in this."

"She's probably at the very least encouraging a relationship between you two," Bobby added.

"We need to dig a little. There's got to be something … *somewhere*." Olivia tapped her fingers on the table as she thought. "How to get a confession from Susan, if she's truly involved …"

Patricia avoided looking at Henry as she suggested, "You could try to woo her, Henry. I think it's safe to say she'd be interested."

"*No*," Henry's reply was adamant. "If there's even the smallest chance she's not involved in this, I don't want to encourage her. Besides, I belong to Catherine. I'm not going to do anything that would appear otherwise. I've already hurt her so much. I won't take a chance of doing more damage."

"That leaves one alternative then," Patricia said. "Snooping."

Henry, Bobby, and Olivia all looked up at Patricia with slightly confused expressions. "Excuse me?" Bobby finally asked.

Patricia rolled her eyes. "Seriously. You can't tell me—"

"What do you have in mind?" Olivia asked, leaning forward eagerly in her chair.

"We dig until we find something." She chewed on her bottom lip as an idea formed. "New Year's Eve would be the best time. Susan's entire family will be at the club."

"Impossible," Henry countered. "Their staff will still be at their residence. If you want to break into her home for evidence, it'll never work." He couldn't believe he was considering the plan, but the hope that this fiasco might all be a scheme plotted by Susan motivated him. "Natalie's place would be more doable."

Patricia replied, "We'd have to get her away from her house."

Henry nodded in resignation, sickness filling his stomach. "I realize that. You'll be too busy running the club that evening. I could take her there to make sure she's out of the house."

"I'm too pregnant to do any dancing, so I could watch her son for the evening while Bobby snooped around," Olivia offered.

"There's one huge flaw to this plan," Bobby interjected. "*Me*. You're relying on a one-armed man to accomplish the most important part of this plan." He ran his hand through his hair. "If you're asking me to break into her home and do the digging, you're doomed."

Henry clasped Bobby's shoulder. "No, Bobby. I'm doomed if we don't try."

Bobby struggled with his insecurity while thinking about Henry's difficult situation. He could only imagine how much Henry was hurting, and guilt over Olivia's plans to pursue Catherine gnawed at him. He nodded reluctantly. "I'm in. I only hope I don't disappoint you."

Once the four committed, making plans for New Year's Eve went well into the early morning hours. As Henry prepared to leave, he couldn't help but feel rejuvenated. He was finally taking some form of action to win back Catherine. Already his heart felt lighter.

Patricia's loud yawn interrupted his thoughts.

"Patricia, it's late. Are you ready for a ride back home?"

"No," Olivia answered first. "Why don't you both stay here? It's so late, and we have enough room."

Henry shook his head. He hadn't stayed the night in this house since Catherine had been recovering from Robert's attack. He wasn't going to stay in her home without her present, granting him permission. "Thanks, but I'm okay to drive home. Bobby, Caleb, and I used to keep later hours than this."

"Well, I'll take you up on that offer to stay the night!" Patricia answered.

Olivia, Bobby, and Patricia stood on the porch and watched Henry's truck taillights disappear down the road. Patricia waited until she could no longer hear his truck's engine before sighing deeply and saying, "Well, I'm glad I dodged *that* bullet."

"Patricia?" Olivia asked.

She kept her focus on the moonlit road as she replied, "He came so close so many times, I thought for sure he'd trip me up and I'd tell him about Michael."

"What about Michael?" Bobby asked.

When Patricia didn't immediately respond, Bobby answered for her. "He's found her, hasn't he?" he asked, wishing Patricia had made this revelation before Henry left.

Patricia's slight nod caused Olivia to grab her hand in disbelief. "Truly?" she whispered.

"Well, he believes he's found her."

"I need to pack!" Olivia turned and started to head back into the house, but Patricia caught her arm.

"No, Liv, not yet. We have to wait. If Natalie's story is fabricated in any way, it's our job to help Henry discover it. We owe it to him."

"We owe it to him to tell him this news!" Bobby countered. "You two haven't seen the full scope of what her absence has done to him. I have ..." He hesitated only a moment. "Forget your plans; I'm going to tell him."

With her free hand, Patricia reached out and grabbed his shirt as he started down the porch steps. "Oh no, you don't! We have to wait, Bobby."

"*Why?*"

"Michael believes he's found her, but he hasn't spoken to her. Don't you think it'd help to know her frame of mind?"

"Seriously? She left town, Patricia. She's refusing to speak with Henry. I think I'm pretty sure I know her frame of mind."

"Bobby," Olivia interjected at hearing his voice rising.

But Bobby wouldn't be deterred. "No, Liv. We're meddling too much. I don't like this, and I don't like keeping things from Henry. If the situation was reversed, and I was looking for you, I'd go mad. Henry *needs* to know we've found her. We owe him the truth on that. We all know how hard-headed Catherine can be. Henry's the only one she'll listen to. And now she's not even listening to him."

"Exactly!" Patricia exclaimed. "She *is* hard-headed and stubborn. It's going to take more than Henry's words to convince her; she doesn't trust them anymore. It'll take proof—proof that's strong enough to guarantee that Susan, or anyone else for that matter, doesn't hurt them again."

Patricia released his shirt only when Bobby gave a reluctant nod.

It's not right. Henry has the most at stake in this battle, and we're blindfolding him for the fight.

FORTY-SEVEN

Catherine stood at the front window in the living room, amazed at the additional snow that had accumulated overnight. Hearing someone enter from the kitchen, she said, "There's a blizzard out there."

"Really?" Edwin's masculine voice grew nearer as he came up behind her. "Maybe for a southern girl," he teased, "but here, that's a dusting."

Catherine gave him an incredulous look. "There's almost a foot of snow out there, Edwin!"

Standing so close to her, Edwin struggled to remain focused on the conversation. It was Sunday morning, and his sole thoughts shouldn't be of this woman. However, she consumed them more with each passing day.

Focus, Edwin!

He pulled his new gloves out of his coat pocket, concentrating on his hands rather than Catherine as he replied, "It's good, then, that you have a new coat to wear. Its thickness should keep you warm." He finally dared to look back at her, his eyes resting on the shoulders of her coat. Even though the coat was given out of necessity, he couldn't ignore the warmness that swelled in his chest each time he saw her wearing it.

"Don't let this bit of snow be a deterrent!" Sarah exclaimed as she whisked in and wedged herself between them. She grabbed their hands as she passed, pulling both of them to the door. "This is perfect weather!"

Catherine pulled free from Sarah's grip at the edge of the porch, which was protected from the snow. Sarah practically danced through the snow as she found her way to the sidewalk. Once there, Sarah stopped and turned back to the rest of the small party.

"Come on, slowpokes! It's just snow."

Irma chuckled as she confidently strode past Catherine and Edwin to meet her daughter. "Be nice to Grace, Sarah. She's obviously not used to this kind of weather."

Watching the older woman on the sidewalk boosted Catherine's confidence. *If she can do this, surely I can too.* Catherine took a bold step from the covered porch and was convinced the earth had moved under her. Throwing out her arms, she twisted and tried to regain her balance, only to spin and fall directly into Edwin's outstretched arms.

Catherine didn't dare move as Edwin securely held her in place. Despite the embarrassment that colored her face, she shyly tilted her head up. As their eyes met, she saw him smile briefly before replacing it with his normal serious expression.

"Obviously," he managed to whisper. "I think maybe we should take the car today, yes?"

Edwin tried hard not to laugh at Catherine as her face clouded over, preparing for an argument. For once, he was glad to have grown up in a place that received so much snow. It made him surefooted, despite his limp—so much so that holding Catherine didn't burden him.

"If your mother can make it in this snow," Catherine huffed as she struggled to regain her footing while ignoring Sarah's and Irma's chuckles, "then so can I."

Edwin bit his lip to keep his own laughter at bay as he helped her. "If you insist …"

"I do," she confirmed. When she finally managed to stand on her own, she looked triumphant.

"Very good," he countered. "Of course, the real test will be when you take a step." Fear flashed across her face, then she stared down at her feet. He held out his crooked arm. "Here, hang on to me. I'll escort you to church."

Hesitating, she realized Irma and Sarah were already walking to church. They'd have to hurry to catch them, and Catherine wasn't confident she could do that without falling again.

"Catherine," Edwin said. His family was far enough down the street that they couldn't hear him. "I won't let you fall."

Catherine found all mirth gone from his eyes, replaced by a deeper promise to protect her from more than the snow.

Edwin watched as wariness crossed Catherine's features. Suddenly, she looked scared and ready to run at the first hint of danger. *Oh, Henry, what have you done to her?*

Not giving her the chance to refuse him, Edwin tucked Catherine's hand in his elbow. They took several tentative steps before her grip on his arm began to loosen.

"Besides," he reassured her as he placed his free hand over hers, "this way, if you fall, I'll go down with you. I can't laugh at you if I'm down in the mix too."

No sooner had Edwin spoken the words than Catherine felt her right foot slide sideways. Instinctively, she tightened her hold on him and leaned on his arm. "Let's not test that theory," she said between gritted teeth.

By the time church services ended, Catherine felt that she had been in constant prayer. From arriving to the service without any more embarrassing spills to listening to the sermon's message about healing in the new year, her silent prayers had been relentless. As the message about forgiving and moving on engraved itself on her heart, Catherine prayed for the courage to do just that.

She loved Henry, despite the wicked turn of events that she could have never foreseen. She had loved him for many, many years. Learning about his son hadn't changed that. While society's expectations held him accountable for his past, Catherine wasn't going to hold that against him. But she couldn't so easily handle the anger and hurt that filled her when she recalled seeing Natalie in his home and hearing her voice on the telephone. That degree of betrayal was unforgivable.

Today's sermon begged to differ.

Okay, it's definitely unforgettable then. We're supposed to forgive and move past these heartaches. But I don't know how. I'm trying ... Catherine shook her head at her own thoughts. *Okay, maybe I'm running rather than trying. But that's all my heart can handle right now. I'm not strong enough for anything more.*

Catherine sensed Edwin next to her as they exited the church. He arched a teasing eyebrow as he offered his arm once more and asked, "Shall we descend the stairs together?"

Noticing that the church's awning ended at the top step, Catherine sighed before giving a slight nod. Irma and Sarah slipped by them without any problem.

"Show-offs," Catherine muttered under her breath as she began to carefully navigate the steps.

Edwin chuckled next to her. "Come, you'll get the hang of it. All you need is time. By the end of the season, you'll be running laps around them."

The expectation about her stay caused Catherine to stumble, and Edwin's firm grip on her kept her from tumbling down the few remaining steps.

"Careful!" he said. "We wouldn't want you tumbling to your death."

As they reached the last step, the memory of Robert meeting his demise at the bottom of her stairs clouded Catherine's vision. She stopped, suddenly only seeing his face and hearing the sound of his gun firing. She had been so afraid of his plans to kill Henry; she had done everything in her power to stop him, ultimately killing him.

His blood was on her hands.

Get it off, get it off, get it off!

Edwin felt Catherine stiffen beside him. He looked over to find her staring at her free hand. "Catherine?" he whispered so only she could hear. "Grace?" He asked a bit more loudly. "Are you all right?"

She refused to pull her attention from her hand.

Edwin saw his mother and sister already across the street. They stopped to wait, but Edwin nodded for them to continue on home. Believing it was due to Catherine's inexperience in the snow, they obeyed. As soon as he saw them walk once more, he turned his attention to Catherine and guided her to the side of the stairs, clear of the churchgoers that were still filing out of the building. He touched her shoulder and turned to face her.

"What is it?" he prodded, wanting nothing more than to wipe away her frown.

She didn't acknowledge hearing him. He watched as she suddenly pulled her arm from his and began tugging at her gloves. It wasn't until she dropped her gloves and plunged both hands into the snow that he realized she was gone, trapped in a memory from her past like she had been on Christmas.

"Blood," he heard her mumble.

Edwin glanced around, thankful that only a few churchgoers remained. He turned so that his body blocked Catherine from their view. When they gave him curious looks, he prayed for forgiveness even as he said, "She must have lost her ring when she slipped her gloves off." He bent down and pretended to search through the snow as the last congregants passed. Only when he was sure no one lingered to watch did he reach out and try to grab her hands.

"Catherine!" he hissed as she tried to fight him. He pulled her to her feet and drew her in close to him, his hands firmly grasping her frozen ones, now red from the numerous plunges in the snow. Grateful his hands were large enough to hold both of Catherine's with only one of his own, he took his free hand and cupped her face. "Catherine! Look at me!" He held her face in place directly in front of him, closing in so that he was the only thing she could see.

Her eyes focused *elsewhere* as she whispered, "Stairs ..."

Oh, God, I mentioned falling down the stairs. I did this. Remorse filled Edwin as he recalled details about the horrible experience Catherine had shared with him.

"Focus on me, Catherine, *please.*" He drew his face closer to her, willing her to look at his eyes.

"Henry," she whimpered.

"He's fine. He's not hurt. He's alive." As much as he hated reassuring her that the man who had broken her heart was all right, he added, "You saved him, Catherine. You *saved* Henry." He removed his hand from her face long enough to remove his own glove then placed it back on her cheek. "Come back to me, Catherine," he whispered, caressing her face and praying the stimulation would help.

It seemed to. Awareness slowly filtered through Catherine's face. He held her close to him, refusing to release her hands, so they appeared to be lovers to anyone who passed. He didn't care what strangers thought. He was focused solely on Catherine.

Catherine looked up to find Edwin holding her hands tightly with one hand while his other hand held her face close to his own. His eyes held an intensity that she didn't know how to interpret. She wasn't sure how she ended up in his embrace or why her hands were gloveless and freezing. She was confused. She remembered coming down the stairs, slipping, and Edwin's words ...

She gasped. *Not again. Don't tell me I had another—*

"Welcome back," Edwin whispered, interrupting her thoughts.

The concern Catherine saw in his face disarmed her. She didn't know whether to cry in embarrassment or take refuge in his comforting touch.

I can do neither. She pulled away, distancing herself as much as possible. "I'm so sorry for that," she apologized.

"I'm sorry too," Edwin countered, reaching to pick up her discarded gloves. "I wasn't thinking when I teased you earlier. This is my fault."

No, this is Robert's.

He held out the gloves to Catherine and said, "Here. Let's get you home and warmed up."

If Edwin saw Catherine's hands tremble as she reached for the gloves, he chose not to point it out. Catherine was grateful. She glanced around her as she hastily put them on. "Where are Irma and Sarah?"

"They figured it might take us a while to get home. They went on ahead of us. Don't worry, they didn't see anything. I told anyone who did see that you were searching for your ring."

Catherine looked at him in surprise. "You lied?"

Edwin contemplated giving her a humorous reply to make her smile but thought better of it. He simply nodded as he returned his hands to the warmth of his own gloves. "Are you ready to make the trek back home?"

Catherine started to nod but stopped when she remembered the promise she had made earlier to Patricia. "I need to make a phone call," she said aloud.

"Catherine," Edwin said cautiously. He started to tell her that it had only been a flashback, Henry was fine, and she didn't need to call anyone to be reassured of that. However, one look in her eyes told him that nothing he said would deter her. Instead, he nodded, adding, "I'll walk you to the phone and wait until you're finished."

"Edwin, it's cold out here. You don't have—"

"Yes, I do," he interrupted. "It'll take you five hours to get home otherwise."

His wink told her he was teasing, and she seized the opportunity to change the subject from the flashbacks that still left her feeling shattered.

* * *

Michael stood a safe distance from the church and nearby phone booth. He had immediately spotted Catherine when she stepped out of the church doors. While a large part of him wanted to rush up to her, hug her in one breath, strangle her in the next, and then curse at her for choosing such a cold location to run away to, he held back at seeing a man at her side. Uneasiness pitted his stomach as he watched the man escort Catherine down the steps and help her as she slipped down the last few steps. From where he stood, he could only read their body language as the man spoke with Catherine, looked over his shoulder at the straggling congregants, and then knelt beside her as she began to dig in the snow.

Something's not right. Michael watched as Catherine continued to dig in the snow, stopping only after the man had made several attempts to stop her. It took the man's bare hand on her face and him speaking to her at an intimate distance to get her to stop.

Is she having a flashback? Her movements, almost frantic, were reminiscent of when she had fled the dance club the night he had triggered a flashback for her. He took an instinctive step toward them, wanting to check on Catherine himself. No sooner had he decided to go to her than she put her gloves back on and allowed the man to escort her to the pay phone.

She's calling Patricia.

Michael couldn't help but smile. He took several steps, closing the distance between himself and his formal pupil while making sure he remained hidden from her view. He wanted more than anything to speak with her, but not in the presence of this man who loomed protectively over her.

As Edwin waited at a respectable distance for Catherine to make her phone call, he shoved his hands in his pockets and ducked his chin into his coat's collar. He felt terrible for causing Catherine to experience the brief flashback, and he wished he knew a way to protect her from them in the future.

I want to protect her from everything. Maybe if I can help create new memories, they'll eventually push out the old ones. Although he seriously doubted Henry would be easy to erase from her heart, he wanted the opportunity to try.

Edwin hoped Catherine wasn't getting too cold as she conversed on the telephone. Today was a cold day to be standing idly outside. The deserted streets were testament to that. He and Catherine were the only ones braving the cold temperatures.

Us and that man, Edwin mused, as he noticed a man standing at a distance, his focus directed toward Catherine. The man stood where Catherine couldn't see him, but he most certainly could see Catherine. Unease crept up Edwin's spine. While the man didn't seem to ogle inappropriately, he kept his attention on her. Edwin watched Catherine from the corner of his eye while keeping his other eye on this mysterious man. As soon as Catherine ended her call, Edwin hurried forward to meet her.

Catherine was surprised to see Edwin so close as she exited the phone booth. "Everything all right?" she asked, seeing a deep frown on his face as his gaze rested on something over her shoulder.

He shook his head as he focused his eyes on Catherine. "Yes, fine. However, I thought someone was watching you," he explained. Seeing Catherine's face pale as she turned to look over her shoulder, he took her arm and tucked it in the crook of his own. "It's nothing, Catherine. They're gone. It must have been my imagination."

"No doubt heightened from the nightmare I told you about," Catherine said, allowing Edwin to lead her safely home, but not before she saw him cast one more backward glance.

Michael smirked as Catherine left with the man who had seen him watching them. He glanced back in Michael's direction once more, but Michael was confident he had hidden himself from view. Michael needed to follow them, despite having learned much in the brief time he had observed them.

It's clear Catherine means something to this guy ... the question is, does he mean something to her?

Before considering how poorly things could go if he was discovered, he waited briefly before following them. Hoping to discover where Catherine had been residing, he also wanted to continue observing the two of them before revealing his presence to Catherine. While they walked, the man kept Catherine's arm tucked tightly in his own, pausing as needed to keep Catherine from falling.

She looked ridiculous as she made her way across the snowy and icy sidewalk, and Michael found himself chuckling at her several times. The man seemed patient with her, allowing himself to bear much of her weight with every slip. Although Henry would have also done his best to protect Catherine, Michael imagined Henry wouldn't be able to resist letting her fall just once.

Of course, Cat would be determined that Henry meet the same fate and would've pulled him down to join her.

The imagined scene brought a sad smile to his lips, and he noticed that the man was now leading Catherine toward the stairs of a full front porch attached to a two-story house. No sooner had the two reached the bottom step than a young woman rushed out the front door, colliding with them and sending all three tumbling into the snow. Michael observed the young woman bursting into laughter, spontaneously making snow angels as she lay deep in the snow. Even the man seemed to be chuckling. He had managed to absorb most of the fall by pulling Catherine into his arms so that she'd fallen against him.

How chivalrous ...

But he didn't find the way the man lingered to be chivalrous at all. He watched with growing concern as the man delayed rising from the ground, keeping Catherine trapped within his arms. Catherine took the initiative to rise, and when they were both on their feet, the man kept his arm near her waist. Although it might have been in preparation for her next fall, Michael doubted that.

It was obvious this man had an interest in Catherine. Although he wasn't close enough to see Catherine's face, Michael observed her body language, grateful that they had had enough dance lessons together for him to distinguish her moods by her movements.

She was hesitant and nervous, and for the first time, Michael regretted not bringing Henry with him.

As the young woman sprang to her feet, she called over her shoulder to

Catherine and the man, "Come on, you two! Mother is packing a lunch for all of us. She's coming with us today."

"With us?" Michael heard Catherine call after the woman as she walked in the direction opposite of where he partially hid.

"Yes. If you two aren't too old, there are some great frozen ponds to explore! I'll meet you all at Winchester's Pond!" Somehow, the woman managed to skip away from them. As Catherine and the man followed her departure with their eyes, Michael used the opportunity to sneak closer to hear their soft conversation more easily.

Catherine wobbled and turned to the man. "Explore?"

Michael heard warmth in the man's voice as he explained, "Sarah means ice skating. There are several ponds that are probably frozen enough to bear ice skaters."

"*Ice skating?*" Catherine asked in disbelief, the emphasis in her words causing her to slip.

The man steadied her in his arms. Once she seemed safe from falling, he answered, "Yes, ice skating. Haven't you ever been?" He kept his arms around her as he waited for a response.

"Look at me!" she demanded, and Michael's heart warmed at hearing the familiar sharpness in her voice. It had been too long since he'd heard it. "Do I look like an expert on the ice?"

The man exploded in full-blown laughter as an older woman joined them from the house. "Oh, Grace, then by all means, we have to take you."

Grace?? Catherine's using her middle name instead of her first. Why? Even as Michael asked the question, he knew why.

She really doesn't want to be found.

"Are you crazy?" Catherine's retort broke into Michael's reflection.

"Not at all," the man replied seriously. "You know that."

"Do you realize how embarrassing it was just to walk home from church? There'll be lots of people skating, won't there?"

"Probably so. You can sit with Mother if you absolutely refuse to skate."

"Edwin! I plan to skate some myself," the older woman retorted.

Catherine groaned, and Edwin smiled. Michael quickly concluded that Edwin and Sarah were siblings, and the children of the woman standing next to Catherine. He was glad to learn that the pond they were heading to would be busy. Michael wanted to follow them and observe them a bit longer, mainly for Henry's sake.

Catherine hadn't been this nervous since her late brother's tribute dance. She glanced at the man beside her, who was serving as her source of strength as she stood at the edge of the frozen pond. Edwin offered his arm and patiently waited for her to take the first step. Catherine couldn't help but reflect on how differently Michael had encouraged her to get out on the dance floor, not allowing her to take her time but rather shining a spotlight on her to urge her to the floor.

If he were here now, he'd probably push me onto the ice. She smiled sadly at the thought. It bothered her that he hadn't been at home when she had called him earlier that afternoon. Her flashback had left her unsettled, and she would have liked to have Michael reassure her that Henry was still okay.

And Henry would be pulling me out on the ice without letting me find my bearings. It wouldn't matter that neither of us knew how to skate; we'd be falling together. She shook her head. *I have to stop this. Henry made his decision ... and it wasn't me.*

"Most people are skating already," Edwin leaned down and whispered. "If you want to try it now, there'll be fewer people watching."

His nearness caused her mind to trip. "And if I f-fall?" she stuttered.

"I won't promise you won't fall. You probably will." He didn't straighten up, and the teasing left his eyes as he added, "But I will be here to get you back on your feet."

Catherine wondered if they were still talking about ice skating. She tore her eyes away from him and down. "But if I stay where it's safe, on solid ground, I won't have to worry about falling."

"You surprise me, Catherine," Edwin responded, whispering her name. "You don't seem like the type of person to cower from taking risks."

She bit her lip, hating how easily his words rendered tears in her eyes. "If you get burned badly enough—"

"Yes, I think we've both had our share of burns. But Catherine," he said, this time confidently taking her hand in his, "we all have our battle scars."

Edwin tugged her hand, helping her onto the ice. In one fluid motion, like a dancer, he turned to face her, skating backwards and never breaking eye contact. He now held both her hands in his, guiding her slowly across the pond as they weaved through other skaters.

Edwin's heart raced as he carefully guided Catherine. Her death grip on his hands meant that if she so much as stumbled, she'd take him down with her. She stared her feet, biting her lower lip at the same time.

"Look at me," Edwin gently encouraged her. "It's easier to keep your eyes focused on my face, since I'm right in front of you."

You sound like Michael.

"Who knew skating would be so much like dancing?" she said, gritting her teeth as she looked up and tried to focus on Edwin.

Edwin couldn't help but chuckle at the pained look on Catherine's face. "Yes," he replied, "but surely you don't look like you're in so much pain when you dance?"

"It's all about trusting your partner," she replied. "I can assure you, I've worn this face on the dance floor a time or two."

"Yes, trust is something that takes a while to build with you."

"Like you have room to talk."

Edwin smiled. "I'll give you that," he responded. He nodded his head toward the edge of the pond to his left. "Look, we made it around once with no injuries. You're doing great."

In disbelief, Catherine glanced to her right, noticing that Irma and Sarah had stepped off the pond and were now waving to them, encouraging her. Someone moved behind them, distracting Catherine from the small cheering section.

Shock racked her body as she gasped at the man standing at a distance. *Michael?*

Forgetting that she stood on ice, she released Edwin's hand, tried to take a step, and fell hard on the ice below her. Pain ripped through her left hip, knee, and elbow, and she let out an involuntary groan.

"Grace!" Sarah called, rushing back out on the ice to help. Edwin was already on his knees beside Catherine.

"Are you okay?" he asked, assisting her to a sitting position. "Where does it hurt?"

"Everywhere," Catherine replied. Her mind was spinning; she had to get off the ice. "Please, help me to my feet."

"That was a hard fall. Maybe you should rest a moment," Sarah countered.

Catherine shook her head, already trying to tuck her feet under her and push herself up. When she tried to bear weight on her feet, her skates slid out from underneath her, and she collapsed into Edwin, bringing him down on his back.

"I'm so sorry!" she cried, frantically trying to get off Edwin and the arms he now had on each side to steady her.

"Hey, calm down. It's okay," he soothed, bringing them both to a sitting position. "Let's take it easy. Let me and Sarah help you."

Catherine could only nod. Pain throbbed on her left side, and the vision of Michael had left her eyes tear-filled. Once she was on her feet, she combed the entrance to the pond, searching for the man who had reminded her of one of her best friends.

He wasn't there. Disappointment, homesickness, and relief filtered through Catherine as she realized the man she had mistaken for Michael was gone. She continued to search for him as Edwin and Sarah helped her off the ice. Irma's, Sarah's, and Edwin's questions about her pain distracted her from the stranger until she was finally able to convince them all that she was fine and only in need of rest.

Irma volunteered to sit with Catherine. Edwin, seeing more than physical pain etched on her face, realized something more was bothering Catherine. "Mother, let me take Grace home. We'll get a head start and will probably arrive at the house no sooner than you and Sarah."

"Very funny, Edwin," Catherine said as she winced when straightening her elbow. "But I think I like that idea. I'm done for the day. You couldn't do anything to convince me to get back on the ice."

As Edwin escorted Catherine from the pond, he noticed her glancing in different directions.

"Looking for someone?" he asked, uneasiness filling him.

She shook her head, allowing Edwin to tuck her arm in his and providing strength for her to lean on. "I saw someone who reminded me … it's nothing. It's left me …"

"Unsettled?" Edwin prompted.

She nodded, pasting a strong smile on her face. "It's nothing, though. Just a figment of my imagination."

Edwin recalled the man standing at a distance from the telephone booth. Apprehension crawled down his spine.

Perhaps it wasn't Catherine's imagination at all.

FORTY-EIGHT

Patricia was just starting to doze off when the telephone's ringing interrupted her rest. She had been expecting Michael to call soon after she had made an excuse for his absence and had ended her noon phone call with Catherine. The fact that it was now late in the evening and well past her desired bedtime didn't make her eager to answer the phone.

"I found her," Michael said after Patricia answered.

"I was expecting you to call much earlier. How is she?"

Patricia heard the hesitation in his voice before he answered, "I'm not sure."

"You're not sure? How did she react when she saw you?"

"I made sure she didn't see me."

"Michael, what are you doing? I thought you went on this hunt to find her and bring her back, or to talk to her at least."

"I did, love, and I still plan to speak with her. But there were ... circumstances that made me feel it might be better to wait."

"Michael, I'm tired. And I'm your wife. Don't stall. I want direct answers."

She heard him sigh through the telephone. "When I first saw her, and I can't be sure, but I believe she might have been having a flashback."

"And you just watched? Michael, what were you thinking?"

"I watched because a gentleman was with her, working hard at bringing her back, if it was indeed a flashback."

Michael's tone told Patricia the unknown man was the cause for concern. "Who was he?"

"I don't know," he replied. Patricia could picture him on the other side of the line, running a frustrated hand through his hair. "He's part of the family she's staying with ... and he has obvious affection for Cat."

"And?"

"I don't know, love. I don't know what this means."

"It means you should have brought Henry with you."

"Yes, maybe. I'm not sure."

Patricia seldom heard uncertainty in Michael's voice. Hearing it now made it even more important to discover the link between Natalie and Susan. "So, what are you going to do now? You can't come back without talking to her."

"I know. I've been keeping my ear to the ground, and I discovered there's a New Year's Eve dance that is host to many businesses. My guess is that she'll be there. I think that might be the best way to approach her—"

"New Year's Eve," Patricia interrupted. "You plan on staying until New Year's Eve?" She didn't hide her disappointment.

"Patricia, I know this complicates things. Especially with the club—"

"The mayor has tasked me with organizing the biggest party this town has ever seen, Michael."

"I know. And if I didn't feel so strongly about that being the best time to speak with Catherine—"

"You'd better have success with this. I'm pregnant and running this New Year's Eve dance without you. I understand your desire to help Cat, but I'm not happy with how it's unfolding." She explained about what had happened when she went to the mayor's home and her suspicion that Susan might have a closer relationship to Natalie than she had let on.

Michael was silent for a minute before answering, "This is interesting, dear. And most likely, you're not far from the mark. You should—"

"I should 'nothing,' Michael. You can't be in charge of everything. You have to choose: either handle Catherine there or handle Susan here. You can't do both." She thought about mentioning Olivia's idea to travel to Catherine in hopes that her child's delivery would lead Henry to Catherine but decided to keep silent for the time being. "Besides Henry, you're the one she'll listen to. So I think you stand a better chance of success by staying put. Let me handle Susan."

Michael's chuckle thawed her heart and made her miss her husband. "If anyone can handle the town villain, love, it's you. But promise me you won't take any unnecessary risks nor do anything to overexert yourself and the baby. I—"

"Michael?" Patricia interrupted.

"Yes?"

"You're doing it again. Focus on meeting with Catherine. We can manage things on this end."

"I love you."

Patricia could hear the smile in his voice. "You'd better," she replied.

* * *

Olivia returned the telephone to its receiver and rested her hands on her rapidly shrinking lap. Although the conversation with Patricia had been brief, Olivia couldn't help but feel a wave of relief wash over her.

He found her!

Once Patricia had spoken those words, it had taken every ounce of self-restraint not to go and immediately pack a suitcase. She missed her best friend dearly and wanted nothing more than to see her again. Only her promise made to Patricia to stay and help with their New Year's Eve plan kept her stationary.

However, she now understood Bobby's desire to share any information with Henry. Seeing the helplessness on his face disappear was something she greatly wanted to witness. Now that they were closer, she wanted Henry to be able to go and sweep Catherine off her feet, heal her heartache, and bring her home. Although Patricia hadn't disclosed the exact city where Michael had found Catherine, Olivia realized she now had the means to make that happen for Henry.

"Let me guess," Bobby said from behind the couch before coming to join her. "He found her?"

Olivia could only nod as she wiped tears of relief from her eyes.

"Was that Patricia?" Bobby waited for his wife to nod in confirmation. "Did she say where they're at?"

"No."

Bobby rubbed his neck and chuckled. "She's a smart one," he said.

"Patricia?"

He nodded. "If she told you where they were, you would have told me, and I would have gone straight to Henry. He would be in his truck heading there before I'd have time to leave his house or hang up the telephone. By withholding the exact location, she's keeping us rooted to this plan of hers."

"She wants Henry to be able to focus on finding out if there's any connection between Susan and Natalie. Knowing Catherine's whereabouts would break that focus."

"Of course it would! As it should!" He leaned over to put his arm around Olivia, drawing her against his chest and shoulder. "I'm glad Michael's found her, but the longer we keep this from Henry … he's going to be furious when he finds out."

"I know," Olivia replied, snuggling into her husband's side. "But if Henry does find her, and Natalie is still here claiming the child is his, will Catherine come back? We have to give Henry some ammunition so he can have a fighting chance. We have to give them both that chance."

"I understand that, I really do. I'm not convinced Henry will agree. I fought with him in Europe. Henry is a soldier. He fights and knows how to overcome obstacles to reach his goal. I pray he won't see what we're doing as an obstacle. God help us if he does."

FORTY-NINE

"It's going to be so much more fun this year!" Sarah exclaimed as she peeled an orange while standing at the kitchen counter. "I can't wait to see you in your Christmas dress, Grace. You'll be beating dance partners away with a stick."

"Will you sit down with that and eat like a normal person?" Edwin asked, trying to ignore the envy filling him at his sister's suggestion.

"You'll have to go shopping with me, Grace," Sarah continued, ignoring her brother. "I was thinking if I could find a dress to complement your green one, that'd be nice."

Catherine smiled at Sarah's excitement. "Sit down, Sarah, before you give your brother—"

"It's too hard to sit still when there's so much to do," Sarah interrupted, grinning. "I'd go out shopping now if it wasn't so late in the evening."

"Spilling orange peels on the floor for us to sweep up won't help," Catherine replied with a hint of humor. Sarah sighed and sat next to Catherine.

"Thank you," Edwin said.

Sarah ignored him. "So, I was thinking if I could find something in red, it would complement your green dress."

The mention of a red dancing dress caused a pain in Catherine's heart. While Sarah prattled on about the New Year's Eve dance, Catherine's mind wandered back to the night she had worn a red dress for dancing. It had been a gift from Michael, and it had meant the world to her. Unfortunately, Robert's attack had tarnished her desire to wear a red dress ever again.

"Choose a different color," Catherine suggested as she took a sip of her coffee. "Everyone else will be wearing red. If you want to stand out, wear a different color. Blue would be great for your complexion."

Sarah beamed at the compliment. "Thank you! And there's so many styles to choose from—"

"Something that flares. It'll give you more room to dance any sort of dance, fast or slow. Slimmer dresses restrict your movement."

"You certainly seem to know a lot about dancing," Irma commented as she brought the coffee pot to the table for refills now that the dinner plates were clean and put away.

Catherine glanced up to find Edwin studying her. She gave a shrug and replied, "A bit," before refocusing on her coffee.

"Oh, you have to give me some pointers!" Sarah exclaimed as she jumped to her feet and grabbed Catherine's hands. "Come on!"

Before Catherine had time to protest, Sarah had pulled Catherine into their living room. Sarah headed toward the record player in the corner of the room, calling over her shoulder as Edwin and Irma joined them, "Help Grace move the furniture."

Catherine gave Edwin a look of helplessness. She motioned to the large sofa and said to Edwin, "Shall we? Irma, you sit in the rocking chair in the corner. There's no need for you to do anything but enjoy the comical site your daughter and I are about to create."

Catherine felt relief when Sarah selected a fast-paced song they could swing dance to. Catherine offered suggestions as best she could, but it wasn't long before everyone was in fits of giggles watching Catherine trying to assume the male's role in the dance.

"I can't handle much more of this," Irma said, wiping tears from her eyes. "You're too funny, girls. I'm going to bed." She allowed Edwin to help her to her feet but shook her head at his offer to help her up the stairs. "I'm not that fragile, son." With a knowing look, she nodded her head back in the direction of the women who had resumed their dancing. "Enjoy it for a while."

Edwin did. He sat back and viewed the playful interaction between Catherine and Sarah that warmed his heart. When their giggling became uncontrollable, he shook his head and headed to the kitchen for a drink of water. "Good night, ladies," he called over his shoulder. "Your silliness is too much for me. I'm off to bed too."

Edwin took his time in the kitchen, surprised at how quickly the music and giggling faded after his departure. He headed back to the kitchen door, aiming to check that everything was all right before going upstairs, but stopped when he heard their whispered conversation.

"All the men there will want to dance with you, Grace."

"Yes, well, I'm not much of a public dancer," Catherine replied hesitantly.

"You'll at least have to dance with Edwin, okay?"

"If he asks."

Edwin heard Sarah giggle before asking Catherine, "And if he wants to dance all of them with you?"

Edwin found he held his breath waiting for Catherine's response.

"Sarah, there'll be plenty of lovely ladies vying for his attention."

Edwin managed to quietly crack open the door in time to see Sarah stand on tiptoe to give Catherine a kiss on her cheek. "Maybe so, but I don't think he'll notice."

Once his sister had retired to bed, he remained hidden as Catherine changed records. She went to stand at the window as "I've Heard That Song Before" played. She dropped her head in her hands, and the heartache radiated through her shoulders.

Before he lost his nerve, Edwin entered through the door. "Do you think I could get a quick lesson too?"

Catherine whirled around to face him. "Edwin, you startled me. I thought you had gone to bed," she clumsily said.

He took a few steps toward her, his eyes never leaving her face. "I was going to." He held out his hand when he reached her.

"I don't know," she said nervously.

"Come on," he whispered. She didn't protest when he took her hand. She kept her eyes downcast as he pulled her close.

Catherine barely breathed as Edwin held her in his arms and began to sway to the music. Despite his limp, he led with confidence. His dancing was good, but it paled in comparison to Henry's. Horror-stricken at comparing the two men, she was thankful when the music stopped. She started to step away, but Edwin held her in place.

"You don't need any practice," she whispered, not meeting his eyes.

With the hand that held hers, he lifted her chin and forced her to look him in the eyes as he said, "On the contrary, I need all the practice I can get to make me strong enough not to fall for you."

His eyes lowered, stopping at her lips, and without thinking, Catherine stared back at his.

What are you doing, Catherine? Stop! Stop! Stop!

As Edwin leaned in to kiss her, Catherine didn't stop him as he lifted her chin up. But as she realized what was happening, she drew her head back slightly. Edwin noticed the hesitation, even as Catherine's eyes remained closed.

He pushed away the disappointment as he released her. However, he didn't distance himself from her. His actions caused her to open her eyes, and he saw relief, fear, and regret in them.

"Good night, Catherine," he said, hating that he was only strong enough to whisper. With every ounce of willpower, he stepped away from her, allowing her to make her exit.

Catherine noticed how he struggled to hide his feelings. Then the stoic mask that she, herself, often wore took its place on his visage. Biting her lower lip, she gave a small nod and headed to the staircase.

She knew he had wanted to kiss her. She knew he was falling for her. She knew he'd respect her wishes and give her as much time as she needed. *But he doesn't know how messed up and shattered I am.* When she reached the bottom of the stairs, she turned back to find Edwin hadn't moved, his back facing her.

"Edwin, I—" Catherine tried to explain.

"Can I ask you something? And can you be totally honest with me?" he interrupted, his face still turned from her.

"Yes."

"Do you hesitate because it's *me*, or because of Henry?"

Catherine tried to form a response. Only when he turned toward her and she saw the emotions warring in his eyes did she find an answer. "Because you're not Henry." She swiped at a rogue tear as she continued, "I loved Henry long before he ever showed an interest in me. I planned to love him the rest of my life. I was engaged to the man and planned to spend the rest of my life with him. I loved him in spite of his failings. He was everything to me."

Edwin turned to face her fully, and his sorrowful eyes pierced her. "What I felt for Henry was deep and true and *strong*. Even though ... even though it ended, it's so hard to forget." She turned away from him and absently stared at the staircase handrail. "It's supposed to be hard to move on. I'm not supposed to be able to this soon, least of all feel tempted to."

"You don't owe Henry anything," Edwin responded.

She shook her head, daring to look back at him. "No, you're right. I don't. But I do owe something to myself. I always took pride in how strong my love was for people ... you show me how weak I really am. And that's not a weakness I'm ready to face."

FIFTY

"Dear God, give me strength," Henry mumbled as he pulled his truck in front of the rental house where Natalie and her son resided. Ever since their meeting at Catherine's house, where they had planned the New Year's Eve investigation, Henry had been trying to prepare himself for the conversation he was about to have. The idea of asking Natalie to the dance turned his stomach, but he didn't have any other ideas.

This will get me closer to Catherine. I have to keep telling myself that.

He had seriously considered stopping by Sal's, despite the early hour, to see if Patricia would permit him to raid the bar for anything that would help give him the courage to do something he thought he'd never do again: take anyone besides Catherine on a date.

It's not a date. I have to make sure she understands that. It'll never be like that.

He hadn't stopped at the club, choosing to rely on prayers to face his battle, just like he had done during his days fighting in Europe. But even if he had chosen to imbibe, the reality of what he was about to do would have sobered him.

Henry struggled internally as he walked up to Natalie's door and rang the doorbell.

"Henry!" Natalie couldn't mask her surprise at finding him at her doorstep. "I—"

"Is this a bad time?" Henry interrupted her, wanting simply to get this conversation over with.

"No, not at all. Never for you, Henry," Natalie answered as she opened the door wide enough for him. "Please, come in. Little Henry is napping, but I can wake him if you'd like."

"No need, Natalie. Let the boy rest. I actually came to talk to you."

Natalie eyed him in disbelief, her hand fiddling nervously with her necklace. "You did? Then this really is a surprise."

Henry sat in the chair that Natalie offered him but found he couldn't look at her as he spoke. "I wanted to ask you if you had plans for New Year's Eve."

Natalie could tell from his body language that he wanted to be anywhere other than here. "I'm a single mother, Henry. The idea of having plans for the holiday is—"

"Would you like to?"

"To what?"

She's not making this easy. "Have plans. I wanted to see how you'd feel about going to the New Year's Eve dance."

There. I did it. He kept his eyes down as he waited for a reply.

Natalie considered his proposal for a long time before finally posing her own question. "Why are you asking me?"

"You said it yourself, you're a single mom. I thought maybe you'd like an evening off."

"I have no one to watch Henry."

"Yes, you do. Olivia has volunteered to watch him."

"Olivia? She's never cared much for me."

"She's Catherine's best friend, Natalie," Henry responded, finally looking up at her.

Natalie's stomach became queasy. Something wasn't right. "Dancing ... that's yours and Catherine's—"

"Yes," Henry interrupted, "it is."

"Have you heard from her?"

"Not as often as I'd like," he replied.

Natalie felt her heart twist at the pain in his eyes. Before thinking, she blurted out, "I'm so sorry, Henry. My behavior that day was unacceptable. I don't know what I was thinking. I wish now that I'd never acted so foolishly."

"Yes, well, nothing now to do but try and clean up the mess that was made." He tried to force a smile. "But I appreciate your apology. I love

Catherine. Nothing has changed in that area. It never will. I don't want you to accept my invitation thinking there may be a reason to assume otherwise. But I realize that I need to work more on having a friendship with you, for little Henry's sake. And what better way to start than going to the dance together?"

"And what happens if Catherine comes back?"

"Then God will have answered my deepest prayer."

Natalie regarded Henry, memorizing the pain that seemed permanently etched on his face—pain that she had created. Guilt over all she'd done permeated her being. She had tried to walk away from this mess so many times, but Susan had always found a way to pull her back in.

"Tell Olivia I appreciate her offer. I'd be happy to go with you to the dance."

Relief and disappointment warred in Henry, but he worked to remain stoic. "I'll pick you all up at eight. We can take Henry to Olivia's together. He'll like playing with Caleb."

Natalie hesitated. "Are you sure that's best? I don't know how he'll react going somewhere he doesn't know."

Henry nodded. "He'll be fine. He seems to adapt well to change."

Natalie paled at his words and was thankful that he didn't seem to notice. "All right, then. Thank you. For all of it."

"Of course. Now, if you'll excuse me, I need to be going." He rose to his feet, taking his leave before Natalie could say anything else.

Henry made it to the dirt road that led to Catherine's house before needing to pull over to be sick.

Even though he'd made it clear to Natalie that his heart still belonged to Catherine, he felt his actions were still a form of betrayal.

It'd better be worth it. This had all better be worth it. I don't know if I can live with myself otherwise.

* * *

"I'm out," Natalie said as she barged past the protesting butler and headed straight for the desk that Susan sat behind.

"Excuse me!" Susan said, rising to her feet. "You can't just barge in here like—"

"I'm *done*," Natalie interrupted her. "I no longer want any part of your game."

"Game?" Susan said, closing the office door and locking it behind her. "This isn't a *game*." She was irritated that Natalie felt she could arrive unannounced and uninvited.

Natalie shook her head. "It isn't working. He still loves her as much as he did the first day. If you ask me, he loves her even more now."

"I'm not asking you. I'm not paying you for your opinion." Susan gave Natalie a tight smile as she continued, "Please, cousin, do tell me what has you so upset."

"Henry's a good man, Susan. Better than you or I deserve. He is absolutely devoted to Catherine. Although he asked me to go to the New Year's Eve dance, he was honest and made sure I understood he'd only ever see me as a friend."

Susan felt a flare of jealousy spring to life. "Wait," she said, eyes narrowing. "What did you say he did?"

"He invited me to the New Year's Eve dance."

"You accepted, right?" Susan demanded, ignoring how it irked her that he was doing exactly what she wanted him to do: go after Natalie.

"Yes, but only as friends. And a friend is what I want to be to him. I'm tired of sabotage."

Susan laughed in delight as a plan formed in her mind. "Sabotage?" she asked, laughing again. "On the contrary, this is perfect."

Natalie looked at her with distrust. "*Perfect*? What are you scheming now?"

Susan shook her head, saying, "There's nothing for you to concern yourself over. I tell you what—go to the dance with Henry. After that, you're free. You can leave. I won't try to stop you or beg you to stay." She reached out and clasped Natalie's hands. "You have my word."

Natalie's suspicions grew. Something wasn't quite right, but she feared that if she questioned Susan, Susan wouldn't be so willing to let her finally leave. *Don't question it, Natalie. You don't have to ruin his life anymore. Take the money, take your son, and* leave.

Susan could hardly wait for Natalie to leave. Once she had confirmed that Natalie's automobile was gone, she set her plan into motion. She picked up the phone and quickly dialed.

"Thank you for calling Freelance Studios," a male's voice greeted her.

"Hello, Stan."

"Susan? Well, well, it seems like ages since I've heard from you."

"I think I have a project for you that will make the gap worth it."

"I'm listening."

Susan smiled. "Good. There's a New Year's Eve event I want you to cover."

"That doesn't sound interesting."

Susan laughed. "Trust me. It will be."

It'll be life-changing. And once the dust settles, I'll be the one here to help Henry pick up the pieces.

FIFTY-ONE

"Sorry I came uninvited," Henry said as he followed Olivia into the living room.

"Nonsense," Bobby said. "Is everything all right?"

Henry nodded. "I thought I'd stay here until I have to pick up Natalie for the dance tonight. If there's any work that needs to be done, I'd be happy to do it."

Bobby couldn't help but chuckle. "There was a time not so long ago when you and I tried everything in our power not to do work around here."

Henry acknowledged Bobby's words, remembering Caleb and wishing his best friend was still with them. "That was a different life. It seems like ages ago."

"Well, I think you're here in the event that we receive a telephone call," Olivia commented as she waddled to the couch.

"You know me too well, Liv," Henry replied. "I figure if she'll call anyone today, it'll be you." *And knowing that I'll be at the club with someone else tonight, I'm really hoping she calls. I need to hear her voice.*

Olivia gave Bobby a pained look before refocusing her attention on Henry. "I'm sorry, Henry. I wish things were different."

Henry nodded and said, "Me too. But I've got to have hope that so long as she keeps contacting someone—you, Michael, anyone from this town—it means she's still attached to us. Even if she's not talking to me, I can't help but pray I'm part of what's keeping her—"

"If she calls," Bobby interrupted, "we'll make sure you speak with her. Privately."

Henry nodded in appreciation. "Have you heard from Patricia?" he asked as he scooped Caleb into his arms and began tickling him. The small boy's giggles brought much-needed smiles to all their faces.

"Well, I think she's ticked Michael isn't here to help, so she's making sure he regrets it by planning the largest party that club has ever seen," Olivia said as she propped her feet up on a cushion. "I bet it makes front page news."

Henry smiled, but the gesture didn't reach his eyes. "He's gone … it's my fault. If I hadn't—"

"Stop it," Bobby interrupted forcefully. "We all know a misunderstanding caused this. You did nothing wrong. And tonight, we're going to make sure no stone goes unturned and see if we can fix it." He gave Henry a stern look as he continued, "You're not the type of person to feel sorry for yourself, so don't start now."

Henry regarded his friends, still feeling helpless despite the evening's plans. Gently setting Caleb on the floor, he nodded his head toward the back window. "I'm going to the barn and muck around a bit. Will you get me if—"

The ringing telephone stopped him mid-sentence. Henry tried to keep the hope buried in his chest as the phone continued to ring.

"Help me up, Bobby!" Olivia exclaimed, trying to scoot herself off the couch. Rather than reaching for the phone once she was on her feet, she deliberately turned the opposite way. "Come on, Bobby, let's go get something to eat. I'm famished."

They gave Henry hopeful looks as they passed. Olivia placed her hand on his arm and gave him a reassuring smile while whispering, "I hope it's her. Give her our love."

The instant the kitchen door closed behind Olivia and Bobby, Henry took a deep breath and lunged for the telephone. He was rewarded with Catherine's voice on the other end.

"Happy New Year, Liv!" He didn't want to speak, fearing her cheerful tone would change the moment she heard his voice.

"Liv?" she asked. "Are you all right?"

"Hello, Catherine …" Henry replied as he heard her sharp intake of breath.

"Henry, I …" her voice trailed off.

"You can speak with Liv in a few minutes. Or maybe more than a few ... however long it takes her to come to the phone." Warmth spread through him as she gave a soft chuckle.

"How is she doing, really? She won't tell me anything."

Henry willed his voice to sound calm and normal, grateful to have a conversation with Catherine. "She's very pregnant, Catherine. She's in good enough spirits, but she's very pregnant."

"Does she need anything?" she asked hesitantly.

"Like everyone here, she needs *you*. I'm not the only one missing you."

It took a long time before Catherine was able to respond. "I ... I called to wish her Happy New Year," she said softly.

"It has to be better than the one we're exiting. I don't want another year like this one."

"Henry—"

"I miss you, Catherine."

"Stop, Henry. We both—"

"I love you," he interrupted again.

She released a sound of frustration and asked, "Is Liv there yet?"

"She's giving us a few minutes."

"We don't need a few minutes."

"Yes, we do. We need to talk. I can't get past five minutes on the phone with you before you hang up on me. We need to talk about what you think happened."

"*Think* happened?" she asked, the pleasantry in her voice dissipating. "You mean how I *saw* Natalie in your home? Wearing only—"

"Catherine, stop being so stubborn and let me explain."

"What are your plans for tonight, Henry?"

The change of conversation surprised him, and he was hesitant to reply. "I'm spending it trying to get you back." Invigorated and hopeful that hearing how he'd planned to discover if there is a connection between Natalie and Susan, he said, "I'm going to Sal's with Natalie so that Bobby—"

"Stop right there." The coldness in her voice told him he had phrased his answer wrong. "You don't need to explain."

"Catherine, I do."

"No, Henry. You can't have both worlds ..." There was a hitch in her voice as she fought back tears. "So, I'm making the decision for you."

"Losing you—I don't choose that! I'll never accept that." When she didn't respond, he continued, "Come home, Catherine. If not for me, then for Liv." He was grasping at straws but desperate enough to offer whatever it would take to get her home. "She needs you here. Won't you at least come and see the baby?"

The long pause that followed gave him hope. *If it takes Liv's pregnancy to get her back here, then I'm going to use it.*

"Midnight," he said suddenly.

"What?" Catherine asked, confused.

"Wherever you're at tonight, I want you to go outside and find the moon at midnight. I'll be doing the same, and for that moment … we'll have that … you and I."

"I'm not promising anything."

Henry smiled, and he hoped she could hear it across the wire. "I'm not asking you to. But the fact that you haven't hung up yet means you're at least listening. And even if you try not to, I'm thinking you'll still throw a glance up at the sky later tonight."

"That confident?"

"Not at all," he replied with honesty. "I'm just praying that hard for it. Confidence left me the day you left town. I have only my prayers to rely on now."

"Prayers?"

Henry's smile widened. He felt that, though the footing was small, he was finally finding one. "Yes, Catherine. Even through this, you're teaching me how to be a better man. And you're teaching me that prayers will get me farther than confidence. This conversation is proof of that."

Henry held his breath, picturing in his mind Catherine on the other end of the line, her brow furrowed in thought. Finally, she spoke. "I need to think about seeing Olivia. I … I don't want to miss … I don't know what to do."

"Come home."

He could hear the tears choking her words as she replied, "You know, the funny thing is, I can't seem to make sense of *you*. What I hear in your voice … it's something so different from what I saw with my own eyes."

"Let me help you reconcile them."

"Henry, stop it!" This time there was no mistaking the sound of her tears. "I don't need smooth words to try and glue my heart back together."

"Yes, actions have always spoken louder than words with you," he conceded. As much as he knew arguing with her might hinder him, he couldn't help but savor the opportunity. "But the problem is, you're only giving me the option of using my words. You're not letting me do anything to *act* on setting things right."

"Are we arguing?"

"Yes!" Henry answered. "And I can't begin to tell you how good that feels. It means we're finally communicating." *Finally.*

"You make it sound like this is my fault."

"You're the one who keeps hanging up!" He bit his tongue regretfully. "Listen, I'm not blaming you. I understand why you feel the way you do, but we're both victims—"

"Both of us? Are you a victim because you were caught?"

"No! Natalie came over uninvited, upset and wanting to talk. I thought she went to the bathroom to compose herself, not search for clothing I had picked out for you in order to parade out in it the moment you arrived."

"Perfect timing," Catherine said, not hiding the bitterness in her voice.

Suddenly, the idea of perfect timing took on new meaning. In light of their suspicions that Susan and Natalie might be collaborating, the timeliness of Catherine's arrival and Natalie's wardrobe change no longer seemed so coincidental.

Henry felt sick. *I have to find out if there's a connection.* The night's plans were now even more important to execute. *Bobby has to find something. He has to.*

"You know everything I went through to get to a point where we were finally together. Do you really think I'd do anything to risk losing that? As hard as we both fought to be together, why would I do anything to destroy that? Catherine, you know me. You know me better than anyone."

"I thought I knew you, but now …" Catherine's voice took on a weariness that dampened his hope. "Listen, tell Liv I'll talk to her soon. I'll call back another time."

He didn't want the call to end. He wanted to share his thoughts about the sinking feeling that Susan was involved, but he was certain she would refuse to listen. Her hurt was too great.

But if this is some plan of Susan's, my wrath will be even greater.

"This isn't over," he said, determination behind his words.

"And if I disagree?"

"It wouldn't be our first argument. I promise you, Catherine. We're far from over."

Henry's promise echoed in her ears as Catherine painstakingly trod from the phone booth back to Sarah, who stood at a distance waiting for her.

"I still don't see why you can't just use our telephone," Sarah said, grabbing Catherine's elbow to keep her from falling on a patch of ice.

"I'm not making long-distance calls from your home. End of discussion," Catherine replied, gritting her teeth as her foot slid. "How you all survive the winters here, I'll never know."

"You'll be able to brag that you did, soon enough," Sarah laughed.

"Thanks for coming with me."

"I think Edwin would have preferred I let him, but he'll have enough time with you at the dance tonight."

"Sarah—"

"I know he's too polite to ask," Sarah interrupted her, "but I make no such claims. Did that phone conversation vex you?"

Henry, despite claiming a lack of confidence, had sounded so certain when he had told her it wasn't over. He had sounded so sincere. She couldn't deny the ache she felt as a repercussion. "Why do you ask?"

"I've noticed you talk with your hands when you're feeling extreme emotions," Sarah said, putting thought into each word.

"And I was talking with my hands?"

"You were talking with your whole body."

Catherine chuckled. "I guess so, then."

They were silent for the remainder of the treacherous walk until they reached the front porch. "Grace," Sarah asked, "is everything all right?"

Catherine grimaced when Sarah called her by her middle name. It reminded her of how far she had distanced herself from Henry, trying to break from the pain of losing him, only to realize during their phone conversation that he was as close to her now as he had ever been. She didn't dare speak as she blinked several times to keep the tears at bay. Finally, she managed a quick nod.

Sarah gave her a sympathetic smile. "Come, let's forget about it for a night, shall we? Tonight, we ring in a new year, with new friends. Cheers to a much better new year."

Yes, Catherine agreed, echoing Henry's sentiments. *I don't want another like this one.*

FIFTY-TWO

No sooner had Henry driven off than Olivia turned to her husband. "Are you ready?"

Bobby took a deep breath before answering, "No. I still think it was a terrible idea to put me in charge of something so important."

Olivia rolled her eyes in frustration. "You are not worthless, Bobby. And you're actually the best person for the job. No one will suspect someone with physical 'limitations,' as you so believe, to be the culprit of a break-in."

"You know, we may not even have to do this. Henry's phone conversation with Cat earlier lasted long enough to give the man hope. He said he has an idea he wants to run by you. And now that we know Michael has found her—"

"Stop it right there. You're a soldier, Bobby!" She crossed her arms over her ample stomach. "You're stronger and smarter than this."

"No," Bobby argued. "I'm not. I've always been the follower. I followed Henry and Caleb from the dance club to Europe."

"You didn't have to fight, but you chose that on your own. That's very courageous, if you ask me."

"Even at the repair shop, I'm the spare. That place would fail without Henry."

Olivia took hold of her husband's face between her hands, forcing him to look at her. "And this plan, this hope to bring Henry and Catherine back together, will fail without *you*. They need you to do this."

He leaned down to kiss her on the lips. "Okay," he murmured.

Olivia nodded resolutely. "Good. While you're out and the children are playing, I'll be packing to get ready for my part of the plan."

"No," Bobby said firmly. He placed his hand on her shoulder. "I know I agreed to you leaving, but I'm having second thoughts." His eyes, filled with concern, traveled to her stomach. "If something happens to you, I would never—"

"Bobby, don't you take this from me. This is what I can do to help," Olivia protested.

"You have to promise me that you'll wait ... at least until we see what the evening brings."

Although the sparks in her eyes threatened to argue with him, she didn't. "Fair enough. But let's get you ready. Once Henry and Natalie drop off Natalie's son, you'll need as much time as possible to take care of business."

* * *

Henry repeated his earlier promise to Catherine to himself as he drove back to Catherine's house with Natalie and David. He was thankful the small, talkative boy sat between him and Natalie. Although Henry had been honest about his feelings when he asked Natalie to the dance, he didn't want to provide any opportunity for her to gain a sense of false hope. Keeping his distance from her was the safest way to prevent any misunderstandings.

"While I appreciate Olivia's willingness to watch Henry for the evening," Natalie said, breaking through Henry's thoughts, "I'm sorry she and Bobby won't be coming along. I understand she loves the dance club as much as the rest of you."

"Well, although she loves to dance, I don't think she has any desire to go into labor early."

"When is she due?" Natalie asked, her hands politely folded in her lap.

"Soon," Henry answered.

They were silent for the next several minutes before Natalie asked, "Do you think Catherine will come back to see her?"

"I pray and am hopeful that's the case," Henry replied without hesitation.

Natalie looked over her son's head to the man driving, to the man who was everything she had always wanted in a man but never had. His gaze never left the road to see the small smile she offered him.

Henry knew he should be making polite conversation on the drive. It would make everything seem less suspicious. Although Natalie hadn't noticed when Henry had slipped into her kitchen, claiming the need for a drink of water, to make sure the back kitchen door was left unlocked, he was still nervous she'd start to suspect something. Henry had wanted to make things easier for Bobby, who had complained that he'd been given the hardest task of the night.

He glanced over to see Natalie watching the road with what seemed a hopeful smile spread across her face. *Oh, dear.* He'd have to spend all evening reiterating that he belonged to Catherine and no one else. His heart wasn't free, and he planned to keep it that way.

Bobby's wrong. He doesn't have the most difficult job of the night. I do.

* * *

Bobby was grateful they resided in a part of the world where snow wasn't a common occurrence. Already feeling clumsy with the task at hand, he shuddered to think of how snow and even rain could easily make incriminating tracks leading to the back of Natalie's house. He had parked his car several blocks away and had walked to Natalie's residence to decrease the chances of being recognized. The town was small enough that *someone* would have recognized his car.

Traversing the sidewalk that led to her home, Bobby was grateful for his military training. Although not as skilled as Henry, he understood the need to blend in with his surroundings and yet appear to be on a casual walk to anyone who might notice him. As much as he wanted to run to complete the assignment as quickly as possible, that would only draw suspicion.

When he finally reached her house, he glanced around to ensure that he wasn't being noticed before slipping down along the small yard adjacent to the side of the house. It took no time to reach the back porch and kitchen door. Henry had assured him that it was unlocked and safe to use as an entrance.

Bravo, Henry. He smiled as he pushed the door open, the hinges so well-oiled they didn't make a sound to announce his arrival. *I can be in and out of here in no time. Once I figure out what I'm looking for ...*

Once inside the house, Bobby checked to make sure all the curtains were drawn closed. He hoped the curtains would minimize any lighting his military-issued flashlight might reveal. Turning it on, he swung the flashlight over his surroundings.

This place is sparse. No wonder she's latching on to Henry. She owns practically nothing.

It took very little time for him to search the living room and kitchen. He was still unsure of what he was looking for, but he prayed he'd find something. He didn't want to think that perhaps Natalie truly was someone trying to reunite her son with his father.

When Bobby entered the single bedroom, he immediately realized it was a shared room. The right side of the room held the child's toys and clothing. A small pallet next to the all the toys indicated his resting place. Sadness sliced through him as he realized how little the boy had.

If Henry knew, he'd be doing something about that.

But Henry didn't know. Henry had always made sure to meet Natalie and her son in public places. Today was the first time Henry had ever been to this house as far as Bobby knew. He would have no idea the child didn't have a bed.

Nor does Natalie, for that matter. He swept his flashlight over the left side of the room to reveal an exact replica of the sleeping situation. Her clothes were kept in small piles, and where her son's toys dominated the center of his side, a few boxes claimed hers.

"As good a place to start as any," he whispered, dropping to his knees and setting the flashlight in a location that would light the box he planned to investigate. The first file he pulled out of the box contained various documents that immediately struck his interest. His eyes took in every detail of the first page, describing the marriage between Natalie Thompson and Edward Collins. Looking at the date of the document, unease filled him.

Natalie's married.

He flipped through the other pages, hoping to find her son's birth certificate. He gave a small cry of triumph when he found it and read aloud, "David Henry Collins, son of Natalie Thompson and Edward Collins."

He was born two years after their wedding date. He's not Henry's. Oh my gosh, he's not Henry's.

Knowing that he couldn't steal the documents, he placed them back in the file as neatly as he could. He had the information needed to support Henry's claim that he didn't remember Natalie.

He was never with her.

Placing the file back in the box, he pulled out another file that contained photographs presumably of Natalie as a child. He leaned closer to the flashlight as he sifted through the photographs. "Jackpot!" he exclaimed as he brought a photograph of Natalie as a teenager closer to the light for further inspection. He'd been around this town long enough to recognize the young girl standing beside Natalie as Susan. While Natalie's maiden name was the same as Susan's, this photograph was solid proof that they were family.

It's proof that Susan is the mastermind behind the entire thing. He fought the urge to take the photograph as evidence. With Susan involved, he didn't want to take into his possession something he'd stolen from her family. Instead, he committed every detail to memory.

When he left the house, he was determined to leave it exactly as he found it with one exception; on his way out, he locked the back kitchen door.

With a triumphant smile on his face, he couldn't wait to share his findings with Henry. He could only imagine the relief his friend would feel at knowing everything had been a hoax.

Susan wanted to destroy Henry and Catherine. Little does she realize, it's now going to lead to war.

For the first time in a long time, Bobby felt extremely hopeful for Henry and Catherine. It pleased him that he'd be an instrumental part of righting the wrong that tore them apart. He wanted to go to the club and share the news with Henry right away, eager to see his friend happy again. But although he couldn't do that, he could at least send Olivia to Catherine. If she was working on Catherine's end and he on Henry's, the two could be back together by the end of the week.

By the time Bobby got to his automobile, he had plans to share his findings with his wife while he helped her pack.

FIFTY-THREE

Catherine studied her image in the full-length mirror as Sarah sat at the vanity and applied last-minute touches of makeup. Sarah had insisted they get ready for the New Year's Eve dance together in her bedroom, and Catherine was doing her best to give Sarah as much sisterly camaraderie as she could. Catherine had giggled with Sarah, had fawned over the younger woman's dress, and had given her liberty to do Catherine's hairstyle.

If Olivia could see me now, she'd tease me to no end for acting like she had when we had first become friends. Catherine's long friendship with Olivia had taught her how *normal* women their age were supposed to act when getting dressed up for a special event. Before Henry, she had despised makeup, fancy dresses, and anything that made a woman feel beautiful. Henry had changed that. Once she was with him, she found her appreciation of those feminine things growing. While she knew she'd never be as adventurous as Olivia nor her old nemesis Susan, seeing Henry's eyes light up in appreciation of a new dress or perfume had made her reconsider self-pampering.

That was no longer the case.

Now she simply went through the motions with Sarah, knowing what part to play. She didn't miss a beat. Although Catherine's heart wasn't in it, she was glad she could pretend well enough to give Sarah an evening of excitement.

"Are you nervous?" Sarah asked as she applied lipstick one final time before dropping the tube in her purse.

"What?" Catherine asked as she put aside thoughts of her pregnant best friend.

Sarah smiled as she rose and indicated the mirror. "You keep holding your stomach as you look at yourself. You're not so nervous you'll be sick, are you?"

Catherine smiled at Sarah's assumption, realizing that she *did* have her hands covering her stomach. "I hadn't realized ... I guess I am, maybe a little."

"Well, there's no need to be," she replied as she stood by Catherine at the mirror. She studied both of their reflections before adding, "You know, he won't be able to take his eyes off you the entire night."

Catherine felt her stomach tighten in knots. *I shouldn't be doing this. I need to get out of this. I shouldn't be dancing. Why on* earth *did I think I could do this?*

Catherine prayed she looked convincing as she rolled her eyes at Sarah. "You're nuts. Remember, I work with your brother. I know how many beautiful women are in his office. I don't think he'll be stuck with me as a partner."

"Who said anything about being stuck?" Sarah asked as she wriggled her eyebrows.

Catherine groaned. "You know what? Maybe this isn't such a good idea. You all should go as a family. I'm not—"

"Stop right there," Sarah said, grabbing Catherine's hand and maintaining a firm grip on it. "You said yourself that you're an employee where Edwin works. This dance is for employees and their families. You're an employee. And you're family *to me*."

Catherine felt her eyes tear up at Sarah's declaration. "You're like a sister to me too," she managed to choke out.

Sarah gave her hand a tug. "Then you have no choice, Grace. You have to come."

Guilt and confusion coursed through Catherine. Before Christmas, Catherine had finished her last day at work intending not to return. But time spent over the holidays with this family had done a number on her heart. She found she was reluctant to leave. Catherine returned Sarah's smile and felt a strong urge to tell the woman everything she'd kept a secret.

I could tell her my real name. I could tell her everything. I could stay.

Henry's promise from earlier in the day cut through her thoughts. There had been so much conviction in his voice, a part of her wanted to defy her broken heart and believe him. His words hadn't been regretful but, rather, determined. He had seemed so confident in his claim of innocence. She had never known him to lie. Catherine forced herself to acknowledge how Henry had immediately told her about Natalie's arrival in town and her claim of him fathering her son. He had been honest from the beginning.

A wave of unease roared through her. Today had been the first time she had remained on the telephone long enough for Henry to offer an explanation. *Was I too rash in leaving like I did?*

"Grace?" Sarah asked, interrupting Catherine's spiraling thoughts.

Sarah stood in the doorway, holding Catherine's hand and looking at her with concern.

"Are you all right?"

"Sarah, I—"

"Are you two ladies finished yet?" Edwin called from the bottom of the stairs. "At this rate, it'll be next year before we get there."

"You're hilarious, brother," Sarah said, rolling her eyes and dragging Catherine down the hall and to the top of the stairs. She made certain she descended the stairs with her body blocking Catherine's. She flashed her brother a knowing smile as she reached the bottom step. "But I promise you, it was worth your wait."

Catherine felt Sarah yank her forward at the young woman's promise. Catherine's foot slipped, and she stumbled forward.

"Sarah!" Edwin scolded Sarah as he swiftly caught Catherine, preventing her from falling. "Be careful!"

Sarah chuckled softly and whispered low enough that her mother couldn't hear from the other side of the room, "I was only helping you get your arms around her sooner. You can thank me later, big brother."

But Edwin had stopped listening to Sarah. After he helped steady Catherine, he held her at arms' length. Her appearance left him speechless. She was radiant. He'd have to remember to compliment Sarah on her choice of color for Catherine when he wasn't so distracted. He couldn't tear his eyes from her. She looked elegant, and the nervousness in her eyes made her even more endearing.

"You're beautiful," he whispered, not attempting to shield his emotions from his face.

Catherine smiled timidly before turning her eyes to the floor and answering, "Thank you. You clean up well yourself."

"Are you two ready yet?" As she helped her mother into her coat by the door, Sarah mimicked, "At this rate, it'll be next year before we get there."

"Lead the way. We're taking the car tonight, and I already have it warming up for us," Edwin called over his shoulder. He waited until his mother and sister were outside on the front porch before he dared to nudge Catherine's chin so she would look up. "Are you all right?"

She nodded. "We should be going." She sidestepped to put distance between them.

Edwin didn't move, blocking her path. He waited until she met his eyes before whispering, "Catherine, you're not fooling me. It's obvious this evening has you feeling out of sorts. I'm not going to ask you what's warring in that beautiful head of yours." Relief slowly began to replace wariness on her face, although a genuine smile had yet to meet her lips. He stepped away long enough to seize her coat and help her slide into it.

"Thank you," she said as she turned her back to him and began to fasten the coat's buttons.

He didn't step away. Instead, he waited until Catherine accepted his offered arm before tucking her in close to his side and saying, "But know that I'm here for you, in whatever way you need me."

* * *

Michael couldn't help but be impressed at the dance hall, although the facility still paled in comparison to his own club. However, he mentally took note of the New Year's Eve decorations as ideas to share with Patricia for next year.

He scanned the room from where he stood, grateful that his intuition had been right. After seeing how close Catherine's companion had stayed to her earlier in the week, Michael had been confident that the man would want to do something special for New Year's Eve. From his hotel, Michael had asked around and discovered that the town had numerous venues open for the holiday. There were so many that he felt the safest way to find Catherine would be to follow her from the house where she was staying.

He had hung around the residence, trying not to appear like a stalker, until he spotted the family leave the house and pile into their vehicle. When he had realized the family was heading to a dance hall, Michael had only been able to smile. He had known that, at some point, Catherine would find her way back to the dance floor.

Now I just need to find her ...

Catherine was grateful that Sarah was such a talkative person. As the family sat around the dance hall dinner table, she knew Sarah's excitement would camouflage her own mixed emotions that currently left her mute. She tried hard to focus on each word Sarah spoke. However, it was impossible as she felt Edwin's gaze on her often.

Edwin nodded at a comment his mother made about the hall's decorations, only halfway listening. His true focus was on Catherine. He watched her picking at the food on her plate, convinced she had only pushed it around so it would appear she had eaten some of it.

"Not hungry?" he asked softly while Sarah turned his mother's attention to the waiters who were serving dessert.

"I'm sorry?" Catherine asked, looking up suddenly.

Edwin nodded to her plate. "You're not eating."

Catherine bit her lip before offering a small smile. She nodded to his plate and replied, "Neither, it seems, are you."

Edwin viewed his half-filled plate and chuckled. "Yes, well, I was being polite and trying to pace my eating to yours. But then I realized you're merely pretending to eat. Saving room for dessert?" Waiters came to the table, promptly removing dinner plates and pressing cakes and puddings into the now vacant places, as though his words had summoned them.

No sooner did the table fill with dessert plates then the band began to play music for the dancing portion of the evening. "Already?" Sarah asked, as she began to frantically stuff dessert in her mouth.

Catherine laughed as Irma scolded, "Slow down, Sarah. They'll be playing all night."

"But I want to be ready when someone comes and asks me to dance," she replied, continuing to plow through her dessert.

"They can't dance with you if you're choking," Irma teased, a smile playing at her lips.

Sarah had just swallowed her last bite when a man suddenly stood next to her. "You certainly ended up at the best-looking table, Edwin," he said, speaking to Edwin while winking at the three women at the table.

Edwin rolled his eyes but politely made introductions. "This is Thomas, a coworker."

"A new coworker," Thomas amended. "This is my first holiday party with the company, so I haven't had the pleasure of meeting your family." He reached out and shook everyone's hand, saving Sarah for last. Once he shook her hand, he continued to hold it.

Bravely plowing on, he said, "I realize the band just started, and you're probably still eating dessert, but I was hoping to have a dance with you."

Sarah shot her mother a triumphant look. "I'm done," she answered promptly. "And I'd be happy to dance with you now."

Thomas beamed as he helped Sarah from the table. "You know, I may try to keep you out there for more than once dance. It's not every day I have such a beautiful woman on my arm."

Sarah's natural blush at Thomas's compliment was charming, and Catherine couldn't help but cast a glance at Edwin. His brotherly concern grew as the two bantered.

"If you dance as well as you dish out compliments, I might let you keep me out there."

"Remember, you're dancing with my sister," Edwin growled.

Sarah stuck her tongue out at her brother as she pulled Thomas onto the dance floor, saying as they passed Edwin, "All bark, no bite."

Catherine laughed at Edwin's reaction to the comment. "Come now, Edwin. What she says is true."

"You would know," he muttered, an intensity briefly flashing in his eyes.

Catherine didn't respond, shifting her gaze to Sarah and Thomas on the dance floor. She joined Irma in chuckling over their moves.

They were both terrible dancers, but the beauty was that neither seemed to care. They exuded a confidence in their clumsiness that Catherine had never had. She had always tried to hide her imperfections and use them as walls to distance herself from the criticism she feared. She had waited until her dancing was near perfect before daring to take a place on the dance floor. How many opportunities to dance with her brother had she lost over the years?

Too many.

If Catherine had only had the confidence to appear weak, she realized with sadness, it would have made her stronger.

And Susan would have never seemed a threat to me ... and perhaps even Natalie.

Edwin rose to his feet, his movements distracting her from her reflections. Catherine looked up to find him standing over her with questioning eyes. "I'd like to ask you to dance," he proposed.

Although she shouldn't have been, Catherine was surprised by his request.

"However," he continued, a smile teasing his lips, "you need to finish your dessert. So, I'll take Mother out on the floor now. When you're finished, if it's all right, we'll dance." He turned and offered his hand to his mother, who gladly took it.

Catherine smiled at the hint of timidity in his voice. "And if I take all night to finish the pudding?" she quipped.

As Edwin led Irma to the dance floor, they passed Catherine, and he bent down to whisper in her ear, "You get one dance to finish it. Then, I'm coming back for you."

Catherine deliberately turned her attention to the untouched dessert.

The musicians played several bars of music before Catherine peeked at the action on the dance floor. Sarah was still having a terrific time being terrible, and Edwin had said something that had caused his mother to throw back her head with laughter.

They're having a great time. Seeing her new friends enjoying themselves on the dance floor reminded her of home. The memories of her evenings shared with Michael, Bobby, Olivia, and Henry at Sal's overwhelmed her. It had taken her some time, but she had finally gotten to the point of laughing on the dance floor like her friends were doing now. Michael had given her the courage to get out on the floor, but Henry had been the one to make her finally—

An achingly familiar voice interrupted her thoughts. "Come now, love … after all that hard work, you're not even using it!"

FIFTY-FOUR

Give Bobby time. I have to give him more time.

Henry played this thought repeatedly as he pulled his truck into the parking lot at Sal's. He didn't like the strange feeling of entering the club when Michael, Bobby, Olivia, and Catherine wouldn't be there. After losing his best friend in Europe, those four had been the tether he needed to stay on the dance floor, with Catherine being the most necessary one of all. Patricia greeted them at the entrance, which was the only part that felt right about this evening.

Together, Henry and Natalie made their way inside the club. While old habits tugged Henry toward the table he always occupied with his friends, he took deliberate steps in the opposite direction, seating them on the other side of the room at a table far from the dance floor.

Saying little to each other, Natalie studied the tablecloth while Henry focused on the dance floor. Finally, Natalie commented, "I understand you're quite the dancer."

Henry gave her a sidelong glance before responding, "Understand it? You didn't already know that? Someone had to tell you?" He watched as Natalie bit her lip nervously.

"I'm just trying to make conversation," she mumbled.

Henry saw the regret in her eyes, and he couldn't help but feel sorry for her. "I'm sorry for snapping at you," he apologized. "This is harder than I thought."

Natalie gave him a sad smile. "I understand. We don't have to go out there, you know. I'm grateful for a night out. I'm perfectly content to stay here and watch." She flinched as a man who'd already had too much to drink stumbled into their table. She waited until he apologized and meandered off in the opposite direction before adding, "Obviously, we'll have enough entertainment sitting right here." She shook her head in disapproval.

Henry framed his words carefully. He indicated the man who had just left their table and asked, "Not your cup of tea?"

Natalie wrinkled her nose. "Absolutely not," she replied. "Never has been. They only allow themselves to get that way to muster up enough courage for a one-night stand." She shivered in disgust. "I hate people like that."

Henry read the sincerity in her actions as his suspicions grew. "I used to be that way, if you remember," he said as Natalie's face paled slightly.

She nodded. "Yes, well, time has obviously changed you for the better." She gave him a smile, adding, "Otherwise, I never would have allowed you to see your son."

"Natalie, when you walked into my shop that first day, telling me about him, you had no idea that I'd changed." He tried to keep at bay his pleasure at seeing her struggling.

Desperately trying to make her case, she declared, "I *knew* you were changed."

"No," Henry argued. He tried to keep the cracks in her argument from giving him hope. "You had no way of knowing."

"Catherine was what told me you had changed," she countered. "You didn't hide anything from her, and I knew she was different than ..." She waved her hand to indicate the rowdier guests.

Natalie flicked her eyes anxiously between him and the dance floor before he finally responded, "You're right. I *am* different. War does that to a person. Losing your best friend, watching him die in your arms, and falling in love with his sister changes a man. Catherine has been very instrumental in that change. *She* made me want to be better, to do better."

As Henry scanned the club, lost in thoughts of Catherine, Natalie's heart broke at the pain she saw on his face, the pain she had inflicted. Realizing she might be making a dire mistake but not caring, she whispered, "You truly love her, don't you?" He gave a silent, confident nod. "And you always will?"

He turned to face her. "I'm sorry, Natalie, but yes. Being here ... she's here. She's everywhere. In every memory I have of this place, this town, my life, she's there. I don't remember my life before her. It's not worth remembering. I thought I'd at least try to loosen up tonight and treat you, but—"

"I appreciate your efforts," Natalie interrupted. She placed a reassuring hand on his arm. "And I understand."

He believed that, for once, she truly did. "I'll be there for little Henry, I promise I will. In every way that I can. But my heart will always be Catherine's."

Natalie watched as his Adam's apple bobbed in an effort to hold back his emotions.

"I almost lost her once before, Natalie. I can't lose her again. Not without a fight."

Natalie heard the promise in his whispered words, and although Henry would never love her like that, she could find hope in men once more. Perhaps someone in her future could love her the way Henry loved Catherine. She nodded. "I see that now. I can never be to you what Catherine is. And you've shown me that the fierceness of your love for her is the only type of love I want for myself. You can't give that to me, so I need to find it with someone else."

Henry reached over and squeezed her hand. "You'll find it," he promised.

She nodded, her eyes tearing up at the gentleness he was showing her—a gentleness most people in her life, family included, had never used with her. She didn't want to let that go. "Can I ask for one thing, though?"

Relief flowed through Henry at realizing Natalie wasn't going to chase him anymore. He offered her a smile. "Of course."

"Can I at least have your friendship? I don't have many friends, and even when you've been furious with me, you've still treated me better than ..." She stopped, unable to continue.

Henry gave her hand another squeeze. "I'd like nothing more than to be your friend, Natalie."

Natalie felt relieved as well. She would no longer pretend to chase Henry. Susan would be furious with her, but she felt better knowing that she was finished playing her cousin's game. "Henry," she began tentatively, "there are some things I need to tell you, but I don't have the courage for it tonight."

Henry didn't pry. He had a sense that whatever she needed to share with him would be vital to his future, but he knew pushing her now might have the opposite effect in getting her to open up. He gave her a small nod.

"Instead," she continued, finding courage from his patience, "can I have a dance with a friend? I haven't danced in so long. If you feel up to it, that is—"

Knowing Natalie would no longer try to stand between him and Catherine, his spirit soared. "Yes, Natalie. I think I can take a friend out on the dance floor. It's easier dancing with a friend than dancing with someone trying to steal me from Catherine." He rose to his feet and offered his hand, already taking steps toward the dance floor.

No longer fending off an ulterior motive, he enjoyed dancing with Natalie. He could treat her like any of his numerous dance partners from his past: a simple dance with no strings attached. He was mindful of hand placements and made sure the dance was clean. There wasn't any way that anyone watching would get the wrong idea about the two of them.

Natalie felt equally free now that she didn't have to place traps for someone she had grown to greatly admire. By stopping her antics, he was willing to be her friend. *I only hope that's still the case after I tell him the truth ... including about Susan.* Of course, he'd be upset, but she also wanted to believe that he'd appreciate her honesty—especially when she would offer to do everything to help him win back his fiancée's love and trust.

She had officially switched sides. Even though Susan would be furious, she knew Susan would have likely tossed her aside either way. She preferred Henry's friendship over family ties to Susan. Seeing the genuine smile on Henry's face that came from her agreement to be only a friend was all she needed to confirm she had made the right choice.

The song ended, and as the pair slowed to a stop, Natalie offered a broad grin. "Thank you for that, Henry. And thank you for your willingness to be my friend."

Natalie had given him the best gift possible, and the once-constant burden of her presence had begun to fade. "Of course."

"To being friends?" Natalie asked, as she offered her hand for him to shake.

Henry took her hand, pulling her into a friendly hug instead. "To being friends."

A couple of hours later, Henry stepped out of the club with Natalie at his side. After their dance, the two had shared a meal while Natalie had asked questions about Catherine. Henry appreciated the opportunity to talk about the woman he loved, and he hadn't hesitated to open up. When he had mentioned his request for Catherine to step out and look at the moon at midnight, Natalie had promptly suggested they leave.

"We don't need to be here to ring in the new year," she had explained. "I'd like to be home in bed by then, and you don't need me or anyone else infringing on your time with Catherine, even if you two are sharing it apart. Let's get out of here."

Now on their way to pick up her son, Natalie prompted, "Tell me more about Catherine. When did you know she was the one?"

Henry mulled over her question as he drove them back to Catherine's house. "That's hard to answer ..." he began. "It was both gradual and very sudden, if that makes any sense. I always knew Catherine was special, even when I teased her relentlessly. Just before I went to war in Europe, I had begun to realize that maybe my definition of special was changing. I didn't see her as the little sister anymore."

"When you left, was it extremely romantic telling her goodbye?"

Henry laughed. "On the contrary. I left with her hating me. But once I was over there, her brother encouraged a miracle to happen. He convinced her to write to me."

"And you fell in love over written correspondence?"

Henry smiled at the memory. "Maybe," he replied. "But not right away. Although what I felt for Catherine was powerful, I fought against it."

"Why?"

He shook his head and replied, "I don't know." He turned the truck onto the well-worn, familiar gravel road. "Looking back now, it was absolute foolishness. I missed so many opportunities to love her earlier on, and there's no good reason for it. But the war and all the horrors it brings—it's sobering. Losing her brother and my best friend, Caleb, made me realize ..."

Natalie waited for him to finish his thought. When it seemed that he wasn't going to continue, she prodded, "Realize what, Henry?"

"It made me realize that I wanted Catherine in my life. Together, we grieved the loss of Caleb. It was through that grief that I realized I didn't want to face another hardship in life without her."

Natalie gave a gentle smile at the passion in his voice. "And then you came home ..."

"But not to a happily-ever-after. I wanted that more than anything, but your friend, Susan, and other barriers worked hard at killing that dream."

"Myself included," Natalie added with regret.

Silence filled the truck as Henry parked in front of Catherine's house. Henry looked up at the sky from where he sat. He knew he'd have plenty of time to get Natalie and little Henry home before midnight. The moon shone brightly. Taking that as a good sign, he said a silent prayer of gratitude. "But it doesn't matter," Henry said, a small smile touching his lips. "The fight's not over."

Natalie smiled at his encouraging words. "No, it's not. A dream doesn't die as long as you're willing to fight for it." *And I'm glad you're willing to fight for her.*

Henry parked his truck at the base of the hill. Even though it was winter, he didn't let the cooler temperatures deter him from his goal. He had been right that he'd have plenty of time to take Natalie home before midnight. When they had picked up her son, Henry had been relieved to see Bobby back home. The cheerfulness in both his and Olivia's voices had told him that Bobby must have found *something* at Natalie's. While he was eager to return and find out what Bobby had discovered, he had told them he'd see them first thing in the morning. He had wanted them to have the rest of the evening to themselves.

Plus, I have a date myself. He climbed the hill where he and Catherine had sat watching Fourth of July fireworks and had later shared a picnic when he had been staying at her home while Bobby and Olivia had been on their honeymoon. This spot was *theirs*, and he wanted to feel as close to Catherine as he could. Memories from both of those times washed over him. Sitting next to her, watching the fireworks cast light on her upturned face, Henry had felt the first noticeable attraction to Catherine. It had bothered him at the time, as Catherine had been nothing like the type of woman he had always been attracted to.

But it wasn't a fluke. If I'd only followed that feeling then, had allowed it to grow instead of spending so much time trying to smother it, perhaps things would be different now. As he reached the top of the hill, he leaned back against an isolated tree and lowered himself to sit on the hard ground, giving no care to the dress clothes he wore. As he sat and stared up at the moon, his mind flipped through all the memories he had of his time with Catherine. They'd been through so much together. The war, Caleb's death, and Robert's attempts on Catherine's life were just a few of the mountainous hurdles they'd had to overcome.

No, Henry admitted reluctantly, *the hurdles brought us together. In the face of losing so much, I realized how much of a treasure Catherine is. I never would have seen that had we not been forced to endure so much. The pressure of it all showed how much of a diamond Catherine is. She never broke under any of it, not until she I thought I was the one destroying us from within.*

Even though the separation was hard to live with, Henry felt that for the first time in a long while, things were looking bright again. His conversation with Catherine earlier in the day had lasted longer than any since she'd left town. He felt she was finally willing to start listening to him. Natalie had agreed to stop pursuing him and to help in any way she could for him to earn back Catherine's trust. Even though Henry didn't know the details, he assumed Bobby had had a productive evening, learning something that would also help him.

God, let this be a sign. Keep her safe until I can reach her. Keep me patient and give me the right words to say to help heal her hurt. And thank you for giving me this moment, this brief pulse in time, to be able to still share something with her, even though she's so far away.

It was well after into the early hours of the morning before he tore his eyes away from the moon.

FIFTY-FIVE

Catherine turned sharply and gasped as she took in the man standing before her.

Michael casually leaned against the neighboring table with his arms crossed. Despite the frown on his face, his eyes were warm, and a smile tried pulling at the corner of his lips.

Catherine didn't think twice as she hurried to her feet, nearly knocking the chair out from under her. "Michael!" she exclaimed. A sob tore through her as she rushed into his now-open arms.

Michael blinked rapidly as his arms trapped Catherine against him. His vision blurred as he fought against the tears. He felt her arms tighten around him, and he knew he'd done the right thing in finding her but regretted not speaking to her sooner.

Catherine closed her eyes as Michael held her in a strong embrace. She had fought waves of homesickness since she had left everything behind, but seeing the man she loved like a brother brought it to a deeper level. *Holding a piece of home makes the pain worse.* She felt his arms tighten around her. He spoke volumes with the simple act.

Reluctantly, Catherine became aware of her situation. She was in a different town, going by a different name. Michael wasn't supposed to be here. She removed herself from his embrace but didn't stop him when he engulfed her hands in his.

"How did you find me?" she finally managed to whisper.

Although Michael smiled, there was undeniable sadness in his eyes. "It was no easy task, I assure you."

He had found her. Suddenly realizing what that meant, Catherine's eyes shifted past Michael's shoulder to the entrance. "Are you alone?" she asked.

Michael observed her darting eyes, relieved that he could still read her. She was wondering about Henry. While she was clearly anxious, he saw a flash of hope as well. "I'm alone, love. He's not here; he doesn't know I've found you," he replied.

Having spoken to Henry earlier in the day, Catherine knew Michael spoke the truth. A stone of bitterness still dropped in her stomach.

Michael freed one hand from Catherine's and used it to lift her chin. Only when Catherine seemed to have control of her emotions and dared to look at him did Michael speak. "We'll talk more on that later," he said, completely releasing her hands and purposefully stepping toward the dance floor. He winked, held out his hand, and asked, "Shall we?"

With the dance floor behind Michael, Catherine saw Edwin come into view. He was still dancing with his mother, but his eyes and full attention were on Catherine. Even from a distance, she saw concern on his face. Not ready to answer the questions she could see forming in Edwin's mind, she returned her focus to Michael.

With a single nod, she took his outreached hand. "But only if you hold off on the questions," she added.

Michael felt an all-too familiar wall shift into place, informing him that her time away hadn't been a vacation. She'd been suffering. Although he had many questions, his desire to dance with his friend was stronger than his curiosity.

"You've been gone a long time, love," he replied coyly. "If you want me to keep silent, you'd better plan on keeping me moving on the floor. Then there's no time for questions."

Despite all the turmoil, confusion, and complications webbed together in her life, Catherine delighted in the small taste of familiar banter. She gave Michael a cocky smile and countered, "Try to keep up, my friend."

That was all the encouragement Michael needed to lead Catherine onto the dance floor and push her through a rigorous dance routine she hadn't experienced since her lessons with him. Subconsciously, she knew what he was doing—he was forcing her to remember. One reason she had started lessons had been an attempt to win Henry, a terrific dancer. The twists, turns, spins, and lifts Michael now performed with Catherine were difficult, and only because they knew each other's styles so well were they able to execute them. She felt out of control in all aspects of her life, so it felt good to finally have control over something, even if it was merely a difficult dance.

For that reason, she wanted Michael to push her more. "Is that all you've got?" she asked in a rush between moves. "You're getting soft, old man."

Michael's eyes glowed in pleasure at the challenge. "You're on, love."

He didn't disappoint Catherine, nor did they disappoint the couples that had cleared the dance floor to circle around them and watch. When the song concluded, Catherine found herself pulled tightly in his arms.

"I've missed you, Cat," he whispered in her ear as applause from the surrounding couples filled the air.

"Me too," Catherine replied sincerely. She turned and made her way off the dance floor as several couples complimented them on their dancing, slowing their escape. Once they cleared the floor, Catherine wanted to control the conversation and keep Michael's questions at bay.

"How's Patricia?"

"Pregnant and irritable," Michael replied, flashing a smile. He took her hand and tucked it into the crook of his arm. "She's breathtakingly perfect that way. But the discussion about her can wait." He ushered her toward the table she had been occupying. The family Michael had seen her with previously was there, waiting for her. The look on the man's face reminded Michael of how Henry had looked at Catherine when she had revealed her skills at her brother's tribute. "Are you going to introduce me to your friends?"

His question brought everything back into focus. They weren't at Sal's Club, and Henry wasn't waiting for her at the table. Even as she stiffened, she felt Michael's determination to have the introduction. "Do I have a choice?" she whispered.

"I can always introduce myself," Michael answered.

"No," she curtly replied. "That won't be necessary." While she tried to sound calm, she was anything but as they neared the table. Seeing Sarah and Irma waiting for her with smiles on their faces, Catherine suddenly realized Michael calling her by her real name was a definite possibility. She didn't want the women to learn of her deceit this way. She wanted to be the one to tell them. "Michael," she whispered frantically as they neared the table, "Edwin knows *everything*, but the others—"

"Grace! That was amazing!" Sarah interrupted as she hurried to close the distance between them.

"Thank you," Catherine replied, trying to ignore the inquisitive look Michael threw her way. "But the true talent lies with my partner. Everyone, this is a friend of mine, Michael. Michael, these are my dear new friends, Irma, Sarah, and Edwin."

Michael warmly offered a greeting and an explanation. "I couldn't believe my eyes when I entered the dance hall tonight and saw Grace." He turned to Catherine, taking in her grateful look. "I'm passing through town on business and thought I'd enjoy some of the holiday festivities. I was elated to discover my dear friend here." He slung his arm around her shoulder and planted a kiss on the top of her head.

Edwin watched the exchange in silence, not daring to speak until he could figure out who this man from Catherine's past was. This man wasn't in her small network of friends she'd made in town since arriving at his doorstep. The familiarity the man showed now, and had shown on the dance floor, told Edwin that the man was an important part of Catherine's former life. He had felt relief when he had heard the man being introduced as Michael. Having seen the way he had handled Catherine on the dance floor, he had at first feared that Henry had found her.

Michael ... the instructor ... the friend who had helped Henry and Catherine get together.

Suddenly, Michael's presence seemed more suspect to Edwin. "What brings you to our sleepy corner of the world?" Edwin asked suddenly, breaking into the conversation his mother had been having with Michael. He held Michael's gaze as the man sized him up before answering.

"Like I said, I'm just passing through. It's been too long since I've seen Grace, but I'm happy to see your family taking such good care of her."

Irma thoughtfully watched the exchange. It was clear to her that Michael wasn't romantically involved with Grace, but she wasn't sure her son could feel that too. "Won't you sit and join us for the evening?" she prodded. Edwin glared at her momentarily, but that was the only indication he objected to her invitation.

"As much as I would love to take you up on your offer," Michael replied, "I'm going to have to decline. I need to get back to my hotel room so that I can call my beautiful wife before the new year rings in." Michael wanted to stay, but he'd already accomplished what he had set out to do for the evening: let Catherine know about his presence. He wanted to speak with her and get answers to his numerous questions, but it would have to wait. "However, I don't want to leave town without having dinner with you, Grace."

"You can come over to our house," Sarah offered, falling for Michael's snare. "Grace lives with us, and you're welcome to come by anytime."

"Of course," Irma agreed.

Michael sent Catherine a questioning look. She gave a single nod before focusing on the table's centerpiece. "I appreciate the invitation," he replied.

"Will it just be you?" Edwin asked. He knew the question sounded odd, but he had to know if anyone else from Catherine's past was in town—particularly Henry. The look his sister and mother gave him told him there was a nicer way to ask, but he didn't care. Seeing Catherine's face pale at his words was enough to convince him he was right in asking. If Henry was in town, Edwin didn't want the man to come near Catherine. She'd suffered enough heartache at his expense.

Michael glanced at Catherine before he replied, "It's just me, my friend." Then, directing his next words to Catherine, he asked, "Grace, are you up for company tomorrow? Then maybe you can show me around town and tell me what all you've been up to. And I can catch you up on my world as well."

Catherine heard the words Michael didn't say. He wanted time to talk with her one-on-one. She remembered how Michael had dealt with her after her brother had been killed in combat, and she knew he'd dissect her again, forcing her to face issues she'd been trying hard to escape and to forget. Michael wasn't going to let her get away with either, and as he looked at her questioningly, she knew he wasn't going to accept her refusal.

And, be honest, Catherine. You don't want to refuse him. You want to see him, even if he will be hard on you.

Catherine gave a small smile. "Of course," she replied. She grabbed her purse, pulling out a small scrap of paper. She scribbled something on it and handed it to him. "Here's the address. Don't forget to give Patricia my love."

Michael took the paper while also seizing Catherine's hand. After planting a light kiss on her knuckles, he grinned and said, "Of course. Good night, Grace. Happy New Year."

Michael's departure left a void in Catherine. In his presence, feelings of *home* had overpowered her. She suddenly felt lost and very much alone. As she watched Michael retreat, she heard Sarah and Irma head back to the dance floor. She assumed Edwin was the man on Irma's arm.

She had assumed wrong. She turned to find Edwin standing right behind her. She could tell by his stance that he was ready to go after Michael or anyone else who threatened her heart. She saw numerous questions swimming in his eyes. She didn't have to put forth any effort to look miserable, so she hoped it would persuade him to not ask questions.

Catherine's pleading eyes convinced him to refrain from bombarding her with questions but, instead, to keep her at his side for the rest of the evening. Confidently, he reached out and took her hand. "Dance with me," he whispered. "I can't dance like Michael—"

"No one can," Catherine interrupted as she allowed Edwin to lead her to the dance floor.

Edwin gave a silent prayer of gratitude as the music shifted to a slow song. Now he needed no excuse to keep Catherine tucked in his embrace as he swayed her around the perimeter of the dance floor. Although he had no answers to the questions that had sprouted when he saw Michael greet Catherine, he realized how unsettled the surprise encounter had left her. While Catherine might not want to talk, he could at least offer support through touch.

"The shop must have been limited in its color selection," Catherine tried to say casually as she commented on Edwin's kerchief for the first time.

"Or maybe Sarah believes we complement each other," he replied. His arms instinctively tightened around her, securing her body against his. In other circumstances, Edwin would never have dreamed of holding a dance partner so intimately.

When she didn't protest his actions, Edwin felt brave enough to ask, "Catherine ... is Henry ...?"

She visibly swallowed and gave a quick shake of her head. "But I don't know anything more. Please, no more questions." Edwin moved the hand that held hers up to her chin, encouraging her to look at him.

He was so close. Catherine noticed his eyes took in her lips before latching onto her own eyes and diving into her soul. She ached, and Edwin stood before her, ready to heal the ache. Michael's unexpected appearance left her mind reeling. *Was it time to go home?* As though reading her thoughts, Edwin's arms tightened around her, encasing her.

Or is this where I need to be? Is this my new home?

When Edwin's kiss came, it was on her forehead. She closed her eyes, allowing her head to rest against his lips and chin. It would be easy to stay safely tucked in his arms. He offered her a new life, one where she didn't have to worry about demons from his past. Even though she didn't love him, she knew she could over time.

But she had to be willing to give him a chance. She could only do that by leaving her first love, her deep love for Henry, behind for good.

Despite the turmoil she felt over Henry, her stomach flipped at the traitorous thought. Without thinking, she tore herself from Edwin's embrace. She looked up at his concerned face, barely seeing it through her blurred vision.

At that moment, the band began to lead the guests in a countdown to midnight.

"Catherine." The single word was a plea, a promise, and patience all wrapped in one.

"I need air," she managed to choke out before turning and rushing from the building. She gently pushed her way past everyone swarming the dance floor with their noisemakers. By the time she reached the entrance, the old year had passed into the new one.

Catherine burst through the doors, frantic for the night air to consume her lungs. She took in deep breaths as she crossed the parking lot to a vacant lot beside the dance hall. She wanted to scream, cry, and rebuild the walls she had used to protect her heart before the war. She wanted the ache to leave her, and she was frustrated that she didn't know how to dislodge it.

She threw an angry look to the heavens, prepared to scream her heart out to God, when her eyes fell on the full moon. Henry had asked her to find it at midnight, in hopes that they'd share this moment. Without realizing it, her emotions had tugged her right to where she needed to be. Even though she hadn't planned it, she was there, looking at the same object in the sky as

Henry. Without giving a thought to the snow below her, she dropped to her knees and let the heartache consume her.

Edwin fought the urge to immediately run after Catherine. Although she clearly wanted time alone, he wouldn't leave her alone for long. As the dance hall erupted into New Year's greetings, he ignored the well wishes and went in search of his sister.

"Happy New Year, Edwin!" Sarah shouted as Edwin came up to her.

He nodded, taking a glass of champagne from her hand and replacing it with his car keys. "You need to take Mother home when you're both ready to leave," he tried to yell over the party noise.

Sarah frowned at the new responsibility she held in her hand. "Is everything okay?"

Edwin nodded, knowing she could hear very little over the noise. "Grace … seems to be having a rough time, so I'm going to make sure she's okay. I doubt she's up for a car full of cheer right now."

Sarah waited until they had made it to a corner of the hall where they could more easily converse. "And you think you're the company she needs?" she asked.

"It's doubtful," Edwin reluctantly agreed. "But until you've had your share of heartbreak, I'm probably the one who best understands." Not giving Sarah the chance to respond, he hurried out the same entrance Catherine had left through.

It took no time to find her, a sobbing, crumpled mess in the snow. Without a verbal warning, he approached her, taking off his coat and adorning her shoulders with it. She offered no sign of surprise nor did she resist when he lifted her to her feet.

He gently took her face in his hands. He related to the confusion and pain he saw in her eyes. He wasn't sure when he had stopped feeling these things himself, but he was fairly confident it had been when Catherine entered his life.

"I'm sorry," Catherine whispered.

"You have no reason to apologize. Let your heart bleed. That's the only way it'll heal."

"I feel so *guilty*," she rasped out.

Her eyes, visible in the bright moonlight, shone with tears. With a slight shake of his head, he replied, "I'm here, Catherine. *I'm* here." He whispered to her, trying to convey promises he hoped she'd understand.

She nodded, a new wealth of tears streaming down her cheeks.

He was here for her no matter what, and he hoped he would be for a long time to come. He wasn't naive enough to think she wasn't currently thinking about Henry. He only hoped the comfort he offered would be strong enough to sustain her through to the other side. With that in mind, he wrapped his arms around her, cradling her head with his chin, and silently greeted the new year.

Fifty-Six

The sun had yet to rise when Bobby, fatigued from the previous evening's events, opened the passenger door for his excited wife. Once they had decided that Olivia would go to Catherine as soon as possible, he had taken his son to his parents' house so he wouldn't have to wake him early.

Lucky little man. I could have used a few more hours of sleep myself.

His wife, on the other hand, seemed to have found her second wind. From the moment he had shared with her that Henry hadn't fathered Natalie's son, she had been going nonstop to prepare for her early-morning departure. Had he allowed her, Bobby was certain Olivia would have preferred to sleep on the train station platform overnight to guarantee she would be on the first train out of town.

"I hope we didn't miss it," Olivia whispered as she took her husband's offered hand and exited the vehicle.

"It's dark, Liv. You're the first passenger here. Everyone else is still asleep. We didn't miss anything," Bobby muttered as he stifled a yawn. He released her hand, grabbed her luggage from the trunk, and led his wife to the platform. "Stay here and keep bundled while I purchase your ticket."

Although Olivia's eagerness would normally have her pacing the platform, she didn't want to do anything that might make her husband change his mind. She sat on a bench with her gloved hands buried in her coat pockets, smiling at the sun starting to peek over the horizon. She couldn't hide her happiness. Although she hated leaving Bobby, she finally felt like she was contributing to bringing her best friend home. She believed her plan was foolproof and couldn't wait to see Catherine's face again.

By the time Bobby returned with Olivia's ticket, the sun had risen enough for her to see the concern written on his face. "Reassure me again that this is a good idea," he pleaded as he sat down next to his wife.

Olivia rolled her eyes, snuggling into his side. "It is. We have proof Henry isn't the father. That means we need to get to Catherine *now*."

"Do you think we should have let him go after her on his own?"

"Don't you dare try to talk me out of this. Besides, we'll be together again soon enough. You and Henry will be joining us."

"I hope not too soon," Bobby countered. "Too soon means something is wrong with the baby."

Olivia patted his hand reassuringly. "And don't forget to check on Patricia from time to time."

"Of course. Taking care of her may be the only thing that keeps Michael from killing me once he finds out what we've done."

Olivia's chuckle filled the otherwise still platform. Suddenly, her eyes turned sad as she whispered, "I'll miss Caleb. I've never been apart from him before. Besides our honeymoon, I mean."

"He'll be fine," Bobby reassured her. "He's got me. However, do whatever you can to get back here sooner rather than later. With only Caleb and me living in the house, I don't know what you ladies will be coming back to."

"What will you tell Caleb?" Olivia asked, trying to overcome the guilt of leaving her son.

"That Mommy needs to visit a very special friend who needs her before his little sibling comes into the world. He knows the baby will be here soon, so hopefully he'll understand that you'll only be gone a short time."

"I promise," Olivia responded.

"Besides, you'll be calling daily, right?"

They whispered words of endearment to each other, stealing kisses as the sun continued to rise. Before they knew it, the train's whistle blew, demanding the early travelers board the train. As eager as Olivia was to get to Catherine, she found herself the last passenger on the platform.

Bobby handed her luggage to one of the attendants, and as Olivia started to board the train, Bobby stopped her. Single-handedly, he spun her around to face him, doing it slowly enough to keep her from falling.

Surprised by the spontaneous action, Olivia grew breathless at the hunger she saw in Bobby's eyes.

"Come now, sweetheart," he said huskily as he leaned in to whisper in her ear. "Henry can't be the only one with romantic train station experiences."

Olivia's body trembled, and before she could utter a response, Bobby's mouth seized hers. When he finally broke the kiss, she wasn't surprised to find tears wet her cheeks. What *did* surprise her was seeing that Bobby's cheeks mirrored hers.

"I care a great deal about Catherine, but you are the most important person in my world, Olivia. No matter what, you take care of yourself. Don't let any harm come to you or our child."

"I promise," Olivia whispered, once again finding it difficult to leave. "I'll telephone as soon as I get there. I love you, Bobby."

She reluctantly allowed Bobby to hand her up to the attendant, who gently ushered her to her seat. "After we're thirty minutes down the track, I'll be sure to have someone come by to offer you refreshments and a newspaper if you'd like to purchase them. Until then, relax. Let us know if we can be of service to you."

Thirty minutes later, Olivia repositioned herself to get more comfortable in the seat. She had refused a beverage but had purchased a newspaper to read in hopes of passing the time more quickly. Once content with her position, she picked up the local newspaper from the seat next to her and spread out the front page to peruse it.

She gasped, and nausea unrelated to her pregnancy suddenly swam in her stomach. Tears filled her eyes as she took a closer look at the article that filled the lower half of the front page: *Mayor's New Year's Eve Fund-raising Dance a Huge Success.*

A close-up, incriminating photograph of Henry hugging Natalie on the dance floor followed the headline.

The hope that had earlier filled Olivia and had spurred her to go to Catherine dimmed. While Olivia couldn't explain the embrace, it spoke volumes on its own, proudly announcing itself as Henry's and Catherine's next big hurdle.

* * *

The commotion on the first floor woke Susan. She had intended to be up early, but once she had received word about the photograph from the New Year's Eve party, she fell into the first truly restful night of sleep she'd had since Henry and Catherine's engagement.

Had she been up earlier, Susan was sure the commotion below wouldn't have escalated to its current level. A woman was screaming at the butler, demanding to see Susan. Susan smiled, knowing that if their guest was this upset, the photograph she had paid a hefty price for was convincing indeed. She snuggled deeper into her pillow.

Let the butler take care of her for now. I'll deal with her after I've had a bit more sleep.

As Susan tried to drift off to sleep, the sound of a hand slapping skin followed by a loud crash assured her that she'd have to deal with the issue sooner rather than later.

Before she could get up, her bedroom door opened with unexpected force. The woman who stood in the doorframe cast a deadly, savage look at Susan, rendering her temporarily speechless.

"Good morning, *cousin*," Susan finally said, stretching as she rose from her bed. "It's a little early for visitors, don't you think?"

"How dare you!" Natalie spat, advancing in the room, closing the door behind her, and locking it. "I should kill you!"

Natalie had always been a pushover, so this threat took Susan by surprise. Trying to mask how it affected her, she barely glanced at Natalie before walking to the window. "Natalie, why are you in such a foul mood? Didn't you have a good New Year's Eve?"

With Susan's back to her, Natalie felt a small fraction of relief as she hurled the town's newspaper at her cousin, hitting her on the back of the head.

Susan whirled, fury now dancing in her eyes as well. "Excuse me! Who do you think—"

"Take a look, Susan! And don't you dare pretend to be surprised by what you see," Natalie screamed, not allowing Susan the upper hand in the conversation.

Susan glared at Natalie as she knelt to pick up the newspaper. She opened it so the front page was in full view. She laid it on her vanity and studied the photograph of Henry and Natalie for several minutes. It was an absolute perfect photograph, exactly what Susan had hoped to capture. While she silently celebrated, she made sure her voice was indifferent when she finally responded, "It could have been better, but it'll do."

"*Excuse me?*" Natalie screamed in disbelief.

Susan shrugged as she neatly folded the paper, making sure it lay with the photograph showing. "It's not a terrible photo of you two. I don't understand why you're so upset about this."

"How selective is your memory?" Natalie whispered with as much venom as when she had been screaming. "My one, single condition in agreeing to do your dirty work was that no photographs be taken. You've made it a thousand times easier for Edward. There's no way I can hide from him in this town after this!" She angrily jerked her arm toward the newspaper.

"I don't know why you're complaining. You've been moaning about wanting out for a while now." Susan also gestured toward the paper. "Well, there you go then. This photograph will do in one day what you couldn't do the entire time you were here. So, your services are no longer needed." She opened her desk drawer and pulled out her checkbook. "I'll write you one more to make sure you shut up and leave town hastily." Susan responded with surprise when Natalie threw an envelope on top of the newspaper.

"Cash," Natalie said with hatred. "I want all of it in cash. I haven't cashed a single check you've written. With you leaving Edward a trail to me, there's no way I'll be able to now. You owe it all to me in hard cash. These checks are worthless."

"Not my problem," Susan hissed.

Natalie reached across the desk, grabbing Susan's hair and yanking her forward. "It *is* your problem. This is proof you paid me to do your dirty work. You pay me cash, burn the checks, and you eliminate a paper trail. It's as much to protect your own neck as it is to protect mine."

"And your son's," Susan added flippantly.

Natalie's eyes narrowed. "He didn't ask for any of this," she said as she took a threatening step toward Susan. "Everything I do is to protect my son. And there's nothing I won't do to protect him."

"Obviously." A hard slap across her face silenced Susan, stunned by

Natalie's actions. When she finally started to protest, Natalie held up a hand to stop her.

"We're through here. Give me what you owe me and I'll leave. I have nothing more to say to you."

As much as Susan wanted to hurl more insults at her cousin, she decided it would be best to give Natalie the money and get her out of her house. Henry would be just as angry, if not more, about the photograph, and Susan needed time to formulate a plan on how to approach him.

"Wait here, dear cousin," Susan spat out as she headed to her bedroom door. "I'll be back in a few minutes with your money." She placed her hand on the doorknob and refused to look at Natalie as she tried to definitively end the conversation, "And then, I want you out of here and gone from this town!"

Natalie, however, felt threatened, fearing much more than Susan's nasty responses. She was determined to have the last word. "I don't know why you started this against Henry, Susan."

Still facing the door, Susan responded, "It's not Henry. It's—"

"Catherine," Natalie finished. "I know. But you're a fool if you think all that you're doing to break Catherine isn't breaking Henry too."

"He's no longer your concern."

"You won't win, you know. No matter how hard you try, you're going to lose this war."

Susan gave a sharp laugh, looking over her shoulder at Natalie. "Oh, dear cousin," she said menacingly, "I'm just getting started."

* * *

Bobby wasn't surprised to see Henry sitting on the front porch when he pulled his car up to the house. He knew Henry had been eager the previous evening to learn what Bobby had discovered at Natalie's home. Bobby *had* been surprised that Henry hadn't returned after taking Natalie and her son home. Seeing as it had been his last night with his wife for a while, Bobby had been grateful. However, Henry's late-night absence had guaranteed his early-morning appearance. Popping into town to buy a cup of coffee and a newspaper had done little to stall the inevitable conversation Bobby was about to have with Henry.

Now Bobby wished he'd taken the time to read the newspaper before returning home.

When he learns about Olivia, he's going to kill me. I can only hope the other news I have for him shields me.

"You're early," Bobby said, trying to muster up his cheeriest smile.

"I could say the same for you," Henry responded, rising from the porch swing. "I just got here."

"You could have gone inside," Bobby said as he met him on the stairs.

"I didn't want to wake up Liv. In her present state, her wrath is not something to mess with. I figured you were on a quick errand, so I thought I'd bide my time here."

Bobby nodded, handing over the newspaper to Henry as he walked past him to open the door.

"Besides," Henry continued, "You can't be too surprised I'm already here. I want to know what you learned last night, and I have my own updates to share with you and Liv."

"Come on in, then," Bobby invited. "I'll get some coffee going, and we can swap information." He expected Henry to be close on his heels, but after entering the house, it took him a minute to realize that wasn't the case. When Bobby turned back, he found Henry in the doorway, frozen in place and deathly pale. Bobby hadn't seen Henry this horror-stricken since Robert had tried killing Catherine.

"Henry?" Bobby asked, taking a tentative step toward his shocked friend.

"*No,*" Henry managed to whisper, his hands gripping the newspaper so tightly it crumpled beneath his fingers. "*How is this possible?*"

Henry made no attempt to show the newspaper to Bobby, so he hurried to look over Henry's shoulder. Bobby couldn't hide his sharp intake of breath at the front-page image.

Bobby groaned as an already messy situation just got messier.

* * *

"I didn't ask for a wake-up call," Michael grumbled as he opened his door to find a hotel employee waiting.

"Of course not, sir," the young man said apologetically. "But you did ask

446

us to wake you should your wife telephone you."

The grogginess in Michael's mind cleared. "Patricia? She called? Is she all right?"

The employee shrugged his shoulders before answering, "I've only been sent to give you the message. She asks that you call her as soon as possible, but I do suggest you wait until you've at least changed your clothes, sir."

Michael only took enough time to follow the employee's suggestion before hurrying down the stairs to the main lobby to make his telephone call. Trying to keep the concern out of his voice as well as his heart from pumping out of his chest, he impatiently waited for his wife to answer.

"Michael?"

"Hello, love," Michael said immediately. "I got the message you called. Are you all right? Is the baby—"

"Will you stop it?" Patricia interrupted. "I'm fine. Nothing's wrong with me or the baby."

Relief flooded Michael. "Good. Then—"

"Have you seen the paper?" she interjected once more.

Although she had a tendency to interrupt him, the somberness in her voice clued him in on a serious issue at hand. "The paper? No, I immediately left my room to talk to you. I haven't had breakfast yet or anything."

"*Find* one, Michael. There's a damaging photograph of Henry ... I don't know how this happened. I want you to find a paper if you can, then call me back. I need you to see this with your own eyes."

The call ended before Michael could say another word. Ignoring his hunger, he went in search of a newspaper.

"Did Henry decide to give up on Catherine and not tell anyone?" Michael hissed from the telephone booth. The newspaper was clutched in his free hand.

"Oh, good, you found one," Patricia replied.

"What is that man thinking? Doesn't he realize how bad this looks?"

"I don't know that he's seen it yet," Patricia said.

Michael took a deep breath before continuing, "This is bad, love."

"You think?"

"I'm supposed to see Cat later today. If she sees this, my presence will make no difference to her." He grumbled in frustration. "I need to know what happened. I need to know *why* this photograph is here. I don't even know if I can unravel this one."

"Don't you think I've already thought that too? I'm on it. I'm heading over to Bobby's now. I'm sure Henry will be there."

"Call me back as soon as you learn anything."

"I will. And Michael? I recommend you hold off on seeing Catherine until I speak with Henry. Maybe wait to bring Olivia with you."

Michael's thoughts were already on his future meeting with Catherine, but the name of her best friend brought him back to the present. "Olivia? What are you talking about?"

"She's on her way to you."

"She's *what*? The woman who's near the end of her pregnancy?" Michael exclaimed.

"That's the one."

"Patricia, what did you do?"

"I don't have time for this. Let Liv explain. I've got work to do."

"*Patricia—*"

"I love you."

Michael fought hard to keep from screaming his frustration. He threw the newspaper at the closed booth door and slammed the phone on the receiver. Things were spiraling out of control. The previous evening had ended with such a promising outlook.

How had one photograph changed everything?

If Catherine sees the photograph, he wasn't sure she'd agree to see him. *She'll be even angrier when she learns Olivia is here rather than safe at home with her husband.*

It wasn't the first time he regretted not bringing Henry. Had he done so, a different photograph would have graced the newspaper. Olivia would be home with her husband, and perhaps they would be several steps closer to Henry's and Catherine's reconciliation.

We wouldn't be going back several steps, that's for certain.

Discouraged, Michael went back to his hotel room. There was nothing for him to do now but wait.

* * *

Despite how late Catherine had gotten to bed, sleep had eluded her. She continually rocked in the rocking chair tucked in the corner of her bedroom, dressed and waiting for the sun to rise. Since encountering Michael, her mind had been in a whirl trying to understand his motives.

There's no way he's here by chance. He's not passing through, and he's not just "checking" in on me. She rose to her feet and began to pace the length of the room, giving no heed to the darkness. She was certain he had a plan. Michael always had a plan. *And it must be an important one if he's willing to leave his pregnant wife home alone.*

Catherine bit her lip as she considered Patricia. When Michael had first learned his wife was pregnant, he had become extremely protective. He hadn't wanted Patricia out of his sight. That he would be in a different city from her took Catherine by surprise.

It angered her too.

He shouldn't have left her. I don't care what he has up his sleeve; no plan that includes me is worth him leaving Patricia's side. He's going back home. After I meet with him, he's taking the train and returning home. She sighed as she focused on the pending conversation she would have with Michael. *How had he found her? Michael had found her, and Henry hadn't. Was Henry even looking?*

I don't want him to! Yet as she thought these words, she knew they weren't true. The part of her heart that still refused to release Henry—the part that loved him despite the heartache—wanted him here, at her doorstep, ready to do battle with whatever obstacle stood in his way of her love.

Catherine resented that part of her heart. She loathed the weakness in herself. She had left him several months ago, and every day she continued to struggle with leaving. The distance hadn't worked in separating them.

Will this pain never fully leave me?

The previous year had ended with her mourning the loss of Henry. Even now, Catherine's eyes grew tearful as she thought about falling apart in Edwin's arms.

Edwin, the one person who hasn't demanded anything. She reflected on the way he had simply come up to her and enfolded her in his arms. He hadn't said a word. As everyone else had shared laughs and kisses to greet the new year, he had simply offered himself to be whatever Catherine had needed him to be. In that moment, she had needed someone to help her stand. Edwin had made sure she had.

As hard as he had seemed at first, Catherine realized soberly, *he isn't. He's protective, demanding, and brutally honest about what he wants, but he's never asked for more than I'm willing to give.*

Catherine rubbed her neck as she continued to brood over Edwin. Although he had never pushed her for more, he had progressively opened more of himself to her. Weeks ago, Edwin would have never dared touch her. Last night, he had no hesitation when he took her in his arms. His confidence had been building.

Edwin's no fool. He knows he's having an effect on me.

Catherine hadn't been prepared to admit that. She looked out her window as the dawn's pink skies slowly appeared. Everyone would be up soon, and despite the hours she'd spent in reflection, she needed more time. She wasn't ready to face them or Michael, for that matter.

Deciding to bring the family breakfast if she could find a place open on New Year's Day, Catherine quietly left her room and tiptoed down the hall, not wanting to wake anyone. As she passed Edwin's closed bedroom door, she thought she heard stirring, causing her to practically bolt down the stairs. Leaving a hastily written note to explain her whereabouts, Catherine put on her new coat as she exited the house.

Edwin watched from his bedroom window as Catherine escaped from the house and hurried down the street. Catherine had had a trying night. As she carefully crossed the icy street, panic suddenly seized him.

Surely she wouldn't leave without saying goodbye? Then he remembered the story Catherine had shared with him of how she had arrived here. For her, a sudden departure was absolutely within the realm of possibility.

He had to stop her.

With an urgency Edwin hadn't felt in years, he dressed and briskly descended the stairs, careful not to wake his mother and sister. His heart was in his throat as he made his way to the front door. For once, he was grateful for the icy conditions outside; it would slow Catherine's pace considerably. Dread filled him as his eyes fell on the console table by the front door with a note propped against the vase.

Edwin couldn't control the tremble in his hand as he picked it up. *No, Catherine, not yet ... not yet.*

Relief burst through him as he read:

Happy New Year!
    I wanted to treat you all to breakfast. I'll be back soon with some food, so don't fill up on Edwin's coffee!

Catherine

With a slight smile still on his lips, Edwin suddenly recognized Catherine's mistake. She hadn't signed it Grace. Whether a slipup or intentional, he wasn't certain, so he wouldn't take the risk of exposing her true identity until he heard it from her lips. Until then, he'd make coffee and wait for her to return.

It was a great comfort to him knowing she would.

"This definitely wasn't my brightest idea," Catherine muttered as she passed by another closed store. Although she figured there'd be closed shops in town, she'd been hopeful to find at least one place she could purchase breakfast items.

Although, to be fair, you've haven't had any bright ideas in a really long time.

Her internal berating ended as she spotted an employee turn the sign in a small donut shop's window, indicating they were open for business. Deciding she'd have little if any luck finding something else open, she hurried inside its door.

The employee had just stepped behind the counter and couldn't hide his surprise when he saw Catherine. "I wasn't expecting any customers until a bit later."

"Am I too early?" Catherine asked as she stomped her feet on the doormat.

"No, not at all, ma'am," the man replied, motioning her forward with his hand. "While I always have good business on New Year's Day, most of my business comes later in the morning. It was a long night for most residents, you know." He winked at her, sweeping his arm along the display

451

case connected to the counter. "Nothing remedies a hangover like my coffee and donuts. What can I get you?"

Catherine chuckled at his good humor. "No coffee, thank you. But I'll taken a dozen donuts," she replied as she began pointing out her selections.

"Thirteenth one is on the house," the man said, "if you sit here for a minute to warm up before heading back out in the cold."

Catherine was happy to oblige.

As she waited for him to box up her order, she stood near the wall heater and nibbled on her free donut. She'd taken only a couple of bites before the front door opened again, and a man with a pile of newspapers entered. "Happy New Year, Cliff," he greeted as he dropped the bundles of newspapers next to his feet.

"Looks like I'm mistaken," Cliff said, offering another wink at Catherine. "There's at least two of you who didn't party too much last night."

"No can do," the man replied, tipping his head politely to Catherine. "News doesn't take a holiday. If anything, it's busier because of it." He accepted the coffee from Cliff after pulling out some newspapers and setting them on the counter. "I've got more than the local newspaper today." He started to rattle off the names of the various newspapers while Catherine reached out for the box of donuts now waiting for her on the counter.

When the man mentioned her hometown, she couldn't help herself. "I'll take one of those," she interrupted, already pulling money from her purse to make the purchase. Her hands trembled slightly as she took the newspaper and folded it against the donut box. She'd wait until later, when she was safely tucked away in her bedroom, to devour news from home. Even though Michael was in town, she was sure there'd be some mention of the club somewhere in the newspaper, especially since this was the first New Year's since Sal's passing. She hoped it had been a successful evening for his business.

Edwin smiled from the kitchen as he heard Catherine entering the house from the front door and reprimanding the icy weather conditions that "almost brought her death." Cradling a coffee mug in his hands, he went to the doorway and leaned against it, watching her kick the air.

"Problems?" he asked with a chuckle.

Catherine spun around to face him, embarrassment reddening her cheeks. She held a box with a newspaper resting on top in both hands. From his vantage point, Edwin could see the box was dented.

"I will *never* understand how your town can think ice, snow, and the like are acceptable." She nodded toward the street on the other side of the door. Turning back to Edwin, who still stood in the doorway with a smile on his face, she held up the box of donuts. "Good thing these will still taste good smashed because that's what you're getting for breakfast: smashed donuts."

This time, Edwin couldn't hold back a loud guffaw as he crossed the room. She looked ridiculously adorable, but he didn't dare tell her that. Instead, he held out the coffee mug. "How about a swap? Take this and warm up. I'll make sure these make it to the kitchen in one piece."

"And lose out on the last leg of my trip? No way." She held the box out of his reach and edged by him. "As much trouble as these were to get here, I'm doing the honors of delivering them to the table."

Edwin contemplated mentioning the signature on her note but thought better of it. Although he figured his sister and mother would be in bed for a while still, he didn't want to risk doing anything to sour Catherine's mood. Last night, he had left her emotionally exhausted. He was pleased to see her current frame of mind.

He gave an appreciative smile as he followed her to the kitchen and said, "You didn't have to do this, but it was very thoughtful of you."

Catherine shrugged as she replied, "I needed to get out for a bit."

He waited until she set the box on the table before handing her the coffee mug. "I'm surprised you found anything open."

"Me too." She took a grateful drink of coffee before adding, "It took me long enough to get these and get back, I thought for sure the whole house would be awake and greeting me with growling stomachs."

"My mother and Sarah will be in bed for a few hours."

"So, we'll have to try hard not to eat *all* the donuts," Catherine replied with a wink.

Edwin gave Catherine's arm a gentle squeeze. He pulled out a chair from the table, saying, "Here, have a seat. I'll get the plates."

Catherine tried to pretend she didn't crave the comfort of his touch. As she took a seat, the additional squeeze on her shoulder brought unwanted tears to her eyes.

"Did it help? Getting out for a bit?" he asked as he released her shoulder and walked to the cabinets.

"I'll feel better when Michael finally tells me why he's here," Catherine responded, sliding the newspaper off the box, desperate to refocus her attention. She stood and shifted the box of donuts to the far side of the table before spreading the newspaper out in front of her.

As Catherine's eyes fell to the bottom portion of the newspaper, everything else fell away. She forgot how to breathe, as oxygen seemed to lodge itself in her throat. Edwin was speaking to her, but she couldn't hear him. Instead, a buzz filled her ears as a cold pain started in her heart and raced through the rest of her body. The words on the paper blurred while the photograph sharpened in contrast.

She forgot about the coffee mug until it slipped from her grip and shattered on the floor.

That was the only encouragement she needed to shatter too.

Edwin had his back toward Catherine, but at the sound of shattering glass, he arrived at her side almost instantly. Taking in her paled complexion and trembling body, he reached out a hand to support the small of her back. "Catherine?"

Catherine didn't respond. With her eyes glued to the newspaper, she didn't hear or acknowledge Edwin beside her. Edwin leaned over to see where her attention lay. Noticing the unfolded paper, Edwin took in the photograph of a couple embracing. "Do you know these people, Catherine?"

He looked at Catherine. If she hadn't been nodding her head, the silent tears streaming down her face would have answered his question. "May I?" he asked, his hand in midair with the intent to pick up the newspaper.

She could only nod.

With one hand still at Catherine's back, Edwin picked up the paper and read, "Henry Bradley and Natalie—"

Catherine's new outburst of tears told Edwin everything he needed to know. He immediately dropped the paper and instinctively pulled Catherine into his arms. The magnitude of her response told him how much she was hurting. She latched onto him so tightly, her grief transported to him through the fingertips that clutched his shirt. Catherine fell apart in his arms as Edwin stood as still as possible, holding her, stroking her hair, and not saying a word. He found his own vision blurred as her pain became his own. Her anguish was so profound that he was astonished when she reacted to the hall clock chiming the top of the hour.

"I don't want anyone to see me this way," she choked out as he felt her stiffen in his arms.

Edwin took that as a plea to protect her, which he had every intention of doing. He slipped his arm under her knees, lifting her off her feet. He ignored the bothersome twinge in his leg as he carried her up the stairs and to her bedroom.

Once there, Edwin dared not speak. He was all too aware of his surroundings as he gently lowered her to the center of the bed. As he released her and started to step away, her grip on his shirt tightened. Frozen in place, he searched her eyes, understanding her silent plea.

Catherine didn't want to be alone.

He held her gaze. *Don't, Edwin. She's broken. Don't take advantage of her damaged heart.* Only when he felt he had fully gained control of his emotions did he nod in understanding. He stepped away from her and closed the bedroom door before going back to the bed.

Focusing on the cause of her pain, a man she obviously still had deep feelings for, sobered Edwin. He repeated Henry's name in his mind as he sat on the bed next to Catherine and gathered her into his arms. Leaning against the headboard, he held her in silence, stroking her hair and back until her tears no longer stained his shirt.

When her small shudders stopped, he dared glance down at her face. She had finally drifted off to sleep. Deep lines of sorrow, some he hadn't seen since he had first met her, had reappeared and somehow multiplied across her face. As gently as he could, he laid her head down on the pillow and slowly slid off the bed. Impulsively, he leaned down and pressed a kiss to her forehead.

Edwin left the room quietly. Questions burned in his mind, and he knew where to turn to for answers. Grateful that his family still slept, he went to the kitchen to clean up the broken mug and retrieve the newspaper. He would take it to his study to pour over the article about Henry. On his way back up the stairs, he couldn't help but steal a glance at the photograph of the man who wielded a dangerous grip on Catherine's heart.

And Edwin couldn't help hating him.

EPILOGUE

Henry,

I don't know why I'm bothering to write this or give you any more of my time. But if it's one thing I've learned in my relationship with you, it's that letters can be therapeutic. It's how I got through the fear of losing you once before ...

But this time, it's real, isn't it? There aren't any mistakes or misunderstandings keeping us apart this time around. No, the only thing that kept this letter from coming sooner is the fact that I'm naive.

And foolish. And very, very stupid.

Somehow, after I saw Natalie in your home, even after I tore myself away from you, my heart still belonged to you. Even after I moved to a different town, even after I tried to give us space, I still found my focus on you. I constantly wondered how you'd react to the experiences I'd been facing without you. As much as I fought it, I gravitated to you. I always telephoned Olivia when you were visiting her. It was as if my heart, despite my mind, always found you. You were still a part of my very soul, despite the physical distance between us.

In the face of all the pain your actions wrecked on my soul, I hate to admit how hope sprouted inside me. Each time we exchanged words, no matter how heated, this devastating hope grew stronger. It brought with it self-doubt, leaving me daring to believe that maybe everything had been a misunderstanding between us. I began to think that leaving might have been hasty ... and that maybe I had been wrong in at least not giving you an opportunity to explain.

Assumptions are dangerous things, and I started to regret with each of your professions of love my refusal to listen to you. And the sincerity I heard each time you told me you loved me ...

It now mocks me.

I hate that I could have been so wrong. Was I so eager to have anyone love me that I gave up the battles I fought so long against you and the love you offered? Loving you from a distance was safest—I can see that now. I was a fool to convince myself otherwise.

And you ... knowing I was so desperate ... did you keep me dangling only until someone better came along? Was Susan right? Looking back now, I can't help but wonder if she was more a friend to me than the villain I always believed her to be. Were her words actually meant to warn me rather than destroy me???

Was I right in my initial belief that you were only with me out of obligation to Caleb, and now your obligation has run its course? Even if you think it hasn't, your actions tell me otherwise.

There's nothing you can say that can erase the embrace I saw on the front page of the newspaper. The smile on your face and how Natalie was nestled into your embrace are two things the photograph can't lie about. So, no matter what you say, your obligation to Caleb, to me, is over.

There's no need to tell you how devastating that photograph was to me. It uprooted that seed of hope and gashed it beyond repair. But the thing is, even though I've cried more tears over this than humanly possible, it's not you to whom I'm now unleashing my anger.

It's me. I hate myself so much right now. I hate the kindness in my heart; I hate the willingness to give you a chance when you came back from the war, thinking you'd changed. You're the same person you've always been. I hate that I knowingly walked into this with my eyes closed. I wasn't blind, but I chose to love you that way.

Foolish, foolish girl. And the worst part? My heart still bleeds for you. I'm the same ridiculous woman who loved you while you spent your time giving your affections to every other woman in town. It's obvious none of that's changed.

I'm as incapable of being loved as I ever was—especially by you.

New Year's Eve made that perfectly clear. I understand that now.

I pray you find what you're looking for, Henry. I hope one day you'll find the love of your life—the woman to whom you'll give your heart. I hope she's everything good in the world and makes you want to be the best you can be. I hope to one day meet her because she'll have to be an amazing person, indeed, to capture your full heart. I thought I was that person at one time, but I realize now that I'm not strong enough to be.

Just wait, Henry, she'll be someone you'll fight for to the end. No amount of distance or number of obstacles will keep you from her. She'll mean so much to you that no amount of hardships will matter. Having her will be reward enough.

I'm sorry, Henry, that I couldn't be enough for you.

Catherine

Her vision blurred as she took the letter, now stained with teardrops that caused smeared words throughout, and folded it between her shaking fingers. Her lips moved quickly as silent words tumbled from them. Catherine was more of an emotional wreck now than she had been when she had received Henry's and Caleb's letters upon Caleb's death or when she'd believed Henry was missing in Europe.

Catherine was ripping out the remainder of her heart by her own words, her own hand, and she found it hard to cope.

Her hands stilled at the sound of footsteps coming to a stop outside her bedroom door. It didn't matter that it was well past the hour that anyone should be awake. So long as the lamp in her bedroom was on, Edwin would continue to check on her, even if it was only stopping at the door. His footsteps simply announced that he was here, ready for her in whatever capacity she needed him. After they gave that reassurance, they'd move away from the door, only to offer more of the same an hour later.

But Catherine didn't need that reassurance. Edwin's presence reminded her of who wasn't here: Henry. Anger and pain flared once again as she placed the letter in between the crumpled pages of the newspaper she'd asked Edwin to return to her. The image of Henry and Natalie was creased repeatedly from the multiple times she'd wadded up the newspaper and thrown it across the room, only to unwrap it once again. Her letter had taken a painstakingly long time to complete as a result. The newspaper spurred her to write the letter, but she had stopped writing every time she found herself drawn to the newspaper across the room. She had hoped by writing down her feelings, she'd be able to calm herself and wrap her mind around everything. But this letter had the opposite effect.

"I hate you, Henry. I hate you, I hate you, I hate you," Catherine whispered. Although she wanted to rage in anger, she quietly opened the drawer to the desk where she sat and gently placed the letter enveloped by the newspaper inside it. She closed it slowly, a new wave of tears surfacing. Her throat burned as she spoke, her next words filling with venom, "But I hate myself even more."

With nothing left in her, she laid her head upon her arms on the desk as silent sobs destroyed the last of her heart.

ACKNOWLEDGMENTS

Karen, thank you for being the best editor *ever*. Even when life left me with little motivation at times, your gentle nudging reminded me that you were there for every step of the process with me. You weren't just there as my editor (but bravo on reminding me you were there by posting comments on my website about waiting for the next book!), you've been there as a friend too. And it was your friendship that helped me get this book out.

Lindsay, thank you for being such a dedicated beta reader—so much so that you would even read chapters on your phone! You've always shown excitement with every step of the process, even when I wasn't so motivated at times. Even now, your enthusiasm over the next book's outline means the world to me.

Becky, you continue to be my "yetter" (and I can tell you my editor appreciates the work you do on the front end). Thanks for being such a huge supporter from the very beginning.

Carrie, whenever I would ask for your feedback and opinion, you always provided the correct answer. Either we have extremely similar preferences in books or you have a superhuman gift in knowing what I need to hear. Thank you for always agreeing with me (even when you didn't).

Ava, thank you for reminding me that even when no one else agrees with me, I should always go with my gut instinct. The cover is what it is because of you.

Jamie, even when I have no idea how to explain what I want in a book cover, you can take my jumbled explanation and create something even better than what I imagined. Your artistry brings life to my words.

Amanda, even when life gets crazy, you always have my back. You push me forward when I tend to want to stay in complacency. Thanks for being my best friend.

Alex, Ann, and Cosette, when the demands of daily life pulled me away from my writing, you still let me keep Catherine tucked safely in my head.

You never begrudged me the time I took to spend with her. I can never thank you enough. Your unconditional love is a balm for my soul.

To my Father in Heaven, you continually keep me in the palm of your hand. Thank you for not letting go.

ABOUT THE AUTHOR

For more than fifteen years, Denise Micka has transformed numerous short-act plays and theatrical scenes into full-length productions for her church. She currently lives in St. Louis with her husband and two daughters. When she's not chauffeuring her daughters to dance and swim classes or Girl Scout meetings (or maybe when she *is*), she's working on the outline of her next book. She loves to write long, 450-plus-page novels but struggles immensely with writing her own bio. *Susan's War* is a sequel to her debut novel *Catherine's War*. Denise welcomes visitors, comments, and bio suggestions at her website, www.denisemicka.com.